WITH DAGGER AND SONG

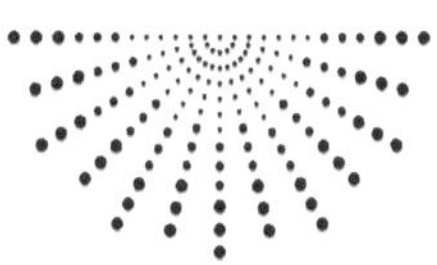

CURSE OF THE CYREN QUEEN BOOK II

WITH DAGGER AND SONG

HELEN SCHEUERER

This one's all yours, Mum.

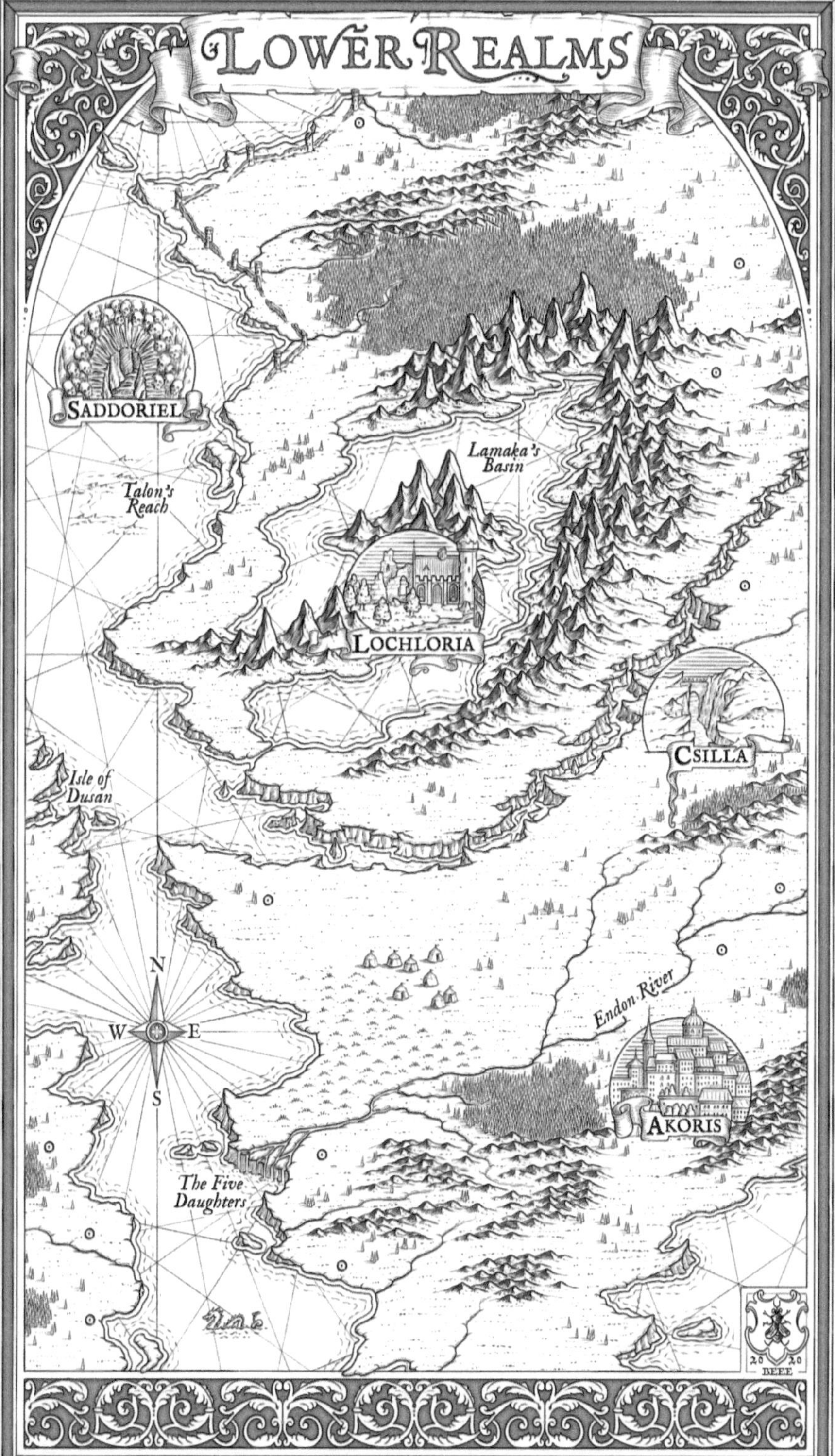

LOWER REALMS
SADDORIEL
Talon's Reach
Lamaka's Basin
LOCHLORIA
CSILLA
Isle of Dusan
N
W E
S
Endon River
AKORIS
The Five Daughters
20 20
BEEE

PROLOGUE

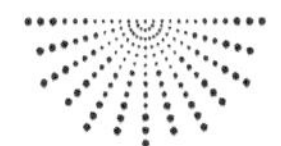

After centuries of imprisonment, half a decade should have passed like a quiet afternoon. But to Cerys, the five years since she'd lain bleeding on her icy cell floor had been the longest of all. She breathed in, recalling the weight of the small, pink-faced bundle in her arms. A piece of her had been taken away that day, a piece she had offered up willingly, and yet she couldn't live without it, or so it had felt.

But live on she did. Far longer than any cyren should. No matter how close to death she managed to get, something tethered her to the realm, always. There would be no relief for her, unless what she had planned all those years ago came to pass.

Someone had cleaned the bars of her cell. The sturdy lengths of yellowed bone that had accumulated all manner of moss and grime now gleamed ivory in the dying torchlight. When had they done that? Likely when she had been passed out on her greying cot in the corner. She had no idea how often, but sometimes a pitying guard would lace her lukewarm gruel with a sedative, just enough to render her unconscious for a day – two, if she was lucky, though she had no way of measuring the hours that passed.

From where she sat cross-legged on the floor, Cerys reached out and traced a finger down one of the clean bars, its surface smooth and unmarred, unlike the walls within. Over the last few weeks – or was it months? – she had re-covered nearly every part of her cage with etchings, some she remembered carving, others she did not. Often, she woke to the soft thrum of pain in her talons, which she found torn and bloody. When her cell was completely covered in markings, she was moved to another, as was the company of dead warlocks that stood outside like statues. It was something to break up the endless passage of time, at least.

She dropped her hand, her gaze lingering on the warlock in the centre of the group, his once-beautiful complexion tinged blue. Though he didn't look like the man she had known, she wanted to reach out and touch him all the same, to cup his face in her hands, to feel the warmth of his skin against her palms. But he had been cold for a long time now.

Cerys closed her eyes, finding what little solace she could in the images that flashed behind her lids. A large hand held hers, danger and adventure entwined around them, a rare fragment of life that moved too fast. A life not contained to the confines of a prison or even the lair itself, but bursting into the realms above: beams of golden sunlight, towering snow-capped mountains and a vast, ancient lake, where the reflection of the stars and moon was so precise, it was unnerving, as though everything were upside down.

The memories stirred something long forgotten resting deep inside Cerys. It seemed to slowly awaken within, and the soft tinkling of musical notes drifted to the forefront of her mind, before forming at her cracked lips. Her throat was raw. She couldn't remember the last time she had spoken aloud, but she knew what threatened to spill from her core: a song. *The* song.

Gravel crunched outside her cell and Cerys' eyes flew open.

Small, chubby hands gripped the bars of bone and wide moss-green eyes blinked at her, bright with curiosity. The nestling tilted her head slightly, her little mouth parting in wonder as she studied the prisoner before her. Waves of dark hair fell to her shoulders, which were pushed back proudly.

Very slowly, so as not to startle the nestling, Cerys stood. She vaguely felt the thin fabric of her shift brush her knees, but her focus was singular. Her chest couldn't contain the swelling of her heart, her eyes couldn't absorb the sight before her fast enough, and for the briefest moment, Cerys stopped wishing time would rush into oblivion. For the first time in centuries, she wished it would stop altogether.

'Rohesia ...' she murmured, the name achingly

familiar. Not an hour had gone by that Cerys hadn't thought of her.

The little cyren's intense green gaze was much like Cerys' own, framed by heavy lashes and sharp with intelligence. Cerys clung to each detail as she would a rope in a sea storm and took a tentative step forward, half expecting the nestling to shriek with fear or bolt away down the dark passages of the prison. She did neither. As small as she was, there was a flicker of recognition in her gaze. Someone had told her exactly *who* her mother was, likely the very person who had brought her to the cell, though Cerys could see no one else present.

Cerys took another step forward and froze; a thin line of gold across Rohesia's forehead had caught her eye. The nestling didn't move as Cerys reached out, a single talon tracing the cool line of metal across her daughter's brow as a vow from half a decade ago echoed in her mind.

'No harm will come to her.'

A lie. For Rohesia wore a circlet, the permanent mark of the *isruhe*. The vermin of the deep. Cerys' swollen heart collapsed into hot liquid, and a raging fury flooded her, rendering her limbs useless, her words inept and her vision blurry. It didn't matter that there was nowhere else a daughter of hers could have ended up, despite whatever promises the visitor had made all those years ago. But seeing it … It made it *different*, more *real* than it had ever been. Centuries ago, when Cerys had wandered Saddoriel freely and proudly, there had been more prisoners – mostly deserters from the Age of Chaos – and so there had been more circlet-wearers. Cerys remembered spotting one or two of them loitering in the shadows, in the outskirts of the lair. But in all her time locked away, she had not met another prisoner, and judging by the quiet of the surrounding cells, she guessed the circlet-wearers were not nearly as common these days, and were likely far more reviled by cyrenkind.

She knew the uncommon was often feared, and fear brought out the worst in cyrens.

'Can you talk?' The nestling spoke suddenly, snatching Cerys from her reverie.

Desperate for contact, Cerys gripped the bars gently, close to where her daughter did the same. 'I can talk,' she said, her voice raw.

Rohesia scanned the etchings on the walls behind Cerys, her posture rigid with intrigue. 'I like to draw, too,' she said, a freely offered kernel of information Cerys would cherish until her last breath.

Cerys licked her dry lips. 'Do you?' It had been so long since a conversation had graced her cell that she couldn't remember how to carry it.

But it didn't seem to matter to her daughter, who nodded enthusiastically. 'They're pretty,' she announced, pointing to the carvings on the wall. 'What are they?'

Cerys couldn't help but stare at her daughter. The very being that had fitted in the crook of her elbow was now this articulate, inquisitive nestling. She showed no fear, no shame in the circlet around her head ... Cerys followed Rohesia's pointed finger to the etchings and her stomach turned. It was too soon to tell her, wasn't it? What if she repeated Cerys' explanation to the wrong cyren? What if with one word, all their plans came undone?

Cerys found her voice. 'Masks.'

Rohesia tilted her head again, her little brow furrowing, as though she were trying to count. 'Why did you draw so many?'

A hollowness opened up inside Cerys. 'Because they remind me of my friends.'

Rohesia's eyes brightened. 'I have friends,' she announced. 'Two best friends. But they don't wear masks.'

And though Cerys was heartened to hear that her daughter was not alone in this godsforsaken lair, darkness pooled within her. She lifted her gaze, meeting the innocent, wide-eyed stare. 'Every cyren wears a mask, Rohesia.'

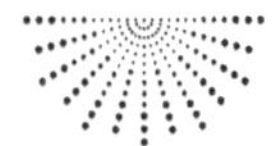

A pearly-grey morning greeted Roh and her four companions as they trekked along the stony shore, across an unknown coast. Colossal cliffs loomed overhead, casting shadows over the black pebbles at the company's feet, the salt spray of the sea kissing their skin. Roh couldn't be sure how far they'd journeyed since crossing the threshold of the cyren territory of Talon's Reach into the lands above almost two weeks ago. There had been no significant landmarks yet, only the winding beach before them. What she did know was that the sky was endless, an infinite patchwork of pale blues and silver clouds, and the crisp breeze that tangled her hair was cool enough to send a rush of goosebumps across her skin.

'Who has the map?' a cold voice cut through the hiss of the waves.

Roh didn't need to turn to identify who'd asked. Finn

Haertel knew damn well she held the map. Not addressing her directly was one of the many ways he'd chosen to undermine her over the course of their recent travels.

'What do you need to know?' she said, refusing to take out the weathered piece of parchment, instead stealing a glance at the human by her side, Odi, who shook his head in frustration.

She heard the intake of breath behind her. 'I need to know *exactly where* you're leading us. Last time I checked, *isruhe*s had little experience navigating,' Finn ground out.

The barb that might once have seen Roh double over didn't sting. What did hurt was the soft snort to Odi's left. Roh's chest constricted. *Harlyn.* Her friend had discovered her own ways of showing her newfound hatred for Roh, which usually came in the form of siding with the highborn, whom she apparently now detested less than she did Roh.

'*Finn,*' snapped another, softer voice, accompanied by the slap of a hand on a leather jerkin. 'That's enough.' It wasn't the first time Yrsa Ward, Roh's final chosen companion, had come to her defence, as though there were something unspoken between them since they had taken on a sea serpent together.

Gold flashed in Roh's mind. The glimmer of scales carving through the turquoise current, the chase of an almighty sea drake ... And then, a different gold – the shine of her circlet, lying broken in two on the marble floor ...

'Well, *it's true.* Who knows where she's taking us? One

of *us* should be the map keeper. We're *Jaktaren*, for Dresmis and Thera's sakes.' Finn's angry words brought Roh back to the cool shore.

With a sigh she relented, rummaging through her inner jacket pocket and pulling out the map. She stopped abruptly and crouched, flattening the parchment and using the round black stones to pin it in place. The others gathered around.

'There,' she snapped, pointing to a southern landmark with her sharp talon. 'The Five Daughters are *there*. There is only *one* direction of travel, unless we decide to take Odi on a scenic detour out to sea. I don't need to be a Jaktaren to navigate that.'

'Oh, really? How far off are we?' Finn sneered, pushing back a strand of chestnut hair that had escaped its knot, his fingers brushing over the zigzag pattern shaved into the side of his head.

Roh gritted her teeth. 'According to *your* initial calculations, we should be there by nightfall. Though with all this bickering, who knows.'

With his mouth set in its usual straight line, Finn didn't deign to respond.

Fury surged through Roh's veins. While she had handpicked the highborn to accompany her on her quest, she had nothing but disdain and loathing for him. It had been *Finn* who had informed the Council of Elders of Odi's true identity as the Prince of Melodies, and she had nearly lost Odi *and* the tournament because of his underhanded, serpentine behaviour.

Roh forced herself to take a deep breath. Regardless of

her personal feelings towards the Jaktaren, she had three gemstones to find and a queendom to solidify. 'I took the advice you gave when we left Saddoriel,' she said as calmly as she could. 'We're taking the secret path up the cliffs by the falls. From there, we trek through the tussock networks, onwards to Akoris. What more do you want?'

The highborn folded his arms over his broad chest. 'I thought I'd made it clear. I want the map.'

Roh got to her feet. 'Tough.' She folded the parchment deliberately, pocketing it once more and starting off again.

To her relief, Odi stepped in line with her, matching her pace. 'I don't know why you two antagonise each other so much.'

'He antagonises me,' Roh argued. 'I rise above it.'

Odi lifted a brow, his amber eyes dancing. 'Is that what you call it?'

'He deserves it,' Roh huffed.

'Then tell me again, why in the name of all the gods did you bring him?'

'I told you – all that scheming, all his Jaktaren knowledge, is on our side.'

Odi heaved his pack higher onto his shoulders and shot her a sceptical look. 'For now.'

Although Roh didn't reply, she was inclined to agree. She liked to think she'd learned from her mistakes and had drawn up a contract for her companions to sign prior to them leaving the cyren territory, which detailed their obligations to her throughout the quest and demanded unwavering loyalty. But there were only so many clauses she could include and there were no doubt plenty of loopholes a Saddorien cyren could find, or create. And the gods only knew whom back in Saddoriel they might be reporting to.

She gave Odi a sideways glance. 'Never trust a cyren, eh?'

'That's what I've heard,' he allowed. But a moment later, he paused, turning to face the sea, shielding his eyes from the misty glare of the horizon. 'The Isle of Dusan,' he said. 'It can't be far off from here.'

Roh winced inwardly, knowing how hard it would be for Odi to be so close to home, and yet so far. 'Why didn't you say anything?'

He shrugged and tugged at his frayed fingerless gloves. 'I couldn't be sure. People from home don't travel this way. For obvious reasons.' He eyed the trio of cyrens behind them.

Roh couldn't blame Odi for his resentment after all he had endured at the hands of her kind. He had been hunted like a wild beast throughout his own lands for his mastery of music, and his stepbrothers remained trapped and were forced to play their fiddles back in the lair. Even now, though he appeared to travel and converse freely, he was outnumbered and compelled to partake in a quest that had nothing to do with him.

It was either this or leave him at the mercy of the council and the lair, Roh told herself, motioning for Odi to keep walking.

The human tore his gaze away from the horizon and

did as she bid, if only to reclaim the distance between him and the Jaktaren behind them.

'*When I'm crowned queen, I will grant you your freedom,*' Roh had vowed to Odi in the dark tunnels of Talon's Reach, and now she wanted to tell him again, to reassure him that she would see him home when all this was over. But with the tournament already unfairly extended and the fight for the three birthstones of Saddoriel ahead, she knew her words would sound hollow, and so she stayed quiet.

They continued onwards in the shadow of the dark cliffs, the tops of which reached up into the clouds. Roh and her companions had yet to find any sign of life along the shores, as though they were the only ones left in all the realms. As a comfortable silence settled between her and Odi, Roh scanned the desolate surroundings. Somehow, the realms beyond the lair weren't what she had imagined. She did not feel liberation or a wild sense of abandon, only the need to push forward. The urgency had not faded since she'd learned of the additional tasks. It thrummed inside her chest, which grew tighter each day as her mind flitted from one possibility to the next.

The competitor will have seven moons to obtain the three birthstones of Saddoriel. The competitor may choose up to four travelling companions to assist their quest. The competitor may be challenged thrice throughout their journey. Once for cunning, once for strength and once for magic, the very virtues cyrenkind reveres ...

The main quest to obtain the birthstones was a constant obsession, as was the question of *when*, not *if*, someone would challenge her. There were many Saddoriens who would happily see her banished from the lair, which was precisely what would happen should she be defeated. As for those who challenged her, glory and riches and elevated station awaited them, should they be named victor. Cunning, strength and magic ... Saddorien cyrens were rife with all three vices and virtues.

Roh sighed, weighed down by these fears, unable to voice them aloud to her companions, knowing they would stay trapped in her mind, where they would only intensify and fester. The outside world could be just as lonely as Saddoriel, it seemed.

Roh's mind began to drift, and, as was its habit, wandered to a pair of wide, green-speckled lilac eyes, blinking at her through the darkness.

'I'm not surprised to see a crown upon your head ...'

Cerys the Elder Slayer. The mad cyren down in the darkest depths of Saddoriel's bone prison, with only her manic carvings of masks etched into the damp walls for company. And yet, the last words she had spoken to Roh were the most lucid she had ever uttered, and had called into question everything Roh had thought she knew about her mother. And then there was the missing quartz dagger, stolen from its usual place in the grasp of a dead water warlock. Roh had spent countless sleepless nights since then pondering it all, each time coming to the same conclusion: none of it made any sense.

Roh walked on, leading her companions across the seemingly endless shore, the stones slipping and crunching uncomfortably beneath her boots. It made for inelegant travelling, though as someone who was usually up to their elbows in bone muck, she wasn't sure it mattered. She adjusted the heavy pack on her back, trying to move the straps from where her skin was already rubbed raw. One thing was for certain: any romantic notions she'd had about the beauty and freedom of the Jaktaren's nomadic way of life had been dispelled. The road was rife with discomfort and an abhorrent lack of privacy —

A streak of gold.

Roh froze, the movement out at sea catching her eye.

It can't be ... Her vision strained as she tried to spot whatever had stirred amidst the currents. Out towards the horizon, sets of waves rolled, crests of white foam atop the darkest blues. And then nothing.

Roh blinked slowly and shook her head in an attempt to rid herself of whatever her imagination had concocted. A mere reaction to her recent traumatic encounter with not only the sea serpent, but its mate, the formidable sea drake. As the images of its outstretched wings and gnashing fangs filled her mind, Roh's stomach dropped, remembering what lay hidden, wrapped in her spare cloak, deep in the pack she carried. A rash decision made in the heat of the moment had been burning a hole of fear in her ever since. She glanced back out to the waves. Perhaps it had made her paranoid, as well ...

She nearly jumped when Yrsa nudged her. The cyren was shorter than most, only reaching Roh's shoulder, but there was the authority of an elder in her white-lashed lilac stare. The zigzag pattern of the Jaktaren guild was shaved into the side of her raven hair, the twin to Finn's marking.

'It's time we took a break,' the highborn said matter-of-factly.

As soon as the words were out of her mouth, fatigue hit Roh, as did the aches along the arches of her feet. She gave a stiff nod. Although its light was muted by a thin film of clouds, the sun was high, which meant they had been travelling for hours already.

Wordlessly, she followed Yrsa away from the lapping tide to the base of the cliffs, easing her pack from her stiff shoulders and lowering herself to the ground, trying to find the most comfortable position atop the uneven stones. Around her, the others did the same. Roh rolled her neck, trying to stretch out the tightness in her muscles. Her body hadn't felt this punished since her first day in the bone workshop back in Saddoriel. Carefully, she pulled her pack in front of her and rummaged through the side pocket for her rations. What little food she had left was stale and bland, but she ate it all the same, chewing mechanically and washing it down with measured sips of water from her canteen. Roh was no expert, but she knew well enough that they would have to find a source of fresh water soon. And food. She glanced up, finding Yrsa gazing knowingly at her. The Jaktaren had clearly come to the same conclusion.

Roh's head snapped to her left as she heard an achingly familiar sound. Harlyn's laugh. Her friend sat beside Odi, her lute case cradled in her lap, her unusual white-blonde hair hanging loose about her shoulders, the smile on her face softening the permanent crease between her brows. Roh tried and failed not to stare. Since when did the human make her friend laugh?

Harlyn looked up, sensing her attention, and without thinking Roh reached across, offering her last piece of flatbread.

A muscle shifted in Harlyn's jaw as she glanced at the food and pointedly turned away.

Roh flushed and hastily packed up the bread. *I can't stand this*, she thought, getting to her feet, shouldering her bag and wandering a short distance from the group. So often throughout her seventeen years she had felt like an outsider, like a pariah to her kind, but *never* with Harlyn. Harlyn and Orson, the friend she had left behind, were her family, her everything. And Roh had ruined that with one sleight of hand and a lie.

She turned her gaze from the open waters to the looming cliffs. At her side, her fingers itched to feel a stick of charcoal between them, scratching at parchment as she sketched shaded shapes to practise her perspective drawings. The contour of the cliff faces before her sparked an array of design ideas. She wanted to jot them down so she wouldn't forget, so when she was Queen of Cyrens, she could commission their creation herself. But quests were not the place for refining artistry. Quests were for damp boots and tight, sunburnt skin, for dirty hair and blisters. A tiny pinprick of fear found a tender, vulnerable spot in Roh's mental armour. What if she lost her skills without practice? What if she forgot the mastery of straight lines and subtle shadowing? Worse still, what if she never became queen?

Seven moons ... That was all the time she had to obtain the birthstones of Saddoriel and ensure her reign. Back in the lair, seven moons would have stretched on and on, but in the realms above, time slipped away quickly and quietly, its swift passage taking her unawares as each new morning dawned.

The sudden crash of a nearby wave upon jagged rocks stilled Roh's fidgeting fingers, its rhythm awakening another longing within her: the desire for music. The mournful notes of the Eery Brothers' fiddles echoing through the lair had faded long ago, and while Roh often found herself gazing hopefully at Harlyn's lute, she didn't have the nerve to ask her friend to play it.

'Bone cleaner.' Finn's hard tone interrupted her thoughts as he stormed towards her, his crossbow gleaming across his back. She supposed it was a preferable alternative to *isruhe*.

'You're not getting the map,' Roh growled.

Fire flared in Finn's gaze. Evidently, he hadn't forgotten their earlier spat; he'd only let his anger fester during their brief reprieve. 'You're an ignorant fool,' he snapped. 'A power-hungry nobody —'

'As opposed to *you*?' Roh retorted, her own fury catching ablaze. 'You only want the map so you can be in control, so you can tell yourself you're still a Jaktaren, better than the likes of me.'

'I don't need a map to tell me that.'

'No? Whatever will you do when I'm your queen? Aren't you worried you're getting off on the wrong foot?'

'No.' Finn lowered his voice, his next words cold. 'You'll *never* be my queen.'

Roh's anger snuffed out as quickly as it had come to life. There would be no peace or agreement between them. She was wasting her breath. Perhaps it had been a mistake to force the Jaktaren on her quest. No matter what contract he'd signed, his loyalty was and always would be to the guild, a guild that did not support her claim to the throne.

'We need to get moving —' Finn's words died on his lips as something caught his attention further down the shore.

Roh followed his line of sight. A massive gull circled overhead, and beneath it was Yrsa, lassoing her sling in wide circles around her head, taking aim. Roh had seen the Jaktaren use her weapon of choice once with great effect in their first trial back in Saddoriel, but this … this was a near impossible shot.

'Five silver marks says she brings it down with one stone,' Finn breathed next to her.

Five silver marks? That's fifty *bronze keys …* Roh wasn't even sure she had ten. She said nothing, biting her lip as Yrsa released the sling and launched a rounded stone, shooting straight for the gull.

A squawk of pain echoed along the cliffs and the bird plummeted to the ground. It landed atop the dark pebbled beach with a thud.

'Told you,' Finn muttered, stalking off towards his fellow Jaktaren.

Roh and her company trekked on, picking up pieces of driftwood where they found them and strapping them to their packs to use for fire fuel later. Hours passed, and as the sun began to dip and Roh's legs were about to give out underneath her, she at last heard the falls. The thunderous roar of water plummeting over the cliffs and hitting the shore below was almost deafening, even from a distance. As they approached the Five Daughters, Roh's neck strained as she looked up. The sheer size of the falls nearly brought her to her knees, the river above carving into the cliff face and rushing down, churning wild white foam as it hit the shore and met the sea. Sneaking a glance at Harlyn and Odi, she saw they were just as awed.

But it was Yrsa Ward who called over the noise, 'Beautiful, isn't it?'

'Yes,' Roh said. 'But we can't make camp here,' she realised, looking at her boots, where sea water foamed at her toes. The tide was coming in.

Yrsa nodded, adjusting the dead gull tied to her pack. 'There's a dry ledge only a little way up. We can sleep there.'

Roh was grateful she had the Jaktaren with her. From their brief interactions over the past few weeks, Roh had learned that Yrsa had travelled the furthest of all the members of her guild, including Finn, who remained stubbornly silent at his friend's side.

'Lead the way,' Roh invited.

To her horror, Yrsa walked straight to the cliff face and reached up, her hands clawing for invisible shelves in the stone.

'She can't be serious.' They were the first words Harlyn had uttered in Roh's direction in days.

But Roh was transfixed on Yrsa's form, scaling the lower part of the cliff. She watched as the fearless Jaktaren hoisted herself up the almost-vertical rock face, her hands finding purchase before she pushed off with her legs.

'Shouldn't she have some sort of rope?' Odi asked loudly, a half-gloved hand covering his mouth.

'She doesn't need a rope.' A note of pride laced Finn's voice. 'And neither do we,' he added. He looked around, as though only just realising that now his friend was climbing, it was he who was left to do the explaining to the bone cleaners and the human. He gave an impatient sigh and motioned for them to follow. They approached the grey stone, jagged in some parts, smooth in others, but from the foot of the cliffs, the tops were lost amidst the orange and gold of the dusky sky above.

'It's just like a ladder,' Finn explained, running his palm along the rock face as Yrsa disappeared from view.

It was Harlyn's turn to scoff.

Finn ignored her. 'You can't see the footholds until you're right up close,' he called over the noise, his talons unsheathing and digging into a tiny ledge. 'It was designed for climbing.'

Roh narrowed her gaze, trying to discern where she might hold on to and where she might slip. Sure enough, Finn was right. There was a pattern of footholds trailing up the cliff. Not an easy feat by any stretch, but not impossible.

Finn stepped back. 'Well, bone cleaner?'

'I hope this isn't the "secret path" up the cliffs you mentioned?' Roh folded her arms over her chest as she strained her neck looking up. It was all very well and good to climb to a ledge, but to climb the entirety of the cliff? She wouldn't force anyone, including herself, to do that.

The highborn clicked his tongue. 'That path starts from the ledge, where Yrsa is now waiting to set up camp.' He gave a pointed look to the water that had begun swirling at their boots. 'You'd best hurry, or the human will be underwater soon. If memory serves, he doesn't like it all that much.'

The image of Odi trapped in a glass tank of water, struggling to keep his head above the surface, came to her. Roh could have hit the Jaktaren. Instead, she tugged Odi towards the footholds. 'You first,' she said.

For once, Odi didn't argue. He simply found his grip and started to climb. Although he made it look easy enough, Roh didn't fail to notice Odi pause several times, clinging to the foothold with one hand while he shook out the other. She cursed herself silently, guilt curdling in her stomach. She had forgotten about the pains that plagued his hands, the very reason why he wore those ridiculous gloves. He'd not explicitly told her what condition he had; she only knew that the pain was chronic, at times debilitating.

It was only when he disappeared to safety that Roh unclenched her own hands. She turned to Harlyn. 'You next.'

Harlyn scowled, opening her mouth to argue, but at the last moment seemed to think better of it. She shook her head and started the ascent.

'Not very popular these days, are you, bone cleaner?' Finn sneered.

Roh resisted the urge to shove him into the incoming tide. She didn't wait for Harlyn to reach the safety of the ledge before she started her own climb. There was no way she was spending a second more alone with Finn Haertel than she had to.

She found purchase easily enough, but the heavy pack weighing her backwards made her nervous. Unsheathing her talons, Roh used them to dig into the gritty cliff face and haul herself up. The rock was cool against her skin in the fading light as she felt around for the next solid foothold. She climbed, feeling a mild sense of satisfaction that Finn was either below, his boots filling with water as the tide came in, or that he too had started the climb and if she fell, she might just take him with her.

At last, she saw the ledge where Yrsa, Odi and Harlyn waited. A large, flat space, the cliff above curved over and up, providing some semblance of shelter from the wind and night chill. Roh's muscles screamed as she used her little remaining upper-body strength to pull herself over the hanging rock. Odi rushed forward to help her, his arms hooking under hers and dragging her away from the edge. Though she was grateful, she wished he'd refrained. It made her look weak.

Finn landed deftly behind her moments later, his boots squelching. 'We'd best set up camp while we still have the light,' he said to Yrsa, as though Roh and the others weren't there. 'I'll start the fire.'

Yrsa nodded, already hunched over the gull she'd killed, plucking its feathers.

Roh stifled a moan as she pushed the straps of her pack away from her aching shoulders and set it down carefully against the cliff face, noting her chipped, dirt-lined talons. They reminded her of another pair of talons she'd seen: Cerys', broken and jagged from her manic wall carvings. Roh pushed the thought aside.

With Odi and Harlyn in the corner talking in hushed voices, Roh went to Yrsa and crouched down close to her.

'Can I help?' she asked, gesturing to the fresh game.

'Well, I suppose … if you're not squeamish …'

Roh scoffed. 'I'm someone who peels flesh from bones for a living. What do you think?'

Yrsa laughed huskily. 'Very well, then.' She handed Roh her machete.

Roh listened as Yrsa told her how to cut the meat. The Jaktaren was surprisingly patient, repeating herself calmly when needed, or taking the blade from Roh and demonstrating particular techniques, though Roh suspected the highborn was holding her at arm's length, albeit in a subtler way than her fellow Jaktaren.

'Who taught you all this?' Roh asked quietly, frowning

as she concentrated on holding the flesh taut while she carved, hoping the practicality of her question would prove too great for Yrsa to ignore.

'It's part of our training. All Jaktaren learn. You have to be able to survive out here.'

'Is that how you learned to use the sling so well?'

Yrsa wordlessly corrected Roh's grip on the machete before answering. 'My aunt Winslow taught me, actually.'

Roh's skin prickled at the name. *Winslow Ward.* So far away from the lair, Roh often forgot that not only was she in the company of two Jaktaren, but also two kin of the Council of Seven Elders. She glanced in Finn's direction, wondering how the council felt about a bone cleaner taking two of their heirs on her deadly quest.

'A Jaktaren must be able to use any weapon,' Yrsa continued. 'But we each have a specialty. Winslow suggested the sling …' Yrsa took the meat from Roh and passed it over to Finn, who was now feeding driftwood into a fiercely burning fire. The sight of it made Roh's chest tighten. Orson always managed the fire in their old sleeping quarters. Roh used to love watching her friend position the kindling with such care, pursing her lips to coax the embers to life with her breath. No one could make a fire like Orson.

Finn took the meat without a word and started preparing to place it over the flames.

'I could teach you, if you like?' Yrsa was saying.

'Teach me?'

'How to use the sling.'

Roh considered this. She didn't know how to wield

any weapon, not to great effect, anyway. She had the natural traits of a cyren – cunning, strength and the ability to manipulate water, although she had failed to sing a note of her deathsong so far.

Roh found herself nodding. 'I'd appreciate that. Thank you.'

Yrsa shrugged. 'It's wise for a queen to have such a skill.'

A queen. The words had slipped so casually from Yrsa's mouth that Roh had nearly missed them.

'She's not a queen,' Finn said, flames illuminating the harsh lines of his jaw and the hardness in his gaze.

'Not yet,' Roh countered, her voice steely.

Finn said nothing.

Roh sighed, turning back to Yrsa. 'It seems you're the only one not at odds with me.'

Yrsa eyed her. 'Don't count on that. I have as much to hold against you. And I'm not overly happy to have been ripped away from Piri.'

'Piri?'

Yrsa's features softened at the name. 'My partner.'

Roh recalled the petite uniform-wearing cyren whom she'd seen kiss Yrsa at the start of the first trial all those weeks ago.

'I'm sorry,' she said, trying to imagine what it might feel like to be separated from someone she cared about deeply. She tucked a loose strand of hair behind her ear, realising that she couldn't really understand how Yrsa felt. She had never cared for another in that way.

'I have the ability to put that aside,' Yrsa told her, 'and

know that it's not personal. Plus, I'm a Jaktaren – my word is my bond. It's a matter of duty.'

Roh sighed. 'Very well.'

Yrsa nodded and got to her feet, moving towards Finn to help.

Roh turned her attention to Harlyn and Odi, who were still sitting in the corner, but were facing each other, playing cards. Roh bit the inside of her cheek, immediately recognising the game.

Harlyn was teaching Odi how to play Thieves.

Watching them, Roh felt hollow, as though there were a gaping, bleeding hole where her heart should be. She couldn't bear it. Which was no doubt exactly Harlyn's intention.

The smell of roasting gull caught in the gentle breeze, but Roh had lost her appetite. She turned to face the sea, where the vast expanse of water met the darkening night sky. She had been waiting her whole life to leave Saddoriel and see such a sight, but now … She stopped herself from glancing back at Harlyn and Odi. Newfound adventure wasn't what she'd thought it would be.

Roh and her companions ate in silence, listening to the rush of the falls. The day had taken its toll on all of them, and it wasn't long before the fire was smothered to embers and bedrolls were unravelled. Roh positioned herself as far away from the others as the ledge would allow.

All at once, it seemed the inky sky had swallowed the

last sliver of sun with a quick, quiet hunger. Now, the black canvas of night yawned before Roh, a smattering of glittering stars blinking down upon her. With a blanket wrapped around her shoulders, she hunched over her pack, carefully sifting through its contents, feeling blindly for the unique texture she had become familiar with. It was only when she could hear the deep, even breathing of each companion that she dared remove the object from her pack. The irony was not lost on her, that secrets had got her into this mess in the first place … and now she clutched a new secret to her heavy heart, bigger, darker and deadlier than the last.

The stolen egg of a sea drake.

CHAPTER TWO

T he soft orange glow of dawn peeking from below the dark horizon came slowly, and as it did, Roh slipped the egg, warm from her body heat, back into her pack before the others stirred —

'We have a problem.'

Roh froze at the sound of Yrsa's voice over the falls. How long had the Jaktaren been awake? Had she seen Roh hunching protectively over her pack? Roh turned and spotted Yrsa a little further along the ledge, peering upwards, apparently perplexed by something else entirely.

'What is it?' Roh asked, getting to her feet.

'It looks like some of the path has collapsed,' Yrsa told her as she continued to search the crevices of the rock face above.

'How bad is it?' Roh asked.

'We can handle it.' Finn was instantly by Yrsa's side,

following her gaze.

'It's not just about us,' Yrsa replied pointedly.

Roh gritted her teeth and without looking up simply said, 'We can handle it.'

Two hours later, Roh regretted it. Her body was slick with sweat and her arms and legs burned with the effort of the steep climb. The echoing roar of the Five Daughters seemed to vibrate through the rock, while the path was steep and narrow, zigzagging up the face of the cliff. In some parts, boulders barred the way or a landslide had wiped out a section of the path altogether, forcing Roh and the others to make death-defying leaps across unstable ground. Scree slid beneath their boots, falling into the eyes of the climber below. Roh had to focus on looking up; any glance down led to a spell of dizziness that threatened to weaken her grip on whatever she was holding and send her plummeting to her death.

'I can't believe we're doing this,' Harlyn called from behind her.

'It was either this or spend weeks travelling around the cliffs and scaling the great dunes of Akoris to the east,' Roh panted. The alternate route would have also meant skipping the gilded plains, where Roh was determined to go. Cerys' words had convinced her that they would find some sort of clue or help there. But there was no way she was about to explain that to Harlyn. She pushed on, ignoring her protesting body and hauling herself further up the deadly path.

But ahead, Yrsa had stopped so suddenly, Roh only just prevented herself from barrelling into her. The Jaktaren was looking out to sea, her mouth agape. Stomach sinking with dread, Roh followed her gaze.

Just before the horizon, a long, powerful body, gold scales glimmering under the water, would shoot out occasionally with a splash.

Roh's heart caught in her throat.

'You see it, too,' Yrsa murmured. 'It's been shadowing us since we left Saddoriel. I think it's holding on to its rage, from when Finn and I attacked it.'

Guilt singed Roh's insides, but she kept her mouth clamped shut. So, she *hadn't* been imagining things back down on the shore.

'At least we're heading inland,' Yrsa added, turning back to the climb.

Roh also tore her eyes away from the creature. They were too far away to see whether it was the sea serpent Yrsa believed it to be, or its mate, the sea drake. Roh silently prayed it was the former. For the latter's wings and legs didn't just carve through water, but air, as well. A sea drake could soar across any land, like the true dragons of old, if it so wished. Roh could only hope that it was too protective of its remaining eggs to leave the sea. But when those drakelings hatched … She shook her head.

Fear continued to churn in Roh's gut as they climbed on. A gasp caught in her throat as her boots slipped across scree and her hands struggled to find purchase. She scrambled, her talons latching onto a foothold at the last second. Inhaling deeply, she paused to gather herself. To fall was to die. But she wouldn't let Harlyn witness her fear, refusing to see the vindication in her friend's eyes as her mistakes highlighted that yet another choice of hers had put them all in mortal peril. Roh forced the rising panic down.

'It's not far to the top,' Yrsa called.

Roh didn't dare risk a glance at her companions below. She focused on each grip, every push off her toes, silently repeating Yrsa's words: *It's not far to the top.* Beads of sweat ran from her hairline, stinging her eyes, and she grimaced, trying to blink away the pain and blurred vision. Anger bubbled in her. At the Council of Seven Elders for unfairly extending the tournament, at Cerys for being so cryptic, at the Law of the Lair for keeping her mentor, Ames, confined to the workshops rather than here with her. But most of all, Roh's anger was for herself. Every decision she had made had led to this moment. Each choice had been hers and hers alone. She could fault no one else.

Roh ground her teeth with the effort it took to haul herself up the sharp incline in the broken path, a grunt of frustration escaping her. *It's not far to the top,* she chanted internally. She had bested some of the most accomplished cyrens in Saddoriel, she had outsmarted some of the most cunning clauses in the Law of the Lair, and she'd defeated a *sea drake*. She would not let this cliff undo her —

A yelp sounded below and Roh nearly lost her grip, her heart suddenly blocking her throat. Without thinking, she looked down. A strangled cry escaped her.

Harlyn had a fistful of Odi's cloak in her talons. The human swayed against the cliff face, arms flailing as he tried to find a hold.

Wild terror flared in his amber eyes.

Harlyn's face reddened as she bore the brunt of his weight with a single hand. 'Stop kicking,' she yelled. 'Stay calm, find a foothold. I've got you.'

Roh expected a panicked retort, but Odi listened. His thrashing movements stilled and a shaking hand extended, palm brushing against the rock until it found purchase.

'There,' Harlyn said. 'I won't let go until you find another.'

Relief cascaded through Roh as Odi's hands and feet dug into the footholds and he started to climb once more. Her own limbs shaking, she forced herself to push on. *It's not far to the top.*

As Roh forced her aching arms to reach up and her feet to push her further towards the sky, her mind sought distraction from the pain and fear.

Odi had nearly died. And Harlyn had saved him. Why? A cyren saving a human was unheard of, at least until Roh had fought for Odi herself in the Queen's Tournament. In the past, Harlyn had made no secret of her disdain for the human, but … Had things changed? Were Odi and Harlyn *friends* now?

Without warning, strong hands gripped Roh and she gave a ragged gasp as she was hauled over the precipice of the cliff.

'What —' Roh wheezed, staggering on liquid legs. Her

gaze fell forward, taking in the expanse of flat, dark sea below the hazy height from which she stood. Lightheaded, muscles at last giving out, she collapsed in the dirt, panting. Her back was wet with sweat beneath the weight of her pack and her hands shook uncontrollably. She did nothing but watch uselessly as Yrsa wrenched the others up over the ledge.

'Never again,' Odi muttered, falling to all fours as though he were about to kiss the earth.

Cradling her pack, Roh found herself looking up at Harlyn. 'Thank you,' she said, with a pointed look at Odi.

But her friend merely dropped her own pack, wincing, and fell to the ground with a moan, lying flat on her back in the dirt.

The Jaktaren were more graceful in their exhaustion. Both Yrsa and Finn simply removed their packs and sat down, stretching out their legs and arms, as though they had just completed a training exercise.

Elbows resting against her pack, Roh ran her fingers through her damp hair, still surprised to find no circlet across her brow. With her eyes closed, she allowed a few moments to gather herself after what they'd all just endured. As her senses came back to her, the sound and smell of fresh rushing water forced her eyes open, and her mouth dropped. They had cleared the cliffs right by the crest of the Five Daughters, where ice-blue water from an immense river churned over the edge into its separate falls and plunged down the jagged rock face.

Roh lurched to her feet, empty water canteen in hand, and stumbled to the river's edge. For a moment, she forgot the presence of the others and fell to her knees on the damp bank, where she cupped the icy water in her palms and brought it to her lips, drinking her fill. The water soothed her swollen tongue and parched throat. She had never tasted anything so good, so pure. Around her, her companions quenched their thirsts and refilled their canteens as well.

'It's such a strange colour,' she murmured, dragging her fingers through the current.

'It's because it comes from the mountains,' Odi said, water dripping from his chin. 'Dust from the glaciers makes it that shade of blue.'

Roh frowned. 'Glaciers?'

But Odi didn't elaborate.

Although it was the last thing she wanted to do, Roh got to her feet and took in the expanse of land before her. A grassy hillside greeted the fast-flowing river, covered in tufts of golden tussock, stretching as far as the eye could see.

'*The gilded plains,*' she breathed, unable to look away. Exhaustion disappeared as she took a step towards the seemingly endless field. For a brief moment, Roh pondered why Saddorien cyrens stayed in the lair their whole lives when there was so much to see beyond. Then, she recalled the strange tether she had felt when she had first tried to leave the passageways with Odi. Perhaps it was an instinctive, preemptive homesickness? She would have to ask Ames when she saw him in Akoris.

Securing her pack on her shoulders, Roh retrieved the map from her pocket and turned expectantly to her companions. Perhaps they were too tired to protest, or perhaps they could see the determination in her eyes and knew it would be no use, but Roh's chest felt light as Odi, Harlyn, Yrsa and Finn hoisted up their own packs in readiness.

After consulting the map, Roh determined that they could follow the Endon River much of the way to Akoris, which would also lead them straight through the mysterious gilded plains. As they put more distance between themselves and the sea, Roh realised that she felt different, that the magic out here was different to that of the currents and tides, to that which linked her to Saddoriel. Walking along the stony shores, she had felt the thrum of cyren power, but atop the cliffs, amidst more arid land … What she felt here was not the same.

Does that mean I'm less likely to find my deathsong, the further away from the lair I travel? Roh pushed the thought to the back of her mind. She could only fret over one thing at a time, and at this moment, she was more concerned with what the gilded plains had to offer her. What was it about the rippling carpet of tussock that had been special enough for Cerys to mention in their last moments together?

The knee-high grasses swished against Roh's legs as she walked on, still clutching the map between her hands. With no more cliffs to scale, her mind wandered to what awaited them in Akoris. She didn't even know *which* of the three birthstones of Saddoriel was in the cyren territory's possession, but at least Ames, her mentor, would be meeting them there.

I could use his 'unofficial' guidance now more than ever, she mused, stumbling as she set off a small rockslide above a larger slip beneath her. She was keenly aware of the silence around her and realised with a start that what she was missing was the simplicity and intimacy of it being just her and Odi, when she hadn't had multiple opposing wills and fractured relationships to deal with. On this new journey, she and Odi hadn't been able to talk how they had before, when it was just them. Roh had become used to freely speaking her mind, but now she felt trapped within it. She gazed out at the tousled tresses of olive and gold stretching before them and her skin prickled, a rush of goosebumps covering her arms.

Frowning, she looked around. There was nothing in sight but hills and grasslands, and yet …

'We're not alone,' she murmured to the group.

The others stiffened around her, craning their necks and straining their eyes to determine what exactly Roh was picking up on. All the while, Cerys' words echoed in her mind: *'You'll find another like him … Another like him amidst the gilded plains.'*

Who exactly will I find here? Roh wondered, her skin still crawling. *Or have they already found me?*

But nothing leaped from the tussock patches. There was no sign of anything out there, leaving Roh feeling foolish. So she continued to walk along the river, her boots sinking into the muddy banks, pushing through the grass that seemed to dance to the rhythm of the current.

As the day wore on, Roh savoured the changing golden hues of the plains at the mercy of the beaming sun. Once again, she found herself pondering the gold of the circlet she had worn her whole life, its broken pieces now lying somewhere back in Saddoriel. She had always been taught to be ashamed of the colour, that it marked her as lesser. But in the weeks that had passed, she had seen much beauty and strength in the colour she had been conditioned to detest.

'Don't you think it's time,' Harlyn drawled from her side, 'to tell us why in the name of all the gods you've taken us this way? There was time enough to go around.'

Roh glanced at her friend. There was nothing kind or forgiving on Harlyn's face, only a challenge, one that had been bubbling up since the day of the final trial in Saddoriel. She paused in the tussock, readying herself for the strike. She'd known it was coming.

'I don't answer to you,' Roh said, steeling herself.

Harlyn laughed darkly. '*You* don't answer to *us*? And what makes you think we answer to *you*, of all cyrens?'

'The fact that you're here at all should give you a hint, Harlyn. I'm your queen.'

'Queen?' Harlyn spat the word as though it were venom on her tongue. 'A traitorous bone cleaner? An *isruhe*? An *isruhe without a deathsong*, no less? You're deluded if you think we will ever bow to you.'

Roh's talons slid out, but she didn't move. She merely sucked in a breath through her teeth. Family always knew which old wounds to press.

'You betrayed me. You betrayed Orson. And then you had the nerve to tear me away from her, to leave her behind as you dragged me along on this joke of a quest for queendom? You're as mad as your mother.'

Roh didn't think. She lashed out, shoving Harlyn viciously.

Harlyn swiped back, talons gleaming.

So it had come to this. Physical blows between them as the Jaktaren and human watched on in silence.

But Roh wasn't done. She had borne Harlyn's hatred and insults with as much dignity and grace as she could muster over the endless days, knowing she deserved them. But to throw Cerys in her face? The image of her music-theatre model lying shattered on the workshop floor filled her mind then, too. She lunged again, forcing Harlyn to stumble back and slip into the shallows of the river. Crimson surged across Roh's vision, the water hissing around her ankles as she advanced on Harlyn. As the river lapped at her skin, she felt its water magic surge and she glanced down at the icy rapids, the scales at her temples warming —

A loud crackling sounded and both Roh and Harlyn froze ankle-deep in the water, fists clenched, looking around wide-eyed. The ear-piercing cracking and popping continued, and Roh whirled around, Harlyn forgotten, as she tried to locate the source of the noise.

'We're not under attack,' Finn said dryly, reaching into a patch of grass. With several snaps, he dislodged something and held out his hand, palm upturned for them all to see. A bunch of red pods popped open before them, filling the air with the same crackling noise.

'Luan seedlings,' he told them. 'They burst when the

sun hits them with a particular heat during this part of the day.' He tossed the pods over his shoulder and glared at Roh and Harlyn. 'Pull yourselves together. At this rate, you'll need no challenger – you'll finish each other off. In case you haven't realised, this isn't the place for lowborn scrapping.'

Roh's cheeks burned with fury – the Jaktaren was right. With a splash, she left Harlyn in the river and found her place at the front of the company, pretending to consult the map.

A half-gloved hand offered her a piece of cured meat.

With a grateful smile, she took it from Odi and chewed the tough, salty fare. 'Thanks,' she said, her fury ebbing away.

Odi shrugged, glancing back at Harlyn, who was tipping the water from her boots.

'Do you think she'll ever speak to me again?' Roh asked quietly.

'Why'd you force her to come? And why just her?'

Roh sighed. 'I could only bring four companions. You counted as one. And Harlyn … I just thought … I don't know what I thought. Maybe that Orson would forgive me sooner? Harlyn was the one who wanted me to fight. *"You can fight. Do the tasks. Find the gems. Become queen, and punish them all …"* Remember?'

'I remember,' Odi said. 'But …'

'But what?' Roh pushed. 'No sense in holding back now, is there?'

Odi gave another infuriating shrug. 'Have you even apologised to her?'

Roh frowned. 'I … She doesn't want to hear it.'

'That sounds like a no to me.'

'But she —'

Odi silenced her with a look, a trick she used to be able to use on him. 'You haven't apologised to me, either,' he ventured.

Roh baulked. '*To you?* Is it wrong for me to have you here? Would you rather have stayed in Saddoriel?'

'I would rather have been granted my freedom, as promised.'

'I had no choice …'

He simply gazed sadly at her. 'Did you *really* try to free me? Or because I had proven myself useful, decided to keep me with you? It wouldn't be the first time you've used a situation to your own advantage.'

'How could you think that? Whose words are these, Odi?' The image of Odi and Harlyn playing cards together flashed before her.

'Mine,' he said. 'Have you even asked Yrsa or Finn what became of *their* humans? Do you even care?'

Roh's words caught in her throat. Against her better judgement, she had long since realised that she *did* care. She remembered helpless young Tess, Yrsa's human, clear as day, and how she'd pulled the girl from the quicksand's death grip. But before Roh could reply, Odi had already fallen back in line with the others.

Reeling from the accusations, Roh tried to lose herself in the sound of the river rushing by, but her thoughts were too loud, dragging her under just as the rapids of the river swept away everything in their path. Was Finn right? Would they all kill each other before she'd even had the chance to obtain a gem? Before someone challenged her? Feeling defeated, she slowed her pace slightly, so Yrsa caught up with her. Despite knowing that the Jaktaren was only being civil towards her out of some rigid notion of duty and self-preservation, Roh longed for conversation that was not laced with hatred. Plus, she suspected that Yrsa had a level of specialist knowledge she sorely needed in her current situation.

As they walked, navigating the plains of tussock, Roh plucked up the last of her energy and courage. 'I always wondered,' she ventured casually. 'What made you choose to focus on vipers for the second trial?'

Yrsa looked up in surprise. 'They've always been a strong symbol in the Ward family. Our line of vipers has been passed down the generations for millennia.'

Roh recalled the box Yrsa had presented to the council, filled with straw and valo beetles and … viper eggs.

'Do the eggs need to be kept warm?' she asked, hoping it didn't sound too out of nowhere.

'Vipers are descendants of the sea serpents. Their blood runs hot because they're supposed to live in the cold, deep waters. The eggs insulate themselves.'

'Then why the valo beetles?'

Yrsa gave a dismissive shrug. 'Disree, my viper, likes them. Apparently, she's developed a taste for bright, shiny things.'

Roh nodded, hoping her questions hadn't raised any suspicion in the Jaktaren. But Yrsa looked unfazed.

Roh turned back, trying to determine how far they'd travelled from the Five Daughters' crests, but instead, spotted Odi and Harlyn passing the lute between them. They weren't playing it, but from the furrow of Harlyn's brow, they were clearly discussing it in depth. A pang of envy twisted in Roh's gut, followed by a shot of alarm.

Why am I jealous? she questioned, turning away sharply and forcing her gaze forward to the winding river and network of gold ahead. *Is it about Odi?* Roh chewed the inside of her cheek, her thoughts spiralling down into the dark depths she was now so intimately familiar with. *Do I ... Do I have feelings for the human?* The question was so ridiculous it nearly sent laughter bubbling from her lips. But why, then, did the sight of him with Harlyn make her gut twist? Why did the familiarity between the pair heat her blood and threaten to unsheathe her talons? Gritting her teeth, she returned her attention to Yrsa.

'So,' she said. 'How does your sling work?'

When the group stopped to rest, Yrsa showed Roh the basics of her chosen weapon. The Jaktaren held out the sling.

'This here is the cradle,' she told Roh without ceremony, pointing to the leather pouch between the two lengths of cord. She flipped open the small purse hanging from her belt and produced a large clay ball. 'It's where you put the stone for firing.' Looping part of the cord around her middle finger and positioning a knot between the others, Yrsa began to swing the weapon in wide circles above her head, gaining speed. 'The length of these cords is tailored to each slinger,' she told Roh. 'If we were to make you one, we'd take your measurements.'

Roh watched the Jaktaren eye up a piece of driftwood on the bank of the river. She released the sling, sending the stone shooting into the damp wood. Splinters flew off upon impact and Roh flinched, imagining the devastation it could cause to flesh and bone. The driftwood was in bits.

'What about close-range combat?' Roh asked.

Yrsa raised a brow and shortened the length of cord between her fingers as she approached the remaining shred of driftwood, positioning another clay ball in the leather pouch. In one swift motion, she brought the cradle and stone crashing into her target. It shattered.

'Gods,' Roh murmured.

'There's a simplicity to this weapon, yes,' Yrsa said. 'But with precision and accuracy, you can shatter any opponent into dust.'

Roh swallowed, silently reminding herself to never get on Yrsa's bad side. 'Can you show me again?'

After their lesson, body aching and hands blistered, Roh wandered further downstream, finding a small pool to bathe in privacy. She had never been overly self-conscious or shy back in the lair, but that was before she had travelled with a human man and a cyren male in such close quarters. Even when she'd shared her chambers with Odi, they'd had a private bathing room. She hadn't experienced true privacy in weeks and she missed it sorely. She washed quickly, hissing at the iciness of the water, which, as Odi had told her, ran from the melting caps of the mountains in the unknown distance to the east. Roh prayed that a hot bath at least awaited her in Akoris. Though the thought of their intended destination brought to light the nagging question that had permanently settled at the back of her mind: once she was in Akoris, how was she supposed to get the birthstone? She didn't even know *which* birthstone the Akorians held. The extended tournament instructions, not surprisingly, had failed to detail the *how* of things.

A branch snapped and Roh's head jerked up, her gaze searching wildly for the source of the noise, remembering the feeling of being followed. She exhaled a sigh of relief as she saw Yrsa approaching the riverbank. The Jaktaren seemed hesitant.

'It's freezing,' Roh offered. 'But you'll feel better after a wash.'

'I don't overly like still water,' Yrsa said.

Roh was surprised. She'd never heard of a cyren who didn't like a certain type of water. 'Why?' she asked.

Yrsa met her gaze for a moment before her eyes fell upon the pool. 'I don't always like what stares back …'

Roh blinked. Whatever she'd been expecting the highborn to say, it hadn't been that.

'I … uh …' Roh wrung her hands.

Yrsa simply waved her away, as though her comment were unimportant, something trivial. Unsure of what to do or say next, Roh retreated into the tussock, where the others sat in silent tension.

The hair on the back of her neck stood up and her

skin prickled again. She turned around slowly, taking in the landscape around them, unable to shake the feeling that they were being watched. Without thinking, she slid her gaze to Finn's, seeking his Jaktaren expertise. Sure enough, his jaw was clenched and his talons were extended, alert and ready.

And yet, nothing happened.

Slowly, they relaxed. With a sigh, Roh sat down, knowing she'd regret not resting her feet soon enough. Massaging her temples and scales, where a tightness had formed, she looked around. Nearby, Odi was hunched over a spare piece of parchment she'd given him days earlier, scribbling away with a battered quill. She craned her neck to see what he was writing, but it was in no language she understood – not Old Saddorien or New, and not the common tongue that humans spoke. Who exactly was he writing to? His father? Surely not his stepmother, who detested him? Roh made a mental note to ask him about it later.

Not far from Odi, Harlyn cradled her lute. Anguish filled Roh at the sight of it, for now would be the perfect time for Harlyn to play. To reinvigorate their group with delicate notes and a comforting melody before the next part of their journey. But once more, Roh didn't have the courage to ask, knowing that at the very least her friend would ignore her, and at the worst, they would come to blows again.

'You shouldn't even have that,' Finn said, watching Harlyn trace the lute's strings.

Roh stifled a groan, sensing the storm brewing within her friend at the very words.

'It's against the Law of the Lair for a cyren to learn human instruments,' Finn continued, jutting out his chin, his nostrils flaring.

'The Law of the Lair can be bent. I'm sure you've had some experience with that, council offspring,' Harlyn retorted, not looking up from her lute.

'You know nothing of my experiences, bone cleaner,' Finn snapped.

'And you know nothing of mine.'

'I know enough. You would break our ancient laws. You would side with human filth —'

'I'm *right here*,' Odi bellowed.

Roh jumped. She had never heard him raise his voice before, had never heard him lose his temper, not like this. She hadn't even realised she'd got to her feet, talons out, ready to intervene. But Odi wasn't done.

'You *worship* the music we create,' he spat at Finn. 'Your whole precious lair thrives off our art. You hunt us down like animals. You need us, and yet you treat us like scum.' He drew a furious, trembling breath. '*Where is Tess? Where is your human? What of the Battalonian, Aillard? What happened to them all?*' Odi stood before Finn now, fists clenched and amber eyes full of fire.

The silence that followed could only mean one thing – whatever had happened to the humans, it wasn't good.

Slowly, Finn stood. He extended a single talon and pressed it to Odi's chest, forcing the human to take a step back, lest it pierce through his shirt and into his flesh.

'Don't think because you have the *isruhe* onside that you're safe.'

'She's your queen.'

Roh's chest swelled with pride.

'No,' Finn said with deadly softness. 'She's not.'

'Oh, for Thera's sake,' Yrsa's clipped voice cut in as she made her way back to them, the ends of her hair dripping. To Roh's surprise, she positioned herself between the two males and faced Odi, offering him something green; a strange, smooth offshoot of a plant. 'Here.'

The palpable tension around them dissipated, curiosity pulsing in its stead.

Bewildered, the human took it from her tentatively, waiting for an explanation.

'For your hands,' she said. 'Break it open and scoop out the sap inside. Massage it into your joints. It should alleviate some of the pain —'

The crunch of dry grass beneath a boot sounded. The five of them fell silent. None of them had moved.

Roh's skin prickled again. This time, she heard a shout. But before she could whirl around, thick hands closed around her arms, pinning them to her sides. She choked as a wet gag was forced over her head and between her teeth. She looked around wildly, panic gripping her heart in its vice-like fist.

A group of cloaked assailants was upon them.

A blur of commotion filled Roh's vision to the left as Yrsa launched her sling into an attacker's face with a sickening crunch, causing an agonising cry. To her right, Finn palmed two daggers and fended off another with vicious slices and a well-aimed kick to the chest. Fear thick in her throat, Roh struggled against her captor. She was a Saddorien cyren, she had to be stronger than her assailant – she coughed into the gag, a chemical tang filling her nostrils. The material had been soaked in something. She thrashed wildly, throwing off her opponent and clawing at the gag, managing to loosen it as she scoured the riverbank for Odi and Harlyn. The cloaked, hooded figures were everywhere, their weapons gleaming in the golden afternoon sun. They shouted in the common tongue, which marked them as human, but they were no ordinary humans – that much was clear enough by the way they moved. Was Roh being challenged?

Is that what this is? It could *be part of an elaborate scheme* ... She struggled against another captor. She had thought a challenger would wait until she had at least reached Akoris, exhausted and depleted. But using humans? That was not the Saddorien way.

No, this can't be a challenge, Roh realised coldly. This was an attack on cyrenkind —

A strangled gasp snagged in Roh's throat as she saw a cloaked man hold a blade to Harlyn's neck. Opposite her, Odi froze mid-grapple with another, surrendering rather than seeing Harlyn killed. Roh surged towards them, talons out, slashing at the hands that grabbed at her. A shriek sounded nearby, but Roh couldn't find its source —

A beautiful, eerie note pierced the air, sending a shockwave out across the skirmish. Roh whirled around, spotting Yrsa, her head tilted to the sky as her deathsong poured from her. It was rich and glorious and full of violence. Roh waited, transfixed by the sound – the first deathsong she'd ever heard used for its actual purpose.

But she gaped in disbelief as the attackers continued their assault, unaffected by Yrsa's magic. That was when she saw them – the talismans around their necks. Similar to the very one that rested against Odi's sternum. At that, Roh was certain: these were no ordinary attackers.

The deathsong was cut off. Four men took Yrsa down and a gag was shoved into her mouth.

'No!' Finn shouted, his eyes wild and hair loose

around his face as he threw a dagger, a scream echoing along the river as the blade sank into the shoulder of one of Yrsa's attackers, blood spurting.

This couldn't be happening. Roh refused to believe it. She was a *Saddorien cyren*, accompanied by two of the most accomplished *Jaktaren* the realms had ever seen. As if in answer, Finn twirled the remaining blade and slashed at another assailant, leaving the second dagger embedded in a man's abdomen and reaching for his crossbow. He fought with a graceful fluidity Roh had never seen and it filled her with hope. As loath as she was to be saved by the arrogant highborn, the alternative was too disgraceful. For her quest to be upended by these strange *humans*...

Finn opened his mouth to call his deathsong. The note that escaped him sent a rush through Roh, the music so delicate, so pure. But there were too many of them and they all wore protective talismans.

Where did they get those? How do they possess cyren magic? Roh started as more hands clamped around her, binding her wrists tightly behind her back, avoiding the slash of her talons and refastening the gag firmly back in place. Whatever it was soaked in nullified her magic, which was snuffed out like a candle. She tried to call out in warning to Finn, but several of the cloaked figures were already upon him. Amidst the violent struggle, he too was gagged.

It was over.

A muffled cry sounded, like that of a wounded animal, and Roh fought against the grip they had on her, craning her neck as she recognised the sound. *Harlyn*. She was on her knees in the tussock, gagged and bound, her eyes filled with pain. Not a physical pain, Roh realised with some relief, but as she saw what Harlyn mourned, despite their differences, Roh's heart broke too.

Harlyn's lute lay smashed in the dirt, its strings sticking out like broken whiskers, its neck snapped nearly in two, dangling uselessly by a shred of wood.

Something trickled down Roh's chest and she looked, finding a long, bloody gash across the top of her breast. *When did that happen?* She hadn't felt a thing, but now, upon sight of it, the hot throb of pain began to pulse.

Around her, their captors checked her and her companions' bonds and gags with cold precision, yanking on ropes and pulling the damp fabric tighter between their teeth. Furious and helpless, Roh writhed against her restraints, trying to work a sharp talon between them. But they were too tight, already rubbing her skin raw. She could do nothing but watch the men as they moved from Yrsa, who stood calmly as their prisoner, to Finn, whose lilac eyes were filled with an icy rage, back to Harlyn, who was still kneeling in the dirt. Of the captured humans Roh had seen in the lair, none had looked like this: armed to the teeth and dressed in leather pants, high boots, leather jerkins and heavy hooded cloaks.

What do you want? Roh needed to scream, but any sound she tried to make caused her to choke, the chemical her gag had been soaked with filling her whole mouth and throat. All this time, Roh had never truly imagined what it would be like to be someone's prisoner. How her own mother felt, trapped behind bars. What it must have been like for Odi in Saddoriel —

Odi. Roh's stomach dropped. She hadn't seen him with the others. But her gaze snagged on the human's familiar lean form and messy toffee hair. He had been separated from the cyrens, bound, but not gagged.

'How are you alive amidst these monsters of the deep?' one of the hooded figures demanded, cradling Finn's crossbow.

Panic spiked within Roh. Odi wasn't with them by choice. In fact, his earlier words had been laced with anger and resentment, and now … now he held the power to determine their fate.

'I …' Odi's shoulders sagged. 'It's hard to explain.'

The hooded man reached out and clasped Odi's protective shell token between his gloved fingers, studying it with intrigue. 'Try,' he said.

Odi seemed to consider this, and then, with his amber eyes glowing, clamped his mouth shut in determination.

Gratitude swarmed through Roh. She didn't know what their captors' intentions were, but she knew very well that upon hearing of the treatment of Odi in Talon's Reach, their apparent low opinion of Saddorien cyrens would not improve.

The cloaked man's voice softened as he spoke his next words. 'I can see you're scared,' he told Odi, glancing at Roh with pure hatred in his eyes. 'And rightly so. But you need not fear us. We will use these sorry creatures to get our own returned to us.'

Odi lifted his chin. 'If your kin went into Saddoriel, they won't come out.'

Roh saw the man's eyes narrow. 'Then we'll kill the cyrens. And figure out what to do with you later —'

A ripping noise dragged Roh's attention away. To her horror, in the now fading light, the cloaked figures had started to rifle through their packs. Sheer terror surged through her.

They're going to find it, she panicked, renewing her fight against her bonds and captor. *They'll find the egg and then we'll truly be done for!* Whoever they were, they'd recognise the mortal peril the egg's presence put them all in. The men would likely slit their throats without a second thought.

'Oi!' her captor shouted as she brought her heel down hard on his toes, trying to buck him off her as one of the men tore through Odi's pack.

Roh cried out as a boot connected with the vulnerable tendons behind her knees and she fell to the ground.

'Looks like there's something this one doesn't want us to find,' her captor said.

You stupid fool, Roh cursed her recklessness.

The search became frenzied, belongings and rations being wrenched from each pack, discarded carelessly in the dirt, before they moved on to the next. Roh flinched as Harlyn's broken lute was tossed aside, her heart creeping further up into her throat as more of the men crowded around and sifted through their things.

They reached her pack and Roh held her breath, her talons digging into the soft flesh of her palms. She tried to stand, to see what they were doing, but she was shoved back down to her knees. She couldn't make out their movements, or each object from her pack as they held it up and examined it before tossing it away —

A sudden shout sounded.

They've found it, Roh thought. *It's over. They'll kill us and take the egg. And I will die out here in the gilded plains, having risked it all on Cerys' cryptic words. Harlyn will die. Finn and Yrsa will die. Perhaps even Odi, too ...*

One of the men beckoned to their leader and the man who had questioned Odi stalked over to the ransackers. The humans whispered inaudibly amongst themselves as their leader considered their bounty.

'This changes everything,' he said. 'We have to take them to *him.*'

Him? Who in the name of all the gods is 'him'? What will 'he' do to us? Roh's mind began the dark descent into spirals. *We'll be killed. And the egg will be sold to the highest bidder, or thrown back into the seas so the drake doesn't come hunting.*

'Get them up,' the leader ordered. 'Get their things. We leave now.'

When Roh struggled again, the point of a sword pinched her back. She had no choice but to walk forward, the thick hand that gripped her arm guiding her roughly across the tussock.

'Where are you taking us?' Odi asked.

After helping their wounded, the hooded men didn't bother to respond as they picked up the discarded belongings and packs, forcing Odi and the cyrens forward at swordpoint.

'How is it that you have cyren magic, then?' Odi asked.

When was Odi going to learn that his incessant questioning was enough to send even the most even-tempered being into a rage?

But the leader laughed darkly, taking his own talisman in his hand. 'You mean this?'

'Yes.'

'This is no *cyren* magic, boy.'

'What —'

'Be silent now. Or you'll find yourself gagged alongside the monsters.'

Wisely, Odi said no more.

They followed the course of the river, the light of dusk bringing the russet and buttery tones of autumn streaking across the sky.

The blood on Roh's chest dried the colour of rust as she walked, becoming itchy across her skin as fear settled in her core, a constant chaperone to her wandering thoughts. As they trekked across the grasslands, Roh felt oddly removed from the situation, as though she were watching the events unfold, happening to someone else, a stranger. With a dark sense of amusement, she realised that the hooded figures were taking them in the exact direction she had planned to lead her company.

Is this what Cerys wanted? Is it a set-up? Is Cerys so deranged that she would send her only daughter to her death? Roh realised with a start that she truly did not know the answer. This was the longest period of time she'd gone without seeing her mother. Had Cerys even noticed that her visits had stopped? Did she remember the crown of bones with the missing birthstones? Roh focused her gaze forward. *I suppose it doesn't matter now.*

'What do you think he'll do?' she heard one of the men hiss.

'No idea. But it means *something*, doesn't it?' said another.

'It's for *him* and *him* alone to decide,' the leader's voice cut in sharply.

'Of course, Captain.'

Frustration coursed through Roh as the men fell silent. She wanted them to drop their guards, to chat freely in front of her and the others. Perhaps then, she'd get a sense for where they were being taken and exactly what threats they faced. If the men continued to gossip, maybe she'd be able to figure out who, in the name of Dresmis and Thera, this 'him' was. But the cloaked men did as their leader bid, the quiet between them intensifying until it became near stifling. Roh could sense Odi was close, his questions likely bubbling to the surface once more.

Evening had almost settled around them when the men forced Roh and the rest away from the river's path. In the distance, Roh could see flames and the narrow plumes of smoke from campfires on the darkening horizon. She was guided through more tussock, the grass scraping against the legs of her pants as their captors slowly closed the gap between them and the settlement ahead.

Roh tried to swallow the thick lump that had lodged itself in her throat, but the gag made it impossible and she coughed violently. She squinted through the dark, now only just able to make out the outlines of Odi, Yrsa, Finn and Harlyn. Would the Jaktaren be planning an escape? Surely they had been trained for this sort of thing, surely they had come up against such challenges throughout all their journeys and travels …? The questions churned in Roh's mind but did not quell the fear roiling in her gut.

The soft glow of multiple fires illuminated the grounds before her and she stared open-mouthed at what looked to be rows and rows of domes sprawling outwards in a circular pattern.

'What is this place?' Odi breathed.

But no one answered.

Upon entry into the settlement, there were humans everywhere. Normal humans, not like the brutes who were manhandling Roh and her companions. She felt their eyes on her, full of suspicion.

'You're in our territory now,' the man holding Roh hissed into her ear. Rage simmered just below the surface of her skin. She wished she could plunge the lot of them beneath the waves and show them just how much she could bend the currents to her will.

The domes were tents, she noted as they passed through the outer rings. All the same size, of the same construction, with a flap of material hanging down across the front. Roh tripped as she was practically dragged through the camp, refusing to acknowledge the stares of the onlookers, instead setting her sights ahead, towards the much larger dome at the centre of the settlement.

Who are they taking us to? Why? Is there a way out? If we escape, what will all this mean for our quest? What of the birthstones? What of the ever-ticking clock of this tournament? The questions flew at Roh with every step closer to the giant dome. As they approached the entrance, she began to thrash against her captor again, trying to pierce him with her unsheathed talons bound at her back.

'Stop,' Odi called out to her. 'It won't help you.' Then he turned his efforts towards the leader. 'Please, you have whatever it is you want. Surely there's no harm in letting us go.'

But that dark laugh sounded again, along with the hum of a dozen whispers. With a rough shove, Roh and the others were pushed through the flap of the dome, into the dimly lit, cavernous space beyond.

Before Roh had a chance to look around, she was forced to her knees again. She winced as hard earth crunched against bone and tender bruises. Before her were a pair of muddy black boots, and her open pack, belongings spilling out, was discarded beside them.

Heart pounding, her gaze trailed up the laces of the boots to the hooded figure who wore them. She bit down on the wet gag, grateful that it stopped her from crying out in anguish.

But it was not the sea-drake egg grasped in dirty hands.

'Tell me,' the man said, his voice rich and deep, his face

still hidden. 'How did a songless cyren come to have this in her possession?'

Roh choked on her gag.

Between his blackened fingers twirled the quartz dagger from Saddoriel's prison.

CHAPTER FOUR

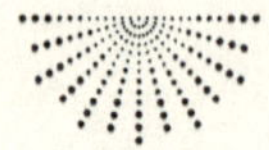

Roh stared at the dagger, its pale-rose hue glinting in the torchlight, the handle of bone gleaming in the man's grip. How did the dagger get here? How did he know she was songless?

Still gagged, all she could do was blink at her interrogator, veiled in shadow.

When her gag was undone, she rasped, 'That's not mine.'

'No?' Something akin to amusement laced the man's tone. 'Then how did it come to be in your possession?'

Roh could feel the searing gazes of disbelief from her companions, but she didn't look away from the stranger standing before her, noting two vicious cutlasses hanging from his worn belt. An icy shiver ran down her spine. She had overcome many obstacles and hardships in the last few months, but if Roh knew one thing for certain, it was that she would not hold up well under duress. Her mind soared back to the last visit she'd had with Cerys; the elation she'd felt at her mother's lucidness … The following plummet of disappointment when madness had claimed Cerys again. And then, the tiny detail … The dead water warlock, who had been there since before Roh could remember. His half-snarl, his blue-tinged skin and the frozen grip of his hand, empty, where a quartz dagger had once lived.

But the man hadn't asked her where the dagger was *from*. 'Well?' he prompted calmly.

'I … I don't know,' Roh stammered, her voice raw.

The stranger kept twirling the dagger, dancing his fingers along the quartz blade and regripping the bone handle.

The pit of fear inside Roh bubbled into something else. Anger. Hot fury at the sight of this bandit playing with something that belonged to the lair as though it were a worthless toy.

'Who are you?' She lifted her chin in defiance. Her intake of breath was audible as the man lifted a hand to his heavy hood. As he lowered the fabric, Roh felt it.

Magic. A whisper of it brushed against her grimy skin. It was different to the magic of Saddoriel – freer. Talon's Reach held its power pressurised and contained, but out here in the vast expanse of the realms, magic, whatever kind, had room to play, to grow. Roh had only heard tales of such power before, the power of a people long ago stamped out by her kind …

'*What* are you?' she whispered, her eyes meeting a grey-blue gaze. Flickering torchlight revealed a crooked, misshapen nose, broken in several places, and a rich complexion smudged with dirt. Dark golden-brown hair fell across the man's harsh face, filth and stubble masking his true age, but Roh guessed he could be no older than thirty or so.

'Do you know what this is? What you've been carrying?' he asked, ignoring her questions.

Roh stared at him, her companions long since forgotten. Was *this* who Cerys had spoken of? *'You'll find another like him ... amidst the gilded plains ...'* Roh had no idea who her manic mother had been talking about, but she was quite certain there was no one like the stranger before her.

'It's a dagger,' Roh said at last, the stupidity of her words sending a hot flush across her cheeks.

She could have sworn the man rolled his eyes. 'It's a historic artefact, prized by my clan above almost all else. I need to know where you got it. *How* you got it.'

A shiver ran down Roh's spine as she recalled the blue-tinged figures who stood opposite her mother's cell. *My clan ...* But that was impossible. He couldn't be speaking of the water warlocks. He couldn't have anything to do with them. That race no longer existed, not since the Scouring of Lochloria. She had been taught that particular history since she was a nestling. Why had Cerys told her to come here? What strange magic swirled about her now? How much could she risk, with not only her life in the balance, but Yrsa, Harlyn, Finn and Odi's, too? How much could she tell this stranger, when she herself didn't understand all the forces at work?

It was Odi who spoke first. 'It was in the prison,' he told the man. 'In Saddoriel. I don't think Roh even knew she had it.'

Roh gritted her teeth. She could have killed him. This was not the time or place for open confessions, not that there ever was one. When was the useless human going to get it through his thick skull?

But Odi's words had snatched the stranger's attention. He inclined his head towards the human. 'Is that so?' he murmured, more to himself than anyone else, peering down at the dagger in his hands.

A moment later, someone cloaked and hooded swept into the dome. Roh only heard the tail end of the message. '… in labour. Your assistance is required.'

As if making a sudden decision, the stranger straightened, blue-grey eyes surveying the group of prisoners. 'I've forgotten myself,' he said. 'Untie our guests,' he told his patrol. 'Show them to the baths, where they may wash. Bring them food and drink in the guest tent.'

'Are you even going to tell us your name?' Roh called out.

The man paused on the threshold of the tent. 'My name is Deodan,' he told them, his cloak trailing behind him as he left.

Roh's body sagged inwards as her binds were cut. She hadn't realised how strained her shoulders had become, or how tight the ropes around her wrists had been, leaving her skin stinging. She got to her feet, watching as her companions were also freed. All but Roh's pack were returned to them. Although Roh could move freely, the thought of these strangers keeping her belongings fed the unease within. She was living on borrowed time. As soon as that egg was discovered, they would be back in binds or worse. Harbouring such an object risked a drake's wrath upon the whole settlement. A fresh, more acute fear flickered within her, too. What would Harlyn and the others do when they found out what she'd hidden from them? How she'd put them at risk, *yet again?* She had seen their faces when the quartz dagger had been revealed – and that hadn't even been her doing. She gritted her teeth as the captors took her pack away, out of sight.

Borrowed time, indeed. Her talons unsheathed, threatening to pierce the soft skin of her palms as she clenched her fists, but there was nothing she could do as they were led through the camp.

They wove through the circular patterns of domes and Roh spat on the ground, trying to rid herself of the horrid taste from the gag, unable to shake the suspicion that it had been soaked in something vile. Finn and Odi were directed down a different path to the male bathing quarters and Roh felt a pang of pity for the human, but Odi seemed too busy taking in his surroundings and his fellow humans to realise he'd been left to fend for himself with the Jaktaren.

A hooded woman guided Roh, Harlyn and Yrsa through a fenced-off area, where inside, steam wafted up from multiple giant wooden tubs and the scent of rosewood soaps filled the air.

'There's cold water over there, if the temperature is

too hot for you. There are also fresh towels,' the woman said, pointing to a table of linens and several barrels lining the fence. 'I'll have someone come back in an hour to show you to your quarters and bring you a meal.'

'Thank you,' Yrsa said.

The woman merely nodded, her hood swishing, and ducked away.

At long last, they were alone. Roh looked to Yrsa and Harlyn in disbelief. 'What is this place?' she whispered, eyeing the tubs and the small burners underneath used to keep the water hot.

'Who cares,' Harlyn said flatly, already peeling off her outer layers.

Roh took in her friend's ragged appearance, and judging by the feel of her own skin, she likely looked no better. She winced as she pulled off her shirt, the fabric having stuck to the gash on her chest.

'Are either of you hurt?' she asked quietly, noting that Yrsa had turned away from them and was deliberating on what item to remove first.

'No,' Harlyn replied, lowering her naked body into one of the tubs with a moan of relief.

Not physically, anyway, Roh thought, spotting the broken lute Harlyn had placed carefully by her pack.

'Yrsa?' she prompted, realising the highborn hadn't replied.

'I'm fine,' she called, hiding her body with a fresh towel.

Roh frowned as she approached her. 'Are you sure? If you need a healer —'

'I'm fine,' Yrsa snapped. It was the first time she'd used anything other than a calm tone with Roh. She sighed, her cheeks reddening. 'I just don't like bathing in public.'

Roh looked around. 'We're not in public.'

'Well … It's not exactly *private*, either,' Yrsa said, still clutching her towel to her chest.

Roh exchanged a rare baffled look with Harlyn. 'We don't care what you look like.'

'I care.'

'Why?' Harlyn blurted out.

Roh was inclined to agree with her. Cyrens were beautiful; it was a fact they'd been taught all their lives. Of all the things Roh questioned and spiralled into, that had never been one of them.

Yrsa didn't reply, but slipped into a different tub, all the while shielding her body from view.

'We're not looking, anyway,' Roh offered, finding her own tub and hissing as the hot water hit her skin. 'Well, Harlyn might.'

A laugh bubbled from Harlyn's mouth, before a look of horror crossed her face, as though she had forgotten how much she hated Roh, just for a moment. She clamped her mouth shut and sank lower into the water.

For a few minutes, only the soft splashing of water could be heard as they bathed. Roh lathered up a bar of soap, relishing the heat and moisture soaking into her skin. Had it only been this morning that she'd yearned for a hot bath? As she ducked below the surface, the rest of the world disappeared and Roh's dark hair floated around her face, the scales at her temples tingling. Her breathing changed to effortlessly draw the air from the water. She blinked, watching the tiny bubbles drift up. *Is it wrong to miss Saddoriel? After having fought so hard to be here? Where even is 'here'?* She couldn't stay trapped in her own mind underwater forever. She broke the surface, pushing her wet hair off her face and finding the others still sitting in their tubs.

'Yrsa?' she asked.

'Hmm?'

'Your deathsong didn't work during the attack, did it?'

'No. They all had talismans, like Odi does.'

'You saw them, too.'

Yrsa nodded from her tub. 'Our deathsongs won't have any power against those.'

'How?' Harlyn chimed in. 'How have they got their hands on our magic?'

'You heard what they said. It's not ours,' Yrsa replied.

'They're obviously lying,' Harlyn said, tipping her head back and pouring a jug of water over her soaped hair.

'Are they?' Roh asked.

Harlyn answered with a glare.

'Isn't it at all possible that they have their own magic? Couldn't you feel it?'

But Harlyn ducked under the water.

Frustrated, Roh turned back to Yrsa. 'They have our weapons, and my pack.'

Yrsa shrugged. 'We're outnumbered. With talismans holding our deathsongs at bay and so many trained fighters in their midst, we wouldn't stand a chance. Not even Finn and I. Plus, there was something on those gags.

I can still taste it. It did something to my song, stifled it somehow.'

'Yes, I tasted that, too. Our only option is to wait, then,' Roh said. 'We wait and hear them out. This Deodan … He obviously wants something.'

'Did you really not know you had that dagger?' Yrsa asked, her gaze flicking to Harlyn, who had resurfaced.

Harlyn seemed to hold her breath.

'I swear it,' Roh said.

That seemed to be good enough for Yrsa, who gave a nod and then reached for her towel and waited for Roh and Harlyn to look away.

'What do you make of that Deodan fellow?' Harlyn asked. Roh saw the question for the kindness it was to Yrsa, drawing the attention away from her, but she grabbed at it all the same, desperate to interact with her old friend with some sense of normality.

'I don't know what to make of him,' Roh said truthfully. 'Once he found out where the dagger had come from, he changed his tune rather quickly.'

After they had finished bathing, a human escorted them to their own dome tent, where fresh bread and a hearty meat stew had been laid out for them.

Finn eyed it all suspiciously.

'If they wanted us dead, we'd be dead already,' Odi told him, reaching for a golden loaf.

A muscle twitched along Finn's jawline, but he said nothing and served himself a bowl of stew.

While Roh awaited her turn, her heart leaped as she spotted her pack in the corner. Someone had returned it. It took all her willpower to remain where she was, instead of running to it and rummaging through its contents. Surely if they'd found the egg, they would have said something by now? She would have been dragged off for an audience with Deodan, no doubt. She exhaled shakily and picked up a plate. She'd have to wait until later to check. All she could do was eat. The gull they'd had yesterday felt like a long time ago.

Picking up the wooden ladle, Roh served herself a generous portion and got comfortable on a bale of hay. Just as she was about to put a stew-soaked piece of bread into her mouth, Finn's steely gaze met her own.

'Are you going to explain the dagger situation?'

Roh lowered the bread back to her plate with a sigh. 'I don't have much to tell you. I didn't take it,' she said, not bothering to lace her words with venom this time. She was too tired.

'Well, where did it come from?' the Jaktaren pushed.

'Outside ... my mother's cell.'

Fury flashed across Finn's face, as it always did when there was any mention of Cerys in his presence. According to him, a death debt needed to be settled between the Haertel family and the Elder Slayer, but Roh knew no more than that. Now was not the time to ask.

'Outside my mother's cell are five dead water warlocks,' she told him, looking to the others as well, her stew losing heat. 'I don't know why. They've been there for as long as I can remember. That dagger ... It has always been in the hand of the one I thought of as the leader. But just before I left Saddoriel, I visited Cerys, and during that visit, I noticed it was gone.'

'Did you tell anyone?' Odi asked.

Roh gave a dark laugh, at last biting into her bread. 'Who would I tell?'

They ate the rest of their meal in silence.

As the night ebbed on, Roh watched her companions prepare their bedrolls. The day had taken its toll on them all and each of them moved heavily, exhaustion dragging at their limbs. Roh didn't fail to notice Harlyn cradling her broken lute. Roh's heart ached for her, knowing exactly how it felt to have the thing you loved most destroyed. She thought of her music-theatre model again, smashed by Harlyn's hand, no less. It didn't stop her stepping towards her friend, words of comfort ready on her tongue.

But it was Odi who reached for the instrument with gentle hands. 'It can be fixed,' he told Harlyn. His hair fell across his eyes as he turned it over, his half-gloved fingers assessing its wounds.

'How?' Harlyn asked, sharply eyeing his every move.

'With the right tools,' he said. 'And the right pair of hands.'

Roh's stomach threatened to send the stew back up. Was it feelings for the human? This was the *second* time she'd questioned what she felt for him, despite considering the very thought absurd. Roh rubbed her tired eyes and turned her back on the pair, only to jump at a touch on her shoulder.

Her head snapped up. She was expecting expecting to see Yrsa, but …

There was no one there. Yrsa and Finn were on the other side of the tent, talking in low voices.

What in the —

She felt the touch on her shoulder again, ever so light, beckoning to her somehow. As quietly as she could, Roh got to her feet and slipped outside the dome.

Magic called to her. Nothing else could explain the reassuring pull of the current that led her through the torchlit rings of domes, towards the centre, where she'd first been brought. Whatever it was, something akin to her inner compass, which she hadn't felt since she'd left Saddoriel, pulled her towards a plume of smoke. The moon was at its highest when she reached the main campfire, where the man called Deodan sat alone, sharpening one of his cutlasses. With each movement, the tinkling of glass sounded from a pouch at his belt, but he didn't seem to mind, or even notice. He glanced up at Roh, unsurprised as she approached, the flames illuminating purple shadows beneath his eyes as he returned to his task.

Fear flickered in Roh's veins, forcing her talons out, and yet that strange force drew her to him and she found herself taking a seat a few feet away.

'Are we your prisoners?' she said.

Deodan didn't look up from his blade, drawing the whetstone across it in a smooth, swift motion. 'I haven't decided yet.'

'Do I not at least deserve to know who my captor is?' she pressed.

He scoffed. 'I told you who I am.'

'I don't care what *your name* is. I want to know *who you are. What* you are,' she added, sensing that foreign magic reaching out towards her, as though trying to gauge her own power.

'That's a lot of information to be demanding for someone who's not giving any information herself.' At last, he placed the whetstone down and looked at her. 'Why should I trust you?'

'Why should *we* trust *you?* Your clansmen attacked us with no provocation and took us hostage —'

'I think centuries of cyren attacks on our kind is provocation enough, don't you?' he interjected. 'And I have since learned there is so much more to you than meets the eye.'

Roh's heart caught in her throat. 'What do you mean?' she said tentatively, trying and failing to swallow.

Deodan nudged something towards her with his boot, something that gleamed ivory against the dirt.

Her crown of bones.

Gods, she had been so worried about them discovering the sea-drake egg that she hadn't even considered the fact that her crown had been stuffed away in her pack as well. She wet her lips with her tongue. 'It's …'

'Oh, I know *precisely* what it is. Now, I'll ask you again: how did you come to have the dagger?'

Roh's fingertips grazed the scales at her temples. He

hadn't been explicit with any threats to her or the others, but she was sharp enough to realise that danger stalked beneath his skin and that feigning ignorance would get her nowhere.

'The human spoke the truth. I don't know *how* it ended up in my pack. But it's from the prison in Saddoriel. From the hands of a dead water warlock who stands preserved there.'

Deodan rubbed at the stubble on his chin and sighed heavily, reaching beneath his cloak and producing the quartz dagger. 'You truly aren't aware of its importance?'

'No.' Roh couldn't read the expression that crossed his face, but she frowned as he leaned down, dragging the dagger through the dirt.

Roh twisted to see what he was doing and froze, the flames casting flickering light across his sketch. 'Who … *Where* have you seen that before?' she breathed.

It was the very same design that Cerys had etched into her cell back in Saddoriel, over and over again. Roh stood, her whole body shaking. 'Who showed you that mask?'

'Mask?' Deodan raised his brows. 'My Queen of Bones, these are *wings* …'

Wings? That couldn't be right. There was no way. Roh had been staring at that damn sketch her entire life. She knew what it was: *a mask*. It always had been. Hadn't it? But even as she attempted to convince herself, doubt crept in like a slow-moving tide. No one had ever told her what Cerys' etchings were, not even Cerys herself, had she?

Roh's throat was dry. 'How do you know they're wings? Why not a mask? Or something else entirely?'

'Because …' Deodan redrew the sketch. 'It's a code that was once used in an ancient alliance.'

Roh shoved her hands in her pockets so Deodan wouldn't see her trembling. 'What do you mean? What alliance?'

'Between our two kinds.'

'What are you talking about?'

'Don't be ignorant, Roh.'

Her name sounded strange on his lips.

Deodan gave a pointed look to the crown of bones at his feet. 'You think news of this hasn't travelled? It has been fifty years since there was even a *chance* of a new cyren ruler. Word spreads fast.'

'But how? This is a *human* village. What do humans care for cyren politics?'

'A great deal if they're interested in keeping their lives. This may be a human village, but it is under my clan's protection. Those under our protection do not go uninformed on the happenings of the realms.'

So, these people aren't his actual clan ... Then what people are? Why is he here? What does he want with me and that dagger? And why are regular humans fearful for their lives? Besides the musicians hunted by the Jaktaren, humans haven't been attacked in centuries. Not since the Age of Chaos ...

He studied her and Roh's breathing hitched as he spoke again. 'So ... You are a songless queen to be, who does not possess the birthstones of Saddoriel.'

'How can you know that?'

'I can feel it, or rather, the lack of it in you. As for the stones' – he picked up the crown – 'that much is obvious. If you had them, they would be in *their* rightful place and this would be in *its* rightful place, atop your head back in Saddoriel. And yet, here we are.'

Roh stumbled over her next choice of words. This man, whoever or *whatever* he was, knew too much. Knew about her lack of deathsong, her darkest fear, the very thing that dragged her into the deep spiral of her mind and kept her from sleep.

'There is no one single thing that defines you,' Deodan started. 'We are the sum of many, forever changing parts. Do not let a lack of song tell you who you are.'

Again, Roh felt a foreign magic reaching out to her, playing with her cyren instincts, whatever cyren power flooded her veins.

'You … you have magic,' she managed, forcing herself to sit back down. It wasn't a question, but it hung between them like one.

'I do not possess it,' Deodan said slowly, before patting the pouch at his belt that clinked at his touch. 'But I can harness it.'

Whatever magic had drawn Roh to Deodan flickered within her, as though it wanted to provoke him. Instinct told her she recognised what he was, but …

'Ask it,' he said, his gaze fixed on hers, alight with challenge.

Roh chewed the inside of her cheek, wringing her hands. 'Are you …?'

'Am I what?'

She swallowed. 'You can't be, though. They're …'

'Gone?' he finished for her, thoughtfully dragging the whetstone across his blade. 'What they *were* is gone. In their place stands something new. The water warlocks are much changed, Roh.'

The breath she'd been holding rushed out of her. Why was she surprised? She had suspected it from the moment that dagger had danced between his fingers, hadn't she? The magic around him – she could *sense* it. And yet … The shocking truth of it pummelled into her.

The water warlocks lived on. She rubbed the chill from her arms.

'You said something about a code and an alliance?' she prompted, her voice raw. 'And this was between cyrens and water warlocks?'

'For a time.' Deodan nodded. 'If you were travelling and wanted to know if you could trust a newcomer, you'd draw half the wings in the dirt and wait to see if they completed the drawing.'

A vision of Cerys' cell formed before Roh – the pattern she'd always thought to be masks etched across every imaginable surface.

'You've seen this drawing before, I take it?' Deodan asked slowly.

Roh stared into the fire until her eyes burned. 'My mother … She knows of it.'

'Cerys the Elder Slayer knew a great deal about water warlocks,' Deodan told her.

Roh's head jerked up. 'You know my mother?'

'*Of* her,' Deodan corrected. 'And as I told you – word of your unique tale has reached the far corners of the realm. *Everyone* knew of Cerys the Elder Slayer, and if they didn't before, they do now, even here in the gilded plains.'

Roh clamped her jaw shut.

'She grew up with them,' Deodan said. 'It's common knowledge.'

'She didn't.' The words were out of Roh's mouth before she could even think. 'Nothing about my mother is *common knowledge.*'

Deodan gave a soft laugh. 'Fair.' He seemed to consider his options, absentmindedly producing the dagger and twirling it between his fingers again. 'Am I right in thinking you make for Akoris?' he asked.

Roh picked at her talons. She supposed it wasn't a massive leap to make if he knew who she was and what she was after. Still, she quickly tried to discern the best course of action and how much information to divulge. Not only was Deodan a stranger, but a man of a race that had a bloody history with her own, and until moments ago, had no longer existed. But …

Slowly, she nodded. 'We do,' she allowed. 'Do you know much about the territory?'

'Enough.'

'I see.'

'I'm not sure you do,' he said lightly. 'How do you intend to get the stones? Do you think you'll simply ask for one and it will be given? Do you know *anything* about your own kind?'

Roh's talons dug into the log beneath her, the events of the tournament crashing into her. Sabotage, trickery, betrayal; the things others had done to her, things she'd done herself …

'I know my own kind well,' she said. 'It makes no difference to my quest.'

'Anything can make a difference to your quest. Including help from the outside.'

Roh laughed. 'Help? Who's going to help me?'

Deodan offered a smile laced with darkness. 'Perhaps I will.'

'And why in Dresmis and Thera's names would you do that?'

'As it so happens, my clan currently resides in the outer villages of Akoris. There are matters I need to see to there.'

'You're telling me there are water warlocks living in a *cyren* territory?'

His eyes were dancing with amusement. 'I told you, we are not what we once were.'

Roh folded her arms over her chest and waited.

Deodan sighed, sheathing the quartz dagger. 'My task was to bring my patrol here and station them with this human settlement. I always meant to return to my clan immediately. I can escort you and your companions across the plains.'

'But what kind of warlock would help a cyren?'

'Perhaps one who recognises that a cyren who carries the quartz dagger, even unknowingly, is no ordinary cyren.'

Roh had no idea what to make of that statement.

Deodan shrugged. 'You may need the protection,' he added.

'Did you not see the two Jaktaren in our midst?'

Deodan exhaled sharply through his nose. 'There are things out there that even Jaktaren cannot face alone.'

'Chief,' someone called. 'Chief, there are reports of a sea drake venturing close to the shoreline.'

'What?' Deodan growled, standing suddenly. 'A *drake?* Is it airborne?'

Roh found herself standing, too. How close was it?

She had assumed that they would be safe on land for a time, guessing that the drake wouldn't want to stray too far from its nest of eggs. But apparently, it was relentless.

A hooded man appeared from the path behind them. 'Not airborne – not yet, anyway, Chief. It's making itself known along the coast, though. That's what the scouts reported, sir.'

Deodan turned to Roh. 'I have to attend to this. Think about my offer.' The water warlock, or whatever he was, left her standing by the dying fire.

Gods, would the drake leave the seas? Even if Deodan *was* a warlock, what could he possibly do against a drake? Roh looked down at the shadows dancing across her crown of bones in the dirt. So far, her foray into potential queendom had felt like one misstep after the next.

Roh picked up the crown. She'd forgotten how smooth it was against her callused hands. She hadn't worn it since her false coronation; she'd wrapped it carefully in a spare cloak and tucked it into her pack. As if she'd wear it travelling, anyway. But now, she studied it for the first time since she'd left the lair. While she had no doubt its intention was to insult her background as a bone cleaner, there was no denying that skilled craftsmanship had gone into its creation. It was beautiful and seamless, in its own horrific way. She traced her fingers across the insets where the gems were missing, Deodan's words echoing in her mind. His offer had been a vague one at best. At worst, the suggestion that a water warlock accompany them … Well, it was worse than a human joining them, wasn't it? But he knew these lands, didn't he?

Roh's mind buzzed with a million questions as she made her way back to the tent, crown still in hand. Was this why Cerys had told her of this place? Had she intended for Roh to meet Deodan? Did they know each other? The walls of Cerys' cell were as clear as ever. Roh could picture the hundreds, even thousands of sketches etched into the stone with broken talons.

Wings. Not masks.

Whatever alliance had once existed between warlock and cyren, she could wrap her head around it, she realised, recalling the mosaic tiles in the Passage of Kings back in Saddoriel. There had been a time when both kinds had lived peacefully, sharing their knowledge, sharing their magic. The lair was still rife with warlock enchantments that made it what it was. The very birthstones themselves had been a joint creation of their two peoples, hadn't they? But Roh's mind went back to the drawings. She could understand an alliance, but what did *wings* mean?

'You look like you've just met the god of death,' Yrsa said, looking up from a pile of small, round stones.

Roh hadn't even realised she'd re-entered their tent. Jars of valo beetles softly illuminated the space. She saw that the others were asleep on their bedrolls, but Yrsa sat to one side, moulding a clay ball between her palms, apparently stocking up on her sling projectiles.

'Where have you been?' the Jaktaren asked.

Roh sat on a stool, weariness pressing down on her.

She studied her crown, holding it in her lap. 'Nowhere,' she replied. 'Just walking around.'

Yrsa's piercing stare told Roh that the highborn didn't believe a word of her half-hearted lie. But she didn't push – she simply continued to add to her pile of stones, clay lining her palms.

Roh watched her, finding comfort in the rhythm of Yrsa's task; the steady roll of her hands, the precision with which she made each ball the same size.

At last, Yrsa placed her final stone by the glowing embers of the fire, and after wiping her hands on a rag, rubbed the back of her neck with a heavy sigh.

Still longing for reassurance and familiarity while Yrsa started to prepare for bed, Roh put her crown aside and got out her sketchbook. This strange tent village with its dome-like shapes had a different sense of beauty about it. From within, Roh appreciated the clever construction, the arching framework that latticed together and held the dome firmly to the ground. These structures were built to last and withstand, and to mirror the hillside across the river. Roh barely registered her fingers guiding the charcoal across the parchment, creating perfect circles and capturing the satisfying symmetry of the domes. There was so much to see, so many details to chronicle. She turned the page to start a new sketch and realised with a jolt of panic that she was running out of parchment. She would have to start drawing in the patches of blank space in her previous work. Turning back through her sketchbook, she found a free corner.

There, she put charcoal to parchment once again and drew the shape she had thought she was so familiar with.

Cerys' mask, which now she couldn't unsee as wings.

The sketch was small, only half the size of her palm, but suddenly its presence on the page didn't sit well with her. She smudged the charcoal with her fingers until the drawing was no longer recognisable and closed her sketchbook with a soft snap.

What am I doing?

Roh had no idea of the hour, but she knew it was late, knew she needed to get her rest before the tribulations of the next day greeted her. She found her bedroll and unravelled it away from the others. When she was sure Yrsa was sleeping deeply, Roh tugged her pack close and reached inside. Her fingertips brushed against the scaly texture of the drake egg.

How did they not find it? she marvelled. Though, she supposed they probably thought they had found everything they needed with her crown of bones and the quartz dagger. She took the egg from her pack and cupped it against her chest, gently stroking its shell. Roh had no idea what had possessed her to steal it from the drake's nest all those weeks ago. She could find no rhyme or reason for it other than *instinct*. She had simply acted.

'*That* is no viper egg,' said a voice from behind her.

Roh jumped, trying to shield the egg from view, but it was too late. Yrsa had seen it. The Jaktaren's mouth hung open, her eyes wide as she took a tentative step towards Roh, blinking rapidly, as though unable to believe the sight before her. There were no signs of sleep on her; she'd been pretending.

'I know,' Roh replied at last.

Yrsa crouched beside Roh and peered at the object in her hands. 'It's truly what I think it is? A sea-drake egg?' she said, trembling fingers reaching out.

Roh shielded it from her touch. 'How do you know that?'

Undeterred, Yrsa didn't take her eyes from the egg. 'I've seen illustrations in books. And it's much too big to be a viper's. I never thought …' She blinked slowly, as the realisation dawned on her. 'That's why it's following us … The drake?' she murmured.

'Yes.' Roh's whole body sagged with the admission. 'I took it during the third trial. The drake chased me back to Saddoriel. I think it has my scent.'

Yrsa let out a low whistle and pushed her hair from her forehead. 'Can I hold it?' The Jaktaren was utterly transfixed by the egg.

Roh realised what was happening. Yrsa's passion for unusual creatures was warring against her sense of duty, and perhaps, just perhaps, Roh could help it win. Reluctantly, she held out the egg to Yrsa, who cupped her hands eagerly, her breath whistling between her teeth as Roh placed it carefully in her palms.

'Gods,' was all Yrsa managed to say, bringing the egg close to her body with the greatest of care. She ran her fingers along its scaly surface in wonder. 'You do realise this is the rarest ancestor of the common viper, don't you?'

'I gathered it was something like that,' Roh replied, glancing nervously around the tent, praying that the others remained deep in sleep.

But Yrsa was barely listening. 'Have you sensed any movement within it?'

Roh looked up in alarm. 'No,' she admitted. 'But I've not had it on me the whole time … for obvious reasons.'

'Mmm …' Yrsa held it up to the light of the valo beetles. 'There's no real way of knowing how long since it was laid. Or how much longer it may incubate,' she said, more to herself than to Roh.

Roh cleared her throat. 'How far do you think a drake can track someone's scent?' she asked abruptly. 'What amount of distance?'

'I don't know much about drakes.'

'But your viper …'

Yrsa's brows shot up. 'So *that's* why you insisted I join you on this quest.' She let out a low, appreciative whistle.

'One of the reasons,' Roh allowed, glancing around at their sleeping companions and back to the egg. 'You won't tell the others, will you?'

At last, Yrsa met Roh's gaze. She inhaled deeply, her eyes darting from the prize she held to the bedrolls in the dim edges of the dome. 'No,' she said, her voice low. 'I won't tell them.'

At last, she handed the egg back to Roh, shaking her head in disbelief.

Relief flooded through Roh's body, and she curled up on her bedroll, bringing the egg to her heart. Yrsa extinguished the lights, and as the last yellow glow faded, the Jaktaren's whisper carried across the darkness.

'Roh?'

'Yes?'

'Can you imagine?'

'What?'

'Having a *sea drake* at your side …' Yrsa's voice was full of wonder – and *excitement*.

For the first time since Roh had left Saddoriel, those feelings sparked within her, too, breathing new life into her tired bones. She nestled into her cloak, feeling lighter than she had in weeks. *Hope* was what it was, she realised. If Yrsa could cope with having a sea-drake egg in their midst, then surely a water warlock would be nothing.

CHAPTER SIX

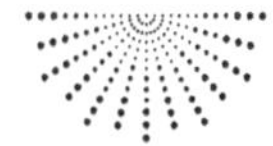

'He's *not* coming with us.' Finn folded his arms over his chest, jaw clenched.

It took all of Roh's willpower to stifle her groan of despair as the dawn rays hit their tent. She had barely got three hours of sleep the night before and she certainly wasn't ready for an all-out battle of wills with the arrogant Haertel bastard.

Roh had told the others what Deodan was, or what she understood him to be, hoping it would not be the core-shaking revelation she suspected. But the declaration that the chieftain was of warlock descent had kickstarted the arguing long before she'd relayed his offer of assistance. Now, the tension was palpable.

Slowly, she got to her feet, not caring that she was only in her loose nightshirt, and folded her own arms as she faced the Jaktaren.

'It's not your decision.' She refused to look away first.

Finn held her stare, his lilac eyes full of unchecked rage. 'And it's not yours alone,' he snapped.

'I'm the leader of this company. The future queen of our kind. If I say we need the chieftain, then we need him.'

Finn closed the gap between them with a single stride. He was so close she could count the freckles across his nose. 'You don't know the first thing about what we need, bone cleaner.'

Roh yielded a step back, uneasy at the fire smouldering in the highborn's gaze.

'I'm with him,' Harlyn added unhelpfully. 'The last thing we need is *another* mouth to feed.'

Roh's chest caved in. Was Harlyn agreeing with Finn just to spite her? Even if it meant they crossed the plains unaided, with a great deal less protection?

Yrsa snorted. 'It's not like you do any of the hunting. I agree with Roh. We need the chieftain's knowledge of the plains. I have not crossed them before and nor has Finn.'

At those words, the fire in Finn's eyes dulled and relief surged through Roh as he shrugged.

'Fine,' he said.

Interesting. Roh watched as he went to his pack and laced up the top. *Perhaps having Yrsa onside will help bring him to heel.* But she knew better than to rub salt in the wound. She turned to the other side of the tent, where Odi held Harlyn's lute in his lap.

'Seeing as we're all giving our opinion, what about you?' she asked.

Odi's cheeks flushed as four sets of eyes went to him. The human glanced between Roh and Harlyn, seeming to weigh up his options. 'Well … Deodan clearly has a deeper respect for human life than any cyren I've met so far, so I think we should bring him along,' he declared.

Harlyn gave a frustrated click of her tongue and stalked out of the tent.

'Good,' Roh said to Odi.

But the human just shrugged and returned his attention to the broken strings of Harlyn's lute.

'We'll get something to eat, then I'll find Deodan,' Roh announced to no one in particular.

As the blush hue of dawn truly settled around the camp, Roh and the others found themselves gathered around the glowing embers and ash of one of the fires, cooking bread. Roh had followed a hooded human's instructions as to how to wrap the raw dough around a long stick and now rotated it over the heat so it cooked evenly.

Around them, the rest of the settlement was stirring and Roh swore she could hear an infant's cry in the near distance —

'We're stronger than you. Smarter, more cunning than you,' Finn was saying, staring daggers at Odi. 'We have the sea at our mercy, more power than you could comprehend. What is it that you offer?'

Just as Roh was about to intervene, Odi laughed. 'You're so much stronger and smarter, are you? Where were all these admirable attributes when we were being attacked? If you're as powerful as you say, then why are we here?'

Finn's nostrils flared, but Odi wasn't done. He casually turned his bread over the hot embers. 'As for what I offer? I create the very thing you cherish most. If that's not power, I don't know what is.'

A memory of rich, mesmerising sound barrelled into Roh, as well as the image of Odi seated at the piano they'd created, his fingers dancing across the bone keys. The melody he had performed was an explosion of feeling, of depth and soul, of yearning and pain, yet it had been beautiful. The most beautiful thing she'd ever heard. Roh had thought of that music every day since, wondering if she'd ever hear it again, devastated at the thought that she might not. Odi was right; if that wasn't power, what was?

The tension was broken by an infant's piercing cry. Roh looked around, trying to imagine what it was like being born in a settlement like this. Though she supposed it was a damn sight better than being born on the floor of a prison cell.

'It's the newborn Deodan helped with last night,' said the human tending to the fire.

As if summoned, Deodan approached, cutlasses swinging at his hips, his hood down, revealing a recently washed face. He looked younger than yesterday.

The chief took the dough offered to him and clapped it around a stick as though he'd done it a hundred times before. 'She makes a lot of noise for such a tiny thing,' he said, nodding vaguely in the direction of the crying, holding his stick over the hot embers. 'But it's good. Means she's got a decent set of lungs on her.'

'What do you know of infants?' Roh asked, frowning. A man who knew of secret alliances and quartz daggers and whose voice was often laced with danger seemed at odds with a man who knew of crying human babies and women in labour.

Deodan shrugged. 'My kind always had an interest in healing, in relieving the pain and suffering of others.'

At the mention of *his kind*, Finn glanced up from the fire, shooting a glare at the chieftain and shaking his head.

Roh ignored the Jaktaren and glanced down at the scabbed gash across her chest and the raised red marks where the ropes had bound her wrists, looking pointedly from the marks of captivity to Deodan. 'Really?'

Deodan's smile had a dark edge. 'That was before.' He pulled his bread away from the embers and tapped it with his fingers, checking to see if it had cooked through. 'Let's have it, then.'

'Have what?' Roh said, mirroring his actions, seeing that her bread had become golden brown in colour.

'Your answer.'

But as Roh fumbled for her words, the distant crying grew louder and she turned to see a young woman jogging towards them, a bundle held carefully in her arms. 'Chief Deodan?' she cried, her face tight with worry.

'What is it, Yalana?' Deodan asked, holding out his stick to Roh as he rose to his feet.

Bewildered, Roh took it, struck by the familiarity of the action, and watched on in fascination.

'She's feverish,' the woman said, pulling the blanket back to reveal a small, pink face.

The clan leader held the bundle with surprising gentleness and touched the backs of his fingers to the crying infant's forehead. 'She's warm.'

'Please, Deodan,' the young woman begged, sheer terror etched across her face. 'My husband … He won't allow your aid, but please.'

Roh frowned. So, even amongst the humans Deodan was protecting, there were those who held the same prejudices as cyrens. She peered over at the squalling infant, so helpless and tiny, so vulnerable. Whatever history her kind shared with Deodan's, whatever he truly was, Roh couldn't understand why someone would refuse help when their child was in trouble.

'It will be alright, Yalana. Here.' Deodan passed the bundle back to her, his hand going to the small pouch at his belt. Its contents clinked as he sifted through it with his fingers, finally producing a tiny vial of liquid. He popped the cork with his thumb and poured the transparent elixir into his palm. But rather than spilling through the gaps between his fingers or sloshing to the ground, it remained cupped in his hand, seemingly hovering just above his skin, as one mass.

Roh heard a gasp, but she didn't know if it had been her or one of the others and she didn't care. She was transfixed by the strange spell unfolding before them, the infant's wails somehow muted by the magic.

Deodan whispered to the floating liquid in his palm, his words inaudible. The mass rippled and rose away from the clan leader's hand, sending droplets spraying as it suddenly cast a wide bubble around them all.

Roh gaped.

'Your husband need not discover you sought my assistance,' Deodan said to the mother as the strange, translucent shield settled into place.

'What does it do?' Roh wondered aloud in disbelief, as she tried to take in the living magic.

Deodan took out a fresh vial and didn't so much as look at her as he replied, 'Keeps prying eyes and ears away. No doubt a handy little spell for someone in a position such as yours.'

He poured water into his hand, whispering again. The liquid came to life in his palm, moulding itself into a shape – no, *blooming* – into a berry-hued flower. It fell softly back into Deodan's cupped palm, which he offered to the woman called Yalana.

'Here,' he said. 'Crush this up and apply it to the little one's brow. It will fend off any fever.'

Yalana threw an arm around Deodan, burying her head in the crook of his neck. 'Thank you. Thank you, Deodan. You've done so much for us. I —'

Deodan patted her on the shoulder. 'It's alright. She's going to be fine. I was just telling this lot here about her good set of lungs.'

The woman flushed and offered a grateful smile, not sparing a glance in the cyrens' direction. 'Thank you.'

The shield around them shimmered and faded. Roh

was still staring after the woman and child when Deodan took his stick back from her. 'Yours is a tad burnt,' he said pointedly, gesturing to her bread, now black. She hadn't realised she'd been holding it over the coals.

'Oh.'

Deodan huffed an amused laugh and handed her his own. 'What was that song you were humming?' he asked.

'What?' Roh said, carefully placing the new bread over the embers.

'As I was conjuring the flower and the baby was crying, you were humming something.'

Baffled, Roh looked to the others. 'Was I?'

Harlyn gave a reluctant nod. 'That nestling tune you always quoted whenever Orson cried.'

The name of their friend hung between them, an open wound, but Roh faced Deodan. 'I didn't even realise I was humming. It's an old lullaby …' Roh removed her bread from the heat once more. The words had been ingrained in her mind forever, but she had no memory of them ever being sung to her.

'Little nestling, little nestling,
'Follow my voice, to the land of sleep.
'Hush, hush, little cyren, so strong yet so small,
'For down in deep Saddoriel, we let no tears fall.'

A strange expression crossed Deodan's face. 'Ah,' he said. 'I am familiar with another … verse.' But he offered no more.

Roh felt Harlyn's eyes on her. Roh knew that she'd recited the lullaby enough to her friend over the years that she too found this utterly unnerving. Roh had been singing the song her whole life and yet it was incomplete?

Deodan took an enthused bite from his freshly cooked bread. 'It's not a lullaby,' he mumbled between chews. 'It's an enchantment.'

Roh faltered. 'Say that again.'

Deodan looked up, frowning, crumbs in his stubble. 'It's an enchantment. A spell. A very old one, to be sure, but an enchantment nonetheless.'

Did he mean that all this time, the only semblance of a normal childhood she had, the lullaby that had taken root in her mind as an infant and never left, was not what it seemed?

She chewed the inside of her cheek. 'What does it do?'

The warlock laughed lightly. 'Nothing untoward, I promise. It was a very common one that new mothers and fathers used to get a reprieve from the constant squalling. It stops the little ones from crying. Soothes them.'

'So, it's warlock magic?'

'It *was* ... Without the water, as you've seen me use, it's just words.'

A deadly calm washed over Roh, a vigorous sense of defiance. It wasn't possible. Why would she know the words to a warlock enchantment, of all things? Why would she know it as a nestling's lullaby? The only plausible reason was that Deodan was mistaken, or he was lying. Either way, she didn't have the time or the patience to try to wrangle the truth from him. *They're just words*, she repeated to herself. She slid the hot bread from her stick with her unsheathed talons and broke it apart, watching the steam rise from the soft crumb.

Deodan dipped his into a pot of honey at his feet. 'So, Queen of Bones, I can offer you horses, provisions and a level of protection, should I join you on the journey. And, of course, a direct route to Akoris. What do you say?'

'I say there's something you're not telling me.'

The clan leader laughed, brushing his hands on the legs of his pants. 'I'd say there are many things yet to be told. But I can get you to Akoris swiftly, and time is of the essence, yes?'

Roh glanced at the others, who were all watching her with keen eyes. 'Yes,' she answered, despite the nagging sensation of things being left unsaid.

Nodding, Deodan stood. 'Then finish your meal and pack your bags. I'll have one of my men ready the horses and supplies. It'll take four, maybe five days to reach Akoris, depending on the conditions.'

'That long?' Finn interjected.

'Just long enough so that your Queen of Bones doesn't arrive delirious. She'll need all her wits about her for dealing with Adriel.'

Adriel ... Roh's skin prickled at the name. The Arch General of Akoris, of whom she knew next to nothing. But her thoughts were interrupted by Finn's retort.

'She's not my queen of anything,' he muttered.

Roh ignored him, but as Deodan turned to leave, he nudged her with his boot, grinning. 'You know you're a queen when someone opposes you that much,' he said. With a final wink, he walked off.

At the gates of the human settlement, Roh stared at the saddled horses before her. She had never seen one in person, let alone six. They very much resembled the backahast herds hailing from Lochloria, majestic and muscular, though these were made of flesh and bone rather than water.

Deodan's men moved around the creatures, strapping packs across their rumps and checking the tack. Roh watched in awe as Yrsa placed a boot in one of the silver stirrups and effortlessly swung herself up and over the saddle. Roh didn't know why she was surprised; the Jaktaren had been trained in everything under the sun, and apparently there was no limit to the skills they possessed. Roh looked at the stirrup on her own horse. Though she wasn't short by any stretch of the imagination, how was she meant to get her foot into it and find balance enough to hoist herself up?

'Roh, here.' Odi bent at her side, interlocking his fingers and offering her a leg boost.

'No,' she said. 'Your hands …'

'They're fine.'

'I'm not adding to your pain,' she told him. Stubbornly, she managed to fit her boot to the stirrup, and very inelegantly scrambled up the side of the horse and into the saddle. To her surprise, Odi easily mounted his own horse, as did Finn. Harlyn accepted the help of one of Deodan's men, who put down a small stool for her to step on. They waited, looking out onto the gilded plains of tussock and the rolling hillside, the Endon River just past their line of sight. Somewhere beyond lay the territory of Akoris, and the first birthstone of Saddoriel.

'Where's Deodan, then?' Roh asked eventually, looking at the unmanned horse, conscious of precious daylight ticking away. Had it not been for Finn's bickering earlier, perhaps they would already be on their way.

'I'm here,' the chieftain called, jogging towards them.

Roh baulked as he approached. In addition to his cutlasses, Deodan wore a black brigandine with silver buckles across his chest and a double scabbard across his back that held a broadsword and a long dagger. Gone was any trace of the gentleness that had healed a tiny infant only an hour before. Here was a warrior, fierce and uncompromising. He fitted in well with the Jaktaren.

Motioning to one of his men, Deodan placed a heavy hand on his shoulder. 'I leave the protection of this village in your hands.'

'Yes, sir. We will guard it well.'

Deodan nodded. 'I'll send word from Akoris.'

With that, in a swift blur of movement, he mounted his horse and guided it to the front of their company. 'Shall we?' he said, a wicked smile on his lips.

'Gods,' Roh muttered as her horse lurched forward. She glanced across at Yrsa, who seemed completely at ease in the saddle. 'Got any tips?'

'Yeah.' Yrsa grinned, their shared secret vivid in her eyes. 'Don't fall off.'

Roh could have sworn she heard a snort of laughter from Harlyn, but her friend kept her eyes forward as she too clung to her reins tightly, face paling as she swayed in the saddle.

'To the river,' Deodan called.

They were on the move.

CHAPTER SEVEN

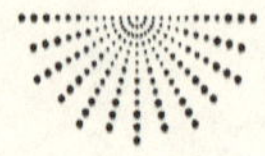

Roh decided she hated horse riding. It took hours just to rejoin the river, and by the time she could hear its rushing waters, her backside, knees and lower spine were aching terribly. She couldn't stand the rocking rhythm of the horse's steps and hated it even more when her mount suddenly lost its footing, causing her to jolt and grip the saddle horn in a panic. While Odi and the Jaktaren looked at home in their saddles, Harlyn looked about as uncomfortable as Roh felt, which in itself was a small comfort. Bone cleaners weren't meant to ride horses across vast networks of tussock.

Future queen, she had to remind herself. She was the *future Queen of Cyrens*. She was no longer a bone cleaner, and no longer did she belong in the songless depths of the lair. Not for the first time since her false coronation, she allowed herself to wonder what the Saddorien cyrens would call her. Queen Delja had been Delja the

Triumphant, the king before her had been Uniir the Blessed, and before that had been Asros the Conqueror. And the very first king had been Taaldin the Great. What would they call her, centuries from now, the second queen in all cyren history?

Roh was distracted by how intently Odi was studying Deodan. The human was clearly fascinated by the armed warrior leading them assuredly across the plains, swaying in his saddle as though he and his horse were one.

'I don't bite,' Deodan called back, sensing the attention.

His skill for noting these small details, and the subtle shift in the atmosphere, unsettled Roh.

He spoke again. 'I'll answer the questions you have, Odi, just stop boring holes in my back.'

Odi flushed but straightened in his saddle, urging his horse forward so it came up alongside Deodan's. 'I want to know how it works,' he said boldly.

'How what works?' Deodan asked.

Roh found herself squeezing her horse's sides with her heels so she could catch up and follow their conversation more closely.

'Warlock magic,' Odi clarified. 'I don't understand it. Are you a human? Can other humans be taught what you know? Can you tell if someone's a warlock from looking at them?'

'Slow down there,' Deodan said, though Roh could hear the smile in his voice. 'All very valid questions. First, warlocks are not human. We are our own kind, our magic inherited from our parents, and their parents before them. A human cannot be taught how to wield magic as we do.'

From the corner of her eye, Roh saw Odi's face fall.

Deodan continued, 'One is born a warlock. You don't get to choose, any more than a cyren chooses to be one. It's in our blood. A belief system and a race, together.' He adjusted his grip on his reins. 'As for being able to tell, perhaps you might have been able to do so once, but no longer. To the naked eye we could be humans, but a warlock can usually sense the power of another.' Deodan glanced at Roh. 'But we have no markings, chosen or otherwise, not like your Jaktaren friends here.'

Odi shot a quick look to the zigzag pattern shaved into the side of Finn's head. 'They're not my friends,' he said quietly, turning back to the chieftain. 'So, I cannot be taught?' A note of dashed hope sounded in his voice.

'Sadly, no, lad. We could teach you our customs, our history, even how we move through the realms now as a new race. But you would never master water magic because the power does not hum within you.'

'I see,' Odi said.

Roh felt a pang of sympathy for her friend. She hadn't stopped to consider that Odi was the only one of their company who did not possess or harness his own magic. Nor had she paused to ponder how vulnerable or weak that might have made him feel over the past few weeks.

'If you're not a human, why are you protecting human villages?' Odi asked abruptly, his gaze filling with suspicion.

Deodan eyed him evenly. 'Because our kind knows what it's like to be left defenceless.'

Those words echoed through Roh's mind louder than she cared to admit. All cyrens knew of the Scouring of Lochloria. They had been taught about it since they were nestlings; they had taken the walk through the Passage of Kings and seen its horrific scenes carved into the mosaics. But it hadn't been until Delja found Roh at Cerys' cell that Roh had learned she had a family connection to the historic tragedy. Somehow, she'd had an uncle who had perished there. Marlow was his name, or so she'd been told. However, since that meeting in the prison she'd thought little of him, unable to make sense of the timeline. How was it that she had an uncle in Lochloria during the Scouring but a mother who was alive in the present? The question was too large for her to fathom, and in the face of the Queen's Tournament, it had been of little consequence. Now, at Deodan's words, she pictured the warlock clans, ambushed in their own homes, exterminated without hesitation. Roh's imagination pulled her through image after image of helpless people being slaughtered —

Sudden movement snatched her from her thoughts as Deodan leaped from his horse. They had reached the swollen banks of the river. His boots sank into the mud with a squelch as he approached the water's edge and crouched, seemingly searching for something.

'I'll need a hand here,' he said to no one in particular, as he dug his hands into the mud, combing through the thick sludge until at last, he dragged a thick chain free.

Finn landed deftly beside his horse and went to the clan leader, his dislike plain on his face.

Does he like anyone but Yrsa? For her part, Roh wasn't getting off her horse for all the world; she didn't know if she'd be able to get back up. Harlyn seemed to be similarly inclined, her usual scowl knitting her brows together.

Wordlessly, Finn pushed back his sleeves, taking the length of chain Deodan offered, and together, Jaktaren and water warlock heaved it, heels sinking deeper into the mud as something from beneath the raging river came to the churning surface.

A bridge.

'There should be an anchor point over there,' Deodan grunted, indicating with a nod.

'There.' Roh pointed, able to see the metal ring from her vantage point.

'I can see it,' Finn ground out, clicking the chain into place and stepping back to see what they'd done, his bare forearms flecked with dirt.

'We cross here,' Deodan said. 'I know you cyrens would manage well enough, but don't forget that you're with a human and six horses. Have patience.' He gave Finn a meaningful look.

'I didn't say a word,' Finn countered.

'You're practically snarling.'

Jaktaren and warlock looked each other up and down, glaring, both armed, both of similar height, and though Finn was the leaner of the two, it meant nothing given his skillset. Roh's patience wore thin.

'Can we ride on?' she called. 'I'd like to get to Akoris and the birthstone before the next century.'

'As you say, Queen of Bones.' Deodan bowed his head mockingly. 'One at a time across the bridge.'

Biting back the urge to snap at the warlock, Roh clenched her teeth and urged her horse across the narrow bridge, the river rushing beneath. From the other bank, she watched the others do the same. It was a strange sight, to say the least, Saddorien cyrens crossing a river on horseback.

When they were all safely across, she guided her horse towards Odi's, planning on asking him how exactly he'd become a master musician as well as a master of horsemanship, but it was Deodan who spoke first, leading their company towards the tussock-covered hills.

'We should talk about Akoris.' He projected his voice so all could hear. 'What do you know of it? Any of you?'

'It's where the mad cyrens go,' Finn offered, edging his horse up alongside Deodan's, as though he wanted to take the lead. 'The ones madder than even those in Saddoriel,' he added, with a pointed glance in Roh's direction.

'I think what you're referring to is their fanaticism,' Deodan muttered.

'Same thing,' Finn said.

Roh recalled the mosaic in the Passage of Kings displaying Uniir the Blessed's imposing figure, depicted on tiles between the goddesses Dresmis and Thera. One of two cyren kings who had changed the course of cyren history forever, the one who'd embedded a blade in his own gut in the name of the gods. The very king whose rule Akorian cyrens admired most – a clan of worshippers. Was that why Deodan had wanted to join them? To oppose the way of life that had seen the Scouring of Lochloria come to pass? But Uniir was dead, defeated by Delja long ago.

'Akoris is a place unlike any other,' Deodan said. 'You would do well to keep your guard up there. Or you may find yourself caught up in its … allure.'

'What do you mean?' Roh pressed. 'Does it bewitch non-cyrens, as Saddoriel does? Lure them in …?'

'I said it was *unlike* any other. But it does have a knack for seduction, only its target is its own kind. Put it this way: it has ways of making you forget there are realms outside, ways of making its inhabitants turn introspective … amongst other concerns.'

The last thing Roh needed was more introspection. She found it hard enough to escape her own thoughts on regular days. She vowed to keep her wits about her in the foreign territory.

'Tell us of Adriel, then,' she requested, suddenly recalling the Arch General's name.

'Adriel.' Deodan said the name as though he were testing it aloud. 'Adriel has a unique nature.'

'Care to be more specific? You've met him?'

'Several times,' Deodan said, clicking his heels into his horse's sides, guiding it effortlessly up a crest in the hillside. 'The Arch General never does anything unless it benefits him. He's a slippery fellow, one who says one thing but means another. Though …' he paused. 'That's not an uncommon trait amongst your kind. He ... has a reputation.'

Roh frowned, frustrated. 'What does that mean?'

Deodan looked uncomfortable. 'It means ...'

'It means he takes advantage,' Finn finished coldly for him. 'Usually of those weaker or of lower stature, which is almost everyone.'

'Isn't that what all you highborns do?' Roh retorted. Adriel sounded like every other noble Roh had met, except perhaps Yrsa, at whom she shot an apologetic glance.

Finn's nostrils flared as he glared at Roh. 'We're nothing like Adriel.'

'No?' Surprised, Roh twisted in her saddle, facing the Jaktaren. 'Have *you* met him?'

'I've only seen him in passing, on his visits to Saddoriel. But I've heard tales about him. Tales bad enough to turn my stomach.'

A shiver raked down Roh's spine. If something was ugly enough to unsettle *Finn* of all cyrens, then something was seriously wrong with the leader of Akoris. She knew she should press for more information, that anything she could learn about the Arch General would help her understand his motives, but something about Finn's words had her turning away. Perhaps there were some things best left unknown.

Yrsa spoke next, eyeing Deodan evenly. 'What business does a warlock descendant have with a cyren leader?' she asked.

'We've had … dealings over the years. We tolerate each other.'

'For what purpose?' Roh asked, her curiosity piquing. If Akoris was what he said it was, he had no place walking through its gates, let alone conversing with the cyren who ran it. And why in the realms would his clan be based there? She had a thousand questions on her lips.

But Deodan took the lead again and said simply, 'My own.'

Roh found Finn's horse directly alongside hers. 'He was an *interesting* choice, bone cleaner,' he muttered.

She rolled her eyes at the Jaktaren. 'So were you.'

'You'll have need of me before the end,' Finn quipped sharply.

'Why do you think you're here?' she countered, nudging her horse onwards, away from his.

The gilded plains were as vast as the day before, stretching on in waves of gold that shivered in the breeze as far as the eye could see. As the company crested the hills rolling towards the blue horizon, Roh tried to imagine what Akoris looked like beyond. It wasn't an enchanted subterranean territory like Saddoriel, she knew that much. According to the map she carried, it was nestled amongst the hills and dunes by the south-east coast. Roh wondered what sort of music they played there. And how was Ames going to get there in time? It had taken Roh and her companions almost two weeks to reach even the gilded plains.

As they rode, Roh's mind wandered and spiralled, as it often did. Though she had slept beneath the stars since she'd left Saddoriel, this type of travelling was new to her – the constant lurch of movement beneath her, the sway of her body in the saddle and the ache at her backside and the base of her spine. But it meant her thoughts were free to roam to the deepest, darkest crevices of her mind. She had trouble controlling them as they flitted from one image or subject to the next with seemingly no prompting. She thought of the crown of bones in her pack, and the sea-drake egg, wrapped carefully in her spare shirt and cloak. Those two objects and her actions to obtain them had caused a tidal wave of consequences that was still washing over the shores and causing quakes across the lands. She wouldn't know how far those tremors would reach for a long time yet.

She thought of Cerys, wondering again if her mother had noticed that her visits to the prison had ceased, or if she was so caught up in scratching *wings* into stone that time hadn't passed in its usual way. Had she even been lucid when she had spoken to Roh the last time they'd seen each other? Or was it all part of the manic persona that had manifested after centuries of imprisonment? Was that the cause of her madness? Or had Cerys' mind always been fated to unhinge? What did that mean for Roh? Was it something that ran through her veins, as Finn and his ilk had implied numerous times?

Roh pondered what might await her in Akoris – the gem, whichever one it was, locked away for certain with some sort of test in its path. And the inevitability of being confronted by a challenger. She knew it was coming; she was not so naive to hope that the offers of prestige and riches would fail to tempt those in lower stations, nor that the wounded pride of those she had defeated in the Queen's Tournament would not spur on the Saddoriens of influence. Though she had won the trials, she knew it was only the beginning.

At the thought of the tournament itself, Roh's mind shifted to an image of Delja, the former Saddorien queen, whose wings marked her as a god incarnate. The very cyren who seemed torn between helping Roh and ruining her.

'Perhaps I couldn't help you when you were born, I couldn't change where the Law of the Lair forced you to go, but perhaps ... Perhaps now I can change where you're going ...' The strain in Delja's voice had told Roh that the former queen knew exactly what it felt like to be trapped for years on end.

Finally, Roh's thoughts went to Orson. Her sweet and gentle friend, her sister. A cyren who had been by her side since she was a nestling, helping her, guiding her through the trials and tribulations of the lair. Orson, who she'd betrayed and left behind.

It was hard to tell how many hours had passed before Deodan allowed a stop. When Roh at last slid from the saddle, her knees buckled as her boots hit the ground. Every muscle in the lower half of her body screamed in protest as she attempted to stretch out her legs and walk normally.

'It takes some getting used to,' Yrsa said sympathetically. 'Best not to sit down right away. Stay on your feet and move around as much as possible. Or it'll be worse tomorrow.'

'Worse?' Harlyn chimed in. 'It can't get worse than this.'

Yrsa laughed. 'Believe me.' She took out her sling. 'Now's a good time to get in some practice, Roh. If you're willing?'

Roh hardly felt like wrapping her mind around learning a new skill, but with the threat of even worse saddle-soreness tomorrow, she found herself nodding. She couldn't deny that the need to be able to defend herself was becoming increasingly paramount.

Roh ignored Harlyn's watchful gaze as Yrsa lengthened the sling's cords to suit Roh's longer arms.

'You have to position this loop over your middle finger, and rest this knot between these fingers.' Yrsa's hands were rough as she showed Roh how to hold the cord for easy release. Looking around the barren landscape, she pointed. 'That rock, there,' she said. 'That can be your target.'

'Hopefully, it's far enough away from the rest of us,' Harlyn called out, arms folded over her chest as she watched, her horse grazing beside her.

Roh was keenly aware of Deodan, Odi and Finn all watching as well, but there was never going to be a private space for her to learn and she was determined to at least gain a basic understanding. The skirmish with Deodan's patrol had left her feeling weak and helpless, sensations that no cyren had any business becoming familiar with. She wouldn't be ambushed like that again; she refused to be a liability to her own companions.

'There are several techniques you can use with the sling. The one you've seen me do before is the spin, where you gain momentum for the stone by circling it above your head. But that's not the easiest manoeuvre to learn. I think perhaps we should start with the overhand method, and once you've got that, we could try for the figure eight. What do you think?'

'You're the expert,' Roh said with a shrug.

'Good. Let's try it without the stone first,' Yrsa said gently, guiding Roh's arm up over her head. 'You want it about there. Hold the cradle in front of you with your less dominant hand, then you'll use your stronger hand and arm to bring it back and over, like this ...'

Roh let Yrsa move her arms into the position and slowly show her the movements.

'It obviously needs to happen much faster than that. You want as much force behind that stone as possible, so it does the most damage when it hits the target. Let me demonstrate.'

Yrsa took the sling, readjusted the cords and the knots, and placed a stone from her pouch in the cradle. In a sudden blur of movement, the sling came up and over her head, sending the stone flying at the rock with incredible speed. Upon impact, the clay ball cracked.

Odi swore.

'Now, if that were someone's face, what do you think would have cracked first?' Yrsa challenged.

Roh winced at the thought.

Yrsa pushed the sling back into Roh's hands. 'You try.'

Roh fitted the loop around her finger and rested the knot between her knuckles like Yrsa had shown her. *Overhand,* she reminded herself and tried to recall in slow motion how the clay ball had shot over Yrsa's head. She held the cradle and stone out in front of her and flung it —

Her projectile went wide. Very wide.

But no one laughed.

'Everyone starts out like that,' Yrsa told her.

Roh couldn't help but glance in Finn's direction.

'Even him,' Yrsa added, following her gaze.

Roh simply nodded. 'Can I try again?'

'Always. That's how you improve.'

Roh found herself lost in the rhythm of their lesson. She enjoyed how each movement stretched out her stiff muscles, enjoyed working towards a goal and seeing just a tiny bit of improvement with each throw. When she finally hit the target, Yrsa showed her how to use the sling in close combat, wielding it almost like a club at an invisible attacker. To Roh's surprise, Harlyn joined in. She guessed her friend was just as keen to learn how to defend herself as Roh was. A helpless cyren was no cyren at all.

'I never thanked you,' Yrsa said suddenly, taking the sling from Roh as they were finishing up their drills.

Roh frowned. 'What for?'

'For saving Tess. For bringing her to me when you

didn't have to. When it would have served you better to let her die.'

Roh saw Harlyn's look of confusion. There had been a lot she'd been unable to share with her friend throughout the tournament, and with Roh's ugly betrayal now out in the open, constantly wedged between them, there had been no opportunity for a debrief.

Roh just shrugged in Yrsa's direction. 'You should really thank Odi,' she admitted.

'I will … I miss that girl.'

Roh thought she'd misheard. Hadn't Yrsa refused to tell Roh and Odi what had become of her human? Hadn't the Jaktaren implied that the poor girl had met an unfortunate fate, as did most humans who had experienced the lure of Saddoriel?

Yrsa must have seen the conflict on her face. 'Tess and I, we became friends. Like you and Odi. We helped each other.'

'Then what happened to her?' Roh pressed, wanting an answer more for Odi than herself. He had pitied the scrappy young thing, had wanted to take her under their wing.

Yrsa shook her head. 'I cannot say.'

'Can't or won't?'

'Both. It's not my place. But thank you for what you did all the same.'

Roh didn't know what to say, but Yrsa wasn't finished.

'I also never thanked you for saving Finn and me … during the last trial of the tournament. If you hadn't dragged us to that cave, we probably would have died.'

Roh met her gaze. 'Probably. I don't suppose you've reminded your friend over there of that?' She jutted her chin in Finn's direction.

'I have.'

'As I recall, he would have preferred to kill me.'

Yrsa gave a sheepish shrug. 'He'll come around, eventually.'

Roh very much doubted that. Shaking her head, she followed Yrsa and Harlyn to where the others were sitting, passing out rations, and decided she wouldn't rehash the conversation to Odi, as it would just upset him. She looked over to where he sat on a rock, his fingers drumming across the top of his thigh as he listened to something Deodan was saying. Odi's fidgeting had frustrated Roh for a long time until she'd discovered that he was simply longing to play the piano. Now she watched him, wishing he could do just that.

Roh ate and drank with the rest, and before she knew it, they were back in their saddles, horses trekking across the grasslands once more.

The journey was punctuated with strained conversation and awkwardness, particularly when someone lagged behind, stopping to relieve themselves within the limited cover of the tussock. As the second dusk fell, Roh spotted an eagle swooping down into the shivering grass and catching a rabbit in its brutal talons.

'That's good,' Finn muttered. 'Means there might be a

warren over there. We could be having roast game tonight.'

Yrsa, ever the huntress, made sure of it with her deadly-accurate sling.

The rise and fall of the sun and moon marked the passing of time across the gilded plains and hillsides. They found streams to water the horses and, at Deodan's instruction, made sure the beasts were well cared for and rubbed down each evening. Every night, Roh slept with the drake egg clutched to her chest beneath her cloak. Yrsa had said the eggs were self-insulating, so she didn't really know why she did it – it just felt right … and perhaps she longed to feel needed.

As the last hours of the fourth day ebbed away and the afternoon heat began to fade, Roh's horse stirred uneasily beneath her. She shortened her reins as Deodan had taught her and tried to calm the beast with long, reassuring strokes down its neck.

'What's the matter?' she murmured, her touch failing to soothe him. He had been a gentle, cooperative horse for the most part over the course of the journey. What had changed?

Roh looked around to see her five companions having similar troubles with their mounts. The horses were skittish, pawing the dirt with their hooves, whinnying and trying to turn back, refusing to crest the next hill.

'Something's wrong,' Roh called to Deodan.

The chieftain nodded and signalled for them to stop. He dismounted and motioned for Roh to do the same.

'What is it?' she asked, approaching him with trepidation.

But Deodan didn't reply. He dropped onto his stomach and began to crawl on his elbows up the hill. Fear pricking at her insides, Roh did the same, following him up the crest, trying not to imagine what would warrant such a cautious move. Together, they peered over the ridge.

Roh clapped a hand over her mouth to stifle the cry of horror that escaped her. Deodan pressed a single finger to his lips, his blue-grey eyes full of warning. For beyond the crest in a valley of golden tussock were several giant creatures. Larger than horses, they prowled the grasslands with a powerful grace, their silvery-black fur and fangs gleaming in the fading light.

Giant wildcats.

'Are those what I think they are?' Odi's voice sounded beside Roh. When had he snuck up here?

It took every ounce of strength not to clap her hand over his big mouth, too. But any sudden movement could draw attention to them, any noise …

'Teerah panthers,' Deodan said, his knuckles turning white as he gripped fistfuls of grass. 'Back away slowly,' he whispered, not taking his eyes off the beasts below as he started to inch his way backwards down the hill.

Blood pounding in her ears, Roh did the same, with Odi at her side. She had to force each limb to move, terror threatening to freeze her in place. Teerah panthers. Of all the legendary creatures of the realms to have stumbled upon … She shook her head in disbelief, breathing heavily through her nose as her talons dug into the dirt and tussock. She was shaking uncontrollably when she and Odi reached the foot of the hill, while the others tried desperately to calm the panicked horses, who had picked up on their fear as well as the scent of the panthers beyond the hill.

Deodan fumbled with his pouch of vials, the little glass containers clinking softly together.

Roh winced at the small sound. Was there some sort of warlock enchantment to deter vicious mythical beasts?

But they hadn't been detected. They were safe. They just had to take a wide berth around the hillside and the valley of panthers.

It's going to be alright, Roh told herself, leading her horse away from the foot of the hill. She sighed quietly in relief as she put distance between herself and the dangerous pride beyond —

Only to hear a vicious, hair-raising growl behind her.

CHAPTER EIGHT

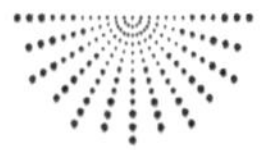

The sound reverberated through Roh's bones and her horse reared on its hind legs with a terrified scream. The reins were wrenched from her hand, nearly ripping her shoulder from its socket, as the horse darted away. The echo of thunderous hooves told her that the other horses had bolted too.

Slowly, Roh turned on her heel.

A lone teerah panther stalked towards her, each step with its giant paws deliberate and predatory. Beside her, Finn raised his crossbow and her heart pounded in her chest.

'Don't,' she hissed, the word like a shard of glass in her throat as she placed a palm atop the weapon and forced the Jaktaren to lower it. 'Have you learned *nothing* from shooting magical beasts bigger than you?'

From the corner of her eye, Roh could see Deodan

fumbling with his vials, but what good would water flowers do here? What would happen when the panther called out to the rest of his pride? They were no match for these creatures.

The beast growled again, sniffing the air around them, its scar-littered coat gleaming across its muscular torso as it considered them with its savage gaze. One by one, Roh and her companions backed away, gathering in a cluster, each of them holding their breath. But Harlyn was slower than the rest, and as she stepped back she stumbled.

A claw swiped out, the movement so fast it blurred with a slash of red.

Harlyn's gut-wrenching scream echoed across the hillside.

Roh darted forward without thinking, throwing herself at her friend.

The teerah panther roared.

Roh's hands gripped Harlyn's shirt in fistfuls, dragging her backwards, to what safety, Roh didn't know. There was no safety here. Blood gushed from the deep gash in Harlyn's arm and she clutched the useless limb to her middle, moaning with pain.

Ice-cold terror washed over Roh as she looked up to the hillcrest, where six other teerah panthers had appeared, and were looking down at them.

Gods, this is it. We'll be torn to shreds by these creatures and our bones will decay in the gilded plains. Roh clutched Harlyn tighter, catching Odi's panicked look as he drew the short sword he had belted at his waist.

'*Now* can we shoot them?' Finn yelled.

But Deodan was emptying vials of liquid into his palm, whispering inaudible enchantments, all the while not tearing his gaze from the pride of encroaching panthers.

Another teerah roar bellowed across the plains – an order. The snarling creatures descended the hillside, fangs gnashing. Roh and her band of companions were simply prey lying exposed, ready for slaughter.

Magic exploded from Deodan's palm. An enormous water whirlwind spiralled towards the pride, towering above the hills, tearing up the tussock as it went. The panthers leaped from its path, roaring, the hurricane's gale and crashing force drowning out their yelps of terror. Deodan sent it chasing after them, threatening to sweep them up into the tempest. Roh felt the magic thrum within her as the beasts scattered, darting across the gilded plains in massive bounds, sending chunks of grass flying and dirt spraying.

Harlyn wheezed in Roh's arms as they watched the teerah panthers flee. The water whirlwind barrelled across the plains with the force of ten thousand rivers and ravaged the land until there was no longer a teerah panther in sight.

Just as suddenly as the magic had burst into being, the cyclone stopped spinning abruptly and water plummeted, as if from a fall, to the ground in a thunderous, cascading wave. Even from a distance, cool droplets sprayed across the company, slowly drawing each of them from their shell of shock.

Roh was on her knees in the dirt, an incredibly pale

Harlyn gripped tightly in her arms. She forced herself to look at her friend's wound and gagged. It was a deep slice into the flesh of Harlyn's forearm, white tissue and tendons poking through the skin.

'What were those?' Harlyn rasped through the pain.

At once Odi was beside Roh, taking Harlyn's uninjured hand between his own half-gloved fingers. 'I've only heard about them in children's stories,' he told her, trying to take her focus away from her wound.

'That was anything *but* a children's story,' Harlyn said, her jaw clenching as Roh helped her sit up.

'There are rumours throughout the realms that there was a tyrant who ruled these lands – perhaps she still does. A human woman with a different kind of magic to cyrens and warlocks. She captured the teerah panthers and tormented them, turned them into vicious monsters to set upon her enemies.'

Roh tried to hide her trembling hands from the others as she looked around for Deodan. They were going to need his healing water flowers before long. But he caught her eye from where he stood a few feet away and subtly shook his head. The vials he held were all empty; he'd used every last one to create the water whirlwind.

Roh ripped one of the sleeves from her shirt and took Harlyn's wounded arm gently in her hands. Blood coursed freely through the gaps in her fingers. 'We have to bind this, Har,' she told her friend.

It felt strange calling Harlyn by her childhood nickname after everything, but Roh didn't know how else to reassure her, to distract her from the pain. 'I have to pull this tight to staunch the bleeding, okay?'

Roh wove the fabric around her friend's arm, red saturating the white material almost instantly, and firmly drew the ends together. Harlyn cried out and Roh felt a tear in her own body, wishing with all her heart that she could remove the pain.

Deodan took Roh away from the others. 'We'll have to set up camp somewhere nearby until she's stable, until we can find the horses. We won't get far without them.'

Roh nodded, not taking her eyes off her friend, whose teeth had started to chatter. 'Will she be alright?'

'Honestly? I don't know. That claw sliced through tendons and nerves, but the greatest risk is infection. That panther could have carved up anything before Harlyn. The wound might start to fester.'

Roh shuddered. 'Can you find the horses? I'll stay with her. I don't want to leave her.'

'If I do, we'll have to make for Akoris at first light. My magic stores are completely depleted and the water from the river isn't potent enough for that level of healing. I can't help her, Roh. Not here.'

Roh still hadn't looked away from Harlyn. Even in the near darkness of early evening, she could see that all colour had drained from Harlyn's face and the wound was still seeping through the makeshift bandage. Roh swallowed the thick lump in her throat, forcing down the swell of emotion. Now was not the time to fall apart. She lit a torch and scoured the deserted hillside for any sort of shelter. It didn't take her long to find one, and while

Deodan and Yrsa called for the horses across the plains, Roh, Odi and Finn moved Harlyn to cover, starting a small fire to keep her chills at bay.

Not even Finn said anything as they worked and Roh was grateful for that small mercy. She was on the brink of breaking and one snide comment from the Jaktaren would send her plummeting over the edge. She could feel it, and from his almost tender movements, it seemed he could feel it, too.

Night had well and truly settled around them, but there was nothing to do aside from wait. The horses had taken their packs and supplies with them, and so there was no food or water to be had but for the single canteen Roh had clipped to her belt. She shared it around with the others, suddenly realising how parched her throat was as her chapped lips touched the cool metal of the canteen. She refused to think about the loss of her pack and all that it contained. Instead, she watched Harlyn intently, her friend drifting in and out of consciousness, the bandage around her arm drenched with blood. She didn't object to Roh's presence, which was a worrying sign in itself.

Odi sat across from Roh and Harlyn, brushing his dark hair from his drawn face as he hunched over Harlyn's broken lute. In the flickering light of the fire, his long fingers picked at the loose strings and used twine to bind the larger fractured pieces together.

Finn remained quiet, prodding occasionally at the flames with a stick and adding fronds of dry tussock. Roh's stomach grumbled loudly, but she didn't register the feeling of hunger. She couldn't eat now even if she wanted to, not with her entire guts churning at the gaping wound in Harlyn's arm. Roh tried to make her as comfortable as possible, folding her cloak and placing it behind Harlyn's head as a pillow. It was all she could do while they waited for Deodan and Yrsa to return.

As the night wore on and the hours ticked by at an excruciatingly slow pace, cold, hard fear settled into her. Harlyn had begun to mutter under her breath, strange murmurings Roh couldn't understand until —

'Maybe he'll be cleaning *my* bones before long,' Harlyn babbled deliriously.

That sent an icy shiver down Roh's spine, fuelling the terror already writhing within her. *What is Harlyn seeing? What if she's never the same again?* And the unthinkable: *What if she dies?*

At some point in the night, Roh drifted into a panicked sleep. She dreamed of Cerys, back in her cell, surrounded by sketches of wings. The sound of the sea drake's screech filled her head, getting louder and louder until she wasn't sure if she was the one screaming. She saw her crown of bones drifting to the bottom of the sea, bubbles of air trailing in its wake through the turquoise waters. She saw the *Tome of Kyeos* floating in its enchanted beam of light in the Vault back in Saddoriel, just waiting for her to open its pages and learn its truths. Finally, a glimmer of light caught her eye and she stepped forward, not quite trusting herself to believe what she saw ... A gem, a shining jewel that seemed to wink at her as she drew closer. A birthstone of Saddoriel. Within her grasp. She didn't hesitate. She snatched it up in her hands, peering down at the Mercy's Topaz in wonder. Nestled in her palm, the birthstone gleamed, growing warmer and warmer the longer she stared. And then it was hot, searing hot, burning through Roh's flesh —

She jolted awake with a strangled cry.

Harlyn's bare shoulder pressed against her hand, heat throbbing from her friend and seeping into Roh's skin.

'Harlyn?' Roh croaked, feeling her forehead with the back of her hand, and swearing at the fever that burned there.

Harlyn's skin was on fire and slick with sweat. At the sound of her voice, both Odi and Finn rushed over, holding Harlyn up as Roh tried to press the canteen of precious water to her lips. The water trickled uselessly down her chin.

'Gods, this can't be happening,' Roh whispered. 'This can't —'

The sound of hooves pounding against the earth cut her off and Roh looked up wildly into the darkness, spotting a lone rider galloping towards them.

Deodan.

Roh scrambled to her feet, nearly getting herself trampled as she ran to him. 'She needs help, Deodan. Now.'

'I only have the one horse,' Deodan said, jumping down from the saddle and approaching the fire. 'Yrsa is rounding up the others, but I thought I should —'

'Take her,' Roh begged. 'Help her.'

'I cannot get her to Akoris in time.'

'Y-you know of somewhere else. Y-you have to,' Roh stammered desperately, gripping the buckles across the water warlock's chest. 'Name your price – just save her.'

'A lesson to hold on to, Rohesia, Queen of Bones. Never promise that which you do not understand.'

'*Please,*' was all Roh managed.

Deodan rubbed the bridge of his crooked nose, his blue-grey eyes pained. Pulling the quartz dagger from somewhere beneath his cloak, he considered it and then Roh, looking between the two, before he sighed. 'There will come a time when I ask something of you, Rohesia,' he said. 'And you will honour your word.'

Roh's breath caught in her throat as Deodan slashed the dagger across his palm and motioned for Roh to offer hers.

Dazed, she held out her hand and felt the sharp sting before she even saw the blade. Deodan turned his palm to face the ground, allowing the blood to drip onto the earth. Ignoring Finn's cursing, Roh did the same.

'Remember this,' Deodan said as he unceremoniously pocketed the dagger and strode forward to Harlyn. Crouching to wrap her good arm around his neck, he picked her up and carried her to his horse. Odi held her upright as Deodan mounted his horse once more, pulling a limp Harlyn up onto the saddle in front of him. He looked down at Roh.

'Follow my tracks south-east to the stream – cross it. You'll find a forest there.'

Ride swiftly, or she'll die – the words were wet on Roh's

lips, but she said nothing as Deodan kicked his horse and left a cloud of dust in his wake.

Roh didn't know how much time had passed when Yrsa returned, three horses in tow. 'We've lost two,' she started, before realising Deodan and Harlyn were gone. 'Where'd they go?' she said, passing Roh's reins to her. Roh found little comfort in the fact that her pack, with its secret contents, remained strapped to the saddle.

'South-east,' Roh told her, foot already in the stirrup. 'We need to go.'

Yrsa didn't question it. She simply passed another set of reins to Finn, while Odi stamped out what was left of the fire.

'Odi, you're with me,' Roh said, mounting her horse and offering her hand. 'Yrsa, Finn, we need to track Deodan and we need to track him fast.'

The Jaktaren were already riding on.

Odi swung himself up into the saddle behind Roh, wrapping his arms around her middle, and she kicked her horse into a canter after the highborns.

No one spoke as they rode through the darkness of the early hours. A thread of Harlyn's life and Deodan's faded magic hung between the separated company, pulling them south-east. Yrsa took the lead, either finding Deodan's tracks in the moonlight, or understanding where exactly they were going.

Roh didn't miss Finn's reluctance at Yrsa's side. 'If

we're going where I think we're going … We shouldn't. Not for a mere bone cleaner.'

Before Roh could bite his head off, Yrsa silenced him with a look. 'We are bound to this quest, and to the company within it.'

Yellowed beams of moonlight illuminated the uneven terrain before them and they rode hard. Roh hardly noticed the close proximity to Odi or his warm breath on the back of her neck. Her thoughts were only of Harlyn, and whether she would survive this. She swore she could smell the tang of her friend's blood in the night air.

The sound of a babbling brook interrupted Roh's reverie and suddenly they were amidst the trees. Yrsa didn't hesitate, lighting a torch and guiding her horse into the dark woods, weaving between the pines. The air was cool and damp beneath the dense canopy that blocked out the inky sky beyond, and the sound of rushing water grew louder. Finally, they reached a small waterfall, where Deodan's horse had its head bowed to the stream and was drinking.

'Through there.' Yrsa pointed. 'Finn and I can't come.'

'What? Why?'

'There's an enchantment against Jaktaren over these rocks,' Yrsa said, dismounting and running a palm across the wet stones. 'We'll have to wait here.'

Is this a trap? Part of a plan to get me away from the companions best equipped to defend me?

Odi slid down from the saddle and offered Roh a hand. She took it, jumping off and approaching the rushing water. If Harlyn was beyond the falls, then beyond the falls Roh would go. She wasn't about to abandon her friend. She didn't like to leave the Jaktaren unattended, but she had no choice, and they hadn't left her, yet.

Hands shaking at her sides, Roh squared her shoulders and stepped through the falls.

CHAPTER NINE

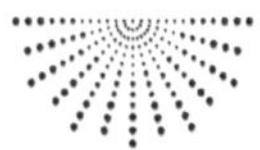

Roh's breath whistled between her teeth as the falls cascaded over her and she stepped through into the cave beyond. The water kissed the scales at her temples, but otherwise left her dry. Odi followed moments later, completely drenched.

A primal instinct stopped Roh from taking another step. Magic simmered here, the same strange magic that was entangled with Deodan, only stronger. Around them were sheets of filmy, enchanted water and walls of stone lined with weapons, hundreds of them, spears in the neatest, most precise lines Roh had ever seen.

Glancing at the veils of water, she knew they shielded something much larger beyond, but all she could see was the narrow cave, reflections of water shimmering across the wet stone.

Where's Harlyn? Where's Deodan? What is the meaning of

this place? She took a tentative step, gravel crunching beneath her boot.

'This way,' she said to Odi, spotting some narrow stone stairs spiralling into darkness.

'How do you know?' Odi whispered.

'There's nowhere else to go,' Roh told him, though she didn't feel half as confident as she sounded.

As she descended the first few steps, her skin prickled. She squinted, trying to find Deodan and Harlyn, but there was nothing other than water and stone.

Until a figure emerged from the shadows. It wasn't Deodan or Harlyn.

'Where are they?' Roh demanded.

The figure closed the gap between them and eyes that mirrored Deodan's blue-grey glared at Roh. A hoarse voice echoed through the caves. 'You've been trusted in a way that I do not yet understand in order to see what you see now. That doesn't mean *I* trust you.'

'Please,' Roh heard herself say, the note of desperation clear as day. She knew from years of playing cards that she shouldn't show her hand this early, but Harlyn's life was on the line. This was a game whose rules she didn't know.

'He took your friend to our healers' quarters.'

Odi nudged Roh. 'Never trust a cyren,' he muttered.

A hollow, scratchy laugh filled the space around them. 'We are no cyrens.'

Indeed, when the older woman lowered her hood and pushed back the silvery hair from her eyes, there were no glimmering scales to be found at her temples. 'When your kind sacked our scholars' city, we had to adapt. We became something else.'

Though Deodan had said as much before they left the human settlement, Roh's stomach churned at the stranger's words. If they weren't water warlocks, what were they?

'Who are you? What is this place?' Roh said, stepping towards the figure.

As she got closer, she saw that the woman was in her seventieth year or so, but she was both fierce and battle-worn. A thick white scar slashed across the width of her throat.

Roh nearly cried out as an eagle swooped through the falls behind the woman and landed seamlessly on her shoulder.

'I do not answer to you, cyren,' said the woman, stroking the bird's chest with the knuckle of her index finger. 'We are our own people.'

'Who is "we"? There's no one here,' Odi said.

Roh silenced him with a look. It didn't matter what they could see – they were definitely not alone. There was far more to this dark place than met the eye.

'While we are different from what we once were,' the woman continued, as if Odi hadn't spoken, 'we still practise the old arts. Follow me.'

Something about that phrase made Roh shiver. What were the old arts? What were they doing to Harlyn? But she and Odi had no choice but to follow the older woman, her cloak trailing behind her, the eagle on her shoulder swivelling its head eerily to stare at them with black eyes.

They trailed down the narrow stairs after the woman. Roh's heart caught in her throat as her treacherous mind raced through all manner of possibilities for what they would find at the end of the path. The nameless woman led them to a cave, where within Harlyn lay unconscious on a bed of stone. Three hooded figures tended to her, while Deodan stood at her side, hands resting on the grips of his cutlasses.

'She's lost a lot of blood,' he said, without looking up. 'And shock has taken hold of her body.'

'Will she —' Roh choked, a wave of emotion hitting her square in the chest. She had been so desperate to find meaning in Cerys' words that she'd risked everything to cross the gilded plains – a place she knew nothing of. A place that might very well have cost Harlyn her life.

'Deodan. A word.' There was only pure command in that hoarse voice.

To Roh's surprise, Deodan bowed his head and instantly ducked away with the older woman without so much as a glance in Roh's direction.

Roh looked up to find Odi watching her. 'Whatever you're thinking,' he said, his face lined with worry, 'don't.'

But Roh was done with waiting around for answers, especially when her best friend lay somewhere between life and death before her. Not pausing for Odi to argue, she slipped from the cave and listened for footsteps.

With all the stealth she could muster, Roh trailed the

two long cloaks around the bend of the narrow stairs, only stopping when she could hear their voices clearly.

'— the meaning of this, Deodan? You bring Saddorien cyrens into our midst? *How dare you* jeopardise all I have worked for these past decades. I have half a mind to banish you back to that pathetic human village you care so much about. You have risked —'

The warlock descendant hadn't put an enchantment in place to stop her from listening, Roh realised with a jolt. Either Deodan was a fool and thought she'd stay obediently put, or … he *meant* for her to hear. And Deodan didn't strike Roh as a fool.

'She had Eadric's dagger,' Deodan said, his words cutting through the woman's fury like a hot blade through butter.

Roh almost lost her footing. *Who is Eadric? Is that the name of the dead warlock outside Cerys' cell?*

'What did you say?' the woman breathed.

'She didn't even know she had it,' Deodan pressed. 'It's a message.'

'More of your speculations?' the woman snapped. 'Suspicions get us nowhere. I will hear no more of your guesswork and I will not have you base any more rash decisions on your wild theories. I have been waiting for this opportunity since before you were even born.'

'I know you have. I have fought many a fight for you because of it. But, perhaps we can do this without so much bloodshed?'

'Bloodshed? You should *want* bloodshed, boy. You

should be hunting after it like a hound on the scent after everything those monsters did to our kin.'

'Bloodshed is never one-sided, Your Supremacy. Perhaps we can achieve our goals *without* becoming the very thing you hate most?'

Supremacy? Roh gaped in the dark. There was only one title like that. *That means the woman with Deodan is ... the Warlock Supreme. The —*

'Roh?' Odi whispered from behind her.

'Shhh!' Roh hissed, panic seizing her. She couldn't be caught here, listening in on the *Warlock Supreme*, for Dresmis and Thera's sakes!

'Harlyn's asking for you,' Odi told her.

Roh was already moving. Whatever Deodan had planned with the supposedly non-existent water warlocks could wait. Harlyn needed her.

Her friend's eyes were bloodshot when Roh reached her, and the usually blue scales at her temples were a dull silver. Harlyn's arm rested on a bed of dark leaves. The wound had been sutured expertly, but the flesh was swollen, threatening to burst the perfect stitches open.

'Har,' Roh croaked, taking her good hand in her grasp.

Harlyn blinked up at her, dazed. 'I'm glad you're here,' she said, her grip weak. 'Where's Orson?'

Something cracked in Roh. She had made a mistake in not bringing their other friend with them. They should never have been separated.

'They said her arm may never have the full function it once did,' Odi murmured in Roh's ear.

A sour taste filled Roh's mouth, knowing that Harlyn's

first questions would be about her ability to play the lute. But for now, all Roh could do was be grateful that her friend was alive, and that she wanted Roh there.

A long arm fell around Roh's shoulders and squeezed her gently. 'She's going to be alright,' Odi told her.

Roh felt herself lean into the comfort of his embrace, relief flooding her body, and together they took up their vigil at Harlyn's side.

Roh awoke with a gasp to a strange magic exploring the cool, damp air around her, tangling with the ancient power that seemed to hum from within her. She staggered forward and Odi's hand shot out to steady her.

I fell asleep standing? She was still on her aching feet beside Harlyn, whose chest rose and fell with shallow gasps.

Deodan stood expectantly at the entrance to the cave. 'We've done all we can for Harlyn,' he said. 'And we've given her all the rest we can allow, but she needs further treatment. If we leave now, we can be in Akoris by daybreak.'

Roh tried to rub the exhaustion from her eyes. 'She can't travel like this.'

'She'll ride with me.'

With Harlyn held gently in Deodan's arms and no sign of the Warlock Supreme, they left the caves and emerged from the waterfall. Roh was half surprised to find the Jaktaren still there, waiting for them in the woodlands with the horses; they'd found one more of the missing animals.

'We make for Akoris,' Roh told them.

Finn and Yrsa simply got to their feet and readied themselves. Roh watched as Odi strapped Harlyn's lute case over his back and mounted her horse.

Moments later, they were riding through the forest. Roh didn't take her eyes off Deodan's back as he rode ahead. She could see Harlyn's limp body jostling in the saddle in front of him. All she could do was hope her friend could hold on a little longer. Daybreak was only a few hours away.

They rode harder than before, sweat gleaming on their horses' necks in the waning moonlight. Deodan led them through the dense woodlands, weaving expertly through the trees, never once faltering. Whatever discomfort Roh had felt at riding before was long forgotten as she urged her mount on through the thick shrubbery, branches scratching at her face as she ducked beneath them too late, spider silk catching in her hair. She didn't care about any of it. She became an extension of her horse, feeling every cantering step beneath her, every stone and fallen bough. The only sound was that of hooves thundering across leaf litter and the occasional hoot of a nocturnal bird somewhere in the distance. Through the gaps in the canopy, Roh could just make out the sliver of moon. *The colour of bone*, she thought.

The terrain was uneven, but the horses were sure-footed and eager, as though sensing their journey was close to ending, with food and water awaiting them.

Around them, the forest started to thin out, with the ground beneath them growing steeper, dipping into slight crests and falls. From what she remembered of the map in her pocket, it told Roh that they were nearing the cyren territory.

At last, the forest ended and dawn spilled its butter-and-blush hues across the land before them, revealing a sprawling hillside city, an enormous monastery with complex structures and peaked domes at its heart.

'Akoris …' Roh murmured, squeezing her horse's sides with her heels, urging him forward.

Deodan nodded. 'I'll see you to the gate.'

As they grew closer, the steady beat of drums could be heard, a rhythm that seemed to thump in time with Roh's very pulse. She could feel it in her chest. Around them, the colours deepened, as though the earth itself were richer here. The russet tones of autumn greeted them as they rode through the hilly outskirts of the territory. Tall, vibrant trees lined everything, their leaves like licks of flame, leading them towards the centre. Villas were stacked on top of one another upon the curved hillside that overlooked the red dunes and the sea on one side, and on the other, the monastery and its various towers. The beat grew louder as at last they approached a heavy set of rusted iron gates.

'The drums of Akoris never sleep,' Deodan murmured.

With a screech, the gate swung inwards and he gestured for Roh to ride through. On the other side, a cyren wearing a crisp, tailored jacket stepped forward. He cut a striking figure.

Roh dismounted, landing softly on the sandy ground.

'Welcome to Akoris, Rohesia of the Bone Cleaners,' the cyren said, a wide smile on his handsome face.

But Roh barely heard his words, for around his neck was an amulet, a gemstone gleaming within.

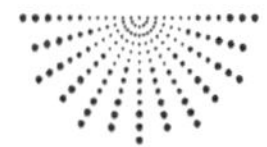

CHAPTER TEN

I t was the Mercy's Topaz – there was no mistaking it. The very first birthstone of Saddoriel winked at Roh in the early-morning light, the colour of rich honey, its magic whispering to her. It was the stone that guided its bearer to sincerity, the gem that showed one the way when lost … Roh fought the overwhelming temptation to snatch it from the cyren's neck with her talons and run as far away from Akoris as possible.

'How do you know who I am?' she managed to ask, tearing her bewitched gaze from the gem.

'We were informed by the council of your unusual situation when the stone was brought to us. Dresmis and Thera speak to me through the Mercy's Topaz and have since shown me many things.'

'You're Adriel,' Roh guessed.

'I am indeed,' he said, sketching an elaborate bow. He

was still smiling, though it didn't quite reach his eyes. 'A mere humble servant of the goddesses and thus, a servant of our Queen of Cyrens.'

Roh scanned his fine clothes, his well-groomed face and the healthy glow of his complexion. Nothing about him said *servant*, that was for sure. His umber hair was swept back from his brow; he was clean-shaven with a prominent jaw and a long, straight nose. The slopes of his face lent him a gentle appearance that did not match his sharp clothes or the curious lilt in his tone.

'You have the pleasure of entering our sacred monastery of Akoris today.' He waved to the grand complex of buildings behind him.

Roh felt her companions dismount behind her, but she didn't look back.

'Come.' Adriel turned. 'You must wish to offer your prayers. I will show you to our great temple.'

'No,' Roh said. 'Our friend needs a healer first.'

Discomfort slid around in Roh's stomach like oil as an expression akin to triumph crossed Adriel's face. He glanced over her shoulder at Harlyn, who lay in Deodan's arms, her complexion sickly yellow.

'Very well,' he said, before his eyes flicked to Deodan. 'Look who it is,' he murmured. 'Come to steal from our sacred pool again, warrior warlock?'

Deodan gave a dark smile. 'You never know, Adriel.'

Warrior warlock. Sacred pool ... Stealing? Roh's skin crawled as she handed her reins to a waiting cyren and shot Deodan a questioning look.

But the chieftain simply smiled at her. 'On second thought, perhaps I'll stay a few days. See to it that my charge is well cared for.'

There hadn't been a moment to question Deodan properly about his magic, not since the teerah panther attack, and there certainly hadn't been a spare second to ask about Eadric. Who was he? Why had his dagger been in Saddoriel's prison and then found in Roh's pack? For the briefest second, Roh considered something. What if *she* had taken it? What if some underlying madness had awoken beneath her skin and *she'd* taken the quartz dagger without her own knowledge? Roh had been so concerned with Deodan and the strangers amongst them that she hadn't considered it might be *her* who was the stranger …

With hundreds of fractured thoughts whirling about in her head, Roh kept her mouth shut as Adriel led them into the strange monastery, the pride of Akoris. The cloisters were lined with candles, intricate stone carvings and iron gates, smaller versions of those outside, leading to what looked like private oratories. As they walked, the drumming continued, so rhythmic it seemed to shape the pace of Roh's thoughts. Her boots scuffed across engraved stone floors and light filtered through stained-glass windows high above. The architect in her marvelled at the structures as they passed, the looming ceilings and decorative archways adorned with artworks of Dresmis and Thera, their wings always outstretched.

'This way,' Adriel told them, turning another corner,

passing a group of cyrens whose robes gaped open at their backs, revealing dark, masterful tattoos mimicking the wings of the goddesses. Roh averted her gaze, feeling as though she was looking upon something she shouldn't.

Adriel opened a pair of double doors with grandiose flair. 'One of the best treatment rooms in Akoris.'

An overpowering aroma of herbs assaulted Roh's senses, stinging her eyes. It was a simple, circular room with a narrow bed in the centre. Plants lined the walls in a vertical garden all around.

'Place her down there. I'll have a healer attend to your friend immediately. Now, if you'd like to accompany me to the temple?'

Roh watched Deodan gently lay Harlyn on the bed, still unconscious. Yellow seeped through the bandage covering her wound and sweat beaded upon her brow.

'I'm staying with her,' Roh said.

'Staying? Here?' Adriel's brows rose. 'Surely you would rather pray to the goddesses for her recovery in our esteemed place of worship?'

Roh ignored the warning stare Deodan was shooting at her from across the room.

'My place is by her side,' she told the Arch General.

Adriel flicked an imaginary piece of dust from his jacket and tugged on his lapels, glancing down to make sure everything was straight. 'Very well. I'll send for our best healer, Incana. The royal quarters are being prepared for you as well.' He sketched another bow and promptly left the room.

Royal quarters ...? Roh had to stop herself looking to

Odi in disbelief. It was the first time someone had referred to her as royal without irony or sarcasm.

'I'm going to wait outside,' Finn announced, his face screwed up at the potent herb scent.

Yrsa followed suit, tugging Odi along with her, which was just as well; the room was small enough without all six of them in it.

'You're playing a risky game with Adriel,' Deodan told Roh when the door clicked closed behind the Jaktaren.

'At this level, every choice is a risk,' Roh ground out, taking Harlyn's hand in hers and looking around the room. She tried to stop herself from feeling overwhelmed. The fact was, she knew very little about Akoris and how it was run. From the brief glimpse she'd had, it didn't look like it was structured in the same way as Saddoriel, with Upper, Mid and Lower Sectors. And Adriel … She didn't know what to make of him. With all the flourishing hand movements and smiling, she should have found him charismatic, but there was something off there. Even his looks … He was definitely handsome, there was no denying that, but he possessed the oily nature of someone who was keenly aware of it and used it to their advantage. Finn's words echoed in her mind: *Tales bad enough to turn my stomach* … The growing unease in Roh's gut told her that the Arch General was not to be trusted. Then there was the matter of the Mercy's Topaz, worn in plain sight, encased in an ugly amulet … A taunt?

Moments later, there was a knock at the doors and a healer peered inside.

'Come in,' Roh told her, stepping back from the stone table to make room.

The healer, Incana, wore a similar open-backed robe to the other Akorian cyrens Roh had seen in the hallways, her skin inked with wings that stretched across her shoulders and continued beneath the folds of the fabric. Roh tried not to stare.

Slowly, Incana carefully unbound the bandages around Harlyn's arm. 'What's happened here? This poor Saddorien,' she said.

Roh winced as the sour smell of the wound hit her, even amidst the pungent aroma of herbs. In a matter of hours, it had festered, the skin hot and red around the seeping stitches.

Deodan answered, 'Teerah panther.'

Roh could have sworn Incana tutted at that, as though it had been a common, easily avoidable situation. The healer made her way around the room, plucking leaves from plants and popping them into a giant mortar at the foot of the bed.

'She's reacted badly to your terrible attempt at magic,' she said to Deodan with a disapproving look.

Deodan folded his arms over his chest and gave a resigned sigh. 'She's *alive* because of my magic.'

'Your magic makes a mockery of true magic.'

Deodan just shook his head. '*True magic?* It never ceases to amaze me how ignorant you cyrens are. What do you think your own magic is based on?'

'Hush,' Incana ordered as she began to mince the various leaves with a large pestle.

Roh watched the exchange, intrigued. Deodan seemed used to the treatment, and while Incana's words said one thing, her face, a mask of calm, said another. Did she truly believe the things she spoke? Roh wasn't sure. Deodan too watched Incana work, as though he had done so before. There was a familiarity between them that was louder in silence than it was in conversation.

Incana finished grinding up the foliage and scooped up the paste in her fingers, not even grimacing as she smeared it directly across Harlyn's foul-smelling wound. A strange fizzing noise sounded and Harlyn's talons shot out suddenly, but she did not awaken.

Roh stared in wonder as the ugly stitches dissolved into flesh before her very eyes. The redness around the gash eased, while the yellow fluid and dried blood evaporated. Skin seemed to knit itself back together, leaving behind a thick, but clean, pink scar.

'Dresmis and Thera were with this one,' Incana said, wiping any remaining paste from Harlyn's skin with a white cloth.

Roh thought she saw a tug of amusement on Deodan's face, but it was gone before she could be sure.

'Will she be alright?' Roh asked, still trying to decipher the unspoken thing between healer and chieftain.

'If the goddesses stay with her, she will recover. She will need lots of rest and she will have to wear a sling for her arm for some time. Exercises must be done daily to rebuild the muscles. There was nerve damage and rot I could not undo. The arm might not have the exact same functionality it had before, but she is lucky.'

'Thank you,' Roh told her.

'Don't thank me. Thank Dresmis and Thera,' Incana said sharply.

'I will,' Roh heard herself say. 'Incana?' she asked, suddenly remembering something.

'What is it?'

'Do you have a treatment for … joint pain? In the hands?'

Incana frowned. 'What ails you?'

'It's not for me,' Roh explained, Odi's half-gloved fingers filling her mind. 'It's for a friend.'

Incana seemed to consider this, scratching her chin, flecks of green paste lining her fingernails. 'I'll have to make something up … I'll send it to the royal quarters before the final meal tonight.'

'I'd appreciate it, thank you. And thank Dresmis and Thera,' Roh added quickly.

Incana nodded approvingly and left.

A moan sounded and Harlyn's eyelids fluttered open. 'Roh?'

'I'm here.'

'Where's Orson?' Harlyn asked, eyes watering.

Roh couldn't remember the last time she'd seen Harlyn cry, not since they were fledglings at least. Of their trio, Orson was the one to show her emotions openly, while as they grew older, Harlyn and Roh tried to be much more stoic. But gone was the bold, reckless cyren with her snide, sarcastic comments and flirtatious ways. Now, Harlyn looked helpless and sad, younger somehow.

'We'll get her back,' Roh said. She didn't know how, she didn't know when, but she knew that whatever happened, she had to reunite their trio, their sisterhood. She hated the thought of Orson all alone without them in Saddoriel, thinking that Roh hadn't deemed her worthy enough of the quest. She hated to think of ascending the throne without both friends, both sisters, by her side. She had made a mistake, and whatever it took, she was going to find a way to right it.

Adriel was waiting for them outside the healers' quarters, Yrsa, Odi and Finn standing in uncomfortable silence at his side, their packs at their feet. Roh had no idea how long she'd been in that stuffy room, but colour had returned to Harlyn's cheeks and she'd managed to keep down half a cup of water, so she didn't care. The door to the treatment room was left ajar and Roh could see the steady rise and fall of Harlyn's chest, thankfully.

'A bold decision,' Adriel claimed, as Roh greeted him with a nod. The topaz flickered in the amulet's setting, as though trying to catch her attention. It had already, its honey hue drinking in Roh's gaze, filling her mind with thoughts of overpowering the Akorian leader. He had no guards with him. Roh and the others could easily snatch the chain from his neck. It was within physical grasp ...

She shook the thought from her head. It was too soon to resort to something like that.

'What was?' She hoisted her own pack onto her shoulder.

'To prioritise your friend ahead of the gods.'

She glowered at him and heard Yrsa scoff. 'What?'

'Choosing your friend over the gods is choosing your personal needs ahead of the needs of your people, who need a holy queen. A ruler who is a descendant of those very gods she should worship.'

'These gods you know so well.' Roh's talons threatened to unsheathe. 'Surely they would rather an innocent civilian live than a cyren attend temple?'

'The gods' wills are their own,' Adriel said blandly.

Roh took a measured breath and decided to skip any remaining formalities. 'I have come for the birthstone of Saddoriel,' she told him, fighting to keep her voice even as dread filled her gut.

'Oh, I know you have. But a queen must *earn* the stones. Dresmis and Thera need to be consulted before we can move forward with this matter.'

'You can't be serious.'

'You'll find that I'm always serious, Rohesia of the Bone Cleaners.'

Roh stopped herself from folding her arms across her chest, guessing that could be seen as confrontational. 'And how will the goddesses be consulted, Arch General?'

Adriel's eyes seemed to brighten at his title. 'Bone cleaners need not know of such rituals.'

'But a future queen should,' Roh countered.

The corner of the Akorian's full lips twitched at the challenge, but he dipped his head in acknowledgement. 'Five days,' he declared. 'I will have five days of prayer in my oratory to confer with our deities. There, I shall learn how you are to earn the stone.'

Five days? Roh would have blurted her outrage aloud, were it not for Odi's gentle elbow to her ribs.

'You will stay in the royal guest quarters for the duration of your time here. I'm sure you'll find it more than adequate,' Adriel said. 'Your friend may rest there for the day.'

'And how do you see us spending the duration of our time in Akoris, while the gods deliberate my worthiness of the topaz?' Roh pressed, failing to keep the edge from her voice.

'As all daughters and sons of Dresmis and Thera spend their time in Akoris – in prayer. You will need a deep connection to the goddesses, should you ascend the throne. You must attend temple with your Akorian kin.'

Gaping, Roh turned to Deodan, who gave her an unhelpful half-shrug. 'I'll watch over Harlyn in your chambers,' he said. 'They don't allow the likes of me in the temple, anyway.'

Roh didn't see any other choice.

'The human will need to accompany them,' Adriel said smoothly. 'Humans are also not permitted in our sacred place of worship.'

Roh glanced at Odi in question and he gave a subtle nod.

'Fine,' she said.

'I'm glad to see Dresmis and Thera have guided you to the right path,' Adriel declared as Deodan held out his hand for Roh's pack. She tried to hide any hesitation on her part and simply passed it over to him. She supposed she'd rather it be in his possession than that of a spy who worked for the Arch General.

A number of Akorian porters appeared to take the rest of their things, and Harlyn was brought out from the treatment room on a stretcher, then taken down another hallway.

'Don't worry, I've got her,' Deodan whispered in Roh's ear before hurrying after them, Odi at his heels.

That left Roh, Finn and Yrsa to attend temple together. 'Lead on, Adriel,' Roh said, willing herself to sound even-tempered, but the Arch General was no fool.

He eyed her testily, straightening his jacket again. 'As you wish.'

The Akorian monastery was breathtaking in its architecture and design, Roh would give the foreign cyrens that much. Real sunlight streamed in through the stained-glass domes in the high ceilings, warming the stones lining the pathways before them. Many doors and gates led off from the main cloistered hallway, and as they walked Adriel pointed some out to them.

'Those are the saunas through there …' He waved his hand towards a set of double doors. 'Where many devotees go to pray until they faint, in the hopes that Dresmis and Thera will meet them in the in-between.'

Roh recoiled at the thought.

But Adriel didn't so much as pause, not even as a high-pitched scream sounded from behind another door. He pointed again and Roh spotted a thin ribbon of what looked to be smoke drifting out into the hallway from beneath the door. 'Over there is the Room of the Lost, where worshippers go to inhale harrowbane. If they are blessed, Dresmis and Thera appear before them and tell them their futures.'

Roh had to bite the inside of her cheek. Since when were Dresmis and Thera *seers*? Her skin crawled as they continued their apparent detour to the temple.

'And that, my dear Saddoriens ...' Adriel waved to a pair of lilac doors covered in mosaic tiles similar to those that adorned the Passage of Kings. 'That is one of the few areas we do not allow guests, so make note.'

That piqued Roh's interest. She craned her neck, trying to commit the doors to memory as they walked on, Adriel's pace quickening.

At last, they arrived at the great temple. Inside the candlelit worship hall, over a hundred cyrens sat cross-legged on the cold marble floor. Hunched over, their tattooed backs were exposed as they prayed, heads bowed. No words were spoken aloud, no chants ringing across the chasm of space as Roh had anticipated, but this was worse. The hair on the back of her neck stood up as somewhere in the distance, the drumming she had become accustomed to, that had settled in her bones, changed its rhythm.

As they made their way through the sea of praying cyrens, Roh saw that an area in the middle had been reserved for her and her small entourage. Saying nothing, she followed Adriel's lead and lowered herself onto her knees, the ice-cold marble floor biting through the thin fabric of her pants. Her glance snagged on the tattooed back in front of her: an intricate mirrored pattern of elaborate, outstretched wings.

Wings, so many wings. Was this the universal symbol for the fanatical? Did the Akorians know that the same symbol was used in Deodan's so-called alliance? Or was it a mere coincidence that the worship of the goddesses centred around the very same symbol? Roh did her best to survey the temple with her head bowed, noting that all the Akorian cyrens prayed with their talons unsheathed in their laps and that the scales at their temples had been darkened with cosmetics to make them stand out.

Beside her, Finn and Yrsa looked out of place in their Jaktaren leathers, but they played their part convincingly enough, heads bowed, as still as the statues that bore down on them from all sides.

Roh couldn't stand the deafening silence of the temple, the drumming only accentuating the lack of words. It was the worst environment for the questions and fears that plagued her mind. A place where they could fester and grow and spiral until a blanket of darkness coated everything in her head. Who was Eadric? How had she come to have his dagger? What was the meaning of these wings that appeared everywhere she looked? What about Harlyn? Would she ever be the same again? Would she ever forgive Roh for what had happened? Would Roh ever bring their trio back together? And what of the Mercy's Topaz? How in the realms was she meant to earn it? Surely she couldn't be expected to spend five whole days praying while her fate was decided for her? And Adriel ... What game was he playing? And for whom? With each beat of the drums, another thought formed in Roh's mind, taking over the former, each more panicked and horror-filled than the last. She hadn't realised she was staring until a wave of goosebumps rushed across her arms, her scales prickling. Roh turned her gaze to her right.

And found Adriel's triumphant eyes upon her.

CHAPTER ELEVEN

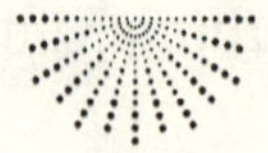

Several hours later, her knees bruised from the marble floor, Roh found herself in the communal Akorian refectory. Several long tables stretched down the length of the enormous room, cyrens packed onto benches elbow to elbow. Hundreds of candles in sconces lined the walls, creating a golden glow in the strange, windowless hall. Beneath them were basins of water for washing. On the tables, vats of soup and stew and potatoes steamed before them, simple food compared to the rich, layered dishes of the Upper Sector of Saddoriel, but hearty.

Roh shifted uncomfortably on the hard bench, suppressing the urge to crane her neck and look for her companions amongst the crowd. Adriel had insisted that she and the others split up *so they could get to know their Akorian brothers and sisters,* but Roh sensed there was more to this request than making new friends. The Arch

General himself was sitting at an elevated table at the far end of the room, an array of children on either side of him. Roh frowned. She hadn't seen any fledglings wandering the passageways, or in the temple, for that matter.

She leaned in to the cyren beside her. 'Who are they?' she asked, nodding to the nestlings and fledglings tucking into their evening meal.

Roh's neighbour gave her a sideways glance and Roh was startled to find Incana the healer next to her. 'They're the Arch General's children, of course.'

Roh baulked. 'All of them? There are almost —'

'A dozen and one,' Incana told her.

Roh scanned the faces. The children ranged from their first years to nearing their majority. They all shared Adriel's striking features. 'But … offspring are so rare. How …?'

'The Arch General is blessed by the goddesses.'

That's one way of putting it, Roh thought. But as she went to make a comment to Incana, she spotted the cyrens standing behind the nestlings and fledglings … A different female stood behind each offspring, only they weren't all wearing traditional Akorian fashions. Roh let her gaze travel from one to the next, confusion rippling through her as she recognised the jewel-belted robes of the highborn Saddoriens on one, and the simple blue pants and tunic of those from the Mid Sector on another. There were other fashions she didn't recognise … *Where have all these cyrens come from?*

Incana followed her stare. 'Adriel's oracles,' she said.

'The Arch General likes to consult oracles from all over the realms.'

Roh blinked rapidly. 'Is that … allowed?'

'In the name of the goddesses? Of course.' Incana was still looking at the females and their stony expressions. 'Saddoriel, Akoris, Csilla, Lochloria … They're all there,' she continued.

'What about the others?' Roh asked, nodding to the woman who wore a cropped shirt, a sliver of stomach exposed above a high-waisted, flowing skirt.

'A Battalonian fashion,' Incana replied. 'And the one next to her? A poor replica of a Valian warrior.'

Roh had heard of the fire continent, but knew nothing of the leather-clad warrior kind, though she supposed the outfit was similar to that of the Jaktaren. She frowned. 'But those are human territories, aren't they?' she wondered aloud. 'The women up there... They're all cyrens.'

'Indeed. The Arch General prides himself on his … knowledge of the realms. This is but one way he can show it …' Incana trailed off, as though she hadn't meant to tell Roh so much. She busied herself with the food.

'So, he dresses them up in …?' Roh hesitated, then tried again. 'Surely the council —'

'Shhh,' Incana hissed.

The lingering quiet around them became all too obvious. Amidst hundreds of Akorians, the conversations were hesitant and soft; even the scrape of cutlery on crockery was timid. That, combined with what she'd just learned about the Arch General, was enough to hinder Roh's appetite. But she hadn't eaten since … When *had* she last eaten? She tried to do a calculation of days and nights past, but it made her head spin. Which was proof enough that she needed to fill her belly, if only to have the strength to face the Akorian leader.

From what Deodan and Finn had said, and what she'd gleaned herself from their all-too-brief encounter, she knew that in order to face Adriel, she had to keep her wits about her. She reached for the soup ladle in the middle of the table.

'I wouldn't eat that,' Incana murmured.

Roh twisted in her seat to face the healer.

'Don't draw attention,' Incana hissed. 'Or it'll find its way to you in one form or another.'

Roh kept her eyes forward, reaching for a chunk of bread. 'What are you talking about?' she said under her breath.

'The soup is laced with potent herbs from the Fields of Dresmis.'

'Why? What do they do?' *And why would Adriel drug his own people?*

'It can have various effects,' Incana said, helping herself to the stew. 'But for the most part, inhibitions are lost and the consumer is compelled to share their truths.'

'It's a truth serum?' Roh gaped. She had never heard of such a thing.

'Of sorts. As for why … What better way to keep hold of your people and ideals than by knowing what truly lies in their hearts?'

The bread turned to a thick, dry lump in Roh's mouth. 'I have to get word to my —'

'*Sit down*,' the healer ordered. 'It's too late and you'll only draw more attention to yourself, and to *me*, I might add.'

'But they —'

'But *nothing*. It will not harm them physically and it'll wear off by morning. You can do nothing now except avoid it yourself.'

'Why are you telling me this?'

'It seems you are a friend of my friend.'

'Who? Ames?' Roh's heart leaped at the thought, willing Ames to appear. He had told her he would meet her in Akoris and he was a cyren of his word. He would be here, perhaps by the —

'Shhh,' the cyren chastised. 'You'll do well to say no names aloud in here. Surely you've noticed not all is what it seems.'

'It never is,' Roh muttered.

'Good. You're learning. Nice to know there's something in that head of yours, after all.'

To Roh's confusion, Incana plastered a sleepy expression upon her face, her body beginning to sway with the beat of the drums. The same was happening to the cyrens around them. Incana reached out for a wooden bowl of finely ground salt and dreamily poured a pile of it between herself and Roh. Slowly, as if in a trance, she flattened the salt with the palm of her hand, creating a glistening canvas. Using a long talon, she drew something.

Half of something, Roh realised, recalling Deodan's words. *'If you were travelling and wanted to know if you could trust a newcomer, you'd draw half the wings in the dirt and wait to see if they completed the drawing.'*

Their mutual friend was *Deodan*, not Ames.

Roh found her hand trembling as she unsheathed her own talon and brought it to the salt, tracing the second half of the sketch into the granules.

A pair of wings.

Almost as soon as Roh had lifted her talon from the table, Incana was blowing the salt away. Roh tensed in her seat, but realised that all around her the Akorians were behaving in the same calm, peculiar manner. Only the sharp gleam in the healer's eyes told Roh that she was acting.

'Always avoid the soup,' Incana whispered, getting to her feet as the drums grew louder and other Akorians gathered at the front of the hall. 'At first meal, avoid the bran.'

The hall was suddenly filled with a flurry of movement and Incana slipped into the crowd. Roh's skin prickled. The candlelight and the bodies of the Akorians seemed to sway to the pulsing beat of the drums.

Peering through the throng of cyrens, Roh spotted Finn one table over. Still seated, his body lurched from side to side, following the enrapturing rhythm. A few places down, Odi's fingers tapped in time against the tabletop. The music and whatever drug they had ingested seemed to take over the entire hall, building and building with each passing moment, matching Roh's pounding heart.

I have to get them out of here.

Shoving a few chunks of bread in her pockets, Roh stood with the rest of the moving Akorians and cautiously made her way over to Finn.

'We have to go,' she hissed.

'Why?' Finn asked, his eyes glazed over, swaying to the drums. 'I like it here.'

'Gods,' Roh muttered, taking him by the elbow and leading him to Odi. She tried not to think about the fact that she was touching a Jaktaren, *Finn Haertel* of all cyrens. His skin was warm against hers.

'Odi,' she called.

The human was gazing at the ceiling, his mouth slightly open in wonder.

She glanced up. There was nothing there.

'Odi, it's time to go.'

At the sight of her, his face broke into a wide smile. 'Roh! There you are!' It was the happiest he'd looked in weeks.

Roh linked her arm through Odi's and pulled him away from the table, Finn at her other side. 'Come on,' she murmured, trying to direct them towards the doors. She'd have to come back for Harlyn and Yrsa, wherever they were, and the warlock —

'Need a hand?' said a deep voice. Deodan appeared at Odi's right.

'Clearly,' Roh retorted with a disbelieving glance at her companions.

Deodan nodded. 'Get back to the quarters. I'll find the others. Follow the main hall until you reach the grand staircase. Follow that all the way to the top and take the first left. You'll find the royal chambers there.'

For a moment, Roh stared after the warrior warlock, as Adriel had called him. Was he affected by the drug? Had he been warned, as she had? Incana was his friend, after all. Or was he simply better at hiding its effects? Or worse, had he known all along and failed to warn them?

Roh glanced back to the podium where Adriel and his ... oracles ... had been. There was no sign of the Arch General, nor his children, nor his collection of females.

Slipping from the hall while the Akorians were in the throes of their dancing, Roh chanted Deodan's directions to herself as she pulled the Jaktaren and the human along with her. She'd be forever grateful to Incana for stopping her from ingesting that soup. She shuddered to think of what she might have done or said.

'Where are you taking us, bone cleaner?' Finn demanded, though his voice was devoid of its usual notes of loathing.

'Somewhere safe,' she said.

'That's nice,' Odi piped up. 'It's good to be safe.'

Finn's eyes went wide with pure surprise, as if the thought had never occurred to him. 'You're right!' He looked younger when he wasn't staring daggers at her.

Roh peered curiously at Odi's relaxed face. 'I try to keep you as safe as I can,' she told him.

'I think I know that,' Odi said, patting her arm absentmindedly.

Roh's brow furrowed, but she kept pulling the pair along, finally reaching the grand staircase Deodan had mentioned.

Gods, they're slow, she cursed as they tackled one step at a time, as though Odi and Finn were learning to walk for the first time.

'Come on,' she coaxed.

'We're doing our best,' Odi said matter-of-factly.

'Yes,' Finn agreed, turning to Roh. 'Why are you putting so much pressure on us?'

Roh hesitated. 'To climb the stairs?'

'Yes. Exactly,' Finn replied, pausing yet again.

Roh took a deep breath. 'Because I want to make sure we get back to the royal quarters.'

'The *royal* quarters …' Finn sounded out the words slowly, as though he were mulling over their meaning.

Roh sighed. 'I *know* you don't think I'm fit to be queen. That I'll never be your —'

'True,' Finn said.

'But that's where we're staying. That's the best place for us at the moment, given your current … state.'

Finn seemed to consider this. 'Alright,' he said.

'Alright?'

Finn nodded. 'The bone cleaner knows best.'

'I'm going to remind you of that later.' Roh resisted the urge to cuff him over the back of the head and yanked on both of their arms, heaving them towards the top of the staircase.

The journey from the refectory to the royal quarters of the monastery took forever, punctuated with strange remarks and observations from Jaktaren and human alike. Roh was sweating by the time they reached the double doors adorned with carvings of Dresmis and Thera.

'Whoa,' Odi said, running his fingers along the markings in wonder.

Roh had to practically push him through the doors, though not before noticing a delicate shimmer around them. Deodan had used an enchantment to protect their privacy, the very same as he had back in the settlement. Somehow, he'd replenished his vials of water magic.

Roh met the warlock's gaze from across the room, a caution on her lips, her eyes darting to the strange shimmer. The last place Deodan should be using warlock magic was in the heart of a cyren territory.

As though sensing her objection, he said, 'Adriel has eyes and ears everywhere. What took you so long?' But his brows shot up as he spotted the two drug-affected young men on either side of her.

'Ah,' Deodan said, lowering himself into a chair in the corner of the room.

The quarters were decorated in true Akorian fashion, the colour palette mirroring the russet tones of the flame trees and dunes beyond the hillside. Archways led from one room to the next, with simple but elegant furnishings in each space.

But Roh started. 'Where's —'

Harlyn emerged from another room and made straight for Roh. She wore a thick sling around her neck, her injured, bandaged arm drawn up to her chest. Her eyes were glazed over in the same way Odi's and Finn's were, but instead of bewilderment, Harlyn's expression was full of sadness. She took Roh's hand in her good one and pulled her aside, eyeing Finn and Deodan suspiciously.

'Do you think we'll ever be friends again?' she asked quietly.

It was everything Roh could do not to crumple at those words. And at the fact that she knew Harlyn would never have uttered them under normal circumstances.

'I'm not sure,' she replied honestly.

'I want to be. I miss you, but I'm so angry, Roh. So, so angry.'

A response eluded Roh. Would Harlyn even remember this conversation come daybreak? Over the years, Roh had heard tales of heartache; she had always just assumed it was about romantic love, not friendships. She had never imagined friendships could hurt this badly. But what did she know of love, anyway?

'Do you think you could ever understand why I cheated? In Thieves?' she ventured. If this was to be the only open and honest conversation she and Harlyn were to have again, then she needed to ask the questions that had plagued her, needed to say the things that spiralled in her mind.

'I think in order to understand it, I would have to imagine myself doing it. And that's just it, Roh. I can't. I would never have thought to do that. Betraying my friends is not in my nature.'

'It wasn't —' Roh stopped herself. She wasn't even

sure what she'd been about to say – that it wasn't in *her* nature? But it had been, or she wouldn't have done it. And it wouldn't have been so premeditated. There were no excuses for her actions, not to her friends, and she needed to come to terms with that. She needed to listen without trying to fight how they felt, or that she was the cause.

'I'm sorry,' Roh said. 'I'm so, so sorry, Har.'

Harlyn nodded. 'I know.' Then, she was rummaging in her pockets. 'I kept it,' she murmured, her fist clenched around something.

Roh frowned, fearful of what other secrets might come between them. 'Kept what …?'

Harlyn's fingers uncurled, revealing two curved pieces of gold.

Roh stopped herself from reaching out to touch the metal. 'My circlet,' she breathed. 'Why?'

Harlyn gave a heavy sigh. 'I wanted to remember the friend I knew, the friend I grew up with.'

'I'm still her,' Roh said, eyeing the pieces of her circlet. 'Things can be the same as they were …'

'Maybe.' Harlyn fitted the pieces together. 'But maybe some things need to be broken before they can be welded back together, to be stronger than ever before.'

Roh stared at her friend, wondering if she knew at all what she was saying. But the moment passed as Harlyn pushed the pieces into Roh's pocket and pointed. 'What's Odi doing over there?'

Roh followed her gaze across the room, spotting Odi sitting cross-legged on the carpet, hunched over sheets of parchment. There was a strange, nestling likeness to her companions, as though they had reverted to their younger selves, still discovering their own bodies, their own emotions and the rest of the realm around them. It would almost be sweet, innocent even, but for the darkness that bled through their all-too-honest questions and the hurt that so clearly still lingered just beneath the surface.

Still holding Roh's hand, Harlyn pulled her across the room to join the human on the floor.

It was the same foreign language Roh had seen Odi use before. Scrawled between, above and below two groups of narrow lines were strange but beautiful markings. He seemed in a trance, the long fingers of his right hand dancing against his thigh while he scribbled with his left.

'What are you doing?' Harlyn asked.

'Writing,' Odi said, not looking up, his dark hair falling into his eyes.

Harlyn picked up a discarded piece of parchment, staring at it hard before passing it to Roh. 'What are you writing?'

'Music.'

'Music? How can you write music?' Roh said, frowning at the strange markings on the page.

'These symbols here resemble notes on the piano,' he told her. 'Reading this, my stepbrothers, Mason and Brooks, will know what keys to play and at what speed to play them.' His fingers still tapped erratically. 'These are songs of my own composition, though they're harder to write without being able to play. I have to imagine the sounds. But … they should help expand my stepbrothers' catalogue of songs while we're gone. It will keep them safe, won't it, Roh?'

Roh's throat tightened at the sound of her name on her friend's lips. 'Yes,' she told him, hoping she projected more confidence than she felt. 'It will keep them safe.'

The truth was, she had no idea what would or would not keep the Eery Brothers safe in Saddoriel.

Beside Odi, Harlyn was swaying to a rhythm Roh couldn't hear, studying each page Odi placed down on the carpet, as though she could truly read the foreign language. 'You're not so bad, human,' she said.

Roh rubbed the bridge of her nose. That was practically a profession of love coming from Harlyn. If Roh hadn't known how affected she was by the drug before, she certainly did now. Roh fought the conflicting impulses within. Part of her wanted to press her companions for information, for clues as to how they might truly feel about her, but the other part of her knew this was unfair, knew it would be taking advantage of them in their weakened, more vulnerable states. As Adriel apparently did to his people. So she stayed quiet, listening and watching as the surreal night slowly unfolded before her, time passing in bizarre conversations and exposed moments.

No wonder the Arch General did this to the Akorians. Cyrens and humans, it seemed, would say anything under the influence of whatever drug laced that soup. What a way to root out any who opposed him, to quell any notions of dissent.

Roh found an armchair in the corner of the room, retreating for a time and cradling her pack in her lap, relieved to find it untouched. She only hoped that Yrsa, wherever she was in the chambers, wasn't spilling her secret of the drake egg to anyone, particularly Finn Haertel. Roh watched her companions, fascinated by the ups and downs of the drug coursing through their bodies. All of them were wide-eyed and moved slowly, precariously, as though they weren't familiar with their own limbs. As she had been for most of the journey, Roh was once again on the outside, on the fringe of her own circle. Harlyn was still sitting with Odi a few feet away, cradling her injured arm to her chest, while Odi had removed his fingerless gloves and was studying his hands intently.

'My greatest fear,' he was saying, 'is not being killed by a cyren. It's that my hands will stop working, that I'll no longer be able to play the piano … I can't fathom what that loss would be like.'

Harlyn nodded. 'I may never play the lute again,' she told him morosely. 'Maybe that's what I deserve after breaking the Law of the Lair to do so in the first place.'

'I don't think that's how it works,' Odi told her, patting her knee.

Gods, I miss that, Roh thought, watching the pair confide in one another. She missed her *friends,* missed being able to tell someone her secrets freely, missed pouring her heart out to her sisters and the reassurance that came with it. That pang of envy she had felt watching Odi and Harlyn before was still there, but now she knew what it was. Not romantic feelings towards the human – that notion was as ridiculous as she had originally thought. It was envy for their friendship, and the fact that they shared that, while she did not. Perhaps this was what Delja had been alluding to back in Saddoriel. That to be queen was to be lonely.

Roh couldn't bear to watch them anymore, to stand idly by while they grew closer and she drifted further away. She got to her feet and went into the next room, where Yrsa and Finn sat by the arching window, completely oblivious to her presence.

'— know you have my unwavering loyalty,' Finn was saying, looking as though he were about to get down on his knees.

What? Roh couldn't help but pause in the doorway. *What about Piri, Yrsa's partner back in Saddoriel?* Roh stopped her own train of thought. It wasn't right to make assumptions. Perhaps they had agreed to have more than one partner. She had no doubt there were things she didn't understand or wasn't privy to. After all, how well did she know Yrsa or Finn – or anyone here, for that matter?

'I know,' Yrsa said softly, taking his hand. 'And while I —'

Finn shook his head. 'There is nothing more to it. I'll be by your side, always. Sacred is the ledger.'

'Sacred is the ledger,' Yrsa murmured, without releasing his hand.

The phrase from the Jaktaren shot ice through Roh's veins. Particularly with Yrsa, it was sometimes easy to forget they belonged to the guild of warriors who hunted human musicians throughout the realms. It was their *ledger* that had almost torn Odi away from Roh, had nearly forced him into a life of musical slavery as it had his stepbrothers. Since Roh had watched Odi play the piano at swordpoint, she'd been at odds with that aspect of cyren culture. And Yrsa and Finn, they belonged there, were still swearing fealty to the guild. Did that mean she couldn't relate to them? Couldn't trust them? Regret churned in her gut. Yrsa had been a great comfort to her during their journey. But this … *Sacred is the ledger* … Roh wasn't sure she could support such a notion anymore.

The Jaktaren were still holding hands and Roh realised that she was intruding on yet another intimate moment. Heat flushed her cheeks and she ducked away into the next room, relieved to find open doors leading to a balcony. She stepped into the cool night, smelling the salt air of the sea that lay beyond the darkness before her. Somewhere out there, a sea drake waited for her, was counting down the days and minutes until its drakelings hatched and it was free to hunt her down.

'What brings you into the shadows, Queen of Bones?' The soft glow of Deodan's pipe sparked to life in the corner.

Roh cursed herself for jumping. 'Nothing.'

'It's always something,' Deodan replied, blowing a stream of smoke from his mouth.

Had the warrior warlock been affected by the drug? It

was too dark out on the balcony to see if his eyes were glazed over like the others', but his words seemed to come out more slowly, more deliberately. Roh could feel him watching her, his lips pursed around his pipe. 'Come to trade secrets and fears in the dark?' he asked.

'What are you still doing here?' she said bluntly. 'I thought you needed to return to your … clan … immediately?'

'Mmm … There have been some delays on that front.' Deodan casually blew a stream of smoke into the cool night air.

'What delays?'

'Surely you do not tire of my company so soon?'

Roh ignored this. 'Why haven't you gone back?'

Deodan sighed. 'Because once I do, I cannot undo it.'

'Oh.' Roh fidgeted. Though she'd travelled with Deodan for a number of days, she still couldn't quite believe the man before her was what he said he was.

Deodan thoughtfully chewed the end of his pipe.

'What was Adriel talking about when he said you stole from the sacred pool?' she asked.

Deodan laughed. 'I use the magic of my kin. The vials of water you've seen me use come from all over the lands, some more powerful than others. Particularly those from the sacred cyren pool in each of the territories. I've been known to slip into the monastery from time to time and help myself.'

'And Adriel allows this?'

'Adriel opts to look the other way. He knows to

punish me would be to incite a wave of violence upon the Akorians that they're in no state to defend against.'

And there it was. The blatant threat his kind posed.

'You don't want that,' Roh said boldly. 'I heard you telling the Warlock Supreme.'

Deodan looked amused. 'So you *were* listening to that little conversation ...'

'You didn't use your fancy spell to hide it.'

'I did not,' Deodan allowed.

'Well?'

The warlock sighed again. 'No, I don't want violence. I see no need for bloodshed, no need for another extermination of life, no matter who the target.' He had moved closer to her, his blue-grey gaze intent as it locked on her.

'You've known Adriel for a long time, then?' she prompted.

'Longer than most.'

'Do you think he believes all that he preaches? Or is it all a play for power?'

Deodan paused. 'That's something I've been grappling with myself for many a year.'

Roh crossed her arms, envisioning the great temple and the bizarre oratories. 'I think he's too smart to believe in all that.'

'Hmm. Perhaps. Or perhaps he was. Sometimes, enough time passes that a man can start to believe his own lies ...'

The thought of that filled Roh with icy terror. Was that

what had happened to Cerys? Delja had alluded to Roh's mother being of sound mind once. Then something had snapped, causing Cerys to go over the edge, never to return. Was that what would happen to Roh? Was it *already* happening? Had she been lying to herself for so long that she was starting to believe her own fantasies? Was she mad for thinking she had a chance at becoming queen? Was she deluded for taking such a risk on her future when she knew next to nothing of her own heritage? The endless questions and the gaping chasm of all she didn't know sent her spiralling. 'Who's Eadric?' she blurted.

A small smile. 'The sharing has been rather one-sided, don't you think?'

Roh couldn't deny that and cursed herself for not asking about Eadric sooner, but Deodan's teasing demeanour grounded her. 'What do you want to know?'

'A bold question. To start? How about … Why are your companions so surly?'

Roh's shoulders sagged. 'It's my own doing,' she admitted. 'I forced them to come on this quest.'

'Mistakes are an essential part of life,' Deodan said. 'Fail hard and fast, I always say. Then do it again. It's the only way to grow.'

When Roh didn't respond, he gently rested a large hand on her forearm. 'We all make mistakes,' he offered.

'Probably not as many as I do.'

'Probably more,' he said, puffing on his pipe.

'Oh? What's your biggest mistake, then?'

Deodan blew a precise stream of smoke into the night

air and tapped the pipe against his stubbled chin as he considered her question. 'That's a tough call.'

'Humour me.'

'Don't think I haven't noticed you've deflected this back onto me, but … Alright. I'd say, swearing fealty to someone before ensuring their vision matched my own. You?'

Roh leaned against the balcony railing. 'It can only be a mistake if you regret it, can't it?'

Deodan huffed a laugh of incredulity. 'We're drifting into murky waters there. I think only you can decide that. But that's not all that bothers you, is it?'

It was not the question Roh was expecting, not that she knew what to expect from the strange warlock descendant before her. His words coaxed her fears to flash before her very eyes. The sea drake's gnashing fangs, Odi in the glass tank, water creeping up his chin, Harlyn's shriek as the teerah panther's teeth closed around her arm … Had he used some sort of magic on her? Was he bringing these fears to the forefront of her mind? There was no vial of water in sight … It was all her.

'Well?' he prompted, relighting his pipe.

'I have many fears.'

'Don't we all?'

'I fear … I fear never finding my deathsong, never having the true magic of a cyren, and in doing so, being a false queen. We have a queen who is a *direct descendant* of the goddesses. Cyrenkind will not settle for a songless ruler.'

'I told you when we met not to let a lack of song

define you. And surely as a musician can play many tunes, a cyren can sing many songs? There's no such thing as a songless cyren.'

Roh thought of the strangled sound she'd made during her last attempt to find her call. She shook her head.

Deodan just shrugged, as though her confession hadn't been worth the wait. 'If you say so.'

They stood there in silence for a time, Deodan puffing away on his pipe as they looked to the stars. Roh felt oddly at ease. It was the longest, most honest conversation she'd had with anyone in some time. And Deodan had been kind, or as kind as a warlock was wont to be.

'Keep your head high, Queen of Bones, lest that crown slip off.' With that, he went inside, leaving Roh standing in the cold, briny wind alone.

CHAPTER TWELVE

Roh awoke to the incessant drumming of Akoris, her sea-drake egg clutched to her chest beneath a silky quilt. Rhythmic, deep breaths sounded beside her, a pattern she'd know anywhere; she'd grown up listening to the sound. Harlyn lay asleep on her back beside Roh, mouth slightly parted, white-blonde hair tousled around her face.

Roh didn't disturb her as she slipped from the bed, tucking the egg back into her pack and pulling the covers up to Harlyn's chin. The others had been awake well into the early hours of the morning. Roh had been the one to insist on them going to bed once the chatter had become more and more slurred and morose. She'd thought they would fight her on it, but all of them, Finn Haertel included, had been led to their respective beds like dazed nestlings. They were asleep by the time their heads had hit their pillows.

Taking her pack, Roh padded quietly across the room to the bathing chamber, closing the door with a soft click behind her. It rivalled the bathing room of her guest quarters back in the Upper Sector of Saddoriel, only there was less gold and more tributes to Dresmis and Thera in the form of waist-high statues. One sat at the foot of the bath, another by the basin, and a third stood in the centre of the room, the perfect place to hang a towel, though Roh doubted the Akorians had thought of that practicality in placing it there. The chamber smelled of incense, although Roh couldn't pinpoint the exact aroma. No hot water had been delivered yet, so she made do with the cold, washing herself as best she could. She tried to scrub the exhaustion from her face, but her eyes felt puffy and there was no escaping the fact that her mind felt like mush. There were no mirrors in this bathing room, but she caught a glimpse of her reflection in the unused bucket of water ... She looked haggard, her face thinner than it had been before, the scar across her face more prominent than ever. Securing a clean towel under her arms, she crouched over her pack, rifling through it, hoping to find one last clean shirt and making a mental note to locate the laundry room —

The door swung inwards.

'W-wait,' she stammered, clutching her towel to her.

Finn's shocked face appeared at the doorframe, taking in her bare shoulders and legs. 'You didn't lock —'

'Get out!' Roh cried, flushing furiously.

'Sorr—'

'*Out!*'

The door slammed and Roh swore softly, the heat spreading across her cheeks. Heart pounding, she went to the door and turned the lock with extra force.

'Gods,' she muttered, looking down at her towel, which hung to mid-thigh.

It could have been worse, she thought. Finn hadn't *seen* anything. But she flushed at the thought of him possibly walking in just moments earlier, when her skin had been utterly bare. Finding her last clean shirt, she changed hurriedly, placing her crown atop her head, and willed herself not to blush when she opened the door.

To his credit, Finn said nothing as she re-entered the room and pushed her pack under the bed. The others were all awake, though bleary-eyed and hunched over. Odi sat at the end of his bed with his head in his hands. Only Deodan was missing.

'How is everyone feeling?' Roh asked tentatively.

Odi looked up, his amber gaze bloodshot and his hair dishevelled. 'What happened?' he croaked.

'You don't remember?'

Yrsa cleared her throat from across the room. 'None of us do.'

Feeling uneasy, Roh went to the window, tucking her hands under her arms. 'The food was drugged,' she told them. 'I wasn't able to warn you from where I was, but I brought you back here. It was quite powerful.'

'You didn't … ingest it?' Harlyn asked, sitting up in bed, pulling her sling over her head and placing her arm in it with a grimace.

Roh shook her head. 'The cyren next to me, she stopped me, but it was too late to get to any of you.'

'Convenient,' Finn scoffed.

Yrsa elbowed him. 'What did we do? What did we say?'

Roh surveyed the room of panicked faces. Knowing how her own spiralling thoughts kept her up at night, planting seeds of fear and doubt deep in her mind, she made a decision.

'Nothing,' she told them. 'You were all just sleepy. We went to bed right after dinner.'

Visible relief flooded their weary faces.

'I feel so strange,' Odi admitted. 'Like I'm hollow on the inside.'

Harlyn grunted in agreement. 'My chest is tight, like I'm worried but I'm not sure why.'

'You're all alright,' Roh said. 'Just don't eat the bran during first meal, or the soup at dinner.'

Deodan emerged from another room, leaning against the doorframe and refilling his pipe. 'Who was this mysterious helper?'

Roh met his gaze and heeded Incana's warning about not using names. 'An ally, I believe.'

Deodan huffed a laugh. 'Good. We need as many of those as we can get in this godsforsaken monastery.'

The group was split up again at first meal, where the atmosphere was forlorn. The Akorians now wore the same exhausted, shameful expressions as Roh's companions – that was, until they tucked into the bowls of bran. Roh watched the cyrens transform from anxiety-filled to bright-eyed and seemingly eager for a day of prayer.

A different type of drug in the mornings, then, she concluded.

When the meal was over, she waited outside the hall for the others, ignoring the stares of the cyrens leaving. Today, she wore her crown of bones, proudly. There was no denying who she was and why she was here. But judging from the sideways glances, the Akorians didn't approve. Roh almost laughed; she was more than used to that.

It was Deodan who found her first. 'It was nice of you,' he said, 'to put them out of their misery, a kindness I didn't expect from a Queen of Bones.'

Roh's stomach churned, the buttered bread she'd eaten threatening to make a reappearance. 'What do you mean?'

'The others, this morning. You spared them the embarrassment.'

Realisation dawned on Roh. 'You weren't affected … You remember.'

'I've been coming here for years. I've learned that lesson the hard way, many a time. Other times I like to relearn it on purpose. Why do you think Adriel knows me so well?'

Anger flared within Roh. 'And you didn't warn us.'

'I've also learned that there is much to discover from

those who spill their truths so freely, so generously. But don't worry, your secret is safe with me.'

I fear never finding my deathsong, never having the true magic of a cyren.

Roh gave him a steely glare as a stone settled into her core: dread. She had let her guard down in front of the warrior warlock, had let him in when she had needed someone most, and now he knew her weak spot. It was a mistake she would never make again, she vowed.

Odi sidled up beside her. 'This place makes my skin crawl,' he said. 'The sooner we get the gem, the better.'

Roh agreed wholeheartedly with him.

A few moments later, when the crowd from the hall had dispersed, Deodan and Odi peeled away as Roh, Harlyn, Finn and Yrsa made their way as expected to the prayer room. Beside Roh, Harlyn was quiet, her usually snarky demeanour subdued. Despite whatever magic Deodan's healers and Incana had worked, Roh knew that Harlyn was far from fully mended. The dark sling around her neck held her wounded arm in place, fashioned with the same thick, glimmering fabric of the Akorians' robes and open-backed dresses. From her gritted teeth, furrowed brow and swollen, bruised fingers that peeked out from beneath the folds of cloth, Roh could tell her friend was still in a great deal of discomfort. All throughout last night, she'd looked longingly to her lute, but it was as though speaking her fears aloud had given them the freedom to sink their claws into her, to deter her ferocious spirit. Roh couldn't help but glance at her with worry whenever Harlyn wasn't looking.

Roh retraced their steps from the day before when Adriel had shown them to the temple, passing the saunas and the strange quarters that expelled smoke from beneath the doors. Then, she paused.

The lilac doors, covered in mosaic tiles, beckoned to her. The very ones Adriel had specified were not for guests to enter.

'Don't.' Yrsa gripped her wrist.

'It must be a test,' Roh argued, starting towards the doors. 'There's something to do with the stone in there.'

Finn ran a talon along the tiles. 'I think the bone cleaner is right.'

It was the last thing Roh expected to come from his mouth.

'You heard what Adriel said,' Yrsa hissed, pulling Roh away. 'They don't allow guests there.'

'But what if it's a *test*, Yrsa?' Finn pressed. He jerked his chin in Roh's direction. 'She can be challenged at any time. What if it's a test of one of the three core elements: cunning, strength, magic?'

'And what if it's not?'

Finn shrugged.

Harlyn merely stood quietly, watching with cautious eyes.

Roh shook off Yrsa's grip. 'We have *five days*,' she stated. '*Five days* of supposed prayer ahead of us, while Adriel plots whatever course of action will suit us least. We'd be fools to sit idly by while he does it. Even if it's not some sort of test, we need to know as much about this place and the cyrens who inhabit it as possible.'

But she knew that now was not the time to be breaking into forbidden rooms. There were too many witnesses; dozens of Akorians wandered through the halls, on their way to the great temple and the numerous oratories. Any number of them could have overheard.

'Later,' she muttered to the others. Harlyn and Yrsa's expressions filled with exasperation.

The exception was Finn Haertel.

'Later,' he murmured in agreement.

Three hours of silent prayers did nothing to quell Roh's anxious impatience. She had received no word or sign of Ames' arrival.

Ames would never break his word, Roh thought. *Not to me* ... But then, what made her special? While she knew that she, Harlyn and Orson were his favourites, they were still just his students. Roh suppressed a sigh. Student or not, he'd been by her side for every milestone, bar this.

Five days. Ames would have five more days to reach Akoris. That would have to be enough.

Taking advantage of the stifling silence, Roh calculated the days and weeks in her mind. It had taken them thirteen days, or thereabouts, to travel from Saddoriel to the gilded plains, and another five to Akoris itself. With *another* five days ahead, it meant she was well over halfway through her first moon of the allotted seven. *Already*. With no birthstone in her possession as yet. Every day they spent in Akoris was a day less they'd have to find and obtain the other birthstones. It was especially frustrating when the one they currently sought was in their very reach, hung around Adriel's neck. She glanced up from her reverent pose of worship, spotting Adriel on the dais at the front where he knelt with his own head bowed, the topaz gleaming against the black of his crisp, tailored shirt.

What goes on in that head? Roh wondered, picturing the nestlings and fledglings at the table last night, who had been nowhere in sight over breakfast. And what of the oracles? Where were they now? Everyone in the temple around her wore identical, backless robes, save for Roh and her companions.

As though sensing her gaze on him, Adriel looked up. Whatever his expression, Roh was certain it was not one of someone whose wholesome connection to the goddesses had just been severed. Adriel's eyes were full of scheming and calculation – Roh knew that look well enough; more often than not, it stared back at her when she gazed upon a mirror.

At last, the prayer session came to an end and the Akorian Arch General stood, taking the hands of his people in his own and regaling them with colourful blessings of Dresmis and Thera. He was wearing a different tailored jacket on this occasion, emerald green this time. When at last the line of worshippers thinned, Roh approached him, noting his smooth movements and easy smile.

'May the goddesses bless you generously,' he said, taking her hands in his as he had with the Akorians. His hands were soft, much softer than hers, and there was something about the touch of his skin that made her feel unclean. Perhaps it was that he clearly hadn't worked a hard day in his life, however long *that* had been so far.

His stare pierced hers while the honey-coloured gem seemed to wink at her, as though it were aware of her desperation to possess it, as though it knew its home was not in the ugly amulet around Adriel's neck, but in the crown of bones atop her head.

Roh sifted through a number of compliant responses to Adriel's blessing …

The goddesses have favoured me with safe passage to Akoris.

I am blessed by your presence – she'd wager he'd like that one.

I am their humble servant …

But she couldn't force the words from her mouth. She pointedly pulled her hands from his grasp. 'One day down,' she heard herself say.

Had fury flickered in his eyes?

But the Arch General's voice was as steady as ever as he said, 'It is the will of the gods, and so it must be. You must prove —'

She inhaled deeply, fighting the raging temper within. 'I proved myself back in Saddoriel. This is a formality.'

'Formalities must be respected, especially by those who wish to rule.'

Roh said no more. She wasn't going to waste time trying to reason with madness, so she slipped away from him, rejoining Harlyn, Finn and Yrsa at the door, her own words echoing in her mind.

One day down.

What she did with the remaining days was up to her.

For the first time, it was Finn's eyes she met. Oddly, he seemed to be the only one in agreement with her, the only one who understood that there was something behind those lilac doors they needed to find, something that was going to test her, to help her obtain the stone. A strange, unspoken truce settled between them as they navigated the crowded halls once more. No words were needed as they disappeared into a giant throng of chattering Akorians, the drumming pounding overhead as they lost the others and ducked away from curious eyes.

In an alcove, they waited in silence, Roh's blood roaring in her ears. She knew there was something in that room, something Adriel didn't want her to see or use against him, and that was exactly what she was going to do. Finn's lilac eyes were alert, his eagerness making him look younger, though Roh had no idea how old he truly was. He couldn't be much older than her, surely?

'Yrsa's going to be furious,' he said at last, catching her eye.

Roh peered out into the emptying hallway. 'I'm sure she'll forgive you. Why are you helping me, anyway?'

'Because as much as it pains me to agree with the human, I can't stand this place. The sooner we're out of here, the better for all of us. And that wretch Adriel is up to something in that room.'

That was a good enough reason for Roh. 'Come on,'

she said, re-entering the hall and following the passageway towards the lilac doors.

She didn't hesitate when she reached them, her fingers gripping the cold metal handle and pushing down. There was no resistance.

The doors were unlocked.

Roh opened one of them a crack and slipped inside, Finn right behind her, his warm breath brushing the back of her neck.

She heard the door click into place before she'd even had a moment to look around the sparse space. But when she turned, the wall behind them was blank.

The room was windowless.

And the doors had vanished.

CHAPTER THIRTEEN

'What is this trickery?' Finn hissed, running his palms across the plain wall where the doors had been.

Roh looked around. The room, a perfect square of smooth, polished tiles, was completely bare.

'There's nothing here,' she murmured, pacing the length of the room in a few short strides, exploring each corner carefully, ensuring she hadn't missed something vital.

'It's a trap,' Finn snapped, pushing his hands against the stone. 'We're trapped.' There was a note of panic in his voice that Roh had never heard there before.

'If we're trapped, we're not in danger,' Roh told him calmly. She had been in far worse scrapes than this, and all of them had taught her that there was always a way out, that where there was a will, there was a way.

Finn gaped at her, his eyes wild. 'There are *no windows*.

No doors. Who knows how long we'll be in here. *Not in danger?* It's sealed with magic, bone cleaner. The others won't be able to find —'

'I didn't think you'd scare so easily,' Roh retorted.

'Don't insult me. I'm not *scared.* I'm telling you —'

'Calm yourself,' she demanded. 'You're a Jaktaren, for Thera's sake.'

'Don't tell me what I am. You obviously aren't grasping —'

'I'm telling you what you are,' Roh cut him off. 'Because it seems you need reminding. I understand the situation. I'm simply trying to figure a way out, which is impossible with all your panicked yammering.'

'I'm not panick—'

'Sounds like panicking to me.' Roh put her hands on her hips and raised a brow in challenge as Finn struggled to argue. His lilac stare was churning with fury as he paced back and forth several times, frustration plain as day on his furrowed features. He swept his hair back before shoving his hands into his pockets.

'I … I don't like enclosed spaces,' he said at last, not meeting Roh's gaze.

Ah. Roh wondered what could have happened to the otherwise fearless Jaktaren to make him claustrophobic, but she didn't ask, didn't push. No good would come from trying to coax out an explanation, here of all places. She had had enough troubles of her own to know that reliving something in the wrong environment could make matters worse by tenfold.

She nodded. 'Fair enough.' Paying the Jaktaren no

heed, she paced the edges of the room, examining the walls and the cornices, anywhere that might hide a hidden trigger or mechanism. 'There will be a way out,' she said, more to herself than to Finn.

'But it's *magic*, bone —'

Roh was on him in an instant. Catching him off guard, she shoved him violently against the wall, her face mere inches away from his. 'Call me "bone cleaner" *one more time*,' she challenged, her talons piercing the thin fabric of his shirt, threatening to sink into his chest.

Finn's eyes narrowed as they met hers. 'Is that a threat?'

'Yes,' she said simply.

For a moment, Finn held her gaze, as though he were about to shove back, as though he were about to call her something worse, but he didn't. The Jaktaren took her gently by the shoulders and stepped away deliberately, breaking eye contact. 'As you were,' he said softly.

Roh's rage dissipated in a huff of annoyance. She had almost *wanted* an all-out brawl. She couldn't think of a better way to channel all her frustration than to beat Finn Haertel to a bloody pulp, even though deep down she knew he'd have her on the floor in seconds. Gritting her teeth, she said no more as she returned to her examination of the room.

Focus, Roh, she told herself.

Over the years in the workshop, she'd seen her fair share of unusual architectural designs, and despite the magic of the vanishing doors, she felt no other sort of enchantment around them. However the stuffy room was containing them, it was now *mechanical,* and she'd find it.

She pressed her hands against various tiles on the ground, knowing there would be a trigger somewhere.

'Is it just me,' Finn breathed, 'or are the walls getting closer?'

'It's just you,' Roh told him, though truthfully, she'd wondered the same only moments before. She quickened her movements, checking every point she could think of, predicting patterns in the tiles and guessing at random. She was getting closer —

There was a loud groan from her left. This time, she *saw* the wall move.

'*Now* do you believe me?' Finn backed up against the opposite wall.

But Roh pulled him away from it. 'That one's moving too,' she told him, keeping her voice steady.

'What?' Alarm made Finn's features sharp. He moved into the centre of the room, eyes wide and chest heaving. His hands were splayed at his sides, as though he meant to bring the enclosing walls to a halt with mere bodily force.

'It's alright,' Roh tried to soothe him, all the while studying the room. 'We'll be fine.'

'You're as mad as the Elder Slayer.' He gulped down air, apparently concerned he might not get enough to his lungs. 'I've heard stories about how madness runs in the blood. This proves it. You're —'

'Haertel,' Roh snapped. 'You are a Saddorien of the

Jaktaren guild.' She laced her words with unyielding command, her eyes boring into his in challenge.

Finn froze, the verbal lashing he'd been in the midst of dying on his lips.

'Am I wrong?' Roh ground out. She combed through her mind for the various design blueprints that had crossed her workbench over the years. Around them, the walls groaned again, inching closer, the threat of being crushed to death becoming more real by the second. Still, Roh glanced at Finn, whose hands trembled at his sides.

'Haertel,' she yelled. 'I said, *am I wrong?*'

His eyes snapped up to hers at once. 'No,' he rasped. 'You're not wrong.'

A blueprint took shape in Roh's mind. It had been a year or more since she had pulled it from a pile of others in the dark and early hours of the morning. A commission from another territory – that was why it had stood out to her. A design for a chamber that could change size, the purpose unknown. There had been numerous flaws in its design, not least of which were the mechanisms.

Roh's shirt was growing damp with sweat and the pads of her fingertips desensitised from pressing against the cold stone. The walls continued to close in, scraping against the floor, crumbling to dust in some parts.

So, they didn't revise the design as per my suggestion, then, she mused. Because of that, in a few years, the walls would need to be replaced entirely. They were slowly eroding away due to poor measurements.

A loud click echoed through the chamber, where Roh pressed a slightly crooked tile in the wall.

The walls came to a screeching halt.

Folding her arms over her chest, she turned to Finn, brows raised. 'You were saying?'

Finn chewed his lower lip. 'We're still trapped.'

'Are we?' Roh went to the back corner of the room and counted from the ground up. 'On my count, press the opposite stone to mine.'

Scowling, Finn got into position as she bid.

'One, two, three —'

Both cyrens pushed against the stones with their full weight.

Another click sounded. The furthest wall slowly scraped backwards, revealing a walkway beyond.

'Come on,' Roh said, tugging Finn by his wrist.

Finn seemed too stunned to object, and he let her lead him from the room.

'Not just a bone cleaner, am I?' she muttered.

A strange calm seemed to have washed over the Jaktaren. It was as though he was a completely different cyren to the one who'd panicked in the room behind them.

'Apparently not,' he murmured as they drew to a stop.

Roh had had no idea what to expect on the other side of the wall, but … She inhaled a deep breath, trying to steady herself as she took in the vast sight before her. She had only ever seen a library in miniature form – the model Estin Ruhne had designed during the second trial of the Queen's Tournament. Though the renowned architect had treated her badly, Roh had nothing but admiration for the cyren's skill and creativity. The model had been beautiful and intricate, a design for a private royal library, but what stood before Roh now …

The wall in front of them was one endless, curved shelf, lined with hundreds, even thousands of volumes. There was a grand staircase on either side, leading to another level and another, where rows and rows of shelves spanned each floor.

Roh took a dazed step forward, her mouth slightly open.

'You've never seen a library before?' Finn asked.

Roh bit back the sharp retort on her tongue as she realised that for once, the question wasn't an insult. There was no note of superiority in the Jaktaren's voice, only curiosity. Finn was waiting expectantly.

She shook her head. 'Back in Saddoriel, there's a trolley that goes around the Lower Sector. The books are borrowed from the library in the Mid Sector, but I've never been there. We're not allowed … Are they all like this?'

Again, there was no spiteful barb as Finn considered the vast space before them. 'I don't know about the Mid Sector, but the library in the Upper Sector is large, though not nearly as large as this. It's renowned for housing rare books rather than many books. I was always told that Akoris has the second-biggest collection of the cyren territories.'

'There's an even larger library?'

Finn sighed. 'There *was*. Lochloria, the scholars' city, used to be famous for its books.'

Lochloria, the home of the water warlocks, of Deodan's ancestors. The territory that had seen the erasure of an entire people.

'Have you been there? In your travels?' Roh asked.

'Once,' he said, but didn't elaborate.

'Can I help you?' said a voice from behind them. A pretty cyren wearing a backless crimson gown approached them, several rolls of parchment cradled in her arms.

'Yes, please,' Roh said before Finn could scare her away with his scowling. 'Could you direct us to the books on the Law of the Lair?'

'Of course,' the librarian replied. 'This way.'

Ignoring Finn's bewildered expression, Roh followed the cyren and her sweeping gown up one of the staircases and through several rows of shelves. She pointed to an entire section.

'These are all the law volumes currently not on loan.'

'There are more?' Roh wondered aloud.

'Yes. Akoris supplies Saddoriel and Csilla with volumes upon request. Books are constantly being exchanged between the three, except for the queen's private collection, of course.'

'Of course,' Roh repeated, though she'd had no idea of the dealings between the cyren territories. It was one of the many reasons she sought answers in books like the heavy volumes before her. She hated feeling ignorant in any situation, but particularly in those pertaining to her future reign. She pushed the topic to the back of her mind, where she had mentally filed her list of things to learn over the next six or so moons.

The librarian's last words suddenly came into focus … *The queen's private collection* … The phrase fuelled a wave of longing in Roh. The collection didn't belong to anyone *right now*, but at the end of all this, it could be *hers*. She wondered where in the queen's residence the library was. Roh had only been there briefly to retrieve Odi after the second trial in the tournament and the rooms had awed her senseless even then. To know that the quarters had its own private library …

The librarian cleared her throat. 'Is that all?'

'If I want to borrow something, how do I do that?' Roh asked.

'Well, you already have Adriel's approval, as you got through the shrinking room.'

Roh stared. So it *had* been a test, of sorts. She felt Finn shift beside her in discomfort at the mere mention of it.

'There's a register by the far exit,' the cyren continued, pointing to the back of the room. 'Just write down the title and your name, and you can take it with you. Bring it back within two weeks.'

Roh hoped to be long gone by then. 'Thank you,' she said, running her fingers along the book spines.

When the librarian was gone, Finn turned to Roh. 'Which book do you want?'

Roh debated keeping quiet on the matter. But the countless spines and numerous titles in various tongues defeated her. 'A volume of *The Law of the Lair*. I think it's number twelve.' She tried to recall the numeral on the spine of the tattered book tucked away in her pack that she'd been lugging around since they'd left Saddoriel. Andwana, the Lower Sector librarian, would be furious to learn that not only had she not returned it on time, she'd taken it from the territory entirely. Perhaps she'd be able to leave it here. Though after she was done with it, there was no way it would match the pristine condition of the Akorian books.

Finn was watching her. 'Why?' he asked.

Roh flipped open a volume and scanned its contents, not entirely sure what she was looking for, but with a feeling she'd know it when she found it. 'If I'm to rule, I need to learn the laws of my people. I need to know everything I can ...'

A queen must know the Law of the Lair better than she knows herself, Delja had told her amidst the Aching Fiirs and laceflower of the Queen's Conservatory, when Roh's dark fears of her origins had nearly got the better of her.

Finn was still staring at her.

'What?' she snapped.

The Jaktaren looked from the book in her hands to the sea of titles before them and rubbed the back of his head, the casual movement seeming to soften his rigid stance. 'You're really serious about this, aren't you?'

'About what?'

'Winning the tournament. Becoming queen.'

'I *did* win the tournament.' But the words didn't have the bite she'd intended. 'And *really serious?*' she repeated his words back to him. 'Have I done something to make you think otherwise?'

Finn leaned against one of the shelves. 'No … Just … I guess I never thought to *study* for it.'

'As someone whose only in-depth education was about the best way to clean bones, the laws of Saddoriel and its territories are downright fascinating.' She sighed. 'You probably don't even have to study,' Roh allowed. 'You probably know far more than I ever will. You're a Jaktaren. An heir of the Council of Seven Elders. They must have taught you *everything*.'

Finn laughed darkly. 'That would mean they actually spent time with me.'

The book was forgotten in Roh's grasp. She had never heard him say anything against his family, or anyone other than her and Odi, for that matter.

'I don't know what I'd do in your position,' he admitted.

Is this a trick? Roh wondered, utterly unsure of this new side the highborn was revealing. For the first time that day, she realised that he wasn't wearing his Jaktaren leathers. Instead, he wore a loose-fitting shirt, the sleeves pushed up to his elbows, revealing tanned, muscular forearms scattered with freckles.

She became incredibly aware of the fact that this was the most time they'd ever spent together alone and the longest Finn had gone without saying degrading things about her. 'Why did *you* enter the tournament?' she asked suspiciously.

Finn's expression changed, his mouth downturned in

what seemed to be regret. 'If you must know, to help Yrsa.'

Roh frowned. 'What do you mean?'

'I never wanted the crown. Yrsa's meant to be ruler, not me. We've been planning it since we were fledglings. Us and Winslow, her aunt. I only entered to watch her back, to help her.'

Roh recalled Finn's vow of unwavering loyalty to Yrsa the night before. *So, it wasn't about romance,* she mused, trying to put the pieces together. It had been about the crown. *But does that mean ...?*

'Is she still ... Does Yrsa still want to be queen?'

'I can't say Yrsa *ever* wanted that for herself. But that's what made her the best choice.'

Roh had never heard him sound so earnest. She hesitated before she spoke next. 'And you don't believe I'll ever be that choice? The best choice, I mean.'

'I don't know you.' Finn straightened, his casual air replaced with a cold, distant voice. 'I only know where you came from, what your mother did.'

Roh felt old resentments resurfacing. Was that it? Was the reprieve from *bone cleaner* and *isruhe* over so soon?

'*No one* knows that. Not really.' She had been thinking about it for some time. Had spent many an hour weighing up the advantages and disadvantages of offering promises too freely. But she spoke in spite of herself: 'Which is why I'll make you a deal.'

Finn's eyes narrowed. 'A deal?'

'Yes,' she said. 'If – no, *when* I have the birthstones of Saddoriel, when I've gained access to the *Tome of Kyeos,*

I'll share that knowledge with you. We can find out exactly what sort of bloody past our families share.'

'And what do you want in return?'

'In the meantime, you stop throwing your abuse and assumptions in my face. Stop fighting with me at every turn. This journey will go faster if we work together instead of *against* one another.'

Finn seemed to mull it over as he faced the shelves and scanned the endless titles before them.

'Here,' he said at last, sliding a book from the shelf and pressing it into her chest. 'Volume twelve.'

Roh supposed that was as close to an agreement as she was going to get.

The next day, after the mandatory three hours of silent prayer, Roh asked Odi to join her for a walk through the surrounding hilly villages of Akoris. She would play Adriel's waiting game to a certain extent, but the later hours of the day were her own and she would spend them as she saw fit. The afternoon was warm and Roh could smell the sea beyond the dunes, the briny breeze tangling in her hair as the pair wandered beneath the flame-leafed trees. She never thought she'd feel relief with a human at her side, but she did with Odi, immense relief. It had been a long time since it had been just the two of them.

'How are your hands?' she asked as they walked.

Odi shrugged. 'Incana brought me some tonic for the pain, which has helped.'

Roh smiled and turned to him, expecting to see that slightly lopsided grin of gratitude, but his gaze remained on the path ahead. Either he wasn't aware she had asked Incana on his behalf or he didn't care. Roh felt suddenly foolish. One nice deed and she expected him to sing her praises?

'— there is no cure for what ails them,' Odi was saying. 'I have to accept that. Just like Harlyn will have to accept her limitations.'

Harlyn's name on his lips made Roh's gut twist. *Why is he bringing up Harlyn? We finally get some time together and he wants to speak of someone who hates me?* Roh knew they were ugly thoughts to have, but she had hoped to have the afternoon to forget about everything pressing down on her shoulders, her broken friendship with Harlyn included. She bit her tongue. She knew whatever she said next would come out all wrong.

Odi seemed to sense it. 'I hate this place,' he told her as they rounded a bend. 'Nothing about it seems right.'

'I know,' Roh agreed. There was an eerie wrongness that stood in stark contrast to the vibrant colours and stunning architecture of the territory. 'And I suspect that Adriel is whittling away my time at the council's instruction. I wish he'd just tell me what he wants for the damn stone. Or what they offered him to do as they bid.'

'Would you try to beat their offer? By promising him something better when you're queen?' Odi asked.

Roh considered this, her mind instantly returning to the image of Adriel sitting at the head of the table, surrounded by his oracles and nestlings.

'Depends what they offered him,' she said.

'Do you mean to tell me there are some things that even *you* would not give, even if it meant securing your reign?'

Roh swallowed, her mouth dry. She was starting to suspect that Odi had been biding his time, waiting to interrogate her. Understandable, she supposed. His future was tied to hers, after all.

'I don't know,' she answered finally.

Odi sighed and she was unsure if her reply had placated or frustrated him. She didn't push the issue further.

'Do you think Csilla will be better?' he asked.

Roh shrugged. 'We'll have to ask Yrsa and Finn, but I hope so.'

They reached the outskirts of the villages, where houses built into the hillside met the sand dunes of the south-east. On the other side, sapphire water glimmered in the afternoon sun, the sea a flat expanse all the way to the horizon.

'Is it so bad for you here?' she heard herself ask. 'As a human? I thought it might be preferable to Saddoriel?' Roh held her breath as the question left her lips. Was it an ignorant thing to ask? Would it drive a wedge between them yet again?

Odi sighed wearily. 'I'm still a human trapped amongst cyrens. While the Akorians are more … subdued, the threat of what they are never goes away. Though the monastery isn't built from human bones, it's still not right, not safe. Honestly? You have no idea what it's been like for me here.'

The anger Roh expected and deserved didn't lace his words. In its place, a profound note of sadness lingered.

'You're right,' she said, shame flooding her face in a wave of heat. 'I've been caught up in my quest, in everything else. We haven't spoken as we did back in Saddoriel, when it was just the two of us. For that, I'm sorry.'

Odi nodded, gazing ahead.

'So tell me,' Roh pressed. 'Tell me what it's been like.'

Odi looked like he meant to protest, but eventually he sighed again. 'It's a different sort of fear here. In Saddoriel, I was constantly on edge, waiting for sabotage, be it by cyren or by the lair itself. I remember falling prey to its lure. It was like I had two bodies: one that followed the lair's call like a moth to a flame, and one that watched on, helplessly, unable to scream. Here … here is different. I don't feel the constant lump of fear in my chest. Most of the time, it's like the Akorians don't even see me as they pass. But then, just as I start to relax, just as I feel at ease, a gaze will slide to mine, utterly aware of what I am, completely predatory, and I'll freeze, cursing myself for my own foolishness. For it's when the prey is most complacent that the viper strikes the hardest.' He swallowed. 'That is what it has been like for me.'

Roh wrung her hands, a cold drop of sweat running between her shoulderblades. 'I'm sorry.'

Odi's shoulders heaved. 'My stepbrothers are still trapped in Saddoriel. And it sounds ludicrous that I might simply return to my father's shop after all of this. What if the Jaktaren continue to hunt me? I'm … I'm worried music will be ruined for me, after everything in the lair.'

His stark honesty hung between them like a bad odour and Roh remembered how he had been forced to play at swordpoint. How her kind had taken the one thing he had loved most and caused him to fear it, to stifle it. The Prince of Melodies, he'd been known as. But if there was one thing Roh knew down to her bones, it was that nothing would return to the way it had been after all this. There would be no going back. Not even for Odi.

'You will never have to endure that again,' she told him. 'You will never have to set foot in the lair again. I'll free your stepbrothers once I'm queen. I'll escort them back to the Isle of Dusan myself if I have to.'

'Roh,' Odi sighed. 'Haven't you learned not to make promises you can't keep?'

Roh didn't reply. She stared out across the sea, marvelling at the rhythm of its sets of waves and how the reflection of the sun sparkled across its surface, until —

A burst of gold a few leagues out from shore shot above the water.

Another second passed and it was gone.

Odi sucked in a breath. 'Was that …?'

'Yes.' Roh stared after it. 'It was.'

. . .

Another evening slipped by. It felt as though a giant hoax were being played upon Roh by the very goddesses she was forced to worship. During those hours of silent, hollow prayer, her mind often turned to Ames. Where was he? Why hadn't he arrived in Akoris yet? She could only play the part of the obedient disciple for so long. For the sake of her sanity, she had also decided not to speculate further about who might challenge her, and how. When she thought of it, panic gripped her insides and refused to let go. She reasoned that any cyren worth their cunning would wait until she had at least attempted to obtain the topaz, wagering on the fact that an attempt would leave her lacking in one way or another. So she boxed up that particular fear, pushing it to a dark corner at the back of her mind. She would worry about the birthstone first and foremost, and would face the rest when the time came.

Soon after their arrival, Roh had convinced Adriel that she and the others needed time to prepare for their greater journey. She'd used his own goddesses against him, insisting that it would dishonour Dresmis and Thera should she not take the time to ready herself. That was the thing about fanaticism: anyone could create false reason out of madness. Instead of attending the afternoon temple sessions, Roh and the others trained. The skirmish with Deodan's clansmen and the run-in with the teerah panther had left Roh feeling vulnerable, something she detested. Never again would she be caught unawares, with no knowledge of self-defence.

The Akorian gardens provided the ideal

environment, with their wide lawns of soft grass onto which Roh could fall inelegantly and an indestructible stone wall perfect for sling-target practice. Yrsa, it seemed, had infinite patience. The Jaktaren took all of them, even Finn, through a series of self-defence drills and hand-to-hand-combat techniques. Roh often found herself watching Finn and Yrsa in awe. The two moved with the grace and fluidity of dancers, and the deadliness of vipers. Roh felt certain that she'd made the right choice in bringing them along. Deodan's style was different, but by no means less effective. He managed to hold his own against the two cyren warriors, much to Finn's frustration. It was clear he was not used to being bested.

With each hour of training with Yrsa, Roh felt herself getting stronger and faster. She would never be as skilled as the Jaktaren, but that didn't mean she couldn't hold her own, and she was well acquainted with hard work. Deodan, however, had a far more ... flirtatious teaching manner. The warrior's eyes glowed with mischief, and though Roh was loath to admit it, his bold comments had her fighting to contain her laughter, especially at the expression they left on Harlyn's face.

During those hours, a simple, easy rhythm formed between the companions, and Roh found that she could even bear Finn's company, as it was not barbed with sharp insults. They had reached a silent truce, for now.

After a vicious round of sparring with Yrsa on their fourth day in Akoris, Roh went to get her water canteen from the refreshments table.

'Training is going well,' Yrsa told her, nodding with approval. 'You're a quick study.'

Roh laughed. 'That's because it beats books and counting bones.'

'I can't argue with you there,' Yrsa allowed.

There was a firm tap on Roh's shoulder, and to her surprise, it was Finn who stood behind her. His loose shirt was untucked and pushed up at the sleeves, while his dishevelled hair was damp at the roots. Colour bloomed on his face from exertion, but he eyed her expectantly.

'You and me, let's go,' he said.

'I just sparred with Yrsa,' Roh told him, nodding to the other Jaktaren and taking a measured step back, wondering if Finn had ever spoken her actual name.

But Finn was shaking his head, loose hair falling into his eyes. He scooped it back with one hand. 'You haven't fought me.'

'But I —'

'You don't get to choose your opponent. Not out in the real world.'

Roh's insides were squirming. She hated to admit that he was right, but the thought of being on the receiving end of his blows was not a tempting one. 'I know, but —'

Yrsa gave her a gentle push towards him, taking the sling from Roh's hand that she'd been clutching so tightly.

Damn Jaktaren, Roh cursed. They were in on his humiliation scheme together. She gritted her teeth as she met Finn in the open square of the garden and noted his stance: feet apart, fists raised to protect his face ...

Great, Roh thought darkly. *Hand-to-hand combat it is.* She took up her position, mirroring the way the Jaktaren stood, but she wasn't going to wait for the oncoming attack. She lunged forward, as Yrsa had shown her, taking a swipe at the side of Finn's head with her fist, while aiming a kick for his legs, hoping to knock them from under him.

Finn blocked the blow with a firm forearm and jumped effortlessly over her lower attack, as though he weighed nothing, his boot shooting out at her. She went sprawling, but caught herself just before she ate dirt, flushing furiously.

'Come on, Roh,' Yrsa cheered. 'You can handle him. Remember what I taught you!'

Don't get angry, don't think too much, just go with your instinct. Those had been Yrsa's words, though these days, Roh was always angry and always thinking too much, so it was a tall order. She rolled her shoulders and took up her position again. She had committed now and there was no way she was letting *Finn Haertel* knock her out in the first round.

Roh attacked, swinging a well-aimed punch at his abdomen. He stepped to the side easily, a slight smirk tugging at his mouth as he waited for her next strike. Roh reined in her temper, feinted left and struck right —

Her blow landed hard on his upper arm.

She grinned. He hadn't been expecting that.

'Pleased with yourself, are you?' he asked, a challenge glinting in his lilac eyes.

'A lowly bone cleaner just hit a *Jaktaren.* I'd say that's

cause for celebration,' she quipped, careful not to drop her guard.

'That won't be happening again.'

Oh, he's angry, Roh mused with infinite satisfaction.

Finn attacked. Blow after blow rained down on Roh and she blocked furiously, her arms a blur of movement before her, protecting her face, protecting her middle. He landed a shot at her kidney, but Roh could have sworn it wasn't as hard as it should have been.

'*Fight back*, Roh!' Yrsa yelled. 'Advance! Aim for the soft parts!'

There was no way she could beat him in hand-to-hand combat. Her handful of training hours had nothing on his years of intense Jaktaren drills and real-world conflicts. Roh scanned her surroundings and hope soared as she spotted something lying in the grass. She made a dive for the wooden training sword and snatched it up triumphantly in her hands.

'That's against the rules,' Finn said, though he looked more amused than irritated.

Roh shrugged. 'Rules are there to be broken.'

'Interesting stance from a supposed queen.'

'Scared?'

Finn huffed a laugh. 'Not in this life.'

Roh gave no warning – she lunged with her wooden blade, aiming for the soft parts, as Yrsa had instructed. Finn jumped back, looking around for something he could use against it, but she didn't give him a second reprieve. At last she had the upper hand. She advanced, ignoring Yrsa and Odi's cheers from the sideline, and thrust her sword forward. Finn evaded her attack again and rolled across the ground, swiping a dagger from a pile of discarded weapons. A *real* dagger, Roh realised, noting the silver gloss of the blade.

'Scared?' he taunted, a wicked grin splitting his face.

'You wish.' She pivoted on her right foot and slashed her sword at Finn's exposed side with all her strength.

Finn's dagger sank into the wooden blade as he blocked her blow, the vibration pulsing up her arm, and she struggled to dislodge her weapon from his. The highborn smirked, victory shining in his eyes as he spun, taking her sword with him and swinging a fist at her —

Roh side-stepped Finn's swipe, leaped into his space and aimed a kick at his groin —

Finn caught her leg midair and twisted. Roh lost her balance, but she'd be damned if she wasn't going to take him down with her. She flung out a hand, grabbing his arm in a death grip, fingers tangling in the sleeve of his shirt. Something ripped loudly, and together, they went crashing to the ground in a heap.

Finn landed on top of her, close enough that his hair tickled her face. For a second, Roh was all too aware of the hard plane of his chest pressing against hers. She could feel his heart thudding against her own. And for a second longer, she couldn't move. Finn's eyes met hers —

Swearing, she shoved him off with all the strength she could muster and practically sprinted back to the safety of the refreshments table.

'I'd call that a draw,' Yrsa said loudly to Roh.

Finn shot her a furious look from across the garden.

Roh gratefully accepted the canteen from Odi. She drank deeply, relishing the cool taste on her parched tongue – only to have it slosh down her front as she caught a flash of bare, tanned skin across the garden.

Finn had taken off his ripped shirt and was using it to mop his brow. Sweat beaded across the muscular planes of his chest and down his carved abdomen, where two grooves ran from where his sword belt sat at his hips, disappearing lower —

Roh looked away, heat flushing her cheeks. She shouldn't be looking at him like that. He was a *Jaktaren*, for Dresmis and Thera's sakes. A *Haertel* no less. He'd made damn sure she was aware of it. She forced herself to turn back to the refreshments, where Yrsa stood, grinning widely.

Roh didn't think it was possible, but her face burned even more.

Yrsa burst out laughing and gave her a comforting pat on the shoulder. 'He's not my type, Majesty,' she said with a wink. 'But I've got a pulse. I can appreciate a decent form when I see one.'

Laughter burst from Roh's lips then, and it was all she could do not to flick her gaze back to the half-naked Jaktaren. Gods, it felt good to laugh.

Roh was grateful for the reprieve until Harlyn cornered her after her training session.

'You're friends with them,' she hissed in disgust. 'You're actually becoming *friends* with the highborns.'

'Har—'

'All our lives they looked down on us, all our lives they

treated us as though we were lesser, and now you're actually *enjoying their company*, those who would call you *isruhe*.'

Roh couldn't believe what she was hearing; her talons slid out. 'They're not the only ones to have called me that, are they?' she said quietly.

Harlyn's face flushed with shame. 'That's different. I —'

'It's not different at all, or perhaps it is,' Roh countered. 'Perhaps it's *worse*. Because you know better than anyone how deep that word cuts.'

'Roh —'

'I can't do this anymore,' Roh told her, shaking her head as she walked away from her friend. She had apologised time and time again for her actions, and she thought she had made her peace with the fact that Harlyn might never forgive her, might never call her friend or sister again. But that didn't mean she had to spend the rest of her life atoning for what she had done in silence, wrapped in grief and guilt, unable to utter a single word, forbidden to speak to another soul. No one had the right to call her an *isruhe*, not even Harlyn. Roh's limbs felt heavy as she walked away. She was so tired of the weight of everything on her shoulders, of carrying so many burdens. It was up to Harlyn to decide whether or not to forgive her, but either way, they had to move on. They could not continue like this.

As Roh made her way to the gardens' exit, a commotion sounded. There was a shout and the clang of steel upon steel —

Running, Roh skidded to a halt at the gates to the courtyard. Akorian guards were tackling a human man to the ground.

'What's going on?' Deodan panted as he caught up and stopped beside her.

'I don't know,' Roh answered, unable to tear her eyes away from the chaos unfolding before them. The Akorians had the man pinned, their blades pointed at his throat.

Deodan craned his neck to see past the guards. 'Shit,' he said, his face crumpling. 'Lars …'

'What is it?' And upon seeing the devastation on Deodan's face: 'You know him …'

'I do.'

'Then why —'

Deodan was already moving, but not towards the human, as Roh expected. The warrior warlock darted away, his cloak trailing behind him as he disappeared into the monastery.

Roh stared after him. *This is how he treats his friends?*

Her attention was dragged back to the courtyard by a shout. The human thrashed and kicked as the guards hauled him away, leaving a cloud of dust and a pulsing, foreboding silence in his wake.

The silence didn't last. A gong rang out across Akoris, the sound vibrating so loudly that Roh had to cover her ears. All around her, cyrens emerged from passageways and doors, all heading in the same direction.

Yrsa, Odi, Harlyn and Finn caught up with her and watched the strange proceedings.

'Where are they all going?' Yrsa asked, frowning after the sweep of Akorian robes and tattooed backs.

'Ah,' said an all-too-familiar voice. 'You're all here. Come, come, we don't want to miss it.' Adriel ushered them in the same direction as the other cyrens.

'Miss what?' Roh pressed.

'The sentencing,' the Arch General replied, as though Roh were a fool. But then he glanced at Odi. 'Perhaps it's best if you return to your quarters,' he said.

'Why?' Odi blurted. 'What's going on?'

Something slithered within Roh, an instinct that told her whatever was unfolding around them now wasn't good, and it certainly wouldn't be good for Odi.

'Just go,' she told him.

'What? You want me to leave? But —'

'Odi, I don't know what's happening, but I don't think you should be here. Please, trust me.'

Odi's amber eyes clouded with anger. 'I am as much a part of this team as any of you. I shouldn't be —'

Team ... The word echoed through Roh for the joyful truth it was. Somewhere along the way, that was what they had become. But there wasn't a moment to savour it.

Harlyn took Odi's arm. 'I'll go back with you,' she said gently.

Odi looked ready for further argument, but Harlyn tugged on his sleeve and they fell away from the group.

Adriel led Roh and the others through the throngs of cyrens still crowding the pathways, taking them towards what looked like a small arena Roh had failed to notice by the monastery. 'That was for the best,' he told her.

'Why?'

But suddenly, there was no need for Adriel to answer. For Roh saw exactly why Odi shouldn't be within a hundred feet of this place. It was indeed a small arena, its seated area packed with cyrens, and in the centre, chained by the ankle, was the human from the courtyard. Deodan's friend. There was no sign of Deodan.

Adriel gestured towards a spare row of seats in the front. 'You'll have a good view of things from there,' he told them. 'If you'll excuse me.'

A good view? Is this some sort of sport?

He left them at the benches, striding in the direction of the helpless human who remained chained before them all.

Roh didn't want to be here, didn't want to watch whatever was about to happen. Her palms had grown clammy. She looked to her companions, but the Jaktaren's faces were as unreadable as stone and Roh realised with a start that she had momentarily forgotten what it was they'd done before they'd started this journey with her. They were used to seeing humans trapped like this. In fact, it was *they* who did the trapping. How could she have forgotten what type of cyrens she travelled with?

'Attention, Akorians and guests,' Adriel's voice boomed out across the arena. 'We have summoned our people here today to bear witness to this human's crime, his sentence as per the Law of the Lair, and ultimately, his death.'

What? Roh felt splinters of wood in her talons as she gripped the bench beneath her.

Adriel pointed to the human in the sand, tugging at the chain around his ankle. 'This man stands accused and found guilty of treason.'

'Treason?' Roh whispered to Yrsa. 'He's not an Akorian, how can he be found guilty of treason?'

The Arch General continued. 'This man conspired to undermine the powers of Dresmis and Thera by making and distributing protective talismans amongst surrounding human villages. Remnants of the very talismans that were used against our kind during the Age of Chaos.'

A unified gasp sounded from around the stands.

'This man,' Adriel shouted, pointing at the human again, 'is part of a rebel movement that conspires to overthrow cyren rule as I speak. He was hunted down by several of Saddoriel's best Jaktaren —'

'*Jaktaren?*' Finn murmured beside Roh, hands gripping his knees. 'That's not Jaktaren work.'

'— and I have just received word from the Council of Seven Elders in Saddoriel of his sentence. He will witness the death chorus.'

A cheer erupted from the Akorians.

Roh felt sick to her stomach. Since she was a nestling, she had been taught about the great cyren power that was the death chorus. It was so revered in their culture and history that she'd envied anyone who'd seen one occur. A death chorus was the embodiment of the ancient magic that flowed through cyren veins, a power feared by all other creatures throughout the realms. But now, Roh tasted bile at the back of her throat. This wasn't what a death chorus was for – preying on a single human. A single deathsong would be more than enough to take his life, and even that wasn't warranted. Deathsongs and death choruses were for *battle*, for war amidst blood-soaked currents and lashing tides. Not this.

She twisted in her seat. *Where's Deodan? He wouldn't allow this to happen to someone he knows. He went to get help,* Roh told herself. But when at last she spotted Deodan's armed figure across the crowd, he was alone, his expression hardened and his blue-grey eyes cold.

A cry sounded from the human as a group of ten robed Akorian females entered the arena.

Adriel nodded to them. 'Proceed.'

Roh was glued to her chair, her voice caught like a thick stone in her throat. She wanted to cry out, to object to the horror she knew was about to come to pass, but she couldn't. She may as well have been one of the frozen statues in the gardens.

Without warning, several heart-stopping notes filled the air. Roh could almost see the sound as it drifted towards the chained man, whose scream had died upon his lips. Now, he simply stared, eyes glazed over as though in a trance as the melody danced around him. Even to Roh, the chorus was hypnotic, designed to fill holes in hearts and lure its prey into the darkness. Utterly transfixed by the cyrens, the man got to his feet, the chain rattling at his ankle as he took a willing step towards them.

But their lilac eyes suddenly went black.

The song pulled tight and a burst of light momentarily

blinded Roh. She squinted, blinking her sight back slowly.

An icy claw raked down the length of her spine and her hand went to her mouth as she saw what remained of the human.

A pile of bones.

CHAPTER FOURTEEN

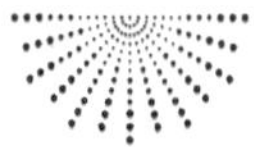

The bone stack looked so small amidst the open space of the arena, still flecked with muscle and blood.

Roh tasted bile on her tongue. There were two hundred and six bones in the human body; she had counted them herself in the workshop. It had seemed a lot at the time, when she was cleaning and sorting them on her small workbench, but now … Her home appeared in her mind. An entire lair built from human skeletons. How many had died to build Saddoriel? Or even just the towering archway at the lair's entrance? The number was unfathomable and the thought of it filled Roh with a horror she'd never known before.

She didn't speak as they made their way back to the royal quarters. Neither did Yrsa or Finn. Roh didn't notice the beautiful stonework of the passageways, didn't hear the beat of the Akorian drums. All she thought of was that pile of bones.

When at last they reached their quarters, Roh suddenly darted forward, throwing herself towards the bathing chamber. The door slammed behind her just as she reached a bucket and was violently ill.

Her body convulsed, bile burning the back of her throat, her eyes stinging as she vomited. Every time there was a reprieve, the pile of bones came to her again, as did the many bones she'd seen before it. Barrels upon barrels of bones, sifting through them with her bare hands and talons, the blood of so many dotting her own skin. She was sick again and again, eyes streaming. It was here, with her head in a bucket, that the realisation came to her. That persistent niggling at the back of her mind that had nagged her since she'd entered the tournament. She had been kept in the dark about her own kind for her whole life. For nearly eighteen years, myth and legend had been taught as fact, as a history to be proud of. The truth was, she knew less about cyrens than she'd ever imagined. The great death chorus. It had taken this long for her to witness it, and now …? She wished she hadn't. The greatest of all the cyren powers, the gift that had won battles, *won wars*, was used on single, helpless individuals? Inflicted upon defenceless humans? And for what?

Roh threw up again, her mind spiralling out of control. She had been complacent and unquestioning, complicit in her ignorance, which she had never tried to overcome.

Is that how a queen would behave? She looked around,

vision swimming, catching glimpses of the Dresmis and Thera statues.

This place ... How has Adriel been allowed to rule it as such? The glazed look of his people flashed in Roh's mind. They had cheered for that poor human's demise. They hadn't flinched at what had happened to him. How many had come before?

And what of Adriel's oracles? Do they want to be there? The costumed women had stayed with Roh since she'd first glimpsed them in the refectory, and the twist in her gut told her she already knew the answer to her questions. *What of their children? When did this begin? For how long has it gone on?* She had been so focused on her own gains that she'd lost sight of the most important part of being a queen ...

The people.

A choked sob escaped Roh. It had to stop. Her own foolish naivety and ignorance would end here. Delja had to have known how Akoris was being run during her reign, but Roh refused to be that kind of queen. She had lived too long as a bone cleaner to watch on and do nothing. As ruler, cyrenkind would be her responsibility. It would be her duty to understand it, to better it.

Roh's stomach clenched painfully, the pile of bones so clear in her mind that the very thought of it made her heave again.

A warm palm pressed against her lower back, rubbing gentle circles, and a delicate hand swept her damp hair from her brow.

'It's alright,' Harlyn told her. 'It's alright.'

Roh didn't have the energy to tell her to go away and she didn't want to. She let her friend hold her hair and rub her back as she emptied the last of her stomach contents into the bucket, panting.

When at last Roh was done, she sat back on the cold tiles, wiping her mouth with the back of her hand. Her watery gaze met Harlyn's softened expression, her friend draping a used towel across the top of the bucket to stop the smell escaping. She sat down on the tiles beside Roh and continued to rub her back.

'I heard,' Harlyn said.

And Roh was grateful, so grateful that she didn't have to explain, so grateful that for a moment she didn't have to relive what she'd just witnessed, and so grateful that Harlyn was finally there with her.

Later, when her stomach had settled, Roh asked Odi to accompany her to the library. She was determined to have answers and she felt a deep need to be with her human friend after what she had seen, forever thankful that he had not seen it.

Odi didn't baulk at the shrinking room. He simply placed his hands on the stones and applied pressure as she instructed. His mood was sombre and Roh knew that one of the others had told him what had happened to the human in the amphitheatre. As the walls groaned to a halt and revealed the library beyond, Roh reached for him.

'Is there anything I can do?' she asked.

'It was just as I said, wasn't it?' His voice was hollow, his eyes haunted. 'The viper struck ...'

Roh felt the gut-wrenching pull of guilt inside her. She had dragged him from one nightmare to the next, with no real thought for his fear or safety. Once, she might have tried to make excuses – that the dead human was a traitor, that not all cyrens did those things. No longer. She squeezed his shoulder gently before letting her hand drop.

'It was exactly as you said,' she agreed.

Again Roh was amidst the towering shelves, craning her neck to spot the librarian weaving through the stacks. The scent of old parchment and leather was comforting somehow, as was the gentle quiet. It seemed that the library was the one place the drums of Akoris didn't pierce, as though it were more sacred than the great temple.

'You're back!' the librarian's voice sounded, her head popping around the corner of a shelf. Her gaze flitted to Odi, curiosity lighting her eyes, though she did not address him.

'Uh, yes. I am ...' Roh managed, getting the distinct impression that the cyren didn't often get company. 'I was wondering if you could tell me where the books are on the Arch Generals? Specifically, those who ruled Akoris after the reign of Uniir the Blessed?'

The librarian's brow furrowed and she thoughtfully tapped her chin, as though she were mentally skimming through a catalogue of books. 'Of course, though I should warn you ... There are many volumes on such an important subject.'

'Do you have a recommendation, then?' Roh asked. 'One that you think is the most accurate, or the most comprehensive?'

The librarian grinned, and for the first time Roh realised that she didn't share the same glazed-over look as the other Akorians. *Strange*, she thought. *Perhaps her occupation doesn't allow for it ...*

'This way.'

Roh and Odi wordlessly followed her billowing crimson robes through the shelves, and Roh found herself wishing she could somehow transport all the information the volumes contained into her own head.

Imagine what having all that knowledge could mean ...

'Here,' the librarian said as she pulled a leather-bound tome from a lower shelf. She glanced again at Odi. 'We don't have any books in the common tongue.'

'That's alright ...' Roh searched her mind for a name, but realised she'd never been given one.

'Mirrah,' the cyren said with a smile. 'Just call out if there's anything else I can assist you with.'

'Thank you, Mirrah.'

As soon as Mirrah had left, Odi turned to Roh. 'Why *did* you bring me?' he asked. 'I'm useless here.'

'You're not useless,' she told him, frowning as she scanned over the extensive table of contents. 'You're here because you have an objective view of cyrenkind.'

Odi scoffed. 'Since when?'

Roh couldn't help but smile at that. 'Well, maybe not *objective*, but certainly not favourable. And I need someone who's going to be honest.'

'About cyrens?'

'About everything.'

Odi raised a single brow. 'What happened to that Saddorien pride of yours?'

Roh exhaled through her nose, finding the chapter she was looking for and flipping to the correct page. 'Perhaps I'm realising there's not much to be proud of.'

That silenced him.

Roh sat down on the floor then and there, in the middle of the aisle. Odi slid down the shelf beside her, watching as she scanned the dense lines of text, thumbing through the pages for a name that jumped out at her.

'I don't know what I'm looking for, exactly,' she explained, tracing the words with her talon as she skimmed a chapter. She paused. 'Here's a vague reference to the Queen's Tournament,' she murmured, more to herself than to Odi. 'It was called The Dawning back then … This one here, it's the one that Delja won, because …' She trailed off.

Placing the book on the ground and smoothing out its pages, Roh rubbed her eyes before glancing across at Odi.

'What?' he asked.

'Well, this *has to be* the tournament Delja won, but it doesn't give any detail about the trials or the victor. It merely says that Uniir the Blessed was dethroned, and upon relinquishing the crown, he declared he stood before the direct ancestor of Dresmis and Thera … Then he stabbed himself.'

'You knew that already, you told me so in the Passage of Kings.'

'I did … but isn't it strange that it doesn't *name* Delja, or anyone? Part of the prestige of entering the tournament is to be immortalised in cyren history …' Roh thought back to her exchange with the former queen at the Vault, before she'd left Saddoriel. According to Delja, history had recorded the seemingly small act of Roh cheating in a game of Thieves, so why would it not record the name of its next ruler? Especially its first and only queen?

Odi was waiting.

Roh turned back to the page and read aloud. *'Following the demise of Uniir the Blessed, the new queen proclaimed that Saddoriel would renounce its doctrines. Any cyren wishing to live by those doctrines could migrate to the cyren territory of Akoris. Religious practices of that fervour would no longer be tolerated in Saddoriel or Talon's Reach.'*

'You already knew that, too, Roh. What are you getting at here?' Odi said with a note of impatience.

'I know, I know,' she muttered. 'I want to know who initially led Akoris after Uniir, and how Adriel came to be Arch General.'

She found the answer on the following page. *'A cyren called Lornell Erbar became the first Arch General of Akoris, chosen by the new queen herself.'*

'How were the territories governed before that, then?' Odi asked.

'Small councils, I think, appointed by the Council of Elders.'

'So that was one of the first things Delja changed …'

'Apparently. But why?'

Odi peeled off his fingerless gloves and began to massage his hands, flexing his fingers with a pained wince. 'Well, arguably, one person – *cyren*, rather – is easier to control than a group. Don't you think?'

'I guess …' She turned the page over, getting lost in the dry detail of the ceremony and various long-winded traditions. 'Surely there's a list of …' She trailed off again, flipping through the thick tome. 'Here!'

'What?' Odi looked up from his hands, alarmed.

'Sorry,' Roh mumbled. 'Seven pages.'

'Seven pages of what?' Odi ground out.

'Of Arch Generals. Since Delja's rule.'

'Well, it is a six-hundred-year period, isn't it? And you said most cyrens don't live that long.'

'True.'

'Has she selected all of them?'

Roh slowly shook her head. 'They're all descendants of the previous Arch General. All of the Erbar line. Adriel is the direct descendant of the very first.'

'Is that unexpected?' Odi asked, chewing a fingernail. 'That is how royalty works in the human realms.'

'I don't know …' But something about it made Roh's skin crawl. She imagined the earlier ancestors of Adriel, passing the fanatical torch to their successors, without a means for intervention from outside the family. Even the cyren rulers had the Queen's Tournament to contend with every five decades, but if the ruler never changed, was there any cause to investigate the running of the other territories?

Mirrah appeared. 'Have you found what you were looking for?'

Roh got to her feet, snapping the book closed. 'Yes, thank you. I'll be borrowing this one.'

'Wonderful. Can I help you with anything else? We have some detailed literature about the history of cyren and human relations, if you're interested?' she offered, with a pointed look at Odi.

'I think we know enough about that,' Odi said sharply.

'As you say,' Mirrah said lightly.

'There is one more thing,' Roh interjected as she made to leave. 'Could you point us towards the books on The Dawning?'

'What era?'

'Uh … The Dawning that Delja won.'

'Hmm … Six centuries ago? That'll be in the Ancient Deep section.' Mirrah seemed to talk more to herself than to Roh or Odi, but she motioned for them to follow her up a narrow, spiral staircase at the back of the room. Once they were two levels above the main library, she wove in and out of shelves with a purposeful stride before stopping abruptly in front of an empty row.

'That's strange,' she murmured, frowning slightly.

'What is?' Odi asked.

A prickling sensation of unease awoke in Roh's gut. She met Mirrah's gaze. 'They're gone, aren't they?'

Mirrah's hand grazed the empty shelf, as though by

dragging her fingers through the dust that had settled there, she could determine the truth of the matter. 'Yes, but … there must be an explanation …' She strode off mid-sentence, towards a lectern at the back of the room. A thick register sat there, along with a handful of quills and a pot of ink.

'Of course,' she sighed, her shoulders sagging with relief. 'They're on loan.'

Odi snorted. 'All of them?'

Roh nudged him. 'Perhaps it's to a classroom …' But even as the words left her mouth, she recalled the promise she'd made to herself. She would not be an ignorant fool any longer.

She adjusted the crown of bones atop her head. 'Who borrowed them?' she asked slowly.

Mirrah shifted uncomfortably, trying to shield the register from Roh's view.

Roh didn't move. 'Who borrowed them?' she repeated, her voice edged with threat.

'I really shouldn't … This is a private document …'

Roh inhaled through her nose and folded her arms over her chest, waiting.

Mirrah caved. 'The queen – I mean, the former queen. They're currently housed in her private collection.'

Roh and Odi returned to their quarters, an unspoken concern pulsing between them. Why would Delja borrow *one of*, let alone *all* the books on The Dawning that she herself had witnessed first-hand? Was she writing her own account of the events? Was it research for some larger project? Surely a queen wouldn't need to do such things herself? Roh hadn't wanted to leave the library, convinced she would find something useful in the numerous tomes. But Odi had insisted that they go, particularly as Mirrah had extinguished the lamps. Tomorrow would be the fifth day of Adriel's mandatory prayers, and Roh needed to be well rested and ready. So, upon her return to the chambers, she sat with the others and spent the next few hours making calculations for their upcoming journey to Csilla. With help from the Jaktaren, she outlined the most effective route from Akoris to Csilla, and from Csilla to Lochloria on her map, relishing the scratch of the quill on parchment. The Arch General had prolonged her time here, but she was determined to use it well. With Yrsa and Finn, Roh had made lists of rations they'd require and had started stockpiling any food items that wouldn't spoil. She had even asked Deodan to scout the best horses in the stables, though the warlock hadn't made an appearance since the death chorus in the amphitheatre. With the exception of the horses, Roh knew they were as prepared as they could be for departure. She had used every spare minute she had to ensure it. And yet, she was restless.

Almost five days had passed, both in the blink of an eye and as though she were watching single grains of sand fall through an hourglass. The waiting gnawed at her. Deep in her gut, she knew that time would have its vengeance, be it by Adriel's hand … or by the gnash of the sea drake's fangs …

. . .

The fifth day arrived at last. Roh attended the morning worship, eagerly awaiting word from Adriel about the birthstone. None came. She reasoned that the day was not yet over, and so waited some more. With each passing hour, her frustration grew. She had played the Arch General's game dutifully, a test of her queenly patience, no doubt Adriel's attempt to slowly whittle away not only the time Roh had left to retrieve the other gems, but Roh's faith in herself as well. And though she had never been known for her patience, Roh had played admirably for her crown. Until now. She was done waiting. She needed to take action.

At the evening meal, as the Akorians succumbed to their inebriations, Roh approached Adriel at the dais, his oracles and their offspring taking their leave at once.

'You have had your five days,' Roh said by way of greeting.

Adriel's face lit up at her words, a genuine smile gracing it, highlighting his handsome features. 'You have done well, Rohesia. I applaud your efforts.'

Roh blinked. Was this the same Arch General she'd spoken to upon her arrival? There was true joy in his eyes, and he seemed genuinely happy that she had passed his test. Could it be that she had misjudged him?

She met his gaze, trying to mask any confusion she felt. 'The birthstone?' she enquired.

Adriel was already nodding. 'Indeed, indeed,' he said

thoughtfully, with no movement towards the topaz, which was where it had always been: around his neck.

Roh exhaled through her nose, dread creeping into her senses. She hadn't misjudged him. It was clear to her that Adriel *wanted* her to ask after the stone that hung in plain sight. She knew he revelled in seeing her conflicted over the thing she needed most, and in the fact that he was the one to hold it over her.

The Arch General laid a gentle hand on her shoulder, his eyes full of a strange earnestness. 'At the eleventh hour, come to my private oratory. I can explain the will of the goddesses to you there.' He smiled again, the sight utterly unnerving. 'You will have the birthstone. We shall see you upon the cyren throne.'

Later, Roh was completely lost in the giant monastery. Adriel's directions had scrambled in her mind and now she had no idea where she was. The only thing she was certain of was the fact that she was walking in circles, and that she practically scared the wits out of a passing porter.

'Excuse me!' Roh virtually shouted.

'Can I help you?' the porter asked.

Roh nodded. 'I need to see Adriel,' she said, knowing he had long since withdrawn from the drug-infused dancing of his people, wherever the refectory was.

'I'm afraid the Arch General has retired for the night.'

'I assure you, he's expecting me,' Roh told the cyren.

The cyren flushed. 'I …'

'Please,' Roh pressed. 'It's important.'

After quickly glancing around the halls, the porter abandoned her duties and motioned for Roh to follow. The poor cyren's movements were stiff with discomfort and she seemed to be permanently on the verge of saying something, but would press her lips together at the last moment.

'You won't get in trouble,' Roh told her, trying to soothe her anxieties. 'I'll make sure of it.'

'No, it's not that.'

'What, then?'

'I ...' But the porter blushed furiously and quickened her pace. 'He's expecting you?' she reconfirmed.

'Yes, but —'

'This way.'

After various staircases and twisting corridors, the porter brought Roh to the doors of Adriel's personal oratory. Roh didn't understand why the young cyren was behaving like this. Surely this was when Adriel was in his best mood? Once all the Akorians were sedated and pliable and he knew all their secrets? And *surely* he'd be glad to see Roh lusting after the topaz again?

Gripping the handle, the porter turned to Roh with a grimace. 'Are you sure you must speak with him now?' she asked again, her eyes lingering on Roh's crown.

'Yes,' Roh insisted. She had to get to the bottom of what in the realms the Arch General wanted. 'I'll join him in prayer if I have to,' she added, trying to ease the porter's concern by pressing a silver mark into her palm.

But the young cyren flushed deeply as she pushed the doors open and waited for Roh to enter.

Instantly, Roh understood the porter's unease.

Candlelight illuminated the space with a soft orange glow. At the far end of the room, Adriel was sprawled on a dark velvet lounge, utterly naked but for an open silk robe and the amulet holding the Mercy's Topaz, resting against his bare chest. Two naked young cyrens sat entwined at his feet, kissing, and another two Akorians were perched on either side of him, their limbs draped across the Arch General.

Roh froze, her feet suddenly rooted to the luscious carpet as the doors clicked closed behind her.

Adriel's gaze lifted to hers, utterly unabashed by his state of undress or the compromising position in which she'd found him. He made no move to cover himself. In fact, he seemed to enjoy that she could see every inch of him.

Roh refused to blush, refused to run for the doors. That was clearly what he wanted. Once again, this was all about power; it always was.

'It's the eleventh hour,' she announced unnecessarily, forcing her voice to remain steady.

'I know.' Adriel's mouth curved into a satisfied smile.

Roh's fists clenched at her sides. 'I've come for the birthstone.'

'I gathered as much.' His voice was as smooth as the silk draped across his body, his fingers curling around the amulet. 'I told you that it will be the will of the goddesses.'

'Somehow, I think the will of the goddesses and your own are entwined.'

Adriel laughed lightly and sat up, the cyrens' caresses falling away from his body. There was no denying the striking form of the Akorian leader as he moved towards her, but Roh kept her gaze at eye level, noting the hint of danger that lingered in his stare.

'I'm sure we can come to some sort of agreement,' he said when he reached her.

Roh narrowed her eyes. 'What are you implying?'

Adriel reached out, tucking a strand of loose hair behind her ear, his cold fingers brushing against her cheek. 'You know *exactly* what I'm implying,' he told her. 'I've never taken a bone cleaner before …'

'I'm not a bone cleaner anymore.' Roh refused to yield a step back.

'I've not taken a future Queen of Cyrens, either.'

'I'm not here to be *taken*,' she spat.

'Then why *are* you here, Rohesia?'

'For the topaz, as you're well aware.'

'And as I've suggested, there's a very simple way to get it.'

'I have completed your five days of prayer.'

'That's not what I was referring to.'

Roh knew exactly what the bastard was referring to, but she also knew full well that a single night with the Arch General would never be just a single night. It would be a decision that, should she become queen, would follow her for centuries in the form of blackmail and innuendo. Once made, it was a decision that she could never take back. *Never trust a cyren,* she'd told Odi countless times.

'A simple solution,' Adriel repeated. 'To obtain the topaz and all the possibilities that come with it.'

Trying her damnedest to quell the fury coursing through her, Roh retorted, 'Nothing is *simple* when it comes to you.'

Adriel was close enough that she could smell the sweet wine on his breath. 'I'll take that as a compliment,' he said.

'Don't. It's not meant as one.'

But Adriel's smug expression didn't falter. He leaned in, cupping the back of her head, and pressed a soft, wet kiss to her lips.

Roh didn't move, didn't recoil. She waited for him to pull back, letting every fibre of rage that had simmered within bubble to the surface. Adriel was a cyren who was used to getting what he wanted. That would end now.

'That was a mistake,' Roh told him, her voice icy, her talons unsheathed at her sides.

'The mistake will be *yours,* bone cleaner, if you don't stay. To defy me is to defy Dresmis and Thera. Together, we can make it near impossible for you to get the stone.'

In a crimson rage and a bloody blur of talons, Roh lost control. A strange note escaped her as the jagged points of her nails sliced through Adriel's skin and pierced his flesh. The Arch General staggered back with a cry of pain, clutching his face, blood leaking from a cut down his eye and several gashes across his chest.

Roh stalked towards him while the naked Akorians

fled the oratory. 'Do your worst, Adriel,' she said, her voice cold. 'Make this test for the topaz the hardest, most dangerous you can think of. Because you'd best believe that when I win, when the crown and its gems are mine, your time here will end.'

Blood had seeped into Adriel's mouth, lining his teeth. 'Do you think it wise, threatening the Arch General of Akoris?'

Roh made for the door, wiping her lips with the back of her hand in disgust. 'Wiser than the Arch General of Akoris threatening the future Queen of Cyrens. I will never forget this.'

Roh left the oratory, but her blinding fury refused to abate. It coursed hotly through her veins, pooling at the centre of her, where she feared it might take root for eternity. In all her seventeen years, she had never, *ever* been treated like that, not even as a lowly bone cleaner. Was *this* what went on here? Akoris was no doubt a place of eerie, ignorant ritual, but was *this* what lay at its core? Was this how the Erbar line had maintained its strength and position over the centuries? Adriel dripped with unchecked entitlement. He possessed the spoiled temperament of a child who lashed out when he was refused. She thought again of the oracles at his table.

His deeds will not go unpunished during my reign, Roh vowed.

By the time she reached the royal quarters, something else had bled into her anger. Panic. She had just threatened the one person who held the key to her future

...

'What is it?' Harlyn asked the second she saw Roh's face.

Roh pictured what she must look like: her cheeks drained of colour, her lower lip swollen from biting it so hard, the blood beneath her unsheathed talons.

'What happened?' her friend pressed.

Roh's insides went cold. The renewed friendship between them was fragile, like a wound that had scabbed over, but with one careless move could be ripped open again to bleed worse than before. What she'd just done … Daring Adriel to make things as difficult as possible … Could that irreparably shatter their friendship?

Sensing the tension, the others had also gathered around, though there was still no sign of Deodan. Finn's stare lingered on Roh's bloodstained talons.

'I did something,' she admitted.

'Did what?' Odi asked tentatively.

'I … I made things worse with Adriel.' She turned her hands over, so they could all see the red smears on her skin.

Finn considered her hands carefully. 'Did you kill him?'

Roh shook her head and flushed as she slowly told them what had unfolded.

Odi was the first to swear. He started to pace, running his hands through his hair, his brow furrowed with worry. 'Gods, Roh … You didn't have to —'

Roh's heart sank. It was as she feared. She should have placated Adriel somehow. At the very least, she shouldn't have bruised his clearly fragile ego. This position they were now in – it was all her fault.

But Yrsa was in Odi's space with one swift step. 'She didn't have to *what?*'

Odi blanched. Yrsa had never shown any aggression towards him before, but at that moment, her lilac eyes blazed with fire, her face mere inches away from his. 'I truly hope you're not suggesting that *Roh* should have changed *her* behaviour?' Yrsa's words were quiet.

'I ... I was just ...' Odi stammered. 'Could she not have at least flattered —'

Roh had never seen Yrsa so angry. 'There is only one way to deal with an attitude like that, and it's certainly not *flattery*,' the Jaktaren snapped. 'Frankly, I'm *shocked* to hear those notions from *your* mouth. I thought you were better than that.' Yrsa surveyed the group with authority, her stare full of challenge. 'I think we can all agree that it was the Arch General's actions that were despicable and that Roh did what she needed to do.'

To Roh's surprise, Finn nodded vigorously, his own talons unsheathed and twitching at his sides. She had expected him to lose his temper with her, to tell her she'd acted rashly and put them all in more danger than she ever had before. But his stance was clear. He stood with Yrsa, and therefore he stood with her, and for that she was grateful.

Roh sought Harlyn's reaction. Her childhood friend had arguably been the one impacted and hurt the worst as a result of Roh's actions. And just as their relationship had started to mend, Roh had lit a fire beneath it once more. Roh swallowed the lump in her throat as Harlyn lifted her gaze.

'Absolutely. Roh did what she had to,' she said, her eyes lustrous. 'Now, do we storm Adriel's oratory, or what?'

Roh gave a tired smile and ran her fingers through her hair. 'I'd like to get out of this godsforsaken monastery, even if it's just for an hour.'

To her right, Yrsa nodded. 'I know just the place,' she said.

CHAPTER FIFTEEN

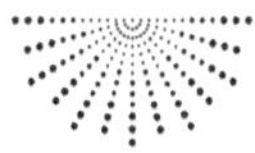

Beyond the great dunes, the sea caves off the coast of Akoris were vast, as though an ancient beast had long ago carved its way through the rock. Glowing algae illuminated the treacherous path in, casting a lavender hue across the jagged edges and sprawling ceilings.

'What are we doing here?' Roh hissed at Yrsa, who'd whisked them away from the monastery. The crash of the waves outside echoed through the caves, the odd shaft of moonlight beaming down through a crack above.

'Yes, Yrsa, what *are* we doing here?' Finn muttered unhappily. 'We shouldn't be bringing *them* here.'

That piqued Roh's interest as she stumbled across the uneven terrain and deep puddles of stagnant water. 'What's here?' she pressed, more to annoy Finn than anything else.

She could hear the smile in Yrsa's voice as she said, 'A sanctuary.'

Roh snorted. 'You and I have very different understandings of the term, in that case.'

'Just wait,' Yrsa replied, motioning for them to keep up. 'The Jaktaren need places to … recover … from their journeys from time to time,' she offered as the cave began to open up.

'*Yrsa*,' Finn warned, his voice low.

She waved him away. 'Over the years, we've learned to get … creative. We've stockpiled all over the realms, for emergencies.'

'Yrsa,' Finn snapped.

She gave him a pointed look. 'If the Arch General propositioning our future queen in exchange for a gemstone isn't an emergency, I don't know what is.'

Roh heard Finn click his tongue in frustration, but he objected no more.

There was a tap on Roh's shoulder and Odi's voice sounded. 'Roh …?'

Her body tensed. Something had soured between them. Roh sifted through the anger that had settled at the pit of her stomach. What he'd said, his reaction to what had happened … It had been wrong, hadn't it? Yrsa's retaliation had told Roh as much, and yet … She couldn't articulate the infuriating lack of control over her feelings. She had no precise words for the rage-inducing sense of injustice that had tightened around her at the shifting of blame. And so, she didn't turn back to hear what her friend had to say. She was no longer interested.

'In here,' Yrsa called, ducking through a narrow fissure.

Roh followed after Finn and gasped at what awaited her on the other side. A grotto illuminated by glowing coral, like what she'd seen in the serpent's nest, with a small pool in the centre. To one side, rocks had been moved to form a long table, where Yrsa was now standing, a wide grin on her face as she lifted numerous bottles from beneath.

'What's your poison?' she said, wriggling a metal goblet at Roh.

'You mean to tell me …' Harlyn caught up, hugging her injured arm to her body and taking in the surroundings with wide eyes. 'That when the good cyrens of Saddoriel think their most prestigious guild is off finding music for the lair, the Jaktaren are just getting drunk in a cave?'

There was a loud pop as Finn uncorked a large green bottle. 'Sometimes we swim too.' He smirked, lifting the bottle to his lips.

Roh met Harlyn's gaze and shook her head. 'So much for *sacred is the ledger.*'

'That doesn't mean what you think it does,' Finn said, his eyes darkening.

'It doesn't?' Roh challenged.

'Not when Yrsa and I say it.'

'Sure. What does it mean, then?'

'None of your business.'

Roh snorted. 'Typical.'

'It's our own code,' Yrsa explained, ignoring Finn's outraged expression. 'We repurposed the guild's pledge for our own years ago, when we realised the Jaktaren were not everything we had been led to believe.'

'Yrsa!' Finn objected loudly. 'That's not for them to know.'

But Yrsa shrugged and pressed a cool goblet into Roh's hand with a wink. 'Roh and I share a few secrets here and there,' she said.

At that, Roh couldn't help but feel lighter than she had in a long time, the weight of everything falling away momentarily. For once, she wasn't on the outside, though she made a mental note to ask Yrsa more about this so-called repurposed pledge later.

'Roh.' Odi's voice brought her right back down to reality. 'Can we talk?'

For the first time since the human's unexpected comments, Roh met his gaze, and at last, let her hurt and disappointment show. 'I don't have anything to say to you,' she said tersely, turning away.

Odi blocked her, stepping right into her path. 'But I have something to say to you – please?'

Roh stopped herself from glancing at Harlyn and the others; she simply waited.

Odi took the opportunity. 'Where I'm from,' he told her, 'folk are quick to blame a woman for a man's actions.'

Roh's blood began to boil.

'It's not something I have ever agreed with,' Odi rushed. 'Though I understand now that my reaction to your tale said otherwise. You are never, nor should you ever be, accountable for someone else's disgusting behaviour. It's not your responsibility to placate a temper or protect an ego. It's just not. I'm sorry, Roh. Deeply sorry. We are friends, you and I … And I should have had your back, as everyone else did.'

The only other sound in the cave was the dripping of water from the ceiling. Odi's words hung between them all, his amber eyes full of earnestness, his plea for forgiveness as plain as day.

Roh didn't have the energy to hold on to her rage, and she knew that she too had learned many things since she'd left the lair. She had learned that sometimes, not everything someone was taught from infancy was the truth of the matter. Odi wasn't a bad person. In fact, for the most part, he'd been better to her than she deserved. Slowly, she nodded, before turning to the others.

'I didn't thank you,' she said, her voice quiet but firm. 'Odi's right. You had my back, *all* of you.' She found herself looking at Finn. 'Even you … I never thought I'd see the day that you would defend a lowly bone cleaner.'

A strange look crossed the Jaktaren's face. 'There's a lot you don't know about me,' he muttered, crossing to where Yrsa had unpacked an array of liquor choices.

Roh started after him. 'I didn't mean —' She stopped herself. What *had* she meant by that comment? 'You're right,' she admitted, standing before him as he studied the labels on various bottles. 'I don't know you at all.' Roh cursed herself. She'd made a mess of things, as usual. 'What I meant to say was: *thank you.*'

'But you're surprised?' he asked in earnest.

'I was,' Roh told him honestly.

He met her gaze, seemingly startled at her candour. 'I

was raised alongside Yrsa,' he told her. 'You weren't aware of that, were you?'

With a sideways glance towards Yrsa, Roh shook her head.

Finn nodded, more to himself than her. 'Her aunt Winslow had more to do with my upbringing than Taro or Bloodwyn.'

Taro or Bloodwyn ... Not Mama and Pa ...

'So you see, being raised by and alongside formidable female cyrens makes you understand the realms more clearly. And their injustices.'

Yrsa gave an exasperated groan. '*Finn*, we came here to have *fun*.' Then she gave him a shove.

'I'm not sure he knows how,' Roh quipped without thinking.

'Fine,' Finn said, a glimmer of mischief crossing his face before he took a long swig of amber-coloured liquor. 'Let's see if the gem hunter has what it takes.'

Roh frowned at the new nickname, though she supposed it was better than *bone cleaner*. 'Has what it takes for *what*?'

Yrsa grinned. 'You'll wish you never asked.'

But Finn was already making for a narrow stone pathway that inclined up the side of the cave. 'Come on, then,' he challenged.

With no idea what she was doing, Roh swiped a bottle from the stone and drank deeply before charging after the arrogant Jaktaren. Whatever she'd drunk heated her from within and her calves burned as she climbed the slippery stone steps taking her higher and higher above the pool. She tried not to look down.

At the top, Finn was waiting expectantly, one eyebrow cocked. 'Well?'

'Well what?'

He moved aside, revealing a dizzying drop to the water below. 'Do you dare?'

Tentatively, Roh leaned over, taking in the horrendous height. 'Are you mad?' she asked, before immediately regretting her choice of words.

Finn didn't comment on madness of any sort. He simply watched as Roh peered down, way down, to the glistening black pool.

How deep is it? What if I hit the bottom and break my legs? Or my neck? Roh didn't even know why she was considering it. Her heart thumped in a quickening percussion as she shuffled closer to the edge for a better look.

'Long drop,' Finn drawled from beside her.

'Has that stopped you?' she asked.

'Nothing stops me.' Finn was at the edge in an instant, not even pausing to remove his boots.

Trying to prevent herself from shaking, Roh pushed her own boots off at the heel. She *knew* there was bravery in *not* bowing to peer pressure, that to simply walk away would demonstrate her unyielding willpower just as much as, if not *more* than jumping would, but … Her skin was tingling with anticipation. As scared as she was, she'd never done something like this before, and she might never get the chance to again. And what bigger regret could she have than to look back and wish differently?

The rocks were cold and wet against the bare soles of her feet as the echoes of Yrsa, Odi and Harlyn's voices trailed up the cave walls and bounced off the ceiling.

Roh turned to Finn. 'Well?' she said, letting her gaze glimmer with challenge. 'Highborns first.'

The corner of Finn's mouth tugged upwards. He reached out, offering her his hand. 'How about together?'

Whatever Roh had been expecting, it hadn't been *this*. She stared at his upturned palm, the callused skin littered with fine, pale scars. She half anticipated that he'd pull it away the moment she moved, but he waited, his hand steady and patient, until at last, she slid her fingers through his.

Lightning bolted through her as her rough skin brushed against his, his grip warm and firm.

Trying to ignore the hitch in her breathing, she didn't look at him as she said, 'On my count?'

'As you like.'

She inhaled deeply. 'One.' She took another step towards the edge. 'Two.' She squared her shoulders, her focus homing in on the utterly surreal sensation of holding the Jaktaren's hand. She couldn't take it anymore. 'Three.'

They leaped.

For the briefest of seconds, Roh was suspended midair, relishing the liberation of momentary weightlessness, of her legs kicking empty space below her. And then she fell. A shriek was ripped from her lungs as she and Finn plummeted from the ridge, her stomach and heart lodged in her throat. Her hand tightened around Finn's as the gap between them and the pool closed fast. Her feet hit the icy water first and then she was plunging into its dark depths. Finn's fingers sprang free of hers.

With a flick of her wrist, Roh bent the water to her will, propelling herself upwards, where she broke the surface with an exhilarated gasp. Blood roared in her ears as she met Finn's lilac gaze.

She grinned. 'Let's do that again.'

For the next hour, Roh, Finn, Yrsa and Odi took turns jumping from the cliff, while Harlyn cheered them on from below, amidst fast-emptying bottles. Roh couldn't remember the last time she'd felt so free, or the last time her cheeks had hurt so much from smiling. Even during normal life, days like these were few and far between as a bone cleaner of Saddoriel.

She collapsed beside Harlyn, who, despite her sling and being unable to join in, had the same glint of glee in her eyes as Roh. Although, Harlyn's were slightly more glazed over.

'Not much for poor little me to do but drink while you lot are cliff diving ...' She gave a sheepish, slanted smile.

Roh laughed as she wrung out her hair. 'I can see that.'

'Orson would love this,' Harlyn sighed.

Roh tensed, readying herself for an incoming slight,

but there was none. Harlyn was simply making an observation, expressing how she missed their friend, as Roh did.

Roh found herself smiling. 'She'd object a hundred times first.'

'*It's too dangerous.*' Harlyn mimicked Orson's voice when it was high-pitched with worry.

Roh added her own impression. '*Ames is due back any minute now.*'

'*You two will be the death of me!*' Harlyn snorted.

A shout sounded and seconds later, a wave of water hit them, drenching them both as Odi broke the surface of the pool, already laughing.

'Didn't want you to miss out, Har,' he said as he lurched from the water, his clothes completely drenched.

Harlyn swore, though there was no real anger in her voice. She took off her sling and squeezed the water from it with one hand. 'When you fools stop jumping like maniacs, I'll have a swim about. Incana said that's one of the best ways to rebuild my strength.'

With a suddenly serious nod, Odi cupped his hands to his mouth and lifted his chin to where Yrsa and Finn stood high above. 'Oi, you two!' he shouted. 'Last jump! Harlyn wants to swim.'

'I can speak for myself, thanks,' Harlyn retorted, though her expression was more of amusement than annoyance.

Odi didn't miss a beat. 'You're welcome,' he quipped, swiping the bottle Roh was holding and taking a long swig. He coughed, wrinkling his nose in disgust as he wiped his mouth with his hand.

'Urgh,' he cried. 'What *is* that?'

Roh gave him a smug smile as she snatched back the bottle and took a drink herself. She didn't know what it was, but she quite liked the sour flavour and tang of citrus. And she definitely liked how it loosened her limbs and quietened her mind.

'Did anyone tell Deodan where we were going?' Odi asked as Yrsa and Finn emerged dripping from the pool.

Roh shook her head. 'He hasn't been around much since ...' She trailed off, the sound of the death chorus and the pile of bones flooding back to her. 'He ... I think he knew the man who was killed,' she explained. 'It must have hit him quite hard.'

'I don't trust the warlock,' Finn cut in, his eyes ruthless and his face all hard lines.

Odi rolled his eyes. *'We know.'*

There was an exasperated sound from the water's edge, where Harlyn was wading in. 'Don't let your tempers get the better of you as soon as I start to enjoy myself.'

Roh gave the empty bottles a pointed look. 'You've been enjoying yourself plenty.'

Harlyn laughed gleefully and dived under, the sound breaking through any remaining tension between them.

Yrsa lifted a fresh bottle to Roh, her eyes aglow with mischief. 'More wine?'

.   .   .

Their time in the caves had to come to an end eventually, and as soon as they stepped foot back on the monastery grounds, a sombreness settled over Roh and her companions. The liquor filled her with restless anxiety, and as more and more statues of the goddesses came into view, dread latched its claws into her. Suddenly, the laughter that had burst from her in the sea caves seemed far away.

The Akorians must be in the temple, she guessed, as they wandered through the empty grounds, their steps falling in time to the beat of the drums in the distance. For a moment, Roh wondered about the drummers, realising she hadn't given them a second thought since arriving. Were they human, as the musicians in Saddoriel were? Hunted down in the human realms and forced into musical slavery for the good of cyrenkind? She thought of Odi's stepbrothers, Mason and Brooks, their faces lined with exhaustion and grief, trapped in a cage of bones ... And yet she couldn't help it. Amidst the pulsating drums of Akoris, she longed for the music of Saddoriel, the rising and falling notes of the fiddle and the harp, the intricate melodies and the way the songs nestled into her chest, filling whatever cracks had formed there.

What does that make me? The question silenced all other thoughts in her mind and hung in the empty space there, demanding to be heard, demanding to be felt. Though she had tried not to, she had thought of the death chorus often since she'd witnessed its devastating effect. Roh had seen the evidence of it all her life, actively participated in the process that came after, but she'd never *understood*, not really. Even now, the thought of it brought bile back up her throat. For her whole life, she had been desperate for the moment she found her deathsong, the very thing that made her a cyren. But to find her deathsong was to do what those Akorians had done to that human. To find her deathsong was to add to the bones of Saddoriel, wasn't it?

As they entered the monastery, a familiar scent filled Roh's nostrils – the sweet, delicate aroma of Deodan's pipe. Sure enough, as they rounded a corner, the warlock was there, sitting on the floor, puffing on his pipe with his long legs stretched out.

'Where have you been?' he asked them, not moving, but noting the damp ends of their hair.

'We should ask you the same thing,' Finn retorted sharply.

'Here and there.' Deodan blew a stream of smoke in the Jaktaren's direction.

Finn rolled his eyes and kept walking, clearly content to let the warlock wallow. Roh wasn't as easily deterred.

'Are you alright?' she asked, the image of that human before the death chorus filling her mind.

Deodan looked from Roh to the others and shrugged, trying and failing to appear nonchalant.

Roh had never lost someone, not in the same acute sense – she had never known her father, nor her mother, really. But she counted herself incredibly lucky that she'd not experienced a deep sense of grief, which was why she turned to Harlyn, Odi and Yrsa.

'I'll meet you back at our quarters,' she said, a polite dismissal.

Odi looked like he meant to argue, but Harlyn pulled him along.

When they were gone, Roh offered the warlock her hand. 'You can't sit here forever. You'll likely get trampled as soon as the prayer session ends.'

Deodan huffed a laugh and put his pipe between his teeth, grasping her hand in his and allowing Roh to help him up.

'I'm sorry,' Roh told him as they walked.

'What for?' Deodan asked without looking at her.

'About your friend,' she said.

There was the briefest of pauses before Deodan replied, 'Thank you.' He continued walking, although not in the direction of their chambers.

Roh fell into step beside him. 'Where are we going?'

'There's something I want to show you.'

Deodan led her along the main passageway, before pulling her down another narrow corridor, twisting and turning so frequently that she was reminded of the lair back home. The passageway was darker than the rest; far fewer sconces lined the walls and there were no windows. Roh couldn't remember taking any stairs to a lower level, but that was where she was: underneath the monastery.

'Where are we going?' she whispered again.

But Deodan didn't reply. He simply kept walking briskly, his cloak flapping behind him.

Only when Roh was well and truly disorientated did

Deodan stop. They were still in a narrow corridor, nothing significant around them except for a small statue of Dresmis and Thera, wings outstretched between them, creating an archway.

Her impatience growing by the minute, Roh had opened her mouth to snap at Deodan when she saw him pull the quartz dagger from his belt.

Roh's blood ran cold. If she hadn't suspected what they were doing was wrong before, her instincts were screaming at her now to run. But she couldn't. Her feet were rooted to the ground and she couldn't take her eyes away from the dagger as Deodan ran a callused hand across the wall beneath the arch and slid the blade of quartz into an unseen lock.

'What are you doing?' she breathed, a wave of goosebumps rushing across her arms as she heard a click from beyond the stone.

Before her eyes, the wall crumbled to dust, and taking a dazed step forward, she gasped at what she saw.

Because she'd seen it before.

Or at least she thought she had, but as Deodan pulled her into the cavernous space by the elbow, the stone reappearing in place behind them, Roh realised it was different.

The Pool of Weeping. Or rather, a smaller version of the one back in Saddoriel. Thick moss carpeted the ground, springing beneath her boots. The drumming was quieter here, a faint rhythmic tapping rather than the pulsating, chest-pounding beat of the main monastery. Even that seemed to fade away as she scanned the grotto before her.

Just like in Saddoriel, the ceiling was vast, looming over an icy-blue pool, though there were no stalactites hanging like knives above. It was the size of a large pond compared to the great pool she had seen in her home lair, and yet it was surrounded by the same weeping willows, whose leaves dangled into the rippling water.

'What are we doing here, Deodan?' she asked in a low voice, releasing his hand.

Deodan smiled. 'I take it from your nervous tone that you've seen the one in Saddoriel, the mother source?'

'I didn't *mean* to. Odi got lost and I —'

Deodan placed a hand solemnly over his heart. 'I won't tell a soul.'

Roh rolled her eyes. 'But … what is this place, then?'

'It's the mirror pool for Akoris. Each of the cyren territories has one. Didn't you learn of them in your lessons?'

Roh shook her head. Surely she'd remember that?

'Hmm … I guess they've stopped teaching those details,' Deodan said, scratching the stubble at his chin.

'Well, how do *you* know of them?'

'Remember that alliance I spoke of? Cyrens and water warlocks used to share information and magic freely. Our kind continues to teach both old and new ways. Cyrens, it seems, have moved to a far more restrictive curriculum.'

'Do you mean …?'

'Do I mean there are things the Council of Seven Elders would rather its own people remained ignorant of? You have the answer to that.'

Roh tried to rub the chill from her arms. She'd known it all too well since leaving Saddoriel. The empty shelf in the Akorian library came to mind. The death chorus on the defenceless human. The wet press of Adriel's lips on hers. Yes, there were a great many things the council would want unknown.

As though reading her thoughts, Deodan nodded. 'A good thing to be aware of as a potential queen.'

'*Future* queen,' Roh corrected, though whether she said it for his education or her own reinforcement, she wasn't sure.

Deodan bowed his head. 'My apologies.'

Roh stuffed her hands in her pockets. 'I take it we're not meant to be here?' she said.

'Not strictly speaking, no. But I'm gathering supplies,' he told her, fumbling with the pouch at his belt and producing several empty vials.

Roh jolted. 'You can't —'

But Deodan went to the water's edge with no hesitation and crouched on the stony bank, lowering the first vial to the rippling surface. Roh didn't know what she expected to happen, especially since every instinct in her was telling her to leave the water alone, to get as far away from this eerie place as possible. But the liquid flowed easily into the glass vial and nothing happened. Roh watched Deodan uneasily as he refilled several containers, slipping them back into his pouch with soft clinks. Unlike in Saddoriel, there was no one else here. No robed figure came to sacrifice an infant's first tears.

She went to the warrior warlock, crouching at his side

and watching him refill his next vial, his supply seemingly endless. 'So … This isn't the same as the one in Saddoriel?'

Deodan shook his head as he pushed the cork in. 'It's a mirror pool, less powerful than the mother source,' he told her. 'Akoris, Csilla and Lochloria all have one for the First Cry. Can't have every nestling born taken to Saddoriel – they'd be fledglings by the time they got there. Of course, the pools have other uses.'

'Such as?'

Deodan gave a casual shrug. 'Selective transport. For the council and the ruler. You can't expect the likes of them to go trekking across the realms, can you? Each pool acts as a portal. Though, I can't imagine that information will sit well with you at the moment.'

It certainly didn't. The near-endless trek across the shores of the Five Daughters, the perilous ascent of the cliffs, the skirmish in the gilded plains and the teerah panther attack … it all came back in a quick succession of images, tinged red with fury. There had been an alternative to all that?

But something caught her eye on the far end of the pool: an iron basket of sorts, raised high on a plinth, its bowl engraved with lines of Old Saddorien, filled with what looked like hay …

'What is that?' Roh pointed to the strange feature.

Deodan followed the line of her finger. 'Ah, that. It's a war beacon, a fire to be lit on the precipice of conflict against your kind. A cyren call to arms. There is one at every pool, and smaller ones all around the cyren territories. When one is lit, the rest around the realms catch ablaze with blue flame, alerting cyrens to the fact that somewhere, they are under attack. The action opens up the mirror pools and allows the cyren armies to be transported to the original source, wherever conflict lies. They haven't been lit since the Age of Chaos – not to my knowledge, anyway.'

Roh's talons and scales tingled in the wake of such a revelation. 'I didn't see one in Saddoriel,' she said at last, still staring at the strange beacon across the water.

'Doesn't mean it's not there, does it? Have a look in those books of yours,' he said. 'You're bound to come across information there. It was long before your time, and mine, but from what I know, it was a great source of pride for your lot. I suppose they're kept even now as a reminder of the unity and strength of cyrenkind ... Or some rubbish like that.'

'Why are there no guards?' Roh was confused as to why such an important place didn't have proper surveillance.

'The pool guards itself,' Deodan murmured, gazing into the icy water.

Roh glanced around. 'It's doing nothing to stop you stealing,' she pointed out.

Deodan trailed his fingers across the surface of the water, watching it ripple outwards. 'Water always recognises its own.' He said it more to himself than to Roh.

'How do you know so much about our kind and our

culture?' she pressed. 'How are you even able to have access to this pool?'

'I certainly don't have *official* access …' Deodan gave a quiet laugh.

'But Adriel is aware that you take from the pools. He said as much when we first got here.'

'Adriel and I, we have a certain … understanding. He allows me to dabble in the sacred pool discreetly and I placate the masses who would oppose him. For now.'

Goosebumps rushed across Roh's skin as the Arch General's name left Deodan's lips.

'Did you know about Adriel?' she asked. 'Before we came here? Did you know what he might try to do?' Deodan hadn't been there when she'd told the others, but the implication was enough.

Deodan's gaze lifted to hers, realisation darkening his eyes. That look alone told Roh all she needed to know.

'I had a feeling. I tried to warn you.'

'Tried?'

'I told you he had a reputation.'

'You could have been a little more specific.'

'Would it have changed anything? I knew you could handle yourself.'

'How?' Roh snapped. 'How could you have known that? I was easily captured by your patrol. You knew I had no deathsong. You knew I couldn't fight.'

'But you can now.'

Roh hadn't realised her talons were out, nor that she was standing in the combat position, feet apart, arms raised. 'That's not the point,' she said. The anger was bitter on her tongue, but she took a step back and lowered her fists with a sigh. 'Who would oppose Adriel, anyway? Seems to me everyone here is rather subdued.'

'You'd be surprised, Queen of Bones. Though I fear the little agreement the Arch General and I share may soon reach its natural end.'

'What does that mean?'

Deodan shrugged. 'Adriel stays locked away in his monastery with his oracles and his worshippers and incense for company. He has no true awareness of the dissent that stirs. He chose his path long ago. It will soon be time for me to choose mine. Leaving him to his vices has been part of a longer strategy.'

Roh gave a dark laugh. 'You should meet my mentor, Ames,' she said. 'You and he both seem to have a fondness for being cryptic.'

'Ames, you say?' A strange expression passed across Deodan's face, but he merely checked a cork in one of his vials and looked out across the glassy pool. 'Tell me something,' he said.

'What?'

'Didn't you wonder more about the enchantment – the lullaby we spoke of?'

Hush, hush, little cyren, listen to my call, For under these starless nights, we let no tears fall ... The tune was on Roh in an instant, though in truth, she had forgotten about it. A lullaby from her infancy had hardly seemed like a priority amidst the rest. But now ...

'What do you mean?' she asked.

'Here of all places, I thought you'd put it together.'

Roh folded her arms around her middle against the sudden chill. *What is he talking about? What am I missing?* She glanced around, searching for clues, taking in the inky darkness of the ceiling and how the water continued to ripple, even though there was no disturbance to its surface but for the fronds of the willow trees.

Whatever Deodan wanted her to realise was on the tip of her tongue, and yet … She couldn't make sense of it. 'I …'

'Why stop a nestling from crying, besides the obvious? Why use *warlock magic*, of all things, to do it? In Saddoriel, of all places? That's a big risk, no?' Deodan prompted. 'Your birth was long after the Scouring, Roh. To use warlock magic in such a way would be treason.' He watched her all too keenly, waiting for the pieces to fall into place.

Roh's skin prickled as the memory of an infant's cry in Saddoriel pierced her mind and she recalled the hooded figure carrying the crying nestling, holding them over the water like a sacrifice.

'Cerys …' Roh shook her head, remembering her mother manic in her cell and dismissing the thought. '*Someone* didn't want me to cry …' Roh's voice was suddenly hoarse. 'Someone didn't want my tears in the Pool of Weeping …?'

'And there it is,' Deodan murmured, satisfied.

Roh's insides felt like a sack of vipers, with dozens sliding around uncomfortably in her gut. 'But why?'

'The First Cry is something all cyrens share, yes?'

Roh nodded.

'Someone wanted you to be different.'

Roh felt the cogs turning in her mind. 'They didn't want my sacrifice to the gods because I'm … an *isruhe*,' she realised aloud.

Deodan shook his head in frustration. 'You let that word have too much power over you.'

'Then what?' Roh snapped.

The water warlock shrugged, his attention returning to the numerous vials he held. 'This may shock you, but I don't know *everything*.'

'Then what *do* you know?'

'I know that you've started to question where you're from and what you've been taught. I know it's time cyrenkind had a leader capable of such reflections. And I know that you'll have more questions than answers before the end.'

Roh suppressed a shudder. So, someone had *potentially* interfered with the most sacred ritual of cyrenkind, the one thing she'd had in common with every Saddorien. What did it mean if a cyren's tears never touched the Pool of Weeping? Did that mean there was something fundamentally wrong with her? The questions tightened in her mind, like a tangled ball of twine, worsening the more she tried to unravel it.

Desperate for some kind of mental anchor, Roh's eyes snagged on the quartz dagger that Deodan had carelessly left sitting atop the pebbled shore. She bent to pick it up, finding it far heavier in her hands than she'd expected, and resisted the urge to run her finger across the clouded, rose-tinged blade.

A name chimed through her like a bell. 'Who's Eadric?' she asked, not taking her eyes from the dagger.

'Someone long gone,' Deodan told her. 'A legend amongst our clans.'

'You didn't know him?'

The warlock shook his head. 'I heard the stories – every child of my generation did. It's largely thanks to him that we still exist. He was the first of the warriors.'

That caught Roh's attention. The first of the new race of water warlocks? She twirled the dagger between her fingers as Deodan himself had done once, waiting for him to continue. But he was silent.

She ground her teeth. Getting information from anyone or anything was like getting blood from a stone, lately. She persevered. 'How did you know to use the dagger to get in? It's been in the Saddorien prison for as long as I can remember.'

Deodan smiled. 'You forget who created these pools to begin with.'

'The water warlocks?'

'Yes, the water warlocks.'

Stones crunched behind them. 'And you, Deodan, forget who has kept them ever since,' Adriel said.

Roh lost her balance on the wet bank, her heart pounding in her throat. Deodan's arm shot out, gripping her elbow and steadying her, pulling her to her feet and slipping the dagger from her grasp as they both faced the Akorian leader. A nasty gash had scabbed across his eye, and the deep V of his jacket revealed a bare chest beneath, where ragged slices were also scabbed over. Roh frowned, realising that he'd chosen not to have a healer tend him, nor was he making any effort to cover them up. He wanted her, and more importantly, everyone else, to see what she'd done to him, to show all of Akoris what a monster she truly was.

'Admiring your handiwork?' he asked, his mouth quirked in a knowing smile.

Deodan glanced in her direction, shock rippling as he realised the wounds were her doing.

'Weren't you told, warlock? Your little Queen of Bones has a violent temperament,' the Arch General said, his voice laced with dark amusement.

Deodan tore his gaze away from Roh and forced a shrug. 'Such is the nature of all cyrens. She's truly a queen to be, it seems.'

'The goddesses tell me we'll find out soon enough.' Adriel's smirk was serpentine now and Roh knew she was about to discover something she would wish to unlearn.

Adriel took a step towards the water's edge. 'They led me here,' he said.

Roh had to bite the inside of her cheek to keep from scoffing. No deity would stoop low enough to converse with the slimy Arch General, of that much she was sure.

Adriel has eyes and ears everywhere. Deodan's words from their first night in the monastery came back to her and she did not doubt them for a second. Her skin had crawled on more than one occasion in these parts.

But Adriel spoke calmly, as though they had all the time in the world to discuss whatever came next, as though the last time he'd seen Roh, she hadn't raked her talons through his flesh.

His gaze went to Deodan, nostrils flaring. 'I'm not surprised at what I find.'

'You know I can't help myself, Adriel,' Deodan replied, the vials he had been holding nowhere in sight.

'But this time you have brought the bone cleaner, the potential future Queen of Cyrens, along with you. Must she witness your depravity?'

As opposed to yours? Roh nearly said.

Deodan merely shrugged. 'Roh should know how the territories are run, don't you agree? It looks like she might have uncovered how you manage your own affairs, Adriel,' he said, with a pointed look at the Arch General's wounds. 'Seems to me as though she was more than a little displeased at the discovery.'

Adriel huffed a laugh. 'What pleases or doesn't please a *bone cleaner* is no concern of mine. My concern is, and always is, the will of the gods.'

It was Roh's turn to laugh, the sound dark and rich and unlike any she'd made before now. 'Your concern is, and always is, yourself,' she spat. 'And I will not be discussed as though I'm not here.'

The bow that Adriel sketched mocked her as his glimmering eyes raked greedily over her.

The white-hot rage within that had seen her talons pierce his flesh hummed in her ears again.

But the Arch General straightened and adjusted his jacket. 'Of course, Rohesia. I simply sought you out to deliver the news personally.'

Roh's blood went cold. 'The news?'

'The goddesses have spoken. They have decided how you are to prove your worthiness of the Mercy's Topaz.'

As if it could hear its name on his tongue, the stone gleamed at Adriel's sternum.

Roh took a step towards the Akorian leader, fighting every urge to unsheathe her talons and drag them across his face a second time. 'How?' was all she said.

She heard Deodan's intake of breath behind her, but Roh waited.

'You are to partake in the Rite of Strothos.'

Although she wasn't sure what that was, Roh knew whatever came next would be a nightmare incarnate, because she had made it so.

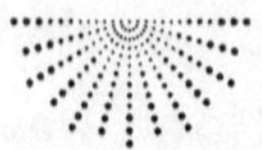

CHAPTER SIXTEEN

'I don't like this,' were the first words from Harlyn's mouth when Roh returned to their quarters and told the others what was required of her to get the birthstone.

In the carpeted foyer, Harlyn, Odi, Finn and Yrsa stood waiting for further explanation, a proposed plan of attack, *anything* that could get Roh out of Adriel's trap. The desperation was clear in both Harlyn and Odi's eyes. But she didn't have anything to offer them, and even Deodan was quiet at her side.

'I can't say I'm all that keen on it, either,' Roh said finally, trying to keep her voice light.

Harlyn ignored her. 'Orson would hate it.'

'Orson didn't want me to do this in the first place.'

Harlyn grabbed her hand, suddenly. 'Because she *loves* you. Because she doesn't want you to die. I wish she was here, if only to help me convince you not to do this.'

Roh wished Harlyn wouldn't bring Orson into it,

especially not in front of Yrsa, Finn and Deodan. They didn't know Orson, didn't know who she was to the two bone cleaners, and it was Roh's fault she wasn't with them now; that fact would never be forgotten.

'There's something not right about this,' Finn interjected. 'There's something he's not telling you.'

Roh knew this, of course. She'd known from the moment she'd seen Adriel's oily smile that there would be something more to the *rite* than simply publicly retrieving the gem from a special pond. Why it was called the Rite of Strothos, she had no idea, and nor did the others, though Deodan had been oddly tight-lipped since leaving the Pool of Weeping. Roh would wager all her bronze keys to Jesmond that he knew more than he was letting on, as always.

Deodan nodded. 'There will *always* be something Adriel's not telling us. And we'll be in the dark until he cares to shed the light.'

'You're encouraging Roh to do this?' Odi blurted out, rage filling his amber eyes.

'I'm encouraging Roh to make her own decision,' Deodan said.

'We are *all* encouraging Roh to make her own decision,' Yrsa said, her voice blanketing over the rest, calming them. Roh hadn't failed to notice that the Jaktaren often had this effect on the turmoil within their group.

Roh felt trapped, as though the walls of the forbidden room were closing in on her again, only this time, she didn't know how to stop them, and she was the one panicking. The ritual Adriel had suggested ... It terrified her. Frustrated, she threw her hands in the air and went to the next room, slumping into an armchair, her whole body caving inwards.

'What if I *don't* do it? What then? We steal the stone? We kill Adriel? We start an Akorian riot? Or perhaps it forfeits my place in this absurd tournament altogether? Am I the only one who sees that there is no other way to get the stone? No other way that gives us the time and freedom we need to obtain the Gauntlet Ruby and the Willow's Sapphire from the other territories as well?'

The others said nothing and defeat sank through her like blood through sand.

'The Rite of Strothos ... Who knows what it'll do to me,' she whispered.

It was Deodan, then, who knelt before her, his warm hands gripping her upper arms. 'You have to feel a connection to who you are *and* what you want, to come back from something like this. If you do, then the stone is yours.'

Her eyes went to his, the blue-grey gaze holding fast with nothing but unwavering faith.

'How can you be sure?' Roh asked, a hollowness yawning wide within.

'Because ...' Deodan's hand rummaged at his side. He produced a leather sheath, with a plaited strap and silver buckle. Pressing it into Roh's hands, he tapped the slender ivory handle protruding from it. 'You'll have this,' he told her.

Roh weighed the piece in her hands and slowly slid

the quartz dagger from its sheath. It felt heavier than when she'd held it at the mirror pool, which seemed like days, not hours ago now. This time, she noticed that her hand fitted to the grip of bone perfectly, as though the shape of it had been moulded to her fingers.

'You're giving this to me?' Roh didn't take her eyes off the blade, the colour of a pale rose, its edges glimmering in the candlelight.

'Consider it on loan,' the warlock said, a glint of amusement in his eyes.

'And what does it have to do with knowing who I am?' The very question had plagued Roh for as long as she could remember. If victory depended on such knowledge, she wasn't sure it was within her grasp at all.

An emotion Roh didn't recognise flitted across Deodan's face before he spoke again, his words carefully considered. 'It found its way to you. There's a connection in that. Just trust that it means something.'

Roh turned the dagger over, the feel of it somehow *right* against the calluses of her palms as Deodan's cryptic words broke around her like a soft wave. Perhaps who she was wasn't about the people who had come before. Perhaps it wasn't a matter of heritage and history, but rather *choice*. Perhaps it was about the people she *chose* to have by her side, and the relentless pursuit of what she wanted, what she believed in, that shaped her the most…

She looked behind the warrior warlock, to the bone cleaner, the human and the two Jaktaren, a group that had been so at odds from the beginning, now slowly knitting together, unified in their outrage, in their support for her.

There was a knock at the door and an Akorian messenger peered into the room. 'Adriel would like to know what you have decided, Rohesia?'

Still holding the quartz dagger, Roh could only look to Harlyn then, to her oldest friend, whose new trust in her was so raw and fragile. 'What do you say?'

Harlyn adjusted the sling around her neck and visibly swallowed before meeting Roh's gaze from across the room. Her worried expression had hardened, a fierce fire catching alight in her eyes. 'Do the tasks, find the gems,' she said.

It wasn't the first time Harlyn had uttered those words, but it was the first time she'd said them knowing the truth about Roh and how she'd got here, and that, more than anything, lit an ember of hope in Roh.

She gave a single nod to the messenger. 'You heard her.'

Roh sat on the end of the bed she had been sharing with Harlyn and stared at the crown of bones in her hands. She felt at odds with it, even more so than she had upon seeing it at her false coronation. It represented so much – all that she could gain, but also everything humanity had lost and continued to lose at the hands of her kind. It left a sour taste in her mouth, but she turned it over, running her fingertips along the smooth insets where the gems should be. Adriel had instructed her to bring it to the rite, though she had no idea why.

When the time came and the messenger returned to escort her to the great temple, she strapped the quartz dagger to her thigh and didn't hesitate. With the others close behind her, Roh placed her crown atop her head and followed the Akorian down the familiar path.

'Your companions may take their place inside the hollow,' the messenger said when they reached the doors. 'You may follow me.'

'The hollow? I thought we were going to the temple?'

'They are one and the same. The temple becomes the hollow upon the Rite of Strothos. You will see.'

'How often is this ritual performed?' Roh pressed, feeling her knees buckle.

The Akorian was holding the doors open for her. 'Every few years or so,' she replied. 'It is a sacred occurrence. You should feel lucky —'

'And what is the catalyst for such an event?' Finn cut in, his voice sharp enough to slice.

The messenger looked at him in surprise. 'When a cyren challenges the will of the goddesses, of course.'

With that, Roh didn't linger. All she could do was acknowledge the worry on her friends' faces with a stiff nod, before entering a separate room, leaving them behind.

It was cold inside; that was the first thing she noticed. The second thing was the virtually transparent shift that had been laid out for her on a table in the centre of the room. Her stomach rolled uneasily, but there was nothing to be done except to strip down. She tried not to think about the size of the temple as she peeled away her weapon and clothes, feeling more and more vulnerable as each layer hit the floor, shivering as she tugged the shift over her bare skin. Roh's hand shook as she re-strapped the dagger to her thigh. Adriel had declared no rules as far as weapons were concerned, and she had learned that what cyrens didn't say was just as important as the words they spoke aloud.

She didn't spare a moment to wonder what donning a warlock artefact in a cyren trial would mean. At this point, she was past caring and would take any help she could get. The leather strap was warm against her chilled skin, and she checked it was secure before letting her shift fall back down to her calves. Goosebumps raced across her arms and she folded them over her chest in part to retain heat, but also to cover herself.

'We are ready for you, Rohesia.' From behind a privacy screen, Adriel's voice cut through the cold and silence like a hot blade. It took every fibre of Roh's willpower not to recoil, but to stand up straight, taking up her crown of bones once more, holding it out to him as he approached her.

He took it from her, eyes assessing her as though she were an animal being prepared for slaughter. 'Shall we proceed?'

Roh didn't trust herself to speak. She didn't know if she could. She motioned for Adriel to show her the way. Behind the screen was an iron door, which opened as she moved towards it. Roh took a deep breath and walked through.

The heat of the great temple greeted her, flushing her exposed skin. She blinked, seeing that the space had been transformed. Where worshippers usually sat on the marble floor, tiles had been removed to reveal a series of steps, leading to an inground bathing pool – indeed, a hollow inside the temple. Dark-green vines coiled around its edges like writhing serpents, reaching into the water, ominous star-shaped leaves floating on the surface. They crept up the steps, too, as though they had a will of their own. The pool was filled to the rim with water as clear as crystal, so that Roh could see the mosaics of Dresmis and Thera lining the bottom. And the Mercy's Topaz waiting for her. There it glowed, sending honey-hued reflections rippling through the water, beckoning to her.

Roh felt eyes on her, hundreds of eyes, on every inch of her, even staring through her. The warm grip of the leather sheath around her thigh gave her little comfort. She couldn't control the tremor in her hands now, could only clasp them in front of her body, trying to hide some of her form from the gawking crowd. She searched the faces for the familiar. Adriel had placed her companions at the very front, so they would have a full view of the rite unfolding. Roh thought she might be sick as she was led down to the pool, feeling smaller than she ever had.

She saw Harlyn first, her friend's face alarm-stricken, taking in Roh's near nakedness. Beside her, Odi's cheeks were red and he looked away immediately. Shame burned in Roh's own cheeks as she closed the gap between herself and the pool.

Until someone blocked the way. Finn, his eyes full of fire. He didn't look away; rather, he looked deeply. He didn't touch her, but he leaned in slowly.

'For millennia, Saddorien cyrens wore those shifts into battle,' he told her.

Roh didn't think she was breathing.

'They needed no armour, no weapons to shield themselves against the realms … They were magic, cunning and power incarnate. And they answered to *no one*.'

His words sank into her like a brand and she clung to them as the drumming began anew and he rejoined the others.

When she reached the water's edge, her hands had stopped trembling and she looked to Adriel, who nodded.

Roh stepped down onto the first submerged step, the lukewarm water reaching her ankles.

'Welcome one and all,' Adriel declared to the crowd. 'Today we will bear witness to the bone cleaner, Rohesia, undertaking the Rite of Strothos. The ritual that is named for the daring cyren who discovered the rare vines —'

Roh could have sworn she heard Deodan snort with disdain. The familiar noise grounded her.

Adriel cleared his throat. '— who discovered the vines that keep us connected to our great goddesses. The Rite of Strothos helps us flush out those who are not worthy. Should Dresmis and Thera deem it so, Rohesia will retrieve the Mercy's Topaz, a crown birthstone of

Saddoriel, from the bottom of the pool, and in doing so, remain heir to the cyren territories for the next part of her quest.' Adriel approached her, the crown of bones between his hands. 'Should our great mothers deem a bone cleaner unworthy of such an honour … A different price will be paid.'

Adriel stood behind Roh and lowered the crown onto her head. She hated the thrum of his body at her back, knowing he was just as likely to put a knife in it.

'We are blessed to witness such a rite, the making of a new queen of cyrenkind … or the demise of an imposter,' Adriel continued, fuelling the anticipation and obsession of the crowd.

A unified cheer echoed throughout the hollow.

What outcome do they cheer for? Roh wondered abstractly, scanning the sea of vacant eyes and hands fisted in fervour.

'Akorians,' Adriel called, his arms outstretched, as though he meant to embrace his entire territory. 'Today we watch history as it is carved before our very eyes by the goddesses.'

Roh had heard enough about the will of the goddesses; she had her own will to contend with. Adriel's words now lost to her, she took another step into the water, and another, and another, the water passing her knees, her thighs, her waist, the shift billowing out around her as the water kissed her skin.

Roh stepped off the ledge and sank to the bottom of the pool.

CHAPTER SEVENTEEN

Strothos' poison shivered across Roh's scales as the crowd disappeared above her and the world went mute. She realised at once that this was not like swimming through the currents of the sea, that this pool had been modified to work with *and against* the cyren nature. Although she could still breathe beneath the surface, she couldn't manipulate the water, couldn't bend it to her will. Instead, the weight, the pressure of an immense body of water pressed all around her in a way she'd never experienced before, almost as though she were human. But it didn't matter, because the Mercy's Topaz was within reach … There on the tiles lining the floor, it glowed, calling out to her.

Roh dived down, parting the water just as Odi would, with her hands and no magic. The water, which she had so often thought of as a living being itself, one that usually listened and answered to her command, was silent. The sensation was surreal as she swam deeper still, towards the hum of the birthstone —

Suddenly, Roh's vision blurred.

And she was no longer in the strange pool.

Fresh air hit her face and the scent of pine and mountains wrapped around her. She didn't know how she knew those smells; she just did. Finding firm ground beneath her feet, Roh took a single step, and then another, the quiet notes of timber wind chimes sounding nearby: music of chance, not precision, unlike anything she had ever heard before. A covered quadrangle of sandstone pavers wrapped around gardens of emerald grass and trees of yellow wattle, flowers falling into a babbling stream that ran through the centre. With the knock of the wind chimes in the cool breeze that danced in Roh's unbound hair, the place was tranquil and beautiful, the arching walkways and unique architecture wondrous. Barefoot, she found herself leaving the path of pavers to walk across the soft grass towards the stream, the delicate flow of water over rocks offering a serene music of its own. When she reached the stream's edge, she looked up, surprised but not scared to find a female cyren sitting on a smooth rock on the opposite bank. Roh stared. Somehow, she felt as though she *knew* her, that some instinctual part of her recognised the stranger. But even after raking through her memories, she couldn't place her. The cyren wore similar garb to the Jaktaren, dark hues and taut leather, but in her arms, she held a squirming bundle, a nestling.

Roh watched on, understanding that the cyren couldn't see her, as though Roh wasn't there at all. Blankets were pulled away from the nestling and Roh realised that the infant wasn't squirming; its tiny body was racked with tremors, its skin discoloured. There was something wrong. The cyren held the infant's limbs by its sides as gently as she could, her own expression pained. But neither nestling nor cyren cried, they only waited for the tremors to pass —

Roh was walking another path now, one she recognised as the path to the Vault, the home of the *Tome of Kyeos*, back in Saddoriel. Delja was not there this time, but the Vault's circular iron door was open as Roh approached it. She held her breath as she passed the threshold into the sacred space, a cylinder of endless shelves holding the endless volumes of cyren history. In the centre, at the Vault's heart, a beam of light glowed, highlighting the great book that hovered there, at long last within Roh's grasp. She reached out with trembling fingers. Finally it was hers – finally she would understand where she had come from, she would know the truth about Cerys and she would have all the answers to the questions that had plagued her for her entire life.

Her fingers slipped through the tome.

That can't be right, she thought, reaching out again.

Roh couldn't touch it. It was as though the tome

floating before her were a mirage, a trick of her mind. Her hands fell straight through it again and she gave a frustrated cry, swiping for it more forcefully this time. Until her eyes snagged on something sitting on a shelf amidst the volumes.

A crown of bones. *Her* crown of bones.

She stared. The insets where the birthstones of Saddoriel should sit were empty, as they had always been. The crown itself was covered in a thin layer of moss, vines growing out from the shelves and wrapping around the bones. Just like the vines that grew over the portcullis of Saddoriel's prison ...

Roh reached for it with clammy hands and —

She knew this place. The familiar scent of bone shavings and dust filled her nostrils and she shifted on her stool, looking around the workshop. She had spent countless hours in this very spot, with Harlyn and Orson at her sides, Ames scolding them from behind his desk at the front of the room. Roh looked down at her workbench, bones littering its surface.

Clean and sort, that was her job. She fell into the old rhythm of it easily, plunging baskets of bones into pungent vinegar water and laying them out to dry, the ivory luminous in the torchlight. She sorted them into piles. Certain bones had particular uses around the lair ... Roh worked without thinking, muscle memory kicking in. She could do this in her sleep —

She froze, staring down not at the bones between her

talons, but at her own hands. They were not *her* hands, they couldn't be … They were withered with age, the knuckles like the gnarled roots of a tree, the veins bulging beneath near-translucent skin. Roh turned them palm up and down again.

What's happening? These aren't my hands.

But they were. They moved as she commanded, they were attached to *her* arms. Without warning, Roh was short of air. She darted to the window and cried out at her reflection. The person who stared back at her in wide-eyed disbelief wasn't her. It was some ancient, hunched-over creature with hollow cheeks and wiry white hair. Beneath her eyes, the skin was dark and sunken, her lips a mere thin line. Panic surged, but she felt weak, too weak to contain it, and her aching knees buckled beneath her.

No, this can't be real, Roh told herself, gripping the windowsill for support.

When she felt she wouldn't collapse, she left the workshop and bones behind, hobbling down another familiar path. In a strange, aged body, the winding tunnels and twisting turns of Talon's Reach were hard to wander. But Roh knew the way just as she knew bones: intimately.

Suddenly she was there, staring between the bars at the face that would be forever etched in her mind, just as the carvings were etched into the stone walls. Lilac eyes flecked with green blinked back at her.

'She hid the stones. The keys to the tome.'

An icy shiver trailed down Roh's spine. She had heard

those words before. Dread crept into her heart like a thief stealing into the night, and with her withered hands, she gripped the bars of bone.

Her mother, Cerys, smiled at her. Utterly unchanged from the last time they'd spoken. No wrinkles lined her face, no ailments crumpled her frame. She was the same ageless cyren she had always been, her hacked hair sticking out at odd angles.

Roh gripped the bars harder, her knuckles burning in pain. 'You …' But as the word escaped her chapped lips, the form within the cell changed and it was not lilac eyes staring back at her, but eyes of moss green. Her own.

As she squinted through the dim light, her breath caught in her throat with a ragged cry.

It wasn't Cerys behind the bars.

It was *her*.

Roh hit the ground hard with long fronds of grass brushing against her skin and the glow of dusk falling around her. She hauled herself up, getting to her feet, swaying slightly, disorientated. A sea of tussock greeted her.

The gilded plains … She frowned, looking around, confused. The Endon River was nowhere in sight or sound, and in the fading light, she had no idea where she might have fallen. And so she began to walk, with no sense of direction, with no purpose, wandering the golden grasslands, her mind fuzzy and her thoughts far away —

A high-pitched scream pierced the silence and suddenly Roh was running. Her bare feet pounded against the earth and she leaped over bundles of tussock, stumbling and staggering as she tried to stay upright. She knew that scream – she had heard it before.

Harlyn.

Harlyn was in her arms, breaths coming in short, shallow gasps.

Roh dry-retched at the sight of her friend's wound. It wasn't a deep gash this time. This time, there was no arm at all, only a bloody pulp at her shoulder. Tears streamed down Harlyn's grimy face, her teeth clenched in agony. 'You …' she panted. 'You did this …'

'No,' Roh begged her. 'No, I can —'

A strangled cry escaped Harlyn and Roh realised with a start that it wasn't just about the pain. She followed Harlyn's gaze forward, to where the Council of Seven Elders stood, Odi held at spearpoint between them.

'Sing,' they commanded Roh. 'Sing your deathsong.'

'But —' *If I sing my deathsong, Odi dies. If I don't sing my deathsong, Odi dies …* None of it made any sense. Roh's heart was pounding and her hands were slick with Harlyn's blood.

'Sing. Sing. Sing,' the elders chanted. 'Sing. Sing. Sing.'

Roh felt the pressure building up within her, terror and longing, pain and comfort, a driving force of magic churning, rising to the surface.

'Sing,' Odi begged, his desperate eyes lined with tears.

She opened her mouth, tilting her head to the darkening sky.

A wailing note escaped her, a sound as ugly as they come.

Roh was small, just a nestling hiding in the shadows, listening. The lowered voice she heard was familiar, but she couldn't quite place it. She squinted through the darkness, but it was no use, so she closed her eyes and focused on the words.

'— that was *not* the plan. Do not let the mask slip now. You know you are watched. Always.'

'She is where she needs to be. We made sure of that.' Cerys' words were clear and cutting, devoid of any dazed, manic notions.

'You think things cannot change?' said the other. 'If there is one thing the last few hundred years have taught us, it's that things do not go to plan.'

'You and I have vastly different experiences of the last few hundred years,' Cerys retorted bitterly.

'I'm aware. So do not let your suffering be for nothing.'

Roh was visiting her mother, standing at the bars of her cell, when the madness returned to Cerys. There was a flash of talons and white-hot pain lanced through Roh's face. Warm blood trickled down her chin and her legs buckled beneath her —

Two inaudible words vibrated against her.

Roh was scooped up into strong arms, before all went black.

. . .

Roh didn't know where she was. She didn't know the room of black, polished marble, so shiny she could see herself on every surface. There was a sudden pressure at her forehead and she fell to her knees. She gasped as cool metal pinched her skin, as a gold circlet was forced back around her head —

Bones were spilling across her lap, hundreds of them, pouring between her talons as she tried to scoop them up. They flooded from an unseen point, circling her, piling on top of her, jabbing into her flesh —

Her shattered music-theatre model was in pieces at her feet.

Harlyn and Odi were screaming at her, 'You care more for your secrets than for us!'

Her book of sketches was burning before her.

She was holding the sea-drake egg, cracks forming in its rough surface.

The shriek of the sea drake pierced her ears, filling her mind until she couldn't tell who was screaming louder.

Image after image crashed into Roh, a tortuous ascension into her worst fears, some she hadn't even known she had. Fear and truth mixed together in a way she couldn't fathom, didn't *want* to fathom.

Roh was drowning. Water filled her lungs as she forgot where she was and how to breathe. Back in the temple's pool, the drug was overwhelming her, the glowing topaz further away than ever. But no – the drug hadn't stopped her from breathing under water. Something was around her throat, tightening. Her eyes bulged – *the vines*. The vines had come alive, had left the edges of the pool and now writhed around her like serpents. A thick coil squeezed at her windpipe. Another crept up her arm, pulling as though to tear it from her shoulder.

Her whole body strained as she reached for the topaz, but the distance between her fingertips and the stone only seemed to increase. Her lungs burned, and for a split second she imagined the vine squeezing her throat so hard that her head popped right off her neck. She batted another vine away with her free hand as another tangled in her hair, the pain sharp as it wrenched her in the opposite direction, threatening to scalp her. She would be torn apart, that was how she'd meet her end, her limbs floating to the surface of a bloodred pool.

Black spots blurred her vision as the vine strangled her. She clawed at it uselessly, her fingers as blunt as a human's – her talons, suppressed by the poison, remained sheathed.

Sheathed. The word rang through her like an answer to a prayer. Her free hand shot through the water to the leather strap around her thigh and closed around the bone handle. She didn't hesitate, not this time. She extracted the quartz dagger, the blade carving through the water to the vine around her other wrist. She sliced through it and lurched to one side as the tension released, leaving the severed vine to sink to the pool floor.

Careful not to cut her own throat, she sliced through the vine choking her, the coil snapping free at once, leaving Roh gasping for the air in the water.

Panicked, she kicked towards the surface, but the vines tangled in her hair dragged her down. Strothos' vines had learned from their mistakes and twisted away from the quartz dagger as Roh brandished it, all the while pulling her deeper into the water. The vines tangled and yanked at her long hair, threatening to rip her scalp from her skull, the pain making her eyes burn. The dark tresses seemed to float before her, the hair that made her inherently Saddorien, made her like her fellow cyrens.

Soft words echoed in her mind.

... Magic, cunning and power incarnate ... Answer to no one ...

Beneath the water, Roh screamed, bubbles escaping her mouth and drifting to the surface she could no longer see.

She would answer to *no one*.

No one would force a circlet back onto her head.

Her hand shot through the water, clutching a fistful of hair that was tangled with the vines. With the quartz dagger, she sawed through it. And the next. And the next. She need not be like every other Saddorien, for she was not the same, and never had been. She sliced through her hair, as she'd seen her own mother do. The vines fell away with the severed tresses, drifting towards the bottom of the pool.

Roh kicked hard, this time propelling herself towards the mosaic tiles of the floor.

Golden light erupted as her fingers brushed against the rough, cold object.

The Mercy's Topaz.

It was enclosed in a setting, stuck there. But this was not the end.

Roh brought the dagger towards the birthstone, sliding it beneath the topaz and leveraging her weight, prising the gem from its hold. At last, her hand closed around the Mercy's Topaz and every vision, every voice in her head fell silent.

Roh was back in Saddoriel, though it was not the lair as she knew it. Hundreds of cyrens gathered at the entrance, the archway of bones standing as tall as ever, but the rest of the lair was different, older. Many of the bone structures that had been in place all of Roh's life were missing, and the fashions ...

The hair on the back of Roh's neck stood up as she recognised the open-backed dresses and robes of the Akorians. Only ... Saddoriens were wearing them.

Although no one paid her any mind, she was jostled as the excited crowd lurched back and forth, anticipation thick in the air.

What's going on? she wondered, trying to get a better look but unable to see over the throngs of cyrens. Then, she was no longer in the fray, but on the outskirts, higher up, looking down at whatever event was unfolding. Nearby stood a group of cyrens, both young and mature, wearing different clothes to those of their counterparts below. They shared a nervous, fidgeting energy, as though something was about to happen, as though they were about to do something dangerous.

Roh approached them quietly, despite knowing they couldn't see her. As she drew closer, her eyes widened and her chest tightened.

Is this another strange dream? Another trick of the drug? Am I dead? She moved closer still, closing the gap between herself and two younger cyrens standing on the fringe of the group.

'Welcome to The Dawning,' boomed a voice like a storm about to break.

Roh almost choked. *The Dawning? This can't possibly be The Dawning ... It hasn't been called that in over six hundred years ...* Again, she noted the strange Akorian fashions. *Is this ... another time?* Roh's gaze went to the two younger cyrens she'd been drawn to before the announcement had begun.

One of them could have been Roh, she looked so similar. They shared the same dark brows and wide, heavy-lidded eyes, the same lithe frame. But this cyren – her eyes were lilac with speckles of green. And suddenly, Roh knew whom she was staring at. Cerys ... And the smaller female at her side, beautiful but self-conscious, was Delja.

Roh couldn't believe what she was seeing. Cerys, before she'd become the Elder Slayer, and Delja, before she had become queen triumphant. But then ...

This is it, Roh realised, looking around at the mass gathering, at The Dawning about to take place. This was the tournament where Delja had won the crown from Uniir the Blessed ... That explained the Akorian robes. The king had been a fanatic.

Roh couldn't help it – she went right up to the two cyrens she had come to know in such complicated ways in the present day. As Roh saw them now, they looked so young; not in their physical appearance – they had not aged much after this moment – but in their eyes. There was a youthful radiance to their lilac gazes that had long since faded from their present-day counterparts. Roh was close enough to smell the sandalwood soap in Cerys' dark, waist-length curls, close enough to reach out and touch the soft skin of her hand, both things she'd never experienced with her mother. But Roh remained still, transfixed by these younger versions of the two intimidating cyrens she knew.

The announcement, performed by none other than Uniir the Blessed himself, Roh realised, was still ongoing, but Cerys and Delja had their heads huddled together.

'Are you scared?' Delja whispered.

'Not with you by my side,' Cerys said with a wink.

'Me either,' Delja replied, though with far less conviction.

Roh gaped. *Cerys and Delja competed in The Dawning as a team?*

'Sangor and Teltah will be the first to get eliminated,' Cerys murmured, scanning their fellow competitors with a critical eye. 'Then —'

Delja sighed. 'I wish Marlow and Sedna were here,' she said, suddenly holding back tears.

Cerys put an arm around her shoulders, squeezing her friend. 'Perhaps they are ...'

But Delja shook her head, taking a steadying breath

and wiping her eyes. 'I'm sorry,' she said. 'They were *your* family.'

'They were *our* family, Deelie.'

Delja sniffed and leaned into her friend's embrace. They stayed like that for a moment, while Uniir droned on about Dresmis and Thera, blessing the impending trials and declaring any forthcoming competitor deaths as a worthy sacrifice to the goddesses.

'Two kings we've seen upon that throne,' Delja snorted. 'Each as mad as the last.'

'Isn't that why we're here?' Cerys said. 'To see *queens* upon the cyren throne, for the first time in history?'

'Yes …' Delja's voice sounded far away. 'Queens.'

'Perhaps one day they will call us *ramehras*,' Cerys said with a grin.

Ramehra … Chosen majesty. Roh recalled the Old Saddorien phrase.

Delja grinned back.

'Competitors.' Uniir's strident tone drowned out all else now. 'Ready yourselves. The trial is about to begin. May Dresmis and Thera guide you well.'

Cerys turned to Delja, her eyes shining and a wicked grin at her mouth. 'Are you ready, Deelie?' she asked.

'If you are, always.'

A gong echoed across Saddoriel and The Dawning began.

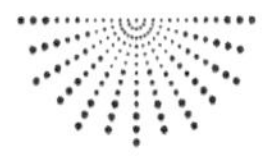

CHAPTER EIGHTEEN

Roh broke the surface of the pool with a ragged gasp, the sound of a gong ringing in her ears. Images of all she'd seen swam before her, blurring her vision. Clumsily, she lurched for the stairs, coughing up water, her lungs burning, her limbs weighted. Her cropped hair stuck to her face.

The vines were real, she realised shakily, her swollen throat pulsing. The drug had overwhelmed her, had stifled her cyren abilities, and at some point, water had flooded her airways as it would a human's. Hadn't it? A Saddorien cyren drowning in a pool barely deep enough to dive into. A humiliation designed by none other than the cruel mind of the spurned Arch General. But she *hadn't* drowned, hadn't allowed the vines to kill her. Here she stood, trembling and weak, but *alive*. She'd found the topaz, had felt its cool edges against her fingers. *But then* ... Her hands were empty; she held no birthstone of

Saddoriel in her grasp. The quartz dagger too had disappeared. With a strangled sob, Roh reached the steps and hauled herself up, not caring that the soaking shift clung to every inch of her, not caring who saw. None of it mattered. She'd failed. After all she'd seen, after everything —

She glanced down, her eyes catching on her reflection. Roh froze.

For at the apex of her crown of bones gleamed the Mercy's Topaz.

The gem shone, sending honey-coloured reflections shimmering from the water's surface across the walls of the temple. All at once, Roh could feel its power thrumming through her, guiding her movements, guiding her gaze around the strange room as she found her footing, ascending the stairs of the pool in a daze.

Strong arms gripped her, folding her into a warm, dry towel. She expected to see Harlyn, but it was Finn Haertel at her side, holding her upright as her legs buckled, shielding her from the throng of eager Akorians.

Bodies closed in, jostling them both, causing Roh to stumble. Finn's arms tightened around her as hands reached for her, invading her space, pressing against her very exposed skin.

'*She is a sign from Dresmis and Thera!*'

'*— survived by the grace of the goddesses!*'

'*— have witnessed the birth of a new descendant —*'

The voices cried out, laced with notes of ecstasy and wonder. Roh flinched as the unsolicited touches continued while she and Finn fought their way from the pool's edge, chaos descending. Cold air kissed the bare nape of her neck and she felt a pang of self-consciousness about her hair – how bad was it?

But then, Roh's skin prickled and instantly she knew why. The brand of Adriel's stare seared from across the hollow. His handsome features were transformed by the ugly upward curl of his lip, and for a second Roh could feel them pressed against hers, all possession and manipulation. She met his gaze, his hatred of her and all she stood for no longer hidden by false smiles and grand gestures. She refused to look away, even as the crowd flung themselves at her and her legs threatened to give out. She would not back down to that monster. He'd stripped her of her clothes and as much of her control and dignity as he could. He'd attempted to force himself on her, tried to take advantage of her youth and her ambition. He'd drugged her, made her face unimaginable horrors. Adriel had tried to break her. And still she'd bested him. Even in *this state*, she'd bested him. She had bested the Arch General's hardest attempt to crush her into nothing. And so, she let him see her – let him witness her resilience, her strength and her relentlessness. This quest was hers and she would see it through until the very end. Adriel's eyes narrowed as an understanding settled between them: when she was done with the birthstones, she would come for him.

He broke the stare and turned on his heel, disappearing through a back door, like the spineless bastard he was.

Yrsa led the battle through the fanatics towards Roh

and Finn, Harlyn, Odi and Deodan close behind her. Together, they fended off the worshippers, pulling Roh into the safety of their huddle. Harlyn made it to Roh's other side, throwing an additional cloak around her shoulders and shoving off an offender with her good arm, swearing loudly.

Roh sagged with relief to see Harlyn's wounded arm in the sling. It had been in her head, the bloody mess, the screaming, the blame …

Leaving wet, poisoned footprints in her wake, Roh let her companions lead her away from the temple, too numb and dazed to speak just yet. The Jaktaren took charge, somehow whisking her away from the pawing crowd and rhythmic chanting that had begun. But when they reached the doors to their quarters, Roh couldn't move another step forward.

Harlyn gently tried to coax her inside, but Roh's feet wouldn't budge.

'I …' Her voice was raw and she couldn't remember the last time she'd spoken aloud. 'I need to feel the sun on me,' she said. The need was so overwhelming that suddenly every moment she was indoors made her feel more and more overwrought.

'But —'

'*Please.*' Roh didn't know *how* she knew what would help, but her skin was crawling with whatever drug had laced the water and a demanding instinct within was telling her to go to the dunes, where the sun was hottest, where the salt spray of the sea would kiss her face and cleanse her skin. She needed to be outside, away from the pulsating drums and incessant chanting that now echoed through the halls of the monastery.

'I'll go ahead to the dunes,' she told the others. 'Could you bring my pack, please, Har? There's something I want to show you all.'

Although her brows knitted together in worry, Harlyn nodded.

With her decision made, Roh couldn't stand to wait a moment longer. Clutching the towel and cloak tightly around her, she set off in a direction she'd never gone before. She was not familiar with the path she was taking, but her steps were assured. She knew where to go.

The Mercy's Topaz, she realised. It was guiding her through the empty corridors of the monastery, away from the crazed singing, towards escape. It was not unlike the inner compass all cyrens had to navigate the lair back home, pulling her along the passageways with gentle tugs showing her the way. But the stone also emitted a wholesome sort of energy, an aura that put Roh at ease as she took its direction, never faltering a single step. She knew in her heart it was taking her the right way, the best way for her.

Soon enough, she found herself at a door that led outside to a small, empty garden. She didn't stop, finding a gate across the path that allowed her to exit the monastery grounds unseen. The stone not only steered true, it held the tidal wave of Roh's thoughts and feelings at bay, as though it knew she needed a blank mind to make this journey. She knew that once she started thinking about all she had seen, the visions and questions would bring her to her knees. So she didn't question it. She felt only gratitude for the stone as the dunes of Akoris came into view, sunlight beaming down upon the glistening sand.

At last she paused at the top of a dune, looking down at the expanse of sea below, the cool breeze filling her aching lungs with briny air. Alone, Roh sat down, the warmth of the sand spreading beneath her, slowly stealing the chill from her skin. She closed her eyes and tilted her head back to face the sun. Everything she'd seen in that pool came flooding back in blurred images behind her lids.

An infant racked with tremors.

A moss-covered crown.

Gnarled, paper-thin hands.

'Sing. Sing. Sing.'

Warm blood trickling down her cheek.

'You care more for your secrets than for us!'

An echo of panic reverberated through Roh as she was unwillingly dragged through the horrors again. But the pressure lifted … The Mercy's Topaz hummed quietly, slowly telling her which visions were true and which merely drug-concocted fears, picking them apart piece by piece, stripping them of their power.

Roh's breath whistled. Cerys and Delja … It was all true. The cyrens had been like sisters, competing as one for the very crown Roh herself now fought for. She recalled their familiarity, their ease with one another, and the fierceness of their friendship.

What happened during The Dawning? What happened that

left one friend behind bars for centuries and the other on the throne?

The question gnawed at Roh as she basked in the sun, still feeling unsettled. Adriel had said something about vines and connecting to the gods, but those words meant nothing at all. Adriel was full of meaningless rubbish. But whatever had laced the pool had turned water, one of the things cyrens loved most, into something to be feared, something that fought against Roh's instincts and power and had left her drowning. She couldn't let the fear of water fester; she wouldn't let Adriel win. Roh looked out to sea – no gold scales in sight.

Shrugging off the towel and cloak, she started down the dune in her damp shift towards the incoming tide, sand sliding beneath her feet. The drugged water of the pool had not soothed and fulfilled her like the salt water of the sea. It had left her hollow and weak. She needed to remind herself of the strength and power of Saddorien cyrens.

When she reached the water, a wave parted at her feet with a gentle hiss. Roh sighed in relief – the seas had not forgotten her. The current called to her and Roh walked out, the tide surging around her, washing the poison and terror from her skin and soul. She traced the lapping surface of the sea with her talons, the caress of a long-lost lover. The water pulsed at her fingertips, as if asking a question. Roh guided it from its body, creating an arching stream before her, her chest threatening to burst as the seas bent to her will, her command. Yes, she was every bit the Saddorien cyren she had always been.

She gazed out to the dark, flat expanse, stretching on to the pale horizon. With the sea drake somewhere out there, she knew re-entering the sea was a risk. She was sure it could sense her somehow, but it was a risk she had to take. The sea belonged to her as she belonged to it, and Roh needed to remember that, needed to feel it deep in her heart and bones after the horrors of the rite. She let the waves wash over her. A cleansing.

When she emerged from the water, the others were waiting for her on the beach. Odi was carrying her pack and Harlyn handed her a fresh towel.

'Thank you.' Roh wrapped it around herself.

'Are you … Are you alright?' At first, Roh thought she had misheard, for it couldn't possibly be *Finn Haertel* asking after her wellbeing.

But it was. And he was waiting for her to answer, his usually harsh face soft with earnestness.

'I don't know,' she replied truthfully.

'What did the stone show you?' Deodan asked, plonking himself down onto the sand.

Roh looked out at the waves cresting the horizon. She wasn't sure she was ready to share what she'd seen; it all cut so close to the bone. But there was something she *was* ready to share, something her companions deserved to know. From the moment she'd broken the surface of that wretched pool, she'd known she could keep the secret no longer. She would not allow secrets to come between them again. Slowly, she took her pack from Odi and set it down in the sand.

'What are you doing?' Harlyn asked.

'I told you, there's something I have to show you.' Roh dug through the contents of her pack, ignoring the clothes and the volume of *The Law of the Lair* from Saddoriel. At last, she found the bundle of her spare cloak and carefully unwrapped it.

She held out the sea-drake egg, its slightly spiked surface shining in the sun. Roh's whole body went tense as she waited.

'Holy gods, Roh …' Harlyn murmured.

Her friends' screams from the rite echoed. *You care more for your secrets than for us!*

'Is that … what I think it is?' Finn asked, taking a step back.

Roh placed the egg in the sand, in full view of everyone. 'It is.'

'Am I the only one who doesn't know what you've got there?' Odi said, frowning at the object.

'It's a sea-drake egg,' Yrsa told him.

'A *what*?'

'Exactly,' Finn said. For once, it seemed he and Odi were in agreement. Finn turned his gaze to Roh, the fragile respect between them thinning by the second. 'What were you thinking?'

'I wasn't. All I knew was that I needed something Delja didn't have.'

Finn's eyes went wide. 'The serpent … The one that's been following us since Saddoriel. It's no serpent, is it?'

Roh shook her head. 'The drake has been stalking the seas, waiting for me.'

Deodan paced, running his fingers through his hair,

while Harlyn threw her good hand up and kicked the sand. '*More secrets*, Roh? What do you think will come of this?'

Another delicate relationship buckled beneath the weight of Roh's many deceptions. She had no words of justification; if she had, she knew they'd be of no use here. Stealing the egg had been an act of desperation and instinct, one she couldn't explain. Instead, Roh went to Harlyn and, mindful of her wounded arm, embraced her firmly.

'It's the last secret,' she whispered weakly. 'I promise.' She wrapped herself around her friend's familiar frame, Harlyn's body warming Roh's cold skin. Roh didn't say anything, but she hoped that the action spoke louder than her words ever could.

Harlyn was stiff in her arms and Roh's heart sank, along with the knowledge that their friendship had crossed an irreparable threshold. But as Roh loosened her grip, Harlyn shifted … and after a moment, she returned Roh's hug.

They all stared at the egg for a time and Roh wondered how something so small could cause such a tidal wave of problems. But as she picked it up, wrapping it once more in her spare cloak, the topaz hummed calmly, as though telling her she wasn't as lost as she thought.

When the initial shock of Roh's revelation had settled, Yrsa wiped her hands on her trousers and faced her. 'Now that we have the stone, what next?'

Roh gave a deep sigh and turned to the rolling waves.

'Next? We ready ourselves for the journey to Csilla. But …' Roh savoured the taste of salt on her lips. 'Right this minute, I just want to listen to the waves. To feel the sea on my skin.'

Yrsa raised a brow. 'It was that bad?' she asked.

'It was worse,' Roh said.

Quiet settled over the companions, before Finn offered his hand. 'Then let's swim.'

This time, when Roh walked into the churning currents, she was not alone.

CHAPTER NINETEEN

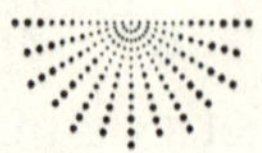

'You were talking in your sleep,' Harlyn told Roh the next morning, both still in the bed they shared as the Akorian sun filtered through the windows.

Roh palmed the sleep from her eyes and sat up reluctantly. Her mind was fuzzy, a dark feeling looming at the forefront, but she didn't know what it was. She must have slept deeply, but the ache in her whole body and the unease within told her the dreams she'd had had left her more exhausted than she'd been the day before, though she couldn't remember them.

'What did I say?'

Harlyn slipped her sling around her neck and rested her arm inside. 'Something about a sick nestling? You were muttering that lullaby.'

An icy shiver raced down Roh's spine, as though someone had dragged a cold talon along the length of her back. She thought she'd made her peace with what she'd seen during the rite, but Adriel's drug had clearly embedded some things in her subconscious. And that lullaby – the enchantment. Why was it following her so?

Harlyn nudged her. 'I said, how are you?'

Without thinking, Roh's hand went to her chopped hair, where the ends hung just below her jaw. Harlyn had done her best to make it even, but Roh was still a stranger to herself when she looked in the mirror. She dropped her hand and shook her head. 'I don't feel right,' she admitted.

'How so?'

'I don't feel like myself … It's like there's a restlessness … like there's something alive in me. I can feel it whispering in my veins …'

Harlyn looked alarmed. She opened and closed her mouth several times before saying, 'If you're not well, we should stay here a few more days. You're probably still recovering from the drug in that ritual. We can't start off on a big journey if you're still weak.'

Though Roh didn't want to, she had to agree with Harlyn. Just sitting in bed and having this conversation was draining her. It was as though a weighted blanket were draped over her senses, over her whole body, hindering the smallest of movements and the simplest of thoughts. What if this was how she was now? What if she never came back fully from the Rite of Strothos?

'You're spiralling,' Harlyn stated firmly, evidently recognising whatever lifelong tells crossed Roh's face as her thoughts descended into chaos. Roh latched on to her friend's words, grateful to have someone at her side who knew her so well. She fell back into the pillows and gave Harlyn a nod. The thought of trekking north across rivers and gorges to Csilla in her current state brought fear bubbling to the surface. She wasn't ready to be vulnerable out in the open. Not yet. Not ever, if she could help it. She reached across to her bedside table, where her crown of bones and the topaz sat. Sand from the dunes had caked some of the more intricate details and it crumbled in her hands as she picked it up. As she placed the crown atop her head, the hum of the birthstone settled around her like calm sea waters and she felt a little more at ease.

'Where are the others?' she asked, looking around the quarters.

'Training in the gardens. They were being loud and I told them you needed to rest.'

Roh hadn't heard a thing. 'Shall we go meet them?'

After Roh and Harlyn had eaten, they found the others in the Akorian gardens. Yrsa was sparring with Deodan, the clang of their swords echoing off the stone walls, while Finn was trying to convince Odi to have a go with his crossbow.

'I can wield a sword just fine,' Odi argued.

'A sword's not always best.'

'Swords are more *versatile* —'

'*You'll* be more versatile, if you'd just learn. Here.' Finn forced the crossbow into Odi's unsuspecting arms.

'There might also be less pressure on your hands,' Yrsa called, blocking a blow from Deodan.

Odi sighed, looking down at the weapon. 'Fine,' he ground out.

Both human and Jaktaren glanced up, noting they now had an audience in Roh and Harlyn, who sat in the shade of one of the many statues of Dresmis and Thera. Roh swore Odi's gaze lingered on her short hair, and she had to stop herself from touching it self-consciously. So she focused on the statue looming down on her and Harlyn. It reminded her of the one that framed the entrance to Saddoriel's great hall. It felt like forever ago that she had been there, the music of the lair swirling around her, dancing with her own magic. Her skin bristled at the thought and she cursed the damn rite. How long until she felt comfortable in her own skin again?

Maybe the drug unhinged something within me ... Is this how the Akorians feel? She had been exposed to a drug for an hour, if that. What was it like to have experienced the effects day in, day out, for an entire lifetime? The thought had bile rising in her throat.

Harlyn squeezed her hand, as though once again sensing that she was teetering on the edge of a descent into darkness. 'What I'd give to see Odi throttle that damn highborn,' she murmured, watching Finn show Odi how to load the crossbow.

The Jaktaren raised Odi's forearm in front of him, resting the weight of the weapon there.

'Then you aim,' he was saying, his face all hard lines

and seriousness, the zigzag pattern in his hair making him harsher.

'Pull the trigger to fire —' Something snapped and the bolt went flying, shooting through the air and colliding with the wall a few yards away, chipping the stone and causing dust to fall along with the bolt.

'Happy?' Odi said with a glare.

Finn frowned at him. 'Is that even where you were aiming?'

'Like I told you,' Odi snapped, shoving the crossbow into Finn's chest. 'I prefer the sword.'

'And I prefer three naked Saddoriens in my bath, but we don't always get what we want, do we?'

Roh's cheeks flushed at the image, but Odi met Finn's expectant gaze. The human tipped his head back and laughed loudly, accepting a new bolt to load into the weapon.

'Well … that's new,' she muttered to Harlyn, who grunted in agreement.

As the day wore on, the restlessness within Roh only increased. She found herself withdrawing from the others, ducking away to flip through the pages of *The Law of the Lair* or to sketch Akorian architecture in the limited blank spaces of her sketchbook, her fingers black with charcoal. She didn't understand how a place of such beauty could be so rotten inside. How the buildings could be so inspired, but built upon lies. Even the statues of Dresmis and Thera that celebrated peace after the wars were false. For how many atrocities had been committed in their names? Even now, the lull of peace within Akoris was artificial, the blanketing of the senses through drugs rather than the liberation of its people. There was only one kind of freedom, and this was not it.

Roh wore the crown of bones constantly, and though she couldn't help but think it looked strange with her cropped hair, the quiet thrum of the topaz's power at its apex lent her some semblance of comfort in that she possessed the stone; she had achieved one part of her quest so far, and that victory meant something to her. Perhaps she was worthy of the cyren crown, after all.

On the balcony of their quarters, Roh sat with the drake egg tucked under her jumper as she tried to skim through as many chapters of the Akorian library book as possible. There was no way she could bring it with her when they left the monastery, and so she tried to cram as much information into her mind as she could. From where she sat in the sun, she spotted Harlyn and Odi inside, bent over the lute, huddled close together. The snarky, trouble-making cyren from the lair was gone. In her place was a thoughtful, even-tempered stranger. Though it would take some magical force beyond reason to get Harlyn to ever admit it.

Odi passed Harlyn the lute, which was in far better shape than it had been in the gilded plains. Odi must have spent hours mending it as best he could without his tools. Roh watched Harlyn take it in her hands and hunch over the instrument, the thing she prized so dearly, the object that had seen her, and Roh and Orson, through their darkest days in the lair. It had taken its own beating on the long journey and recovered. Surely its own tale was enough to inspire Harlyn? But the crease in her brow was deep, the muscles of her jaw clenched as she cradled the lute's body to her own and poised her hands to play. There was a rigidity, a strain in Harlyn's arm where there had never been before. Sadness and pain contorted her features as she attempted to strum her fingers across the strings. Harlyn's body sagged and she stared at the instrument, as though estranged from the very thing she'd created.

The stick of charcoal in Roh's hands snapped. *What if she never plays again?* Roh wondered, watching as her friend extended her wounded arm with a grimace and passed the instrument back to Odi. Even from a distance, Roh could see the fresh pink skin of the thick scar and could only imagine the knots of pain lumped together beneath the flesh.

'It will take time,' Odi said. 'All good things do.'

Roh had heard Odi say something like that before; she only hoped the human was right.

Roh stayed on the balcony until evening fell around her, the air cool against her heated skin, tickling the bare nape of her neck. When she went inside, everyone was there, waiting for her. They'd had food delivered to their quarters and set up a picnic-style meal on the floor of the living room. Roh looked around, taking in the faces lined with worry and the space left for her next to Harlyn. She was touched. Her companions had given her space to process her thoughts, but she was not alone.

Harlyn patted the cushion at her side. 'Come, Roh. Sit.'

Roh did as her friend bid, allowing Harlyn to push a plate into her hands, piled high with bread, meat and cheese.

'We guessed you'd rather not eat in the refectory,' Deodan said with a grin.

Roh recalled the throng of bodies pressing in around her, hands reaching out and touching her without her permission, tugging at the ends of her hair in wonder. She considered how she was feeling: fragile, introverted. If she could curl up into herself and hide, she would. Deodan was right: the last thing she wanted was to be the centre of attention in a hall full of fanatics. She gave him a grateful look and picked at a piece of bread.

'May I?' Yrsa asked, pointing to the drake egg in Roh's lap.

Without hesitation, Roh passed it to her.

They all watched as Yrsa cupped the egg, running her palms across it, her brow furrowed in concentration. 'It's getting warmer,' she said.

Roh nodded. 'I thought the same.'

'It means it's getting close …' Yrsa passed back the egg. 'Have you thought about what to do when it hatches?'

Roh gnawed at the inside of her cheek. The truth was, she knew nothing of sea drakes or serpents. She didn't even have experience with vipers, like Yrsa did. She had taken the egg from its nest on an impulse, a voice inside her head telling her it was the right thing to do. But that didn't mean she had any inkling of knowledge regarding rearing drakelings.

'I tried to find information in the library,' Roh replied, her voice surprisingly reserved. 'But all the books there … They just tell the same story – how one of Asros' consorts, Freya, defended the lair against a drake when the king and Saddorien Army were away, fighting during the Age of Chaos. She threw a dagger at it. It's one of the reasons the people called her *ramehra*. But apart from that, there was no practical information about *raising* drakes, as you might imagine.'

'Perhaps you'll be the first.' Yrsa laughed lightly, shaking her head. 'Well, vipers are notoriously independent from the moment they hatch, but drakelings … From what I know of the legends, they're not as solitary.' Thankfully, Yrsa didn't press the issue further.

'How are you feeling, Roh?' Deodan asked, offering her a jug of wine.

Roh's grip faltered, causing it to slosh onto the blanket beneath them. Before she even had time to put the jug down, Odi was already pressing a cloth into the dark stain.

'I feel different,' she admitted, watching as Odi poured her a goblet of wine without a word and set it down before her.

'We need to find out more about what they put in that water,' Yrsa said determinedly.

But Roh shook her head. 'We need to ready ourselves for the journey.'

'Roh, this morning you agreed,' Harlyn objected.

The idea of the journey still terrified her, but she had no doubt that was exactly what Adriel wanted. He had designed this challenge to whittle away precious days while she hesitated and second-guessed herself. Yes, the thought of leaving scared her, but the thought of staying scared her more.

'I know what I said. But we need to get to the next stone. We should leave tomorrow.'

'*Tomorrow?* Roh, you're not well enough.'

'We don't have the luxury of time, Har. Ames isn't coming. He would have been here by now.' Deep down, Roh had been aware of that for some time. 'We can't afford to wait around. I feel … I feel this sense of urgency. We have to make our move. And soon.'

'Is that what the stone is telling you?' Odi asked, staring at the topaz in Roh's crown.

Harlyn fell silent.

Roh considered this. 'The stone doesn't *tell* me things as such … It's just a feeling. A pull in a certain direction, a humming of sorts …'

'Well, that's good enough for me.' Deodan wiped his hands on the legs of his trousers and got to his feet. 'I'll send word to Adriel. We can have supplies and horses ready by first light tomorrow.'

'Thank you,' Roh told him. She made another decision, her skin still crawling. 'Deodan,' she called out after him.

He paused in the doorway.

'Do you know how to get word to Incana, the healer?' she asked. 'I wish to see her before we go.' Roh made sure to give Harlyn's slinged arm a pointed look.

Understanding filled Deodan's eyes and he nodded, taking his leave.

At least he thinks *he understands*, Roh reflected.

The rest of them ate their meal with a newfound ease between them. There were no snarky comments or bitter asides, only gentle, amiable chatter and the preemptive passing of dishes. The dynamic had shifted somehow and the relief Roh felt was immeasurable. The others huddled around her map, checking the routes to Csilla they'd plotted and calculating the rations they'd need and the safest spots to rest.

Roh sat back and watched, her skin tingling. Her senses had heightened since the rite; sound in particular was sharper than ever to her ears. Though her friends weren't speaking at a high volume, she had to excuse herself.

In the bathing chamber, she pressed her forehead to the cool tiles on the wall, breathing in deeply. Something on the vanity caught her eye: a looking glass. Without thinking, she picked it up and lifted it to her face, staring at her reflection. Ignoring her cropped hair, she saw that the scales at her temples had darkened and she could have sworn there was a tinge of lilac in her moss-green eyes. Both signs of a maturing cyren, of leaving her fledgling nature behind, and yet … She still hadn't learned her deathsong.

Would she ever? The question had dug its talons deep into her heart, so much so that it had found her during the Rite of Strothos. That strangled, ugly sound she'd made haunted her. She had not only failed herself in that instance, but Harlyn and Odi as well. She knew it had only happened in her mind at the mercy of a drug she didn't understand, but the depth of her sense of failure knew no bounds, knew no reason.

Roh traced her scales with her talons and then the jagged scar down her face. She'd thought that leaving the lair and embarking on such a journey might have lit some sort of fire within her, something to fuel the spark of a deathsong. If not those things, then surely obtaining the Mercy's Topaz meant something? But she felt nothing, not even a hint of a single note. And after she'd witnessed the death chorus, she hadn't tried.

She had been a bone cleaner all her life. She had designed *entire residences* out of bones. How had she never come to question, to really interrogate what that meant? Her eyes went to her crown, an intricate work of art, also a symbol of all that was wrong with cyrenkind. There was nothing cunning or powerful about what Adriel had ordered done to that poor human. To prey upon the weak was to *be weak*. And to be weak was not in the nature of a cyren. Or so she'd always been taught.

She studied her reflection again. This time, there was no lilac in her eyes and her scales were the same sea-blue hue they'd always been.

Is this it? Is this the start of the madness unravelling me from within?

Later, in the safety of darkness, Roh whispered to Harlyn, 'What if I never find it?'

'Find what?' Harlyn mumbled, half asleep.

'My deathsong.'

Harlyn patted her arm clumsily. 'You will.'

'But what if —'

'Roh, Ames told me a tale about some Saddorien battalion leader who didn't find hers until her fifth decade. And hers —'

'Was the most powerful in all our history,' Roh finished for her. Ames had told her the same story. What had her name been? It was on the tip of Roh's tongue —

A soft snore sounded. Harlyn was fast asleep.

At a late and silent hour, a soft knock sounded at their door. Upon opening it, Roh was not surprised to find the healer, Incana, standing there.

'You asked to see me?' she said in a low voice.

Roh gave a nod and led her through their quarters, out onto the balcony, where she knew Deodan's protective enchantment extended. If she squinted in the dark, she could still see it shimmering.

'We won't be overheard,' she reassured her guest, whose eyes were darting around in suspicion.

'I thought this was about your friend's arm,' Incana said.

Roh shook her head, suddenly unable to bear the thought of standing still, so she paced the balcony as she spoke. 'You warned me of the drugged food,' she started.

'I did,' the healer allowed. 'For that you are welcome.'

Roh sifted through her memories, her stomach sinking. 'I don't think I did thank you.'

'Well, you didn't ask me here to do so, did you?'

'No, but you do have my thanks, for what they're worth.'

'The gratitude of a Saddorien is always worth something,' Incana said. 'But tell me, then, why am I here?'

Roh paused her pacing. 'Do you know what drugs are used in the meals?' she asked. 'Where Adriel gets them from?'

'The Fields of Dresmis,' Incana replied.

'Will you tell me how I can find them?'

The healer eyed her warily. 'I might,' she said. 'What's it to you?'

It felt as though it had barely been an hour when Roh woke to someone gently shaking her shoulder. Yrsa.

'Come,' said the Jaktaren. 'We have to get our things. The horses will be ready within the next quarter-hour. It's nearly sunrise.'

Roh stifled a moan as she hauled herself from the warmth of the pillows and blankets. She had no idea how long she'd stayed up talking and plotting with Incana, but she felt every lost minute of sleep now. Beside her, Harlyn was far less gracious, swearing and muttering under her breath, her hair a bird's nest atop her head.

Bleary-eyed like the rest, Roh packed her final belongings, fixed her hair as best she could and forced down a few meagre pieces of fruit for breakfast.

Rose and lavender hues streaked the sky as the companions shouldered their packs and left the great monastery while its inhabitants still slept. At the gates, their horses awaited them, saddlebags filled with supplies for the journey ahead. As tired as she felt, she was relieved to be leaving Akoris and its drums behind.

Roh mounted her horse, settling herself in the saddle, boots in the stirrups, hands gripping the reins. *I never thought I'd be so glad to be riding again*, she mused as her horse lurched forward, seeming as eager as she was to rid herself of the uneasy atmosphere of Akoris.

Though it was barely daybreak, Roh was surprised that Adriel hadn't turned up to see them off. It was unlike him to not want to have the last word. She had expected some sort of smug, unsettling farewell from him, but there was no sign of the Akorian Arch General, and for that she was glad. It made putting her plans in place far simpler.

Around Roh, the others mounted their rides as well and before them the gates swung open. The tightness in Roh's chest dislodged as she pressed her heels into her horse's sides and they started forward —

'Wait!' cried a strangely familiar voice from behind.

Roh's eyes went straight to Harlyn, who was twisting in her saddle, disbelief etched on her face.

'Roh, wait!' it called again.

Roh steered her horse in a semicircle, searching the grounds for the source. *It can't be ...* The owner of that voice was thousands of leagues away.

But in her heart, she knew she wasn't hallucinating as Jesmond, the fledgling bone-cleaner apprentice from Saddoriel, ran towards them.

'What ... what are you doing here, Jes?' Roh managed, when Jesmond skidded to a halt, almost colliding with her horse.

Jesmond hunched over, hands on knees, gasping. There wasn't a second to ask how in the realm Jesmond had got to Akoris, or why she was there, because the youngster thrust a crumpled piece of parchment up at Roh.

Any plans Roh had made fell away.

'The Council of Elders and their entourage will be here by sundown,' Jesmond panted. 'You're being challenged.'

Back in the Akorian royal quarters, Roh hurled her rations bag across the room, its contents scattering on the carpet. She should have *known*. She *had* known. Adriel had had this up his stupidly tailored sleeve the whole time, a fallback plan, in case she somehow managed to get her hands on the Mercy's Topaz. She had known this was coming and had pushed it to the back of her mind like a fool. How could she have forgotten that everyone wanted her to fail? *Everyone.*

Talons out, she looked wildly about the room, desperate to grab something else and shred it into a million pieces. It wasn't *fair*. She had bested her fellow competitors back in Saddoriel in *three* separate trials, she'd nearly lost her best friend to a teerah panther in the gilded plains, she had defeated the Rite of Strothos, and at last she had been about to leave this horrible place behind … Now *this*? She couldn't bear it. She wouldn't —

'Roh ...' Odi watched her from the doorway.

'If you tell me to calm down,' Roh panted, her hands in her hair, 'I'm not sure what I'll do ...'

Odi opened his mouth but froze in shock, staring at her as though she were a different creature.

A lump suddenly formed in her throat as she realised why. Letting go of her cropped hair, she fell to her knees. 'I look like her, don't I?' she said, her voice small.

Odi knelt before her. 'You still look like Roh to me,' he told her, brushing a strand of hair from her brow.

Roh felt her whole body sag.

'And I'm not going to tell you to calm down,' Odi said reassuringly.

'What, then?'

'It's horseshit,' he spat, his words as venomous as hers. 'Complete and utter horseshit that they can do this.'

At his outrage, the storm of fury within Roh guttered. She hadn't realised how much she needed someone to be on her side at that moment. She threw her arms around him and held him tight. 'Thank you,' she murmured.

At first rigid, Odi seemed to relax into the embrace, drawing his arms over her back. Roh couldn't remember the last time someone had outwardly offered her any sort of physical comfort. She hadn't realised how utterly alone she'd felt these past few weeks. She rested against Odi's lean frame, and for the first time noticed that he smelled of jasmine.

He tried to peer into her face. 'Roh, are you —'

'What's going on?' said a voice from the door.

Harlyn.

Roh didn't know why, but she pushed Odi back, putting as much space between them as possible. 'Nothing,' she said quickly, but as soon as the words had left her mouth, she realised they made her look guilty – of what she wasn't sure.

Pink bloomed on Harlyn's cheeks, but she didn't say anything else. She simply placed her pack down. Roh reached for her, but Deodan's voice cut through the chamber.

'So, now we know why Adriel didn't offer any farewell blessings,' he drawled, throwing himself unceremoniously into an armchair. The warrior warlock glanced between the trio, as though picking up on the palpable tension between them. He shot Roh a bemused smirk before picking at the dirt beneath his fingernails.

'He's a bastard,' he continued. 'But you beat his antics once, Roh. You can beat them again.'

Roh wasn't so sure. Then it dawned on her.

'We don't know who invoked the challenge, do we?' she asked.

Finn strode in, dumping his pack on the ground and running his hands through his hair with a frustrated sigh. 'Could be anyone. But my silver marks are on Zokez.'

'Really?' Roh started. She hadn't thought of the other highborn competitor since he'd forfeited the serpent-scale hunt.

'He was royally pissed that a bone cleaner came out on top,' Finn told her as he went to the drinks tray and poured some amber liquid into a glass.

'As I recall, he wasn't the only one.'

Finn shrugged unapologetically. 'He'll be looking to restore his family's reputation after forfeiting. That sort of shame sticks for generations.'

'I think we can expect that you'll be challenged all three times, Roh,' Yrsa offered. 'The question is, which category does this fall under – cunning, strength or magic?'

Roh's stomach lurched. She had no deathsong, therefore if it was magic the council wanted a display of, she would lose without question. As for the other categories … She wasn't sure she'd fare much better there, either, not in her strange, weakened state. Running a finger down the ridge of scarring on her face, she suppressed a heavy sigh.

With the sea-drake egg tucked away in her satchel, Roh slipped from the royal quarters alone and followed the birthstone's guidance through the quieter passageways of the monastery. A flurry of movement had descended upon Akoris. Paying her no heed, cyrens rushed about, arms piled high with decorative banners, draping garlands of flowers around the numerous statues of Dresmis and Thera, washing the stained-glass windows and carrying stacks of chairs down the corridors.

She didn't know why she was surprised. Saddorien and Akorian cyrens alike appreciated making a grand spectacle of things. Once she'd been excited by such antics, but now … Roh ducked beneath a small archway and left the monastery, shaking her head.

Though she hadn't made the conscious decision to do so, Roh headed through the town towards the dunes. The windswept ridges mirrored the playful cresting waves on the shoreline, golden, rippled and soft. When she reached them, she removed her boots and let her feet sink into the shifting warmth of the sand. What she wouldn't give to be as carefree as she'd felt leaping from the ledge in the sea caves with the others … Why did that afternoon feel so long ago? So out of reach? She breathed in deeply as she walked, finding something inherently soothing about the briny air on her skin and the roll of the waves across the shore. It was beautifully desolate out here, and for a moment she pretended she was the only cyren left in all the realms, marvelling at the kingdom at her feet.

Atop one of the steepest dunes, Roh sat down, pulling the sea-drake egg into her lap, running her hands across its heated shell.

'Soon,' she told it, 'you'll see all of this for yourself.'

Beneath her palm, the egg pulsed hot.

Roh started, almost losing her grip on it and sending it tumbling down the dune.

'What in the realms …' she murmured, examining the egg. 'You … you can hear me,' she said in wonder. She'd kept it close from the moment she'd snatched it from the nest. Had it been listening this whole time? Did the creature within *know her*? 'Show me you can hear me.'

Nothing happened.

Roh sighed heavily. Apparently, the drakeling she held had a stubborn streak of its own.

She wasn't sure how long she sat there, the afternoon

sun soaking into her skin, but she let her thoughts run freely from one to the next, an unstoppable current inside her head, barrelling into her like waves. The image of her mother as a young cyren filled her mind, eyes glistening and alert, and the sound of her voice as she said, *'Are you ready, Deelie?'*

What had happened between that moment and now? Why had Ames never told her about The Dawning? Did he know? He seemed to know everything else, why not this? And where was he? He'd given her his word that he'd meet her here, and yet she'd gone through it all without him. Her thoughts returned to Cerys and Delja as she stroked the egg, questions churning. Only the *Tome of Kyeos* could tell her the whole truth, which meant she had to get through this next challenge. Magic, cunning or strength ... Which would it be? She hadn't tried her deathsong since she'd witnessed the death chorus. The pile of bones appeared before her again. Her reaction to it hadn't been natural for a cyren. Even now, the thought of it sent a shiver down her spine. Was she so averse to her own kind's magic? Why couldn't she cope with it? Perhaps there *was* something wrong with her. The stalking feeling beneath her skin certainly supported that theory. Whether it had been the drug used in the Rite of Strothos, or whether her undoing was natural, inevitable even, she was slowly understanding where her choices had led her, where her fears stemmed from ... The restlessness within stirred fervently, as though it were building up, as though she needed to —

Roh tilted her head to the sky and closed her eyes

against the glare of the sun. Her mouth parted and a sound escaped. Not a strangled noise like before, not a cry to shrink away from, but a note. Singular and poignant, laced with sorrow and longing, as clear as the sun was against the pale-blue sky.

The note was followed by another, and another.

All at once, magic rushed into Roh, coursing within her like a river breaking through a dam, restlessness dancing with it, escaping through song, *through her*. Several notes. She knew in her very core that they belonged to her and her alone.

Something tickled the side of her foot and she jumped, scrambling back, her eyes flying open.

A flower. A small lilac bloom was sprouting from the sand, swaying in the gentle breeze.

Was that there before? Roh wondered, squinting at the delicate petals. She plucked it, examining the flower between her talons —

'Thought I'd find you here,' Harlyn's voice interrupted.

The sand shifted beside Roh as her friend sat down and took the flower from her. 'Pretty,' she said, twirling it between her fingers.

'Hmm …' Roh agreed, weighing up whether or not to tell Harlyn what had just happened. She wasn't sure she knew herself.

Harlyn reached across and pushed Roh's hair from her brow, tucking the lilac bloom behind her ear. 'Funny where life can flourish, isn't it?' she said with a smile.

Slowly, Roh smiled back. She wanted to say something about how it was like their friendship, how it had shrivelled up in the barren space of Roh's betrayal, but in time it had survived nevertheless, to come back stronger, more resilient than ever before. But Harlyn had already turned her gaze to the seas and was removing her sling, stretching out her arm with a grimace.

'How is it?' Roh asked, nodding to the bandage.

Harlyn tugged at the fabric, the bandage falling away in a ribbon. A thick, nasty pink scar lined her forearm. 'I rather like it,' she told Roh.

'So you should. How many cyrens can say they fought off a teerah panther?'

Harlyn laughed. 'It'd better make me popular back home.'

'You're already popular.'

'More popular, then.'

'I suppose you can never have too many friends,' Roh said with a grin.

'Who said I was talking about friends?' Harlyn quipped, producing a tin of salve from her pocket.

Roh took it from her and unscrewed the lid, scooping a generous lump from within and smoothing it across Harlyn's scarred skin. As gently as she could, she rubbed the treatment into her friend's wound, working in sweeping circles as she'd seen Harlyn do before.

'Do you miss home?' she asked, knowing that it was she who had ripped Harlyn away from the lair.

Harlyn shrugged. 'I miss Orson,' she said thoughtfully. 'But look where we are, Roh …' She gestured to the open sea and sky. 'Think of all we've seen.'

A few feet away, sand shifted, causing a small slide down the dune.

Roh thrust the egg back in the satchel and scanned their surroundings. 'Someone's here,' she whispered.

Harlyn shook her head in disbelief, unable to suppress a smile. 'Can't you guess who?' she said. 'Tell me, who's the one person who always manages to sneak up on us unawares?'

Frowning, Roh looked around and spotted a familiar grin. 'Jes,' she said, as the fledgling approached and plonked herself in the sand next to them.

'Afternoon, Roh,' Jesmond greeted her. 'Or should I call you "Majesty"?' she asked with a wink.

Roh huffed a laugh. 'Not quite yet.'

'No? That crown of bones suits you well enough.'

'What are you doing here, Jes?' Harlyn retorted. Roh knew her friend was trying to sound irritated, but she hadn't pulled it off. She sounded amused, even a little glad for the fledgling's presence.

'Well, I delivered my message already. So, you could say I missed your company, Har.' She batted her eyelashes at Harlyn, who shoved her away, clicking her tongue.

'Would you keep it in your pants, for Dresmis' sake?'

'You and I, we're inevitable,' Jesmond announced with an arrogant smirk.

'You're insufferable,' Harlyn snapped.

Roh couldn't help laughing. Their verbal sparring made her feel at home, until the reality of why Jesmond was here sank in.

'What can you tell us of the challenge?' she asked. 'Do you know who called for it?'

For the first time in her life, Roh saw Jesmond look uncomfortable. 'I can't say,' she told them.

'Was it Zokez?' Harlyn demanded.

Jesmond grimaced. 'I can't say.'

'You mean you won't. You won't help Roh.' Harlyn clenched fistfuls of sand.

'No. I mean I *can't*. They used some sort of magic to stop me from helping,' Jesmond told them. 'You know I wish I could help. I'm a bone cleaner, too. Plus, imagine the commissions I'd get back home if I had some input into how this would all sway. I'd give you a percentage, of course.'

'Ever the opportunist,' Roh said.

'*Tchah*,' Jesmond replied. 'Takes one to know one.'

'Can you tell us who's coming?' Roh pressed, desperate for any information that might help her stay ahead.

'And how you managed to weasel your way in,' Harlyn added.

Jesmond shook her head.

Roh swore. 'You can't even say if Ames is coming? He said he would.'

Jesmond gave a non-committal shrug and Harlyn threw her handfuls of sand into the wind. 'What good are you, then?'

'Plenty good,' Jesmond replied, unfazed as usual. 'You'll find out for yourself one day.'

Roh made an exasperated noise. Ames had been teaching the youngster his cryptic retorts, it seemed.

'What were you holding in your lap before, anyway?' Jesmond asked, peering towards Roh's satchel.

'Nothing,' she said quickly.

Jesmond gave a shrewd smile well beyond her years. 'Your Thieves face never fooled me before.'

'You knew about the card game?' Harlyn turned to her, pink blooming on her cheeks.

'Of course I did,' Jesmond scoffed. 'It's my job to be informed.'

Harlyn snorted. 'It's your job to be a bone cleaner.'

'Some of us like to dream big,' Jesmond said pointedly, gesturing to Roh's crown.

Roh was trying not to think about the tournament and challenges. 'What news from Saddoriel?' she asked.

'Oh, you know, the usual. Cleaning bones, taking bets. Trying to stay up to date with what's going on out here.'

'How can you?' Harlyn scowled.

'I listen to the whispers. Then try to work out which are lies and which are truth. Everything filters down from the Upper Sector, eventually. I saw you still have your human, so that rumour was true.'

'He's not *my* human,' Roh corrected, with a glance at Harlyn.

Sharp as ever, Jesmond noted the look between them but said nothing. Instead, her mouth dropped open in shock as she pointed. 'What in the realms is *that*?'

An elegant bird made entirely of water flew towards them, wet beads hitting their skin as it flapped its wings before their faces. It dropped a small scroll of damp parchment at Roh's feet.

'It must be from Deodan,' Roh said, watching the bird in wonder.

'Well, what does it say?' Harlyn nudged her.

Roh unravelled the scroll and read aloud: '*Get back to the monastery. Delja and her entourage arrive within the hour.*'

'Oh yeah.' Jesmond feigned slapping her forehead in mock recollection. 'I was meant to tell you that.'

Harlyn cuffed her around the back of her head.

The water bird gave a satisfied cry and ruptured into a thousand droplets, a fine mist kissing Roh's face. Jesmond was still staring, bewildered by the foreign magic. But Roh scrunched the scroll in her hand and got to her feet, dusting the sand from her clothes.

'Shall we?' she said, offering Harlyn a hand up.

Harlyn's grip was strong in hers. 'Let's go see which Saddorien wretch has dared to challenge you.'

By the time they arrived back at the monastery, there was no possibility of getting changed or stashing the drake egg safely back in their quarters. Roh, Harlyn and Jesmond found themselves swept up in the crowds surging towards the refectory. Noticing the crown of bones and the Mercy's Topaz amongst them, the Akorians gave Roh and the others space, but not without reaching out to touch her, as though skin-to-skin contact would somehow bless them, just as Roh herself had been blessed by the goddesses, apparently.

The refectory had been transformed; the front wall was gone, opening up into a secondary hall with a large, long table running perpendicular to the rest. A table for the council and those it deemed worthy of their company, no doubt. Garlands of flowers hung from every imaginable surface and banners preached age-old cyren adages: *Mighty is the law. Sacred is the ledger.*

'There you are.' Adriel's smooth hand gripped Roh's arm and guided her away from her friends. 'We've been waiting for you. The council is due any moment.'

Roh wrenched her arm from the Arch General's grip with a hiss. 'Don't you remember what happened the last time you touched me without my permission?' she growled.

Adriel gave her an even look, his eyes flicking to the topaz. 'Don't you?' But his grip fell away.

Roh hauled up her mental walls, refusing to let images from the rite flood her thoughts at such a critical time. She gestured for Adriel to lead the way, hoping Harlyn remembered to warn Jesmond about the food.

Adriel led her towards the long, empty table at the front, adorned with silver cloches and elaborate glass decanters full of rich red wine. Everything was much more decadent than usual.

A drumroll sounded from the edges of the hall, and Roh at last spotted the humans who beat them. They wore the same glazed expressions that the Akorians wore after supper and first meal. Roh didn't know which was worse, to be so drugged you were no longer aware of the shackles, or to be all too aware of the bars of bone a cage was made from.

'Cyrens of Akoris,' Adriel called, his voice projecting to the far corners of the hall, his arms outstretched grandly, as though he could entrance the whole room. 'This evening we welcome the Council of Seven Elders, Delja the Triumphant and their guests into our humble abode. Please give our esteemed Saddorien brothers and sisters the reception they deserve.'

Every Akorian in the hall stood and eagerly turned to the grand doors. The drumming intensified and dancers appeared in the aisles, swaying to the beat of the drums and twirling colourful ribbons through their talons.

Roh's breathing hitched as Delja appeared in the doorway, her wings outstretched behind her in all their glory. At the sight of her, the Akorians burst into wild applause and screaming. For Delja the Triumphant was the embodiment of the goddesses they so fervently worshipped, a direct descendant, here in their midst. It didn't matter that her crown was in question, that for all intents and purposes she was no longer a queen. For what was a mere queen in the presence of a goddess? With a small smile, Delja tucked her wings behind her back and crossed the threshold into the hall. The Council of Seven Elders emerged from beyond and trailed her, their luxurious robes belted with jewels gleaming in stark comparison to the plainer dress of the Akorians. Time slowed as they moved through the hall, looking fiercer than Roh could ever recall. She saw Winslow Ward first, who looked nothing like Yrsa. It occurred to Roh that she knew nothing about why Yrsa had been raised by her aunt, or even on which side of Yrsa's parentage Winslow fell. Roh's thoughts didn't wander for long, though, as she spotted Elder Colter, the head of the Jaktaren guild and the keeper of Saddoriel's laws. The Haertels entered last – Finn's formidable parents. Their expressions were as severe as ever, but as they drew closer, Roh realised that Finn didn't resemble them as closely as she'd initially thought.

She clasped her hands behind her back to keep from wringing them. She peered beyond the council and spotted more familiar faces … The tournament's previous competitors were in attendance: Neith, Estin, Arcelia, Savalise, Miriald, Darden, Ferron and even Lillas. But Roh's eyes fell upon Zokez, who shot her a searing look, sneering at her cropped hair, before his gaze lingered on her crown and the Mercy's Topaz sitting proudly in one of the three apexes. Finn had been right; the highborn was *not happy* about her victory. The fire in his stare awoke whatever magic stalked beneath her skin and she glared back. If he was to challenge her, then so be it. He hadn't dared to take on the sea serpent when she had. She could outdo him again.

Behind the former competitors were more familiar faces still. Roh's heart soared at the sight of Ames. Though the cyren looked older than she remembered, he was here, just as he had promised. She made a mental note to comment on the lateness of the hour, as he so often did with vigour whenever she was a mere few minutes late to the workshop, but for now … He was here. He could help her get through this, whatever *this* was. And though she didn't think it was at all possible, her chest swelled further still. She almost couldn't believe her eyes, for beside Ames was a face she had missed from the second she'd left the lair: *Orson*. How could she have ever doubted that Orson would forgive her? There would always be love and friendship between them – they were *sisters*. Roh let her happiness radiate from her smile. It didn't matter that they were all here to see her challenged. She had everyone she needed by her side. She could do this. She could *win*. She scanned the rest of the hall and by some miracle found Harlyn's elated face. They beamed at each other.

'So, you passed Adriel's test …' A melodic voice curled around Roh's ear.

She found herself staring into the lilac eyes of Delja the Triumphant, who was taking the seat to her right.

'I did,' Roh said, struggling to find her voice as she lowered herself into her chair. Roh knew so much more than when they had last spoken, but that knowledge had only raised more questions and Delja was the only one who could answer them. She longed to ask about The Dawning, about how it had all ended, about Cerys and how she'd earned her shackles and cell. But around them, the Saddorien entourage were finding their seats and servants were pouring generous goblets of wine.

On the opposite side of the table, a few seats down, was Ames. Roh tried to catch his eye, but her mentor was looking everywhere except at her. An Akorian tapped him on the shoulder and pushed Jesmond towards him.

Roh could almost hear his exasperated sigh from where she sat. Trust Jesmond to be causing trouble already. Ames pulled the youngster into the seat beside him with an incredulous glare.

'What is that unruly apprentice bone cleaner doing here?' Estin Ruhne demanded from her seat.

Ames bowed his head in the architect's direction. 'I couldn't trust her left to her own devices back in the lair. She is my charge. My apologies for any inconvenience she causes.'

Jesmond rolled her eyes and reached for the soup.

No! Roh wanted to shout, but she couldn't make a scene, not here. Surely Harlyn had warned the fledgling about —

Jesmond spooned a generous helping into her bowl and raised it to Roh in salute with a wink. Roh sank back in her seat. Jesmond *did* know. And clearly, she wanted to experience the drug herself.

Before Ames could stop her, she'd downed the whole bowl and sat back with a grin.

Roh couldn't help smiling as Ames pinched the bridge of his nose, trying to subdue his temper. It seemed Jesmond was capable of enraging the older cyren just as much as the 'trio of terrors' had been when they were younger.

At the thought of their trio, Roh scanned the length of the table for Orson, spotting her down the far end and sighing with relief. Orson sat with Arcelia Bellfast, their former lessons master, who had shown Roh much kindness during the tournament. No doubt she'd look after Orson amongst the vipers just as well. Roh couldn't help but watch Orson a little longer, grateful for the one silver lining this damned challenge had offered her: the chance to make amends with her friend. If Harlyn could forgive her, then there was no doubt that Orson could as well. Roh was determined to make things right between them, perhaps even find a loophole in the rules so Orson could join their quest. Amidst the terror she felt at the impending challenge, Orson's presence gave her hope. She'd have to find a moment after the feast to speak with her alone.

Roh's skin prickled and she became keenly aware of Delja's gaze. She turned to find the honey hues of the topaz reflecting in the former queen's eyes.

'Was that the cost?' Delja asked, gesturing to Roh's uneven hair, her plate untouched before her.

Roh's throat was suddenly dry and itchy, and she struggled to swallow. She'd known she would see Delja again, but she hadn't prepared for it, hadn't worked out what she wanted to say, what she wanted to ask the cyren who'd teamed up with her mother over six hundred years ago to fight for a version of the crown she now wore. And she wasn't sure what she was willing to tell the former queen. Delja had claimed she wanted to help Roh, but what was Roh herself always telling Odi?

Roh steeled herself. 'Do you really care, *Deelie?*'

Delja flinched, as though the name had been a stinging slap to the face. She reached for a goblet of wine and drank deeply. 'It has been a long, long time since anyone has called me by that name ...' The former queen was as still as death, her goblet suspended before her, crimson staining her lips. Her expression was faraway, haunted, as though her mind had slipped back to another time, another place, to another green-eyed companion at her side.

The surrounding feast carried on, unaware of any slip into the darkness. While the dinner was underway, neither Roh nor Delja touched the lavish foods before them. Further down the table, Roh could see Taro and Bloodwyn Haertel with their heads bowed together, whispering, the intensity of which made her shift in her seat. Yrsa's aunt, Winslow Ward, sat opposite them, accepting a basket of bread from Neith, the water runner who'd attempted to sabotage Roh so many times during the tournament. Roh clung desperately to the small realities in the hope of anchoring herself to the present moment. She'd underestimated Neith; perhaps it was her, not Zokez, who'd called the challenge here. Roh scanned the Saddorien faces. It could be any one of them.

'Do you know which element the challenge involves?' Roh whispered to Delja. If the former queen was truly an ally, then let her prove it.

'I can't tell you that,' Delja replied.

Roh's heart sank. It was as she suspected; Delja's offers of help had been nothing but empty words.

A gong sounded and the drumming and dancing ceased abruptly. Adriel stood, glass in hand, a snakelike smile upon his face. 'We all know why we are here, gathered together for this momentous feast,' he said, arms outstretched again. 'Akoris has been graced with the honour of hosting a challenge for the pending crown ... Rohesia of the Bone Cleaners, bearer of the Mercy's Topaz, please stand and come forward to meet your opponent.'

Roh felt the blood drain from her face and her limbs went heavy as she forced herself to her feet. The strange restlessness beneath her skin stirred as she approached Adriel like she would an executioner, and he eyed her as an executioner would his victim.

'Should Rohesia emerge victorious from this challenge, she and her cohort may continue on their quest for the remaining birthstones of Saddoriel. Her opponent will lose their place in the lair and will be turned out to the outside realms. Should Rohesia fail, she will lose the crown and gem she has fought to possess. And she and her companions will be banished from the cyren territories.'

Roh's stomach curdled and she tucked her hands behind her back to hide the tremors that suddenly racked her body. *Banished?* There had been no mention of such stakes until now. Roh was not only to risk herself, but the others as well?

Adriel rested a large hand on her shoulder and Roh could feel the icy cold of his fingers through the fabric of her shirt.

'Rohesia, meet your challenger,' he said, turning her slightly to face the table as the scrape of a chair sliding back sounded.

'Orson of the Bone Cleaners.'

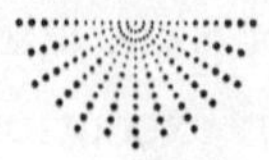

Orson. The name reverberated through Roh's whole body, threatening to crack through her very core. It had to be a mistake, *didn't it?* From where she stood before the masses of Akorians and Saddoriens, Roh took in the young, round face, once so familiar to her, now that of a stranger. Her wide-set, almost-lilac eyes were dark with hatred, and any softness in her features was long gone.

'Orson?' Roh croaked, her knees buckling.

Orson's talons wrapped around the stem of a goblet and she lifted her drink in mock salute to Roh.

'The challenge will take place tomorrow at sundown,' Adriel was saying to the crowd, but Roh could barely hear him. It was as though she and Orson were the only ones in the hall; everything else seemed inconceivably distant. Blood roared in her ears, the revelation refusing to sink in. The Orson she knew would *never* do something like this. Something was incredibly wrong.

A mistake. There's no other explanation but for it all to be a horrible mistake. Or it's a dream ... Roh pinched her arm, hard. The pain bit into her flesh but nothing before her changed. This was no dream, no drug-infused vision.

When Roh's gaze fell upon her friend once more, she saw that Orson's eyes were still cold and her nostrils flared with loathing. She hadn't taken her eyes off Roh since her name had been announced.

As Orson's full lips curved into a smirk, it dawned on Roh: Orson was *enjoying* this. She was savouring every moment as her betrayal pierced right through Roh's heart. Just as Roh's betrayal had done to her.

Numb, Roh returned to her seat, Delja peering into her face, brow furrowed in concern. 'Are you —'

But Roh didn't look at her. She couldn't. She had pushed Orson to this and now, no matter what happened, no one would emerge completely victorious. Their trio would never be the same again. How naive had she been to think she could put the broken pieces back together to make a whole? Roh kept her eyes on her empty plate, all too aware of the eyes boring into her around the room. She didn't even dare look for Harlyn, worried at what she might find there.

At last, when servants came to clear the plates, Roh took the first opportunity to slip away from the hall, the topaz guiding her to a porter's entrance at the back. Outside, the air was cool and she leaned against a stone wall, feeling as though she might collapse then and there.

'Rohesia.'

She would know that voice anywhere. 'You came,' she said to Ames by way of greeting. 'A little later than expected,' she added.

Ames grimaced, noting but saying nothing of her hair. 'It was not as I planned. I had to claim you as my ward. I'm here in a guardian capacity – as you've not reached your majority yet, you have the right to one, according to the law. It was the only way I could excuse myself from my duties to the bone cleaners. But come, we cannot talk here. The crowds will disperse soon enough.'

Roh felt a tug from the topaz that told her he was right. 'This way,' she said, starting off down the nearest path.

'No, we need to —'

She cut Ames off. 'Trust me.'

And oddly, he did.

Mentor and student wove hurriedly through the outer gardens of the monastery and into the streets beyond. Roh had thought she might return to the dunes, but the topaz led her somewhere else entirely. She hadn't had the opportunity to fully explore the cobbled streets of the Akorian city, but she led with complete confidence in the birthstone; it had not steered her wrong yet. Night had fallen and cyrens from all walks of life lingered on the narrow paths, quietly conversing by the water fountains. As she put more distance between herself and that godsforsaken monastery, Roh felt relief that her reactions were no longer being monitored or used as a sick form of entertainment.

'So, you're my guardian?' she ventured at last.

Ames raised a brow. 'I was when you were a nestling,' he said. 'And so I am again for the duration of your quest.'

'If there was no other way for you to be here, how in the realms did Jesmond manage it?'

Roh's mentor inhaled deeply and shot her a long-suffering look. 'Jesmond is my ward, as well. You know this – she has been since she was little. I cannot leave her unsupervised in Saddoriel.' He glanced around warily. 'I suspect that particular law was more strongly enforced so my attention here would be split.'

'Oh?' Roh prompted. It was *very* unlike Ames to voice any sort of suspicion or criticism of the council, least of all to her.

But he didn't elaborate.

'Where's Jesmond now, then? Surely you cannot supervise her while you're here with me?'

'Arcelia Bellfast has agreed to room with her tonight. The troublemaker gorged on that drug-laced soup, and to my knowledge passed out shortly after the announcement. I *had* hoped she might be able to assist you in some way. The girl has an uncanny knack for hearing what she shouldn't …'

Roh came to an abrupt stop outside a tavern door and frowned up at the faded sign swaying in the breeze.

Ames was frowning too, only his expression was directed at her. 'How did you know to come here?' he demanded.

Roh pointed to the birthstone set in her crown.

Ames made a disgruntled noise.

'What is it?'

'This is where I'm staying,' he said. 'You might consider removing your crown for the time being.'

Reluctantly, Roh took it off and tucked it into her satchel, careful not to reveal the bag's existing contents to Ames.

'After you,' Ames said, pushing the door open for her.

Feeling self-conscious, Roh entered the tavern first, a wave of smells hitting her nose all at once. A mix of sweet and sour liquor left a strange but not unpleasant tang in the air, while the warm aroma of freshly baked bread made Roh's empty stomach grumble.

'We'll take the corner booth if it's free, Calla,' Ames said from behind her.

A delicate cyren wearing an apron over her open-backed dress appeared at their side and guided them to a quiet corner of the establishment.

'When you have a moment, ale and two meals, please,' Ames added as they slid into their seats, eyeing Roh and immediately understanding that there was no way she could have eaten anything back at the refectory.

'Very good, Master Ames.'

'You're known here?' Roh asked, intrigued, as Calla returned to the kitchen.

'I told you, this is where I'm staying.'

'Not for the first time, it seems.'

'No, not for the first time.'

Roh leaned back in the leather seat. 'Why are you not staying in Akoris proper? In the monastery with the rest of the entourage?'

'I don't fare well in Akoris.'

Roh frowned. 'What do you mean?'

'I meant what I said, Roh.'

Roh bit back an angry retort. She had hardly *fared well* in Akoris, and yet she'd stayed within its walls with everyone else, not realising there were other options. She rested her elbows on the table. 'Fine,' she huffed. 'Why have you not come sooner? You said you'd meet us here.'

'I said that I would find a way to meet you here, and I did.'

Anger bubbled. 'You implied it would be to help, not to watch me take on my childhood friend in a challenge.'

'There were no implications. Only the words you heard.'

Roh's talons dug into the table. 'Spin it however you want, Ames, but we both know what you meant when you said you'd meet us here.'

'Watch it,' her mentor growled. 'Do we not have more pressing matters to discuss?' Ames considered her with his weathered gaze. 'You're alive, at least. Deodan got my message, then.'

Roh started at the mention of the warrior warlock's name. 'Message? What are you talking about?'

Ames reached into his cloak and placed something on the table between them.

Roh blinked. And blinked again.

The quartz dagger.

Shock barrelled into her and her hands went to her head, running through her hair in disbelief. '*You* took that from the prison? *You* put that in my pack?'

'I did. I was hoping you'd run into Deodan in the plains and —'

'What *in the realms* is going on, Ames?' Roh had never spoken to him like that before. She had always pushed back, especially as she'd got older and her patience had thinned, but she'd never raised her voice to him, had never dared. But now … now, this was bigger than mentor and student. Now, Roh's crown was on the line and she would speak to him as she saw fit. Ames had involved her in a larger scheme and hadn't had the decency to tell her about it. 'I could have been killed.'

'I know.' Regret laced Ames' words, a note Roh had never heard in his voice. 'Believe me, I knew the risks and I did not take them lightly, Rohesia. You were not killed, likely because you had this very object.'

Roh's mouth fell open, suddenly unable to string together a full sentence. Mentor or not, he had no right to make decisions like that about her and her life, or her companions, whose lives she'd also put in jeopardy. The rite, the challenge, Orson, and now this? It was all becoming too much, and again that restlessness within surged and Roh could hardly breathe —

'Rohesia, look at me.'

Roh's gaze snapped up to his, tethering her to the present.

'Do not lose yourself just yet. I am a *friend*. Deodan is a *friend*. Were we not, you would be dead,' Ames explained, his voice lowered. 'There are things that cannot be said aloud within the passages of Saddoriel and so I did what I could to show Deodan who you are without committing words to a page, hoping you would cross paths in the gilded plains. I knew he would recognise the dagger. It's a revered object amongst those clans.'

'He did. Recognise it, I mean.'

'I know. Hence why I have found it again in my possession. I spoke with Deodan just before the feast.'

Roh stared. 'So you *know him*?' Her mind was reeling, remembering how Deodan had looked strangely at her when she had mentioned Ames by the mirror pool.

'I knew *of him*, of his existence. We had never met. It was his ancestors whom I knew. Long ago.'

'Well, when you spoke, what could you have possibly had to say? That you've both enjoyed using me as a pawn in your cyren–warlock games? Did you have a big laugh about the fact that I thought warlocks didn't even exist? You've known all along and *you* were the one to take us to our lessons. You've never corrected any of our supposed education about the outcome of the Scouring of Lochloria —'

'*Lower your voice,*' Ames hissed. But his tone softened when he spoke again. 'You weren't corrected because there was no need to do so. Deodan and his clan are not the same kind that used to run the scholars' city.'

Roh ignored the strange inflection of emotion in her mentor's tone. Gods, she was angry. She'd been angry for some time, and now, sitting before the cyren she'd known the longest, it was all bubbling to the surface.

'Horseshit,' Roh countered, favouring Odi's expression. 'I've seen him use his magic.'

'What difference would it have made to your life,

Rohesia?' Ames asked sadly. 'None. The fact of the matter is that there are very few cyrens left who are aware of the entire truth about their kind and they have learned over the centuries that to speak of such things is to sign a death warrant. The histories have been kept in a way that prolongs cyren culture. But now is not the time to delve into the hows and whys of the past, Rohesia. I thought Deodan could help you and he did. Hiding the dagger in your pack was the only way to show him that he could trust you, without me having to explain everything to you in the lair itself. Don't you see? It was the only way to keep you safe.'

Roh was was rendered powerless beneath the lack of control – there was so much she wanted to know, so much she *deserved* to know that was constantly being dangled before her then snatched away. It only fed that fire within, that determination to complete the quest, to access the *Tome of Kyeos*. The lies, the misdirection and cryptic words would all fall away and she'd be left with the truth, whatever that might be. Only then could things change.

Ames changed tack. 'I'm sorry about Orson,' he said, his voice rich with sorrow. 'I realise how much she means to you.'

Roh narrowed her eyes, wishing she could hold the topaz to determine his sincerity. 'Did you know? About the challenge?'

Ames shook his head. 'Not until it was formally announced back in Saddoriel. We didn't understand how hurt she was, it seems.'

Roh picked at her talons, her gaze lowered to the table. 'No matter who wins tomorrow, one of us will never return to Saddoriel. And if *I* lose, Harlyn and the Jaktaren will have no place to go. Odi will be captured and forced to play piano in the lair until he can play no more … I lose either way.'

'It was designed to feel like that, yes.'

Roh allowed herself a heavy sigh. 'Whatever happens, I have to live with it. I set all of this in motion.'

'That you did,' Ames agreed. 'But that doesn't mean you're not allowed to feel it.'

Calla appeared at the end of their table and placed two bowls of steaming stew before them and two mugs of frothy ale.

'Thank you,' Ames told her, pressing two silver marks into her palm.

She gave a grateful smile and left them.

'Thank you,' Roh said, realising that she had no coin with her.

Ames waved her away, as though this weren't the very first time he'd bought her something.

Roh let the silence settle between them as they ate. She dug into her meal, finally not concerned about what was drugged and what was safe; she hadn't eaten well in weeks. The ale was cold and fresh on her tongue, but she paced herself, knowing she needed a clear mind for what came next.

'Ames …?'

'Hmm?' he grunted between mouthfuls.

'When I touched the Mercy's Topaz, I saw Cerys and Delja.'

He looked up sharply. 'You did?'

'They were competing in The Dawning. I realise you know more than you've ever told me. But I'm asking you, please, tell me now.'

Ames reached for his mug of ale, a slight tremor quaking his hand. 'Delja Silvah and Cerys Irons knew each other from when they were nestlings,' he told her, wiping his mouth with the back of his hand. 'They met during the early years of Saddorien mandatory lessons. Delja was the youngest in a big but mostly absent family, and Cerys … Well, she befriended Delja as she befriended everyone. She brought her home, and they became fast friends, sisters, even. Delja became their family's ward of sorts, after a time.'

Her throat was dry. 'Irons …? My family name is *Irons?*'

Ames' gaze met hers. 'Was.'

Why does it sound so familiar? Cerys had certainly never mentioned it, nor had Delja … It had been stripped from Cerys the moment she'd been put in that prison, so why would anyone have heard that name before? Least of all Roh?

Calla added more wood to the fire at the heart of the tavern, bathing the room in flickering golden light. The quartz dagger glinted against the timber surface of the table, catching Roh's eye.

'What else?' she pressed. 'What else will you tell me? Do you know who owned that dagger?'

'Now is not —'

'Who is Eadric, Ames? Tell me that much, at least. I'm tired of stumbling through the dark.'

Ames pushed the dagger towards her. 'I'll tell you when you win the challenge.'

'What?' she blustered. 'That's not fair!'

'Who said anything about fair?' Ames scorned. Any emotion he'd shown was gone, his usual mask of annoyance back in place. 'We're Saddorien cyrens.'

'So that's it? You're just going to leave me with this damned crown of bones and no information, even though it's at the tips of your talons?' Roh's own talons were out and digging into the table, splinters of timber peeking from beneath them. Fury coursed through her like a raging river ready to burst its banks and obliterate all in its path.

Ames was watching her, his expression unreadable, his gaze cool. 'That's exactly what I'm going to do.' He drained the last of his ale and got to his feet, his grey robes fluttering to the floor. 'Get some sleep. You've got a challenge to win tomorrow.'

'And what about Orson? If I win, that means she's out of Saddoriel for good.'

'That was her decision. Just as cheating to get into the tournament was yours. That's the thing about choices, Rohesia. Once you've made them, you own them for life.'

Furious, Roh left the tavern. Everything Ames had told her, and not told her, swirled in her head. Her family name was *Irons* ... She should feel triumphant in that knowledge. How many lowborns discovered they had a family name? A word that anchored them to the history of their kind? A name that offered what she'd never had before: a feeling of belonging.

Irons ... She felt as though a piece of the puzzle were hidden at the back of her mind, just out of reach. She could see the lock, but had misplaced the key. However, that wasn't the only thing that had sparked a flicker of recognition. Ames' voice ... It had always been known to her; she'd grown up listening to his lessons, his scoldings, and on occasion, his words of encouragement. But there was something more ...

Roh slipped her hand into her satchel, her fingers brushing against the Mercy's Topaz. Upon contact with the birthstone, it came to her. One of the visions she'd had during the Rite of Strothos. The white-hot pain carving through her face. The words of Cerys' visitor.

'Do not let the mask slip now ...'

Ames. It had been *Ames* with Cerys.

Right before Cerys had attacked her own daughter. Why?

'You shouldn't wander the streets alone,' a voice cut through her reverie. Finn stood waiting outside, his hands in his pockets, leaning against the stone wall of a building, a glare ready for her on his face.

'You've got a target on your back,' he said irritably, pushing off the wall with his heel.

'What do you care?' she snapped. But she saved him the trouble of answering with some speech about how *isruhe*s were nothing to the likes of him, by quickly asking, 'How'd you find me, anyway?'

Finn paused, peering into her face. 'What's wrong? You look like you've seen a spirit return from the afterlife.'

Without thinking, Roh's hand went to her scar, tracing its jagged shape down her face. 'I …' She didn't know what to say. And if she did, she didn't know that Finn was the one to say it to, especially given that there was a secondary scar that crisscrossed over the original, courtesy of the Jaktaren. But Finn was still watching her, his brow furrowed in what looked to be concern.

'I was … I was just thinking about this,' she said carefully, running her fingers over the scar again.

To her surprise, Finn nodded. 'We all have them.'

'Oh …'

'You should be familiar with my most recent one,' he added.

Roh baulked. 'What?' She wasn't familiar with *any* part of Finn Haertel.

But Finn was lifting his shirt, revealing that carved abdomen of his. The lamplight above cast a soft glow upon his olive skin and Roh found herself taking a step towards him. A raised, thick, pink scar ran across the width of his stomach in an almost-perfect straight line.

'From the sea serpent's tail.' Roh reached out as the bone-rattling roar of the creature echoed in her mind. Her fingertips met the smooth, scarred skin, heat thrumming from Finn's body. Gently, she traced the length of it. 'I remember …'

There was a sharp intake of breath and goosebumps

rushed across Finn's skin beneath Roh's touch. 'I … I never thanked you,' he murmured.

Roh's fingers lingered across the scar. 'No, you didn't.'

'Thank you,' Finn said, his voice raw. 'I didn't deserve it, but you saved my life that day.'

Roh's face was suddenly hot. Unsure of what to say next, she stepped back, flushing, and Finn instantly dropped his shirt.

'Sorry,' she mumbled, praying that the dim lamplight was enough to hide her burning face.

'It's fine.' He busied himself adjusting the strap of his crossbow. 'How'd you get yours, anyway?'

Roh went cold, feeling her defensive walls slide up into place, a fortress. 'I don't know …' And she didn't, not truly. There was a chance she would never know. Roh looked down the near-empty street. 'So, how did you find me here?' she asked, pushing all thoughts of Finn's warm body from her mind.

'I'm a Jaktaren, remember? Tracking is one of many skills in my arsenal.'

Roh withheld a rude retort. 'We'd best get back.'

'Wait,' he said, grabbing her arm. 'Here.' He thrust a page of crinkled parchment at her.

Frowning, Roh smoothed it out against the wall, noting one edge was cut straight, the other ripped, as though it had been torn from … 'Where did you get this?'

Finn shrugged. 'The library.'

Roh was taken aback. 'The *Akorian* library? Where you panicked in the shrinking room?'

'I did *not* panic,' Finn retorted, leaning all too casually against the wall. 'Just read it, will you?'

Roh scanned the printed page. It showed a detailed illustration of an intricate vine sprouting star-shaped leaves. Diagrams showed how the plant could be crushed into a powder for mass use. Legs weak, she rested her shoulder on the cool stone, needing its support. 'This is the drug they used in the rite?'

'Yes, it is. I've heard you say a few times that you weren't feeling right and it just got me thinking. Adriel's the sort of gift that keeps on giving, isn't he? It seemed out of character that there would be no other consequences of that stupid rite.'

Roh scanned the block of text. 'This says it could be in my body for years. That it could alter the course of my development, my cyren nature. Even … my mind.'

Finn was nodding, his usually hard lilac gaze soft with sympathy. 'I know, but look.' He pointed to a footnote. 'That says there is a type of leaf that grows in the eastern mountain pass that acts as an antidote.'

Roh's gaze slid to his. 'The eastern mountain pass? All our planning sees us going *around* the mountains on the way to Csilla, not *through* them.'

The Jaktaren shrugged. 'Plans can be changed.'

'I …'

'It's your body,' Finn told her. 'Your mind. Therefore it's your choice.'

Roh found herself chewing the inside of her cheek. 'I was already worried,' she admitted. 'About …'

'What happened to Cerys the Slayer?' he finished for her.

'I would have said "my mother", but yes. What if this tips the scales? Or what if there's a clock on me now?'

'I don't know,' he told her. 'No one can know what's to come. That's why we tackle this day first. Then the next, then the next.'

She met Finn's gaze, the tension unfurling from her as she unclenched her fists. 'That sounds simple enough.'

He broke their eye contact first. 'Sure,' he shrugged, 'we just do that over and over again until we die.'

A laugh burst from Roh. '*What?* You can't be serious. That's how you end a pep talk?'

Finn frowned. 'I don't do pep talks.'

But his words faded as something caught Roh's eye and she squinted at a familiar figure down a nearby laneway. Two cutlasses glimmered in the torchlight and a heavy cloak trailed behind.

'He's been slipping away all week,' Finn murmured, following her gaze.

'Where?' Roh asked, craning her neck to keep Deodan in sight.

Finn raised his brows. 'I thought you two shared all your secrets.'

'Apparently not this one,' Roh said, starting after the warlock. He was already turning a corner.

'What are you doing?' Finn exclaimed, hurrying after her.

'I'm done with being kept in the dark,' she snapped.

Together, Roh and Finn hurried through the emptying

streets of Akoris, trying not to lose the mysterious warrior warlock. *What in the realm is he up to?* Roh surged around another corner and down a dark alley. Her heart pounded as they gave chase. She was determined to uncover at least one damned secret this evening. She would not go into that challenge as ignorant and helpless as she felt now.

Finn slowed to a jog, not as out of breath as Roh. 'We've lost him,' he said, kicking a stone in frustration.

'I thought tracking was "one of many skills in your arsenal",' Roh quipped, waiting for the words to sink in.

And sink in they did.

'Fine,' Finn said. 'You want to see what a Saddorien Jaktaren can do? Let's go.'

Without waiting for her response, Finn charged down the alley, scanning the dirt path before them. Roh started after him, pleased that at least one thing had worked in her favour and secretly satisfied that she'd sufficiently riled up the highborn. It almost made her forget about Orson's mock salute and the threat of violence in her once-kind eyes. Almost.

'Hurry up,' Finn called.

Roh suppressed a smile, deciding it was best not to mention that even from her satchel, the topaz was leading her in exactly the same direction.

The moon was high when they were well and truly deep in the heart of the city. The buildings and structures were surreal to Roh.

Strange that cyrens who have the freedom to live outside the lair choose to live in such compact, winding quarters, she thought abstractly as she followed Finn around another bend.

At last, they came to a stop outside an ordinary-looking door.

'In there,' Finn said.

Roh grasped the handle and the door swung inwards with almost no pressure. *Odd ...* But she didn't wait for Finn's objections to come tumbling towards her. She stepped inside.

The door merely opened up to a steep staircase reaching down into the dark. Roh could hear voices echoing along whatever passageway lay beyond.

'Coming?' she asked Finn without looking back.

She heard him mutter a curse as he followed her.

There were no railings on either side of the narrow staircase, so in the dim light, Roh used both hands against the cool stone walls to keep her balance as best she could. She could still feel the reassuring pulse of the topaz from her satchel, and so, determined to find answers, she pushed through the dark, with Finn at her back.

When they reached the lower floor, Roh followed the stone and the sound of voices trailing from where a crack of light escaped beneath another door. She realised that either side of her now were shelves with rows and rows of bottles, containing what, she had no idea. As they reached where the light was escaping from, Finn unsheathed a short blade.

Roh pushed the door gently and it swung inwards just a crack, revealing a sliver of the room beyond. It was well lit, a private cellar – the walls lined with hundreds of bottles of wine, the room packed full of folk dressed like Deodan, fully armed, wearing hooded cloaks. Roh's eyes narrowed as she spotted spears that looked all too familiar. Spears she remembered seeing in the cave where Deodan had taken Harlyn.

'What's going on?' she whispered to Finn.

The Jaktaren's eyes were wide as he pressed a single finger to his lips and they watched as an older woman took to the small platform at the front of the cellar. Not just any woman, Roh realised. *The Warlock Supreme.* The very one Deodan had argued with back in the cave, her eagle still sitting proudly on her shoulder, its sharp eyes utterly menacing.

The woman hit her spear to the ground several times and the chatter ceased.

'We know why we are gathered here,' she began, her eyes narrowing as she critically scanned her audience.

It was no ordinary audience, Roh realised. The throng of people before the speaker were warlocks ...

'How is this possible?' Roh kept her voice low, stopping herself from gripping Finn's arm. 'An entire force of warlocks living freely in Akoris?'

'Enchantments, disguises,' Finn murmured, not taking his eyes off the woman before them. 'They use all manner of trickery.'

It's not possible, Roh thought.

But the Warlock Supreme cleared her throat. 'Akoris is worse than ever before. Adriel keeps his people drugged and ignorant. There is no official cyren ruler. At long last, Delja has no access to the tome. During the

Scouring of Lochloria, our people were weak. But we have changed, adapted. As warrior warlocks, we will *never* be weak again. Now is our chance to *strike* —'

A cheer broke out across the room.

'And reclaim what was ours.'

Goosebumps rushed across Roh's arms.

'It won't be long until the terror tempests hit the seas again.'

'But, Your Supremacy,' someone called. 'We have long since learned not to rely on the storm seasons. They are infamously irregular —'

The Warlock Supreme cut the man off. 'There has not been a terror tempest in over five decades. Our spies in the Csillan gorges have reported that the storms are brewing behind the mountains as we speak. Once they begin, there will be no stopping them and Talon's Reach and all its networks of tunnels will be vulnerable. When the seas split apart, we will be ready, warriors.'

Roh's skin was clammy. *A terror tempest? The seas splitting apart?* She wasn't sure she was breathing. How could she, when this barbaric warlock was threatening her home with magic she'd never heard of?

'Glad you could make it, Queen of Bones,' a voice drawled from behind her. Roh jumped as the door swung completely inwards, bathing her and Finn in light.

A unified gasp sounded from within as Deodan pushed them both forward into the cellar, revealing them fully to the clan of warrior warlocks.

'You knew she was there?' the Warlock Supreme hissed, her face etched with rage. 'She has the topaz!'

Finn threw a protective arm in front of Roh and tried to pull her back towards the door, but the warlock clan swarmed them in an instant, spears pointed threateningly.

They were surrounded.

Roh cursed herself for leaving her quarters without a weapon to defend herself with, now she knew how. *A mistake I'll never make again*, she vowed.

'It's the daughter of Cerys the Slayer!' someone cried.

'If it weren't for them, Lars would still be alive!'

'Kill them both and take the stone!' yelled another.

'Nay, kill the Jaktaren and take the Bone Queen hostage —'

It appeared that word of Roh's heritage had travelled as far and wide as she had herself.

'That's enough,' Deodan's voice boomed out across the room. 'She is under my protection. They both are.'

A wave of shock flooded the chamber. Gasps and whispers sounded all around Roh while she herself gaped at Deodan.

'What's going on, Deodan?' she hissed, his grip tight around her arm. 'What are these terror tempests? What is this attack for?'

But the warrior warlock ignored her and instead addressed his clan. 'If Roh fails to defeat her fellow bone cleaner in tomorrow's challenge, power will immediately return to Delja. We *cannot have that*. We *need* Roh,' Deodan said loudly, dropping Roh's arm and approaching the platform where the Warlock Supreme glared down at him.

A sickening combination of fury and terror surged in Roh's gut. What game was Deodan playing? Why had he let them listen out of sight, only to reveal them?

Deodan bowed his head and lifted three fingers to his left shoulder in some sort of foreign salute. 'Mother —'

Mother?

Finn swore beside Roh. 'That lying sack of shit. We should never have let him come with us,' he hissed, angling his body towards the door, his knuckles white as he gripped his blade hard. 'He's been plotting against us this whole time. The whole of Saddoriel is at stake —'

'Mother,' Deodan continued. 'Roh is *our chance*. She can help our kind find their way home without bloodshed. Our home was stolen, our kin slaughtered. No more of us need to die with the right cyren queen at the helm.'

The Warlock Supreme barked a harsh laugh. 'You're just like your father. An unrealistic dreamer, fated to doom our clans to the likes of our —'

A sudden song filled the air, coursing between the warlocks and toying with Roh's own restless magic. Her gaze snapped to Finn, whose head was tilted to the ceiling, his mouth open as he called his deathsong. Roh could *see it*. Waves of golden magic poured from the Jaktaren. It was beautiful, a sound so rich and vibrant —

Screams pierced the air. A glass shattered.

Finn was tackled to the ground, his song cut short.

'See what monsters they are! They would turn us to nothing but bone right here!' a man yelled, pointing his spear at Finn's throat. Roh could see the Jaktaren's pulse jumping beneath his skin.

'We have talismans against your kind,' a young woman said, her fist clenched around a token at her neck.

'Perhaps against one of our kind,' Finn sneered. 'But I'd like to see you face the death chorus.'

'See?' someone yelled. 'First Lars, now us! They would use their song weapons against anyone – man, woman or child!'

The Jaktaren glowered. 'Anyone who threatens a cyren forfeits their —'

'Finn!' Roh shouted. He was goading them, to what purpose she didn't know. They were vastly outnumbered, and whatever magic Finn possessed was clearly nullified by their warlock enchantments.

'That's enough,' Deodan called, cutting through the crowd and removing the spear from the Jaktaren's throat. He offered his hand to help Finn up, but the highborn batted it away, getting to his feet and moving to stand at Roh's side once more.

'What is your plan, Deodan?' the Warlock Supreme said, her voice filled with unspoken threats. 'You would put the fate of our kind in the talons of these vicious monsters?'

'Who are you calling *monster*?' Finn spat. 'You're the unnatural —'

Roh brought her heel down on his foot. There was no end to the ingrained prejudices here.

Finn shot her a scathing look but shut his mouth.

The Warlock Supreme's lips curled into a satisfied sneer. 'Well?' she said to Deodan.

'Lars was *not* their doing. It was Adriel's, as it always is. Roh herself has vowed to unseat him,' Deodan said, projecting his voice across the cellar. 'Our friend Lars knew the risk in the work he did for us, and I will mourn his passing as I would my own family. But Roh and her companions are blameless in his death.'

The Warlock Supreme's eyes narrowed. 'All I hear is a cyren sympathiser with no plan.'

'I do have a plan.' Deodan squared his shoulders and met his mother's glare. 'I suggest we vote.'

'Vote? On what, exactly?'

'Whether to release Roh so she can face the challenge, to support her claim to the cyren crown.'

The Warlock Supreme scoffed. 'Or?'

'Or to take the topaz from her and start the rebellion you so desperately crave. To let the terror tempests reign and make your move.'

Roh tried to swallow the thick lump in her throat. She didn't dare look at Finn. Somehow, their lives had ended up in the hands of a clan of warlocks who detested their kind. And the Warlock Supreme knew it.

'Fine,' she said tersely. 'Vote.'

There was nothing Roh could do but stand there. Deodan hadn't specified what would happen to her and Finn if they chose to take the birthstone, a deliberate, skilful loophole on his part, no doubt. But what would it matter? If the warlocks took the stone, she was done for, she and all her friends were. Around her, she could hear the murmurs of the clan …

'— why would we replace Delja the Tyrant with a dirty-blooded bone cleaner?'

'— if it avoids mass loss of life then shouldn't we —'

'— if the bone cleaner is decent, she'll *give* us the stone —'

Deodan cleared his throat and the chamber fell silent. 'All those in favour of taking the stone by force?'

Roh felt sick as she watched hand after hand reach for the ceiling. There were so many against her —

Deodan surveyed the room and nodded to himself. 'All those in favour of releasing the cyrens.'

Roh's talons dug into her palms. Hands rose. Ten. Then twenty. Then thirty. She held her breath as the votes slowly, miraculously, tipped in her favour.

How? She gazed at Deodan in wonder. He had a loyal following, it seemed.

'Then it is settled,' he announced. 'Rohesia the bone cleaner and Finn Haertel go free. With the stone.'

Where Roh rested a palm against her satchel, the gem pulsed gently within, as though to reassure her that his words were sincere.

'After you, Queen of Bones,' Deodan said, gesturing towards the open door.

Roh narrowed her eyes. While the warrior warlock might have been responsible for their freedom, he was also responsible for putting them in this position in the first place. It was his clan who were plotting against Saddoriel with these so-called terror tempests.

Deodan led them from the cellar out onto the street again. As soon as they were clear of the warlock headquarters, Roh rounded on him.

'What in the realms are you playing at?' she barked.

He looked at her, his blue-grey gaze steely. 'Did you really think I didn't know you were following me? The Jaktaren's skills are rusty.'

'You bastard.' Finn lunged for Deodan, but Roh blocked him with an arm across his chest. Deodan wasn't through and she would hear the full extent of his betrayal.

'You have gone only where I have led you, Roh. And tonight, I led you here. I needed the clans to pick a side, once and for all. I needed to see what lasting goodness there was in warlocks.'

'At the risk of my life? And Finn's? And my crown?' Roh was outraged.

'Yes,' Deodan said simply. 'I risked everything tonight. But I needed to know, so I forced their hand.'

Roh nearly choked. 'Is that supposed to *comfort* me? You wormed your way onto our quest, all the while plotting to take —'

'*Retake*,' Deodan corrected. 'Retake what was ours.'

'What if that vote hadn't swung your way? You gambled the cyren crown and our lives back there, you untrustworthy swine.' Finn took a threatening step towards Deodan.

Similar fury coursed through Roh, hot and untamed. Her talons itched to slice into the warrior warlock – she wanted him to bleed for this, and her fingers twitched at her sides, ready to lunge for him. But she had always known, hadn't she? That Deodan's motives were his own. Somehow, in between their quiet conversations and shared secrets, she'd let herself forget it. Had she really believed that a Saddorien cyren could be friends with a water warlock? Had she truly been that naive? Even so, Deodan's deceit left her feeling hollow and raw.

'This isn't over,' she promised him before turning to Finn. 'Come on.'

The Jaktaren glared menacingly at the warlock but said nothing as he turned on his heel and followed Roh down the street.

'Do you know anything of these terror tempests?' Roh asked him at last.

Finn shook his head. 'Nothing. I've never even heard the term before.'

A sour taste spread across Roh's tongue. 'We have to find out. We have to know if Saddoriel is in real danger.'

As the pair entered the monastery grounds, the dawn was blood red.

The day of the challenge had arrived in a single betrayal and the blink of an eye.

CHAPTER TWENTY-TWO

When Roh and Finn reached the royal quarters, the others were awake, waiting.

'Where have you been?' Harlyn exclaimed, rushing to Roh and throwing her arms around her.

Exhausted, Roh returned the embrace. 'It's a long story,' she said, sinking into one of the lounges and explaining. The others echoed her shock at Deodan's betrayal, muttering curses and pacing wildly. While Roh spoke, Finn stood leaning against the doorway to the balcony, shaking his head, his fury palpable. But Roh needed to put all that aside in the face of the upcoming challenge.

As though reading her mind, Harlyn offered a sympathetic grimace. 'I can't believe it's *Orson*, Roh ...'

'I know. Have you seen her?'

'No.' Harlyn shook her head. 'I tried. I wanted to reason with her, but she wouldn't see me.'

'I'm so sorry, Har. It's all my fault. I drove her to this.'

'You don't know that,' Odi interjected, pressing a hot mug of tea into Roh's hands.

She took it gratefully, the scent of peppermint filling her nostrils. 'Don't I?'

'This could have been her plan all along,' Yrsa offered carefully.

'What? Don't be ridiculous.'

'I'm not,' Yrsa said. 'She could have studied the laws, realised that if you won, there would be an extension of the tournament and the opportunity to challenge. If she knew that, she knew she could skip the initial trials altogether and bide her time.'

Roh shot Harlyn a look of disbelief.

But Harlyn shrugged. 'We've been talking about it for hours. We underestimated Orson before. It'd be a mistake to underestimate her again. Maybe she's the most cunning of us all.'

'If that's the case, we're done for,' Roh told them, taking a sip of tea, savouring the warmth that spread down her throat and into her belly. She looked to Harlyn again. 'You realise what this means, don't you?'

Harlyn nodded slowly. 'It's either us or Orson.'

'If you want to be with her, I won't hold it against you, Har.'

'The way I see it, you and I have made amends. Orson has just put me back in the position I was in – in a bloody mess. That's on her. We *should have* all been on the same side together.' Harlyn adjusted the sling around her neck. 'We could have been, until now. I'm not going anywhere.'

Though she tried to hide it, relief flooded through Roh. She wasn't sure she could handle it if Harlyn left now, not after everything they had been through. Next, she turned to Yrsa and Finn.

'You understand what this means for you, too?'

'Yes,' Yrsa replied. 'If you lose, we lose our positions in Saddoriel. We'll be banished from the cyren territories. We will no longer be Jaktaren.'

Though Roh was sure the Council of Seven Elders would find some loophole that would allow their heirs to return, she placed her mug on the side table and wrung her hands. 'I'm sorry to have put you in that position. I didn't know it would come to this. If you want to return to Saddoriel, I'll free you from the contracts you signed.'

A thick silence settled around the room, and at last, Roh turned to Odi.

'You could go now, if you wanted. But I'd wager they'd just send more Jaktaren after you. You're the biggest prize on the ledger.'

Amber eyes met moss green. 'You think it's safest to stay with you?'

'Safest? No,' Roh told him truthfully. 'But I think it's the only way you stand a chance of getting the freedom you want. If I make it to the end of all this, I'll strike your name from the pages and tear the damn ledger in two.'

Shock rippled across Odi's face and he picked at the loose threads of his fingerless gloves. 'We've been in this together since the start,' he said slowly. 'Looks like I'll be with you till the end.'

A frustrated click of the tongue sounded. 'Well, if the *human's* staying, then so am I,' Finn declared stubbornly.

Yrsa grinned. 'Me too. Who needs the lair, anyway?'

Even with a unified front, the minutes and hours passed at a glacial pace. Roh wandered about the quarters aimlessly, obsessively checking the clock on the mantel, glancing out the windows at the height of the sun. She hadn't slept since the night before last, and even then it had been a troubled sleep, plagued by thoughts of the impending journey that hadn't come to pass. Now, memories of Orson filled her mind …

A young Orson showing both Roh and Harlyn around the workshop for the first time, both nestlings' noses scrunched up in disgust as they surveyed the various tools and buckets of foul-smelling liquids.

'You'll get used to it,' Orson had said, reassuringly patting their shoulders. *'Roh! Don't touch that, it's sharp!'*

Another time, Ames had confiscated a set of stones from Roh when she was supposed to be practising her common tongue. Orson had comforted her, slipping her a handful of candied nuts. *'He means well,'* she had whispered. *'You'll get your set back soon enough – he just wants you to learn.'*

One afternoon, when Harlyn was in rare tears after an older crush had rebuffed her, Roh had watched Orson fold the younger cyren into a long, unwavering embrace. *'There'll come a time when you'll be the one to turn away would-be suitors. The pain will pass.'*

Orson had always been there for them. Always reassuring, always right. They'd all done so much together, experienced every high and low as a trio. They'd shared a life.

Until Roh had broken it apart.

The image of Orson's tear-filled eyes filled her mind. *'You ... you cheated us,'* she had said.

And Roh had.

Not even sketching on the last blank page of her pad distracted her. She found Harlyn on the balcony, practising strengthening exercises for her wounded arm. 'Do you think she'd see *both* of us?' Roh ventured.

Harlyn looked up, beads of sweat glistening on her brow as she lowered a small weight to the ground. 'I don't know. Do you think that's a good idea?'

'I don't think any of this is a good idea ... But it can't be worse than facing her in the challenge without having tried. Maybe we can change her mind.'

Harlyn dabbed her face with a towel and met Roh's gaze. 'Then let's try.'

Roh followed Harlyn to a part of the monastery she'd never been before, where all the Saddoriens were staying in guest quarters.

'Must be strange for her,' Roh said. 'Having rooms to herself after the Lower Sector.'

'It was strange for me, but I had you,' Harlyn offered. 'I'm surprised they didn't make her share with Neith – the two lowborns together. But I suppose she's doing them all a favour, isn't she, by challenging you?'

Roh shrugged. 'I don't know whose motives her actions reflect anymore. Or which option is worse.'

'This is it. This door here,' Harlyn said, pulling Roh to a stop. 'Are you ready? Do you have an idea of what you want to say?'

'Not really,' Roh admitted. 'But … we're here now.' She raised a fist to the door and knocked.

The cyren who greeted them looked like Orson, even smelled like Orson, but the mask of cold and hatred she wore was utterly foreign. It was a surreal moment of disconnect for Roh as she studied her friend's face.

'I was wondering when you'd come,' Orson said, her top lip curled in a sneer.

'I came before. You refused me,' Harlyn said.

'Didn't feel right without our Roh present,' Orson said coolly, her eyes critically scanning Roh's cropped hair with a dark glint of amusement.

'Aren't you going to invite us inside, at least?' Harlyn made to cross her arms but stopped, as she couldn't do so with the sling around her neck.

Orson snickered at the injury. 'No doubt that's because of Roh. And no, I won't be inviting you in.'

'Actually, it was a teerah panther,' Harlyn retorted.

The momentary shock on Orson's face softened her features, and for the briefest second, she looked like herself.

Harlyn gave a satisfied smirk. But Roh took advantage of the moment. They hadn't come here to put more walls up between them; they had come to tear them down, to see if there was some way they could all come back from this together.

'Orson,' Roh implored. 'We can make this right. You don't have to do this. We can figure it out —'

'Make this right?' Orson's nostrils flared. 'Don't tell me you've found your moral compass after all, Roh? I suppose that's what they say, isn't it? That it's easier to ask for forgiveness than for permission.'

Each word was icier than the last, laced with a venom Roh had never heard in her friend's voice before.

'I'm sorry,' Roh said, realising that despite what Orson had said, she never had actually asked for forgiveness – there'd been no time – but perhaps …

'You're not,' Orson told her. 'You'd change nothing. You got what you wanted.' Her gaze flicked to the crown and the gem that shone there. 'For now,' she added.

A chill took hold of Roh's bones. 'Why have you done this?'

The mask slid back in place. 'Why?' she sneered. 'It is no worse than what you did.' There was no sign of her trademark tears or emotion, just cold calculation and determination. Orson seemed to sense Roh searching for it on her face.

'You thought I was some simpering fool,' she said. 'Both of you.' She gave Harlyn a pointed look, gathering herself up. '*Poor, fragile Orson,*' she spat. 'You thought you were so much better, so much stronger. More Saddorien than I could ever be.'

'That's not true,' Roh argued. They'd *never* thought that … Had they? But Orson wasn't done.

'How could you think me so weak, when neither of you knows your deathsong? You're the pitiful ones – even Ames thought so.'

'What are you talking about?' Roh demanded.

'The two orphan nestlings needing guidance, needing a big sister? You think I wanted you nipping at my heels for over a decade?'

Roh exchanged a glance with Harlyn. *This can't be true ... her* friend's eyes said. It was one thing for Orson to resent Roh's actions, but surely ... surely she hadn't resented their friendship for all this time? The past ten years of lessons, late-night whisperings and helping each other at the workshop couldn't all be lies ... Could they?

Orson was shaking her head as she watched the questions roll through Roh. 'Letting that incessant internal chatter get the better of you, Roh?'

Roh's stomach roiled as she realised ... Orson was no ordinary opponent. She was someone who *knew her,* better than anyone. Someone who knew exactly what buttons to push, someone who knew that Roh was her own worst enemy.

But Roh refused to accept that this cruel, cold cyren was the friend she'd known for the better part of her life. 'Orson, please, it's not too late. You can withdraw your challenge. We can all still have a home to go back to when this is over.'

Orson laughed darkly. 'There is no "we".'

'And was it me who made sure of that, or you? Was this what you wanted all along? Was this always the plan?' Yrsa and Odi's suspicions came tumbling out of Roh.

'The not knowing will eat away at you, won't it?'

'Orson …'

'I'm going to enjoy crushing you to pieces,' Orson told her. 'Just as I enjoyed smashing your stupid theatre model to bits.'

Roh blinked at her.

'Oh.' Orson smiled. 'You thought it was Harlyn?'

Harlyn was tugging Roh's sleeve. 'Come on. We won't change her mind.'

'You chose your side quickly, didn't you, Har?' Orson retorted, her icy gaze flicking between the two of them.

'You forced my hand.'

'Nobody forces a Saddorien cyren's hand.'

'Orson —'

'There's no way out now. I'll see you at sundown.' Orson slammed the door in their faces.

'I'm sorry,' Roh told Harlyn when they stood on the balcony of their quarters alone once more. 'I did think it was you.' She had worked on that music-theatre model for months – the one thing that had been hers, that had given her a sense of purpose and creativity amidst the gore and monotony of cleaning bones. She'd prided herself on that work. Had even dared to dream that it might actually be something one day …

'I let you think that,' Harlyn admitted. 'I was angry enough that it didn't matter which one of us had done it.'

Roh sighed. She understood that. 'What do you make of her? Has she been planning this from the start?'

'I have no idea.'

'She could just be saying those things to hurt us, because she's hurting.'

'She could be …'

Roh pinched the bridge of her nose. 'What are we going to do?'

Harlyn slung her good arm around Roh's shoulders. '*You* are going to beat her in the challenge.'

'I am?'

'You'd better. Or else we're all homeless.'

'No pressure, huh?'

An escort arrived for Roh just before sundown. She wore a simple tunic, pants and belt, with her crown atop her head, savouring the comforting thrum of the topaz as she followed the servant down several unfamiliar corridors to an unknown outdoor area. Roh found herself at an open-air gallery, which was not only crammed with cyrens, but statues as well. Placed above the grassy ground and golden leaves were towering sculptures of Dresmis and Thera. Busts, torsos, full figures in an array of poses, crafted from an array of materials: marble, bronze, stone … as though …

'These are offerings from all over the realms,' her escort explained.

'Offerings?'

'Well, tokens of victory.'

'You mean they were stolen?'

'*Won*,' the cyren corrected her. 'This way.' He led her

through the maze of statues, the differing styles telling Roh that they were indeed from all over the realms. Some were chipped or broken completely, as though in some instances they had been taken by force.

She peered up between the numerous wings, and above, the first streak of rose gold graced the sky. Sundown was nearly upon them.

They reached the heart of the gallery, where the Council of Seven Elders and the whole of Akoris, it seemed, were waiting. A long table had been placed in the only open space large enough to accommodate it and the council sat behind it, each wearing a blank expression, with their hands clasped before them. Roh's gaze lingered on Finn's parents, Bloodwyn and Taro Haertel. There were definite similarities between them and their offspring, but centuries of existence had honed their features with sharper, crueller details. Winslow Ward, Yrsa's aunt, sat at the far left end of the table, her mouth just a thin line, betraying nothing. Was she different from the others? She had raised Yrsa, after all. Finn, too, according to what he'd told Roh. The others, Roh wasn't so familiar with, only knowing them by name and jurisdiction. Though she knew that it was Erdites Colter, the elder in charge of the Law of the Lair and the Jaktaren, that she had to watch out for. She had no doubt it had been he who'd put the additional clause in the tournament contract about *questionable heritage*. He eyed her with unmasked dislike, his talons unsheathed, the zigzag line shaved through his head making him appear all the more severe.

Finally, Roh noticed Delja standing to the far right, not seated at the table, her face solemn, her wings tucked neatly behind her. She locked eyes with Roh from across the way, her gaze filled with understanding, with warmth. The words exchanged between the former queen and her mother before The Dawning came back to Roh.

'Are you scared?'

'Not with you by my side ...'

Whatever had come to pass between Delja and Cerys, Delja was here, at Roh's side. She had to find comfort in that. She took a deep breath.

Where is —

Roh didn't know how she'd missed Adriel. He stood on a raised dais behind the Council of Seven Elders, framed by two statues of Dresmis and Thera in all their glory, their outstretched arms creating an arch over him, as though he himself were godlike. His lips curved with a smug smile when he spotted her, his eyes resting upon the crown on her head.

Roh pushed down the fear that rose in her chest. This was not the time to panic. She saw Orson emerge from the shadows. Someone had loaned her clothes similar to the Jaktaren leathers, so different from the loose-fitting fabrics of the bone cleaners. Once, Roh might have said the form-fitting style was too harsh for her friend, but not now. Orson looked lethal.

The drumming had begun anew, but Roh didn't take her eyes off Orson and Adriel, her skin crawling.

'Rohesia,' Adriel called. 'You have been challenged by your fellow bone cleaner. You will remove your crown.'

Though she'd suspected she would be required to do so to avoid any unfair advantages, the loss of the topaz's guidance was still a blow. She said nothing as she reached for her crown and placed it carefully on the cushion offered. When it had first been presented to her back in Saddoriel, she'd seen the bones as a slight to her upbringing, a jibe at her *questionable heritage*. But … now it was hers. It belonged to her as she belonged to it. She had fought tooth and talon to win it and she'd be damned if she lost it now.

Cunning, strength, magic – the key virtues of cyrenkind. Roh had them all.

No matter what this challenge holds, I will prevail, she told herself. Pushing thoughts of friendship and betrayal, of warlocks and tempests from her mind, she looked for familiar faces to ground her, as she had done in all her previous trials back in the lair. To her relief, she spotted Odi, Finn, Yrsa and Harlyn close by. And Ames at Harlyn's side. They were with her. There was no sign of the traitor Deodan.

A gong sounded and Adriel cleared his throat unnecessarily. 'This will be a battle of cunning …'

Roh ignored her hammering heart and inhaled deeply and steadily through her nose. She could be cunning. She had already proved as much by standing where she stood.

Adriel continued. 'This challenge will consist of three riddles: a cyren tradition going back numerous millennia.'

Roh's heart sank. *Riddles?* She was no good at riddles. Her mind had long ago developed the terrifying habit of going completely blank as soon as a question was posed. Ames had told them riddles as nestlings that she'd never figured out. Putting abstract pieces of mental puzzles together was no strength of hers. She could work with her hands, she could design buildings and take things apart, but riddles ...? Something niggled at the back of her mind. Riddles were a feat of wit, not cunning, surely? Which meant that the demonstration of cunning would lie elsewhere in the challenge ...

Adriel was pacing, clearly eager to get the main event underway. 'The opponent to answer each riddle first wins a point. You know the stakes.'

The mere mention of the stakes drove a knife of fear further into Roh's heart and she turned away from her band of companions to face her challenger. Cold, wide-set eyes met her own as they were led to their positions before the council. Determination hardened her former friend's face.

'As a sign of respect, you will embrace your opponent,' Adriel said, clasping his hands behind his back and waiting expectantly.

What? Roh didn't let her surprise show as she took a step towards Orson. They had embraced countless times over the course of their lifelong friendship. Roh knew how Orson's soft body felt against her, how long she usually held on and the smell of the soap she used to wash her hair. But the cyren she embraced now was all hard lines and rigidness. A firm hand clapped her on the back twice, perfunctory, before they broke apart, unrecognisable to one another.

Whether Orson's choices had been reactionary or part of a long-hatched plan, it didn't matter now. They were both here. And only one of them would return to Saddoriel.

CHAPTER TWENTY-THREE

A team of servants came forward carrying two writhing hessian sacks and Roh's breath whistled between her teeth. Even Orson's steely expression faltered as the bags were placed on the ground before them. A long prong was used to pry the fabric away from whatever wriggled within.

A hiss sounded and a forked tongue peeked from one of the sacks, before an enormous triangular head emerged, its beady eyes immediately fixating on Roh. The serpent that left the bag was no ordinary viper. Its smooth, scaly body was as thick as one of Roh's legs. *Thicker.* Its tongue continued to flicker, as though tasting her fear in the air around it.

'Pythons,' Adriel announced. 'Imported from the jungles east of Csilla, just for this challenge.'

'Gods,' Roh couldn't help muttering as the reptile

slithered towards her. Perspiration dampened the back of her shirt. *How can I be sweating so much already?*

Adriel's smile was as serpentine as the snakes before her. 'They're to encourage you …'

'Encourage us to what?' Roh snapped.

'Answer faster.'

Roh forced herself to remain rooted to the spot as *both* pythons propelled their powerful bodies in her direction. She glanced at the council. Why were *both* creatures fixating on her, when the point had obviously been to have one python per competitor? When the snakes reached her, neither struck as a viper might. They didn't make any sudden movements. Instead, one slowly coiled around her boots, its forked tongue flickering at her ankles. It wrapped around her there, as though it had all the time in the world, as though it were considering a slow and painful death for her. Its vice-like grip tightened around her. The other slithered behind her and she was too terrified to twist to keep it in view. Had Adriel really imported these creatures from afar simply to entertain himself? Roh knew the answer to that and so refused to squirm.

When do we get to the riddles?

Roh glanced at Orson, but her former friend's gaze was ruthless and unsurprised, her eyes following the snakes with a cool curiosity.

'Are you ready?' Adriel asked.

'Let's just get this over with,' Roh muttered, fists clenched at her sides.

Adriel pressed his long fingers together. 'Very well,' he said as he surveyed both competitors. 'The first riddle is as follows …'

Roh could already feel her mind seizing up, the panic wrapping around her brain as the python was now wrapping around her, squeezing her bones. Roh willed Adriel to remain silent, knowing that whatever words he spoke next would send her into a pit of mental quicksand, sucking any logical thoughts under, leaving only useless blanks behind.

Adriel looked triumphant, his eyes glinting with pleasure as he took in her scarred, pale face and the deadly creatures at her legs. He cleared his throat.

'*In graves we gather. But the living we support. Small and large, movement of every sort.*'

Panic spiked through Roh's heart, the words already jumbled in her mind. *Graves. Movement. Gather.* She had to decipher it, had to stay calm, to register the riddle and solve it. As if sensing her fear, the python she could see squeezed around her calves and her mind went blank. Utterly blank. For a moment, she couldn't see the council, nor the crowd of Akorians. They were only grey blurs before her. She was shutting down. After every trial, after all she had endured to get here, was she to come undone at a handful of words? Would she forever be the almost-queen?

She didn't dare look at Orson, knowing that whatever expression her former friend wore would merely distract her, would get inside her already useless head.

'I will repeat it once more.' Adriel's voice sounded far away. '*In graves we gather. But the living we support. Small and large, movement of every sort.*'

The python slithered further up Roh's body and she closed her eyes. She needed to think, to break down the riddle. And not just the riddle, but who had spoken it. This challenge was about cunning, but she'd wager it was not just the cunning of the opponents. It was never that simple with cyrens.

What gathers in graves? Mourners? No. Corpses? But a corpse doesn't support anything that lives ... Or does it? What feasts on a corpse? Insects? Scavengers ...? Roh kept her eyes closed, ignoring the tightening press of the python around her thighs now, ignoring the prickling sensation at the back of her neck and the sticky dampness between her shoulderblades. She tried to push the fact from her mind that creatures like these crushed and suffocated their prey. What if she wasn't able to answer the first riddle? Would she be left to be squeezed to death? And why in the realms were *both* snakes fixated on her?

Focus, she chastised herself. The second half of the riddle didn't quite match her answer to the first, did it? *Insects and scavengers can be small and large, I suppose ... And movement of every sort ... Flying creatures, crawling creatures* ... But something didn't feel right about those possibilities. Something in Roh's gut told her the answer was within reach, perhaps right at her very fingertips ...

She chanced a glance at Orson, who was murmuring to herself, sweat beading at her brow, despite the fact that nothing was squeezing her half to death —

Roh gasped as the python wrapped around her stomach, its grip tighter still where there were no bones to keep it at bay. She looked around desperately for any sort of inspiration, something that might catapult the answer right into the forefront of her mind and rid her of the oncoming attack. She still couldn't see the creature behind her, but she could feel its presence, as though it were biding its time. No one objected, no one intervened. That wasn't the way of cyrenkind.

She felt like she was going to be sick. The python had clenched so hard around her middle, forcing her organs to shift into unnatural positions. She glanced down to see that her fingers were swelling ...

In graves we gather ... It couldn't end like this. Not after everything she had been through. The hunt through the Saddoriel water forest, jagged coral shooting towards her face to maim her, losing Odi to the council and getting him back, racing through the seas with a sea serpent in pursuit ...

Orson's gleeful expression sent a new spike of fear into Roh, and almost instantly she knew why. Roh stifled a moan of panic as she felt the weight of the second python against her calves, inching up her back —

Her eyes shot to Orson's as the realisation dawned on her. It wasn't sweat that drenched her back, but something else ... Something that Orson had planted there during their forced embrace. Roh couldn't help but gape at her former friend. She had never done something like this before, something so underhanded, so ... cunning. Orson wasn't like that, wasn't like the rest of the

Saddoriens. She was kind and considerate and … But that wasn't the Orson who stood before Roh now. The new Orson had known in advance about the snakes. Somehow, she'd found out about what the Council of Elders had been planning and had wielded the knowledge against Roh as she would a blade. Orson had done whatever she could to ensure the pythons fixated on Roh instead of her. A new icy wave of realisation shuddered through Roh. Orson had done exactly what *she* had done in that game of Thieves all those months ago …

'Gods,' Roh breathed, feeling her eyes bulge. There was a popping sound as her silver belt buckle broke from the leather beneath the creatures' grip and clattered to the floor. Each trial blurred before her as both pythons closed around her ribs, already bruising with their powerful bodies, threatening to break the ridges of bone —

Roh's eyes flew to her crown, where Adriel had placed it before Delja on a velvet cushion.

In graves we gather. But the living we support. Small and large, movement of every sort.

'*Bones*,' she rasped. 'The answer is bones.'

Adriel's eyes snapped to hers. His cold expression was unreadable. Roh felt like she was drowning again, though this time, her lungs burned with the poisoned water of waiting. She'd answered impulsively, foolishly. Ames was likely shaking his head in the crowd. Where was her so-called Saddorien cunning?

'Rohesia is correct.'

At that final word, the giant pythons fell away from her and a ragged gasp of relief broke from Roh. Panting, she pressed a gentle hand to her ribs to find them tender, definitely bruised, if not fractured. She reached for the wet patch on her back, but when her fingers came away from the soaked fabric, she could see nothing but clear moisture. Whatever Orson had put there … Roh would have to ask Yrsa later. But right now, it didn't matter. She had been *right*. After a moment, sounds came crashing into her; not just any sounds – applause, shouts of victory from the Akorians. How many times had she daydreamed about cyrens cheering her on during the first tournament? How many times had she wished to be the object of her kind's admiration rather than something they reviled? It had never happened … Until now. The Akorians were on their feet, fists striking the air, hands cupped to their mouths as they called out to her.

'Goddess incarnate!'

'Wise daughter of Dresmis!'

'The goddesses have guided her!'

But it didn't feel how Roh had imagined. There was a sourness to the experience. They weren't applauding *her*. They didn't *know* her.

I was right, she told herself, *that's what matters*. She couldn't lose her cool. She wasn't at the finish line yet. There were two more riddles, two more opportunities to lose all she had fought for.

She didn't acknowledge Orson. And she refused to take her eyes off Adriel, the underhanded bastard.

A strange scent wafted towards her. Incense laced with something familiar.

Porters walked towards them, holding swaying lanterns, silvery smoke escaping them. Roh's knees went weak and she staggered. *Gods. It's the same drug they laced the pool with in the Rite of Strothos. I can't ... I can't be exposed to this again ...*

As panic took hold once more, the pythons eyed her eagerly. Only they didn't start at her feet like before. This time, both rose up, their thick bodies more than capable of keeping themselves upright as they considered her.

Gods, I have to get these things away from me. Her unsteady hands went to the buttons of her shirt. She was only wearing a camisole beneath, but if it meant taking the pythons' focus off her ... Careful not to move too suddenly and provoke an attack, Roh undid the buttons of her shirt and slipped it from her shoulders, all too aware of the crowd's eyes on her, the impending second riddle and the incense that was growing stronger and stronger in her nostrils; she could taste it at the back of her throat.

Bunching her wet shirt in her hand, she threw it at Orson's feet.

Her former friend looked from the pile of fabric to Roh in horror. Smug satisfaction bloomed in Roh as the snakes eased off her and trained their beady gazes on Orson. But the small victory didn't last. Roh swayed. The drug was flooding her senses, jarring her concentration, pulling her attention in every direction. Even the slightest movement caught her eye and tugged her thoughts away from the glaring serpents and Adriel.

It felt as though the world around her had gone mute, the same way it had when she had been submerged in the hollow, but no visions swam before her. She saw no maimed Harlyn or withered, imprisoned version of herself … Roh blinked slowly, trying to regain her focus, using the statues of Dresmis and Thera to anchor herself.

'— *her heart I am red —*'

Roh jolted in shock. *Adriel's already started the riddle.*

'— *In your hand I am black. Unwanted, discarded, I am grey. What am I?*'

Dazed, she waited. He'd repeated the first one. He had to repeat the second, didn't he? Or had he already said it twice while Roh had been lost in her own head? Gods, if she missed this one … While the pythons had split their attention between both opponents now, one still swayed an arm's length before Roh, its stare intense.

The thick incense tickled the back of her throat and she coughed violently. Was she going to drown again somehow? Was this —

'*My master is not alive, yet she needs to breathe. In her heart I am red. In your hand I am black. Unwanted, discarded, I am grey. What am I?*'

The last words echoed in Roh's mind. *What am I? What am I?* She didn't know what she was. She only knew that she was drifting. The answer to Adriel's riddle floated somewhere in the incense-filled air around her, only she couldn't grasp it. So close but intangible. The smoke danced with the restlessness beneath her skin and she became untethered from the hall of statues, from the challenge unfolding without her. It was no doubt affecting Orson, too, but Roh already had so much in her system. The incense was somehow dislodging whatever remained in her body, essentially doubling, even *tripling* whatever dose laced the smoky air. She could almost see into her own body – the essence of the Strothos vines was a silvery substance, awakening within. Particles of it floated around her organs, joined by the new dose she was inhaling. Her tongue was furry in her mouth and she felt as though she were moving at half speed with heavy limbs, while everyone else carried on as usual around her.

Something shiny at her boots caught her attention. Her belt buckle. Its reflection shimmered against one of the statues by Orson. It was Yrsa's voice that came to her then: *Disree, my viper ... Apparently, she's developed a taste for bright, shiny things ...*

Perhaps pythons have similar proclivities, Roh mused abstractly. Using the toe of her boot, she manoeuvred the belt buckle so that its reflection hit Orson square in the chest. Both pythons' gazes snapped to the flicker of light and Roh sighed with relief as the snake before her eased itself onto its belly and made for Orson ...

You have to focus, Roh told herself. She stared at her hands, palms upturned, talons unsheathed. *Not alive, yet needs to breathe ... Red at heart, black in hand ... My master is not alive ... Red, black, grey ...* But the incense was clouding her thoughts. The colours swam in her vision, red, black, grey, each bleeding into the next. She staggered —

'— answer is: charcoal.' Orson's voice brought Roh

crashing down from wherever she'd been floating. Charcoal? *Of course* it was charcoal. And *of course* Orson was the one to answer it first. Orson, the cyren who tended to their fire back in the Saddorien rooms. The only one who liked to go near it, who relished feeding kindling to the hungry flames, the one who had watched Roh sketch with a stick of charcoal in that very same flickering firelight for years on end.

'That is correct,' Adriel allowed.

As they had done with Roh, the snakes fell away from Orson, but Roh was hardly paying attention. A rumble from the crowd sounded. Jeering. The slap of rotten fruit hit the ground by Orson's feet. Dissent. Roh knew how that felt. She almost felt sorry for her former friend. *Almost.* Roh glanced down at her hands – smudges of black still on her fingers. How could she have been so stupid? Adriel had designed these riddles to torment her. She should have known.

The haze of incense cleared and Roh was left blinking, shocked. She had lost a round. *Lost.* Her trick with the belt buckle hadn't been enough.

She refused to look at Orson, knowing she'd find a taunting smile she didn't recognise. Roh didn't need to feel any more unhinged than she already did. They were on even footing. Her initial victory had been rendered irrelevant. All that mattered now was what came next. Her knees quaked. The first to answer correctly would win the last challenge. They were mere moments away from one of them being banished from the cyren territories and thrown out into the wilderness of the realms beyond.

It will not be me, Roh vowed. *It will not be me.* Perhaps if she told herself that enough, it would become prophetic. *It will not be me*, she chanted again, trying not to fidget as the pythons slithered back to their masters, apparently done with tormenting both her and Orson. The Arch General motioned to a porter and Roh's heart lodged itself in her throat as a fabric-covered trolley was wheeled to the front.

'Rohesia and Orson of the Bone Cleaners, you are tied,' Adriel stated unnecessarily. 'This last riddle will determine our victor and the potential course of the cyren monarchy.' He lifted the cloth away from the tray with a flourish.

Roh took a step forward. Three bowls of clear liquid sat atop a tray. One with a small silver fish swimming circles within it. Roh's hands trembled at her sides and she stuffed them into her pockets. She couldn't help but glance at Ames and Harlyn, who both shifted nervously, straining their necks to see what the bowls held.

Adriel's voice called Roh back. *'What begins, but ceases to end, yet ends all that begins?'* He turned a small hourglass and the sand began to run.

Another hourglass flashed before Roh then. The giant one that had hovered over her first-ever trial in the Queen's Tournament. A lifetime ago. She had come so far since that moment. She found Odi's gaze in the crowd, understanding filling his amber eyes. He too had been taken back to the hunt in the water forest, it seemed. But they were in Akoris now, faced with a riddle and a former friend seeking vengeance.

There was nothing for her to do but approach the bowls. Each looked like it contained water, though she didn't understand why there was a single fish in one … *What in the realms …*

'Do we have to drink the one we think is the answer?' Orson spoke suddenly, nearly causing Roh to jump.

'You must act in a way the answer dictates.'

Roh rolled her eyes. *Classic Adriel horseshit*, as Odi would say. She leaned down and sniffed each bowl, trying to detect any clue she could, though the smell of incense was still trapped in her nostrils.

Orson copied her actions, though Roh was sure neither one of them had any idea what they were actually looking for.

'*What begins, but ceases to end, yet ends all that begins?*' Adriel said again, his expression smug, as always.

Roh wanted to flip the trolley onto him and shatter the bowls. How had Delja allowed someone like him to stay in power for so long? Roh's temper unfurled and fury coursed through her veins, along with whatever cyren magic and poison had awoken within her. Not even the Council of Seven Elders were so detestable.

She examined the bowls again. *There has to be some sort of hint here.* But with the exception of the fish circling, the bowls were identical, containing exactly the same amount of what Roh could only assume was water.

The sand in the hourglass fell in a steady stream,

creating a small hill in the lower half. Gods, she didn't have time for this.

Time – time had once begun and was yet to cease ... No, that couldn't be right, that was too simple. Adriel would never place the answer before her just like that. And then, how did the bowls come into it? There was going to be some sort of catch, some other snare that could trip her up ... Roh inhaled deeply through the front of her camisole, using it as a filter, trying to rid herself of the lingering sickly-sweet notes of incense. She bent at the waist again, sniffing the first bowl. She couldn't detect any aroma. Moving to the next one, the bowl with the fish, she breathed in deeply. Twice. And then to the third. There, she lingered. Was she imagining it? Ever so subtle ... Simultaneously sweet and bitter ... Roh repeated her actions at the first and again, the second and third.

I can't be imagining it, can I? Her mind went to the Rite of Strothos. *Well, there's a high chance I* could *be imagining things, given everything that I've ingested over the last week. But ... surely ... I would know that scent anywhere?*

The sand was running thin in the top half of the hourglass, and beside her, Orson was pacing in a panic.

Roh steeled herself. If it was indeed what she thought it was in that bowl ... Then what?

What begins, but ceases to end, yet ends all that begins?

Countless images swam before Roh as she tried to sift through an array of possibilities, each triggering the next, each more unlikely than the last ... But then, this challenge wasn't *just* about answering riddles, was it? It was about *cunning*, about the very root of cyren nature.

She looked to Orson, the cyren Roh had thought she knew best of all. They had grown up together, cried and laughed and bled together. Roh knew every one of Orson's tells, but more importantly ... Orson knew every one of Roh's ...

There was a solution here, or at least a manoeuvre that could *help* Roh win, but ... It would mean severing that last delicate thread, if there even was one left between Orson and her.

You can justify anything if you try hard enough, she thought, as the idea bloomed fully in her mind. What came next would be a matter of doing whatever it took to win, the consequences be damned. Roh had made that choice before, and she knew in her heart she would make it again long before her time was done.

She took a steadying breath and studied her opponent. Her friend's posture, which was usually straight and rigid when she was confident, was slightly slouched, her shoulders rolled inwards. Roh let her eyes dart to the statues around them, widening them slightly as though pieces of the puzzle were falling into place for her. *The answer is right in front of us,* she willed her surprised gaze to say. For a split second, Roh was back in the workshop with Orson, the vacant place in the Queen's Tournament hanging between them along with the cards of the thief's temptation. It had been just the two of them then, as it was now.

Roh chewed the inside of her cheek, hard enough to draw blood, glancing nervously at the statues before opening her mouth to speak —

'The gods,' Orson blurted. Roh turned to see her former friend's face flushing.

Roh's own face bloomed with heat. Had she made a mistake? Now that Orson had spoken the words aloud … Was it possible that the crown would never rest atop her head again? Would she wander the realms of man and warlock, banished from her home, the root of all her friends' hatred as they too stumbled through the barren outside lands?

'What say you, Rohesia?' Adriel called.

The final grains were falling in the hourglass.

Roh swallowed as the last pieces came together in her mind. There was no room for error.

'Well?' Adriel pressed.

Roh picked up the third bowl – the mingled sweet and bitter scent was undeniable. She poured its contents into the bowl with the fish.

'Death,' she said. 'The answer is death.'

As the final grain fell through the hourglass, the little silver fish floated belly-up to the surface of the water, poisoned by coral larkspur.

The gallery went silent, every gaze homing in on the bowl. Roh refused to let her knees buckle as she met Adriel's stare and waited. The Arch General's lips twitched. Roh couldn't tell if he was containing a smile of victory or warring with himself. Time stood still until —

There was a loud mechanical groan as one of the statues twisted on its plinth, revealing a dark passageway beyond.

When it ceased moving, Adriel still hadn't spoken, still

hadn't declared a victor. It was Delja's melodic voice that filled the gallery.

'I believe Orson of the Bone Cleaners is required to leave Akoris,' she announced.

A sour taste spread across Roh's tongue. She had won. *Death* had been the answer. But that meant ...

Orson's face drained of colour as an Akorian guard pushed her towards the tunnel, the two pythons from earlier now slithering again at her heels.

A primal, piercing scream echoed amongst the statues of the goddesses. A sound that came from deep within the soul. Roh whirled around to see Orson's mother, whom she hadn't noticed before, fighting against the hold of several guards.

Gods!

'*Meesha,*' Orson's mother cried, tears streaming down her face, her talons clawing at the Akorians who came between her and her daughter. '*Meesha!* Oh gods, don't make her do this!'

The New Saddorien word was drenched in anguish, in terror. *My love, my love!*

But Orson was already in the mouth of the passageway. And her ma gave a bone-rattling gasp, layered with all kinds of grief Roh didn't understand. The older cyren fell to her knees. '*Meesha,*' she sobbed again.

Roh trembled. *This wasn't the agreement.* The loser was to be banished, not hunted by giant snakes in the dark. Roh lunged forward. She wouldn't allow it, there was no way —

A firm hand shot out and held her back by the

shoulders. 'Do *not* interfere,' Ames said in her ear. 'It's only more ammunition they can use against you.'

Roh didn't care. This was *Orson*, for the gods' sakes!

Another hand, softer, found hers. Harlyn. 'Leave her,' her friend said. 'This was her choice. You jeopardise yourself, all of us, if you go after her.'

'Adriel?' Delja waited for confirmation from the Arch General, who gave a single, unhappy nod.

Orson didn't look at Roh, didn't look at her sobbing mother. She made a point of avoiding them altogether as she squared her shoulders and faced the newly revealed tunnel.

Roh was hardly breathing. Who knew where the tunnel ended up in the surrounding lands? And Orson would enter it with nothing but the clothes on her back and the monsters at her heels.

Adriel approached Orson and rested a hand on her shoulder, not an offering of comfort, but a threat. 'I hereby declare Rohesia the victor of this challenge. Orson of the Saddorien bone cleaners, you are hereby banished from all cyren territories. Should you return to Saddoriel or Akoris, or should you seek help in Csilla or Lochloria, you will face certain death. Let it be known.'

A soft cry escaped Roh, but she didn't move.

'Your banishment concludes this challenge. Leave now or face the wrath of the council.'

'We'll never see her again, will we?' Roh whispered to Harlyn, clutching at the pain blooming within her.

'Good riddance,' Harlyn hissed. But Harlyn's anger

only made the pain worse, for Roh knew it for what it really was: a mask for her own despair.

So many words lodged in Roh's throat and she fought desperately to free her voice, to call out to their friend.

But Orson walked into the dark mouth of the tunnel and didn't turn back. Not for her former friends, not for her screaming mother.

Roh shuddered as she watched her go. Victory had never tasted so bitter.

CHAPTER TWENTY-FOUR

All at once, Akorians threatened to swarm Roh, their bodies closing in, pressing against hers, stifling the air she so desperately needed to think clearly. Harlyn was pulled away from her and her friend's eyes widened in panic as Roh was dragged deeper into the fray.

'Don't worry,' Roh called out to her. 'Get out of here before someone knocks your arm —' And then she was swept away, whispers buzzing in her ears like a swarm of insects poised to sting. She didn't fight the movement – it was pointless against the unified sway of the crowd.

Silence fell. Roh craned her neck, trying to find the source of the Akorians' new focus. The throng of cyrens parted, revealing a figure who walked towards her.

Delja.

She held Roh's crown of bones between her talons before her, each step slow and deliberate. The Akorians watched her in awe, taking in the great wings tucked behind her back, and the glittering lilac of her gaze. When she reached Roh, she stopped and smiled, warm and understanding. She, too, in many ways, had been where Roh now stood. The former queen lifted the crown, the topaz gleaming in its setting.

'Congratulations,' Delja murmured, placing the crown on Roh's head, an acknowledgement of the new reign to be, a blessing from old queen to new.

Applause thundered around them, but Roh concentrated on the humming magic of the topaz.

'I will speak with you now,' she told Delja, deliberately phrasing her words as a command, from a future queen to a former one.

'Somewhere a little more private, I hope?' Delja whispered, utterly unfazed by the insatiable flock of Akorians crying out, their tattooed backs bared to her. 'And quickly – no doubt we will depart for Saddoriel within the hour.'

With the help of the topaz, Roh managed to guide them away from the crowds and into an antechamber.

'You did well, Rohesia,' Delja said, a soft smile tugging at her mouth.

'At the expense of my friend,' Roh replied, the sting of it still sharp and bleeding. 'Again.'

'You will come to find that sacrifices must always be made.' Delja gazed upon the crown and held out her hands. 'May I?' she asked.

It seemed a strange request given that she'd just placed it on Roh, but Roh could find no reason to object, and so she passed her the crown and the topaz it housed.

'Is that what you told my mother? That sacrifices must be made?' Roh asked sharply.

Delja's eyes, flecked with the golden reflection of the gem, shot up to her. 'What?'

'When you were in The Dawning.'

Delja studied the crown as she turned it over. 'So it *did* show you that.'

'Some.'

Delja sighed. 'It's actually what Cerys said *to me*. Before she tried to kill me. And her brother, Marlow.'

'What?' Roh's hand went to her scar.

'We had seen the wretched consequences of two wars and couldn't bear it. For too long, we'd been toiling our lives and the lives of others away in the army. Saddoriel did not prosper under the reign of kings. We vowed it could go on no longer. So together, we plotted and bided our time, and at long last, we entered The Dawning … together.' Delja inhaled, her eyes lined with tears. 'We defeated our fellow opponents and emerged victors of one of the most brutal Dawnings in our whole history. We were about to be crowned joint rulers of Saddoriel and cyrenkind, but Cerys … It wasn't something she wanted to share in the end. A sickness took hold of her. Winning The Dawning wasn't enough for your mother. She wanted full autonomy, complete power.'

Roh's mind threatened to cave in under the weight of what she had learned. They'd won *together*. In another life, Roh might have been the daughter of a queen. The seventeen years she'd spent as a bone cleaner flashed before her eyes, and then what could have been swept in … A fine education, feasts and galas, private quarters of her own with magical veils to the seas. She would have grown up alongside Yrsa and Finn, a cyren princess … But that life had never come to pass.

A sickness. Roh's blood ran cold and the brutal words of Taro Haertel filled her mind: *'The offspring of such a beast in the dungeons is bound to share the same foul blood.'*

Perhaps the Rite of Strothos hadn't weakened her. What if it was her own mind? What if the same madness that plagued Cerys flowed through her own veins as well? The restlessness she'd felt beneath her skin, the strange deathsong notes that had poured from her atop the dunes … What exactly would cyrenkind do with a mad queen? The spiral of thoughts sucked Roh into a dark, vicious whirlpool. She clawed and kicked with all the strength she had, but she couldn't escape it, couldn't find a place to break through.

Delja continued, 'Cerys went to the Council of Seven Elders, knowing she had always been the more popular of the two of us, and pleaded her case. Despite our joint victory, there couldn't and would never be dual leadership of the cyren territories. Only one. Only her. There were those who agreed with her, those who had never warmed to me, but … those who objected … Well, they perished.'

Roh's throat was too dry. 'How?' she croaked, though she already knew.

'At the deathsong of the mighty Cerys Irons.'

Irons ... A name that once would have belonged to Roh, too. A name that had been snatched away, left to crumble to dust in Saddoriel's prison.

Delja winced, the tale clearly bringing painful memories to the surface. 'She used our sacred magic against our own kind, yes. Cerys' song was so strong that our immunity as cyrens didn't matter. She targeted the elders and one by one, they fell. I managed to stop her before she wiped out the entire council, but that's when she turned on Marlow and me. The two people who loved her the most. Then, the damage was done. I couldn't protect her any longer. As I told you before, the course of our history changed forever.'

'She was imprisoned and you were recognised as the rightful queen?'

'I was. And the new council members were selected from Saddoriel's founding families.'

'And that's when your wings manifested?'

'Yes. A blinding agony tore through me when I was presented to Uniir the Blessed, the former king of Saddoriel. The wings ripped through my very being and into this world ...' Delja winced as she recalled the pain. 'It was recognition from the goddesses themselves, according to lore. I was told it was why I was able to stop her, that my heritage was the only thing that prevented her from turning me into a pile of bones.' Regret shone in Delja's eyes.

Roh recalled the vision and the words Ames had spoken to her in the tavern. 'She was your family ...'

Delja nodded. 'It never ceases to astound me ... all

the beautifully wretched ways we can break each other. How those we love ultimately cause the worst of our pain.'

Slowly, Roh reached out and took the crown from Delja's grasp, the bones and gem suddenly feeling heavier than before as she placed it back on her head.

The former queen leaned in close, her fingertips brushing Roh's loose hair from her brow. 'Allow me,' she murmured, straightening the crown. The action felt so familiar, so intimate, that Roh froze.

Delja smiled sadly. 'In another life, you could have been a niece to me – a foster daughter, even.'

Something in Roh shifted when her gaze met Delja's. She could have been staring into a looking glass: before her stood a lonely orphan, forgotten by a family long ago lost. They had both hurt and been hurt, cut from the same cloth of ambition, cunning and desperation.

Delja sniffed. 'I have asked you before, and I will ask again now – will you let me help you? I want you to be the queen your mother never could be.'

'But ... why?' Roh croaked.

Delja's smile was full of sadness. 'I am tired, Rohesia. And a tired queen makes mistakes. It is time for someone fresh and vibrant. It is time for you.'

Roh's hands were trembling as Delja took them in her own, her palms soft and strong. Roh was still reeling from Orson's betrayal and banishment, and she had nearly lost Harlyn, too. And Ames' broken promises and cryptic nature had put up a wall between them. Roh needed this. She needed guidance, someone in her corner, someone who understood where she was from and what she had endured.

She took a deep breath, at last feeling as though the air was completely filling her lungs, and leaned into the former queen's warm embrace.

CHAPTER TWENTY-FIVE

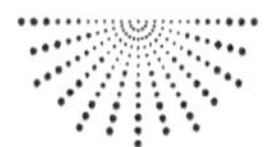

There was almost as much fanfare for the Council of Elders' departure as there had been for their arrival. Only this time, Roh was going to see how exactly the company travelled through the mirror Pool of Weeping.

Delja had been right. Within the hour, the entire entourage gathered around the pool's bank, stepping over the roots of the weeping willows, while Roh searched wildly for Ames. He owed her answers – he couldn't just leave. Panic soaring, she cornered him by yet another winged statue.

'Who's Eadric?' she demanded.

'Rohesia, not now —'

'Now is the *only time*, Ames. And you promised. I made it through the challenge, despite what it cost me, so you will tell me what you know, despite whatever it will cost you.'

Ames looked taken aback and he glanced around before bowing his head in defeat. 'Eadric …' he told her softly, 'was your father.'

Roh stared. The image of the snarling blue-tinged warlock opposite her mother's cell filled her mind.

Ames watched her thoughts flit across her face and he nodded in confirmation.

'My father … was a water warlock? *The* water warlock from the prison?' Roh felt sick. 'How?' she croaked.

'They knew each other as children. A long time ago, it was different between our kinds. Your mother was raised alongside many warlocks in the scholars' city.'

'She grew up in Lochloria?' Hadn't Deodan said as much?

Ames nodded again. 'She left Saddoriel's schooling when she was quite young. Your grandmother had duties in Lochloria.'

'How do you know so much about her?' Roh pressed.

'I have picked things up over the years.'

'That's not an answer.'

'That's all the answer you'll get. Don't forget your place, Rohesia. You're not queen yet.'

'I am *almost* queen,' she ground out. 'Some would do well to remember that, for when the time comes, I'll remember how I was treated.'

Ames eyed her warily. 'Sentiments like that make for shortsighted rulers.'

Roh's face heated instantly as shame filled her. What was she thinking, threatening Ames?

His face softened, as though he could sense the regret

coursing through her. He turned his back to the pool, shielding himself and her from any onlookers. From his cloak, he produced the quartz dagger once more. 'This belonged to your father.' He pressed it into her palm. 'It is one of two. A pair forged at the very beginning of our kinds.'

A fissure formed across Roh's heart. 'Where is the other? Please don't tell me it's another object I have to find.'

'It will find you.'

'Ames ... I can't do this. I can't keep living in the dark, surrounded by whispers and secrets.' She didn't hide her desperation.

Ames' gaze was unflinching as he spoke, his voice lowered. 'There is no limit to what you can do or what you can endure, Rohesia.'

The fissure across her heart deepened, a ragged fault line threatening to crack her wide open. 'How do you know?' she whispered. She had never felt so weak, so alone, so powerless. *How can I take any more?*

Ames' intense stare did not falter. 'Birthed by a cyren, fathered by a warlock, named for a human girl ... Maybe you are the one to bring us together, after all.'

Roh blinked at her mentor, her fragile chest suddenly forgotten. She hadn't heard him right, there was no way —

The mirror Pool of Weeping rippled, sending a pulse of magic outwards, momentarily stunning Roh. The Council of Seven Elders, Delja and the rest of the entourage were readying themselves.

'We are out of time,' Ames said. Roh swore she saw a flicker of relief cross his weathered face.

'But —'

'Soon enough, you'll learn it all.'

'Only if I win.'

'Then win,' Ames said simply.

Roh almost let out a shriek of fury as she gripped Ames' bony arm. 'Saddoriel is under threat,' she blurted.

Ames' eyes narrowed as they slid to where Roh clutched him. 'What are you talking about?'

'Terror tempests.'

Roh didn't miss the flicker of recognition that passed across her mentor's face. 'Those storms haven't raged in over fifty years.'

'I heard —'

'Saddoriel has been under threat since the dawn of time,' Ames said coolly. 'The most powerful territories always are. And they beat back their attackers time and time again. Let the matter rest, Rohesia.'

Jesmond appeared at Roh's side. 'Nice work with the challenge,' she said with an approving nod. 'I'll let the punters back home know you're still in it.'

Roh felt Ames detach himself from her and step away.

'How kind of you,' Roh said drily to Jesmond.

'Sorry about Orson, though,' Jesmond added with a shrug.

'Are you?'

'Not particularly. Pretty low move from her, if you ask me.'

'No one asked you,' Ames snapped, glancing across the

shore of the pool to where Orson's mother stood alone, her eyes red-rimmed and hollow. 'Say your farewells, Jesmond,' he added. 'We can't delay the council any longer.'

Jesmond rolled her eyes and turned to Roh. 'You've got a little following back in the Lower Sector.'

Roh raised her brows. 'I do? I thought everyone preferred Neith?' The banners with the water runner's name scrawled across them were a sharp memory. She could still feel the sting of seeing them for the first time and realising her own kind didn't support her.

'Word got out about her being a two-faced backstabber.'

'Oh? And how did that happen?'

'No idea.' Jesmond winked. 'Where's Harlyn?'

Roh scanned their surroundings and pointed. Harlyn was standing next to Odi, their heads close together as they discussed something intently.

Jesmond studied the pair.

'Sorry, Jes,' Roh found herself saying. 'I know you have a soft spot for her.'

But the youngster didn't look fazed. 'It's not our time yet,' she said with a grin, leaving Roh baffled at her resilience and self-assuredness. Perhaps there was something to be learned from the fledgling.

'Tell her goodbye from me, will you?'

'Sure, Jes.'

With a final nod, Jesmond turned to Ames and gave a resigned sigh. 'Back to the lair of bones we go, then.'

Ames shook his head in disbelief before offering her

his arm. Jesmond took it and Roh watched as her mentor led the youngster to where the others were waiting at the edge of the pool.

Someone slammed into Roh as they passed, sending her sprawling. She only just caught herself before she ate dirt. Palms stinging, she got to her feet, her head spinning.

Zokez Rasaat stood before her, his lilac eyes narrowed with malice.

'What do you want?' Roh's patience was on its last legs.

The highborn's talons were unsheathed at his sides and his nostrils flared as he stared her down, his eyes raking over her in disgust, as though she were a slab of meat he was about to carve into. '*What do I want?* I want you *gone*, bone cleaner,' he spat. 'You are an insult to Saddoriel, to all of cyrenkind.'

'That's old news,' Roh muttered, dusting off her pants and attempting to leave.

A sharp pain pierced her upper arm and Roh looked down to see Zokez's hand clamped around her, warm blood trickling down her skin from where his talons cut into her flesh. She jerked away, hissing as the talons cut deeper, but his grip was like that of the python's: unshakeable.

'I am not the only one who feels this way,' he hissed in her ear.

Hot fear pulsed through her, but Roh didn't flinch. 'Again,' she said icily, 'that's old news. Do you have anything of importance to tell me, Rasaat?'

His grip tightened, his talons digging deeper into Roh's skin, and her eyes watered at the pain. Blood ran down her arm freely, but still she didn't yield.

Zokez's voice was low, laced with the dark promise of violence. 'You will lose everything you hold dear before your time is done, *isruhe*.'

There was a blur of movement, followed by a cry of pain and anguish from the highborn.

Finn Haertel's fist had collided with Zokez's face.

Sprawled on the pebbles, clutching his bleeding nose, Zokez gaped at the Jaktaren. 'What in the name of —'

But Finn didn't offer an explanation. He merely stared down at his fellow highborn, his face contorted with dislike.

'Finn, what the …?' Zokez examined the red pooling in his palm in shock.

'Zokez!' a sharp voice rang out, echoing across the water. The Council Elder, Koras Rasaat, looked utterly mortified as he called out to his son.

The highborn scrambled to his feet, the flushed disbelief on his face transforming into anger as he wiped the blood from his nose. 'Of course,' he said, his swelling nose barely able to scrunch up in disgust. 'Of course you're an *isruhe* sympathiser. The two misfits of Saddoriel, coming together.' Zokez laughed darkly, taking pleasure in something Roh couldn't understand. He sneered at Finn. 'A new queen won't make you whole, Haertel. Especially not an *isruhe*.'

Finn made to lunge for the highborn again, but Zokez scurried away like the coward he was, leaving

Finn with his battered fist clenched and his chest heaving.

'I remember you calling me the same foul name,' Roh said, when Finn came to stand at her side, rubbing his grazed knuckles.

He didn't take his eyes off the entourage before them. 'I will never call you that name again.'

Finn's parents, Taro and Bloodwyn Haertel, whose stony expressions betrayed nothing, walked forward into the water.

'What did he mean, "won't make you whole"?' Roh asked.

Finn's eyes were on his parents as the water began to swirl around them. 'No idea,' he said.

The pool suddenly parted around the elders.

What in the realms …?

Roh's shocked gaze met Delja's from across the shore. The former queen smiled at her, the new bond between them warming Roh from within.

Alarm crossed Delja's face and she mouthed something to Roh.

Fear spiked as Roh squinted, trying to make out her words. *What is she trying to say?* A single word. Once. Twice. Her face taut with urgency.

Roh started with realisation. *Dagger.*

Roh looked down. She was still holding the quartz dagger that Ames had given her, out in the open, for all the realm to see. Hurriedly, she stuffed it into her pocket, instantly wondering who had spotted it in her grasp.

'Wait!' shouted a familiar voice. Odi bolted forward,

pressing sheets of parchment into Ames' hands. 'Music,' he panted. 'For the fiddlers.' He darted away before Ames had a chance to respond.

'If we're all ready?' Taro Haertel said icily, eyeing Ames as he tucked the papers into the folds of his robes.

Ames gave a stiff nod.

As if in tune with the Council Elder's thoughts, the water of the mirror pool parted completely, allowing the whole entourage to walk down into the basin, where at the bottom, a shimmering portal was revealed.

Roh swore under her breath, knowing in her gut that it would bring the council straight to the Pool of Weeping in Saddoriel. Instead of sharing that power with their potential future queen, they were forcing her to trek across the realms and face angry clans, teerah panthers and Dresmis knew what else that lay ahead. Her fury simmered in her veins as she watched the council and their cohort disappear through the portal and the water of the pool surge back in place in a violent wave. Seconds later, it was as though the Saddoriens had never been there, the surface of the water still but for a few ripples.

A gentle hand gripped Roh's shoulder and she turned, finding Deodan behind her. Dark circles shadowed his eyes and he looked more dishevelled than usual. On her other side, Finn stiffened. They hadn't seen the warrior warlock since the night before, when his clan had nearly stolen the topaz from her.

'And so now you know,' he said.

Roh found herself blinking up at the warrior warlock who had somehow embroiled himself in her quest. The words he'd spoken before the Rite of Strothos came back to her: *You have to feel a connection to who you are ... to come back from something like this ...* He'd said it just before handing her the quartz dagger, *her father's* dagger. He'd known to whom it had belonged this whole time.

'*Now I know?*' she spat back at him, her fury coiling together, willing her to mark him as a target. 'Get out of here,' Roh said coldly.

'I'm sorry. I wanted Ames to be the one to tell you. It was only right.'

'What does that mean —' Roh cut herself off. 'Actually, *I don't care.* I don't care what it means or what you want. I don't care about your clan or these so-called storms. Just leave me be. You've done enough.' She stared him down, talons unsheathed, letting the fiery fury that had simmered below boil to the surface at last. Magic rushed through her and it was all she could do to stop herself from tipping her head to the ceiling and opening her mouth to sing.

'You should care ...' Deodan started.

But Finn shoved the warrior warlock towards the exit. 'You heard her.'

'Roh?' Harlyn asked, gently gripping her arm as Jaktaren and warlock faded into the distance.

Roh focused on her friend. 'It's been a long day,' she managed, the drying blood on her arm itching.

Harlyn nodded. 'I know.'

Numb, Roh let Harlyn guide her from the mirror pool. She felt herself caving inwards as every blow from the past few weeks hit her at once, threatening to open that fissure that kept cracking wider within. They had lost Orson, and now here she was, a potential ruler of cyrens, with glimpses into truths long past, facing the threat of storms she did not understand, with two Jaktaren, a bone cleaner and a human in tow ...

A water warlock had been her father. She had been named after a human girl. Both species that, until recently, she'd only known as weaker and lesser. And what of the Warlock Supreme? Deodan's mother, who was ready to go to war with cyrenkind, who had every weapon imaginable to cut through their song attacks and defences ...

'— in the morning,' Harlyn was saying as she pushed open the doors to their quarters.

Dazed, Roh staggered inside and Harlyn grabbed her, leading her to the lounge and sitting her down as though she were a lost nestling. 'Roh?'

Roh shook her head. 'Sorry. I didn't hear you.'

'I was just saying that we should leave in the morning. Put as much distance between us and this place as possible. I can send word —'

'No, don't send word. Anything like that gives Adriel the upper hand. We order as much food as we can to our chambers tonight, pretend we're celebrating, and pack our own supplies. Let's be at the stables before dawn and leave before first light. We tell Adriel none of it.'

'I like it,' Yrsa said as she entered the room. It was only when the Jaktaren threw a blanket around Roh's shoulders that she realised she was shivering. Now that she had finally stopped moving, her body felt battered.

Sure enough, when she peeked beneath her camisole, she saw mottled bruises around her ribs, where the python had threatened to squeeze the life out of her.

'I'll get you a cold compress for that,' Yrsa told her, looking at the splotches of purple and blue across Roh's skin.

Roh didn't know when she fell asleep, or how, given the whirlwind of thoughts churning through her mind. At one point, she felt the press of a wet towel against her ribs and someone wiping the blood from her arm, but she didn't open her eyes. She was too far under, where countless memories barrelled into her. Cerys, the sea drake, the piano she and Odi had built, the Eery Brothers playing their fiddles in a cage of bones, the human who had been lured to his own demise by the death chorus, statues of Dresmis and Thera, the Akorian library, the dunes and the hot sweeping winds ... All the while, the same set of words hummed in her ears:

Maybe you are the one to bring us together, after all ...

CHAPTER TWENTY-SIX

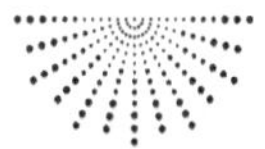

Roh woke to the sound of the others packing and the click of the door closing. Finn had returned from somewhere, a brilliant bruise blooming high on his left cheek that he certainly hadn't received from Zokez. Deodan was nowhere in sight and Roh didn't have the strength to ask what had happened. *Good riddance.*

Wordlessly, she got up and went to the bathing room to wash. She didn't bother to look at her reflection; she already knew she looked as terrible as she felt. It was surreal, packing up again as they had done once before, but this time Roh felt no lingering sense of paranoia. Adriel couldn't stop them. At last, they would put Akoris behind them.

'I've been thinking,' Odi said from the corner of the room as Roh emerged. He was wrapping Harlyn's lute in some sort of protective canvas.

'About?'

'When I was trapped in the queen's quarters and I looked at that book?'

Roh's brow furrowed as she tried to sift through her memories. 'Oh.' They had been sitting on the floor of her quarters in the Upper Sector when Odi had first told her about it. 'The *Tome of Kyeos*?' Odi had stolen a glimpse of the ancient tome while he had been locked away with a piano in Delja's chambers. 'I forgot you'd seen it,' Roh murmured.

'It showed me Orson, remember? She was all alone … Do you think it was warning me about the riddle challenge? She's all alone in the realms now.'

Roh tried not to picture Orson blindly wandering the lands. 'If it had been, it didn't do much good, did it?'

'I guess not.' Odi shrugged.

Roh returned to packing her bag, carefully tucking the drake egg into her spare cloak and ensuring it had plenty of cushioning lest it be knocked on the journey. Harlyn and Odi had packed their supplies while she slept and she felt a surge of gratitude for her friends. Especially when Harlyn threw her a spare loaf of bread to eat after hearing her stomach growl.

As Roh packed away the last of her spare clothes, Yrsa approached her with a handful of cloth. 'Do you have a moment?' she asked.

'Of course. What is it?'

'I … uh … I made you this.' Yrsa pulled back a fold of fabric, revealing a freshly woven sling and a new leather pouch of stones. 'Figured you should have your own, now you know how to use it.' She pressed the small bundle into Roh's hands.

'You made this?' Roh said in wonder, fitting the loop to her finger and testing its length. Yrsa had estimated perfectly.

'What'd you think I was doing, knitting socks?' Yrsa grinned.

Roh huffed a laugh. 'No, knitting and socks aren't what come to mind when I think of you. But thank you. I love it.'

Yrsa gave her another grin and left to finish packing.

After a final sweep of the quarters, Roh and her companions shouldered their packs and supplies and headed to the stables. In the dark and quiet hours of the morning, they saddled their horses. Roh inhaled the scent of hay and manure, grateful that it cut through any lingering memory of the incense aroma. She tightened the girth of her saddle as Yrsa had shown her before and adjusted the length of the stirrups before filling the saddlebags with her rations and water canteen. Leading her horse out of the stables, towards the gates, Roh realised how eager she was to get back on the road, to breathe in the crisp air of the plains, and how determined she was to feel a sense of progress as distance was covered, one step at a time.

A few moments later, Finn, Yrsa, Harlyn and Odi were all ready. Roh mounted her horse and motioned for the Akorian guard to open the gates.

With her crown sitting proudly in place, Roh guided her horse to stand alongside Finn's. She reached into her pocket and produced a piece of folded parchment, holding it out to him.

Frowning, Finn took it. 'What's this?'

Roh shrugged. 'You said you wanted the map …'

Finn unfolded the yellowed page and, peering down at the markings, he smiled widely. A true smile, one that revealed a dimple in his left cheek Roh hadn't seen before. She decided it suited him.

At last, the heavy slabs of rusted iron swung inwards and Roh didn't hesitate, pressing her horse's sides with her heels. No one stopped them as they left the monastery behind, but Akoris seemed to say its own farewell as golden leaves from the flame trees fell from the sky.

The further they rode from Akoris, the lighter Roh began to feel. She hadn't realised how much the place itself had burdened her, and though she was sad to leave the sight of the sea, she felt stronger with each passing step. The sun warmed her back and the cool breeze kissed her skin as she swayed to the rhythmic stride of the horse beneath her, finding that the saddle had moulded to her shape during their last journey and wasn't nearly as uncomfortable as it had once been.

They were passing through vast fields of golden crops when Harlyn spoke.

'Can you smell that?' Her nose wrinkled, her eyes narrowing.

Roh twisted in her saddle, looking west, knowing what she would find there.

Smoke billowed in the distance, marring the crisp blue canvas of the horizon.

'What is that?' Yrsa said, shielding her eyes from the sun's glare.

Roh watched the smoke pour into the sky. 'The Fields of Dresmis; Adriel's crop of wild draketail,' she answered with no small sense of satisfaction. 'It's the hallucinogenic plant he used on you all on our first night here. The one he uses on his people every night. And that' – she pointed to another billow of smoke several leagues south – 'is his store of monk's thorn, the herb he laces the bran with each morning.'

She watched the blazes for a moment, a weight inside her lifting. 'He'll have a hard time drugging his people into submission now.'

The others gaped at her, but Roh simply rode on.

Finn led their entourage, proudly clutching the map in his hands whenever he paused to check their position against the height of the sun and his compass. They rode for the Endon River, the first body of water that split the lands between Akoris and Csilla. They had crossed it once before, to the west, after leaving Deodan's clan of humans in the gilded plains. Roh looked to her companions, relishing the comfortable quiet that had settled between them, so different from the resentment they had all clung to when they'd first journeyed over these lands. She found herself riding alongside Odi.

'I've been meaning to tell you,' she said, leaning towards him so he could hear over the horses.

'Tell me what?' he asked with raised brows.

'I found out something recently.'

'Oh?'

'Apparently, I was named after a human.'

Surprise flashed across Odi's face before he said, 'Surely that's not the worst thing?'

Roh took in his features and his straight-backed posture, resilient as ever. 'No,' she told him. 'I suppose it's not.'

Only a few hours had passed when Finn signalled for them to stop. As soon as he did, Roh heard what he had: hooves thundering towards them.

In an instant, Finn had his crossbow loaded and aimed, Yrsa had her sling at the ready and Odi had unsheathed his sword. Roh prepared her new sling, almost eager for a chance to use it, and Harlyn palmed a small fighting knife in her good hand.

Dust clouded their pursuer.

'Halt!' Roh shouted as whoever it was closed the gap between them.

The horse gave a high-pitched whinny as its rider drew its reins up short and they skidded to a stop in the dirt.

A hooded figure dismounted and approached them. 'I'm sorry,' he said, pulling back his hood. 'I didn't mean to alarm you.'

'Deodan,' Roh breathed, the name tasting sour in her mouth.

'What are you doing here?' Finn said sharply. 'I thought we decided it was best that you remain behind.' Roh's gaze flicked to the bruise on Finn's face. They had done more than exchange words.

'*You* decided that,' Deodan retorted before facing Roh, revealing a split and swollen lip. 'I want to come with you.'

Roh snorted. 'Why should we have you with us? You misled us about who you are. You put us in a position where my crown was nearly taken from me and our lives were at risk. Your kind are rallying against ours and plotting the fall of our homeland.'

'I know,' he replied. 'And for that I'm sorry. But I want you to understand ... My people had *everything* taken from them. That is the bitterness you sensed in the Warlock Supreme.'

'You mean, in your mother,' Roh corrected.

'Yes,' Deodan allowed. 'My mother. She – we – had our home, our families and even our magic stolen from us. Our talents, our enchantments and talismans were used against us, after promises were made. They're all still used in Saddoriel to this day. Even the birthstones you seek are of warlock creation.'

'Whatever the truth may be, I'm not allowing you to join us only to have you stab me in the back and take what I have fought for.'

'We don't want the gems, Roh. We just want our home

back. And hopefully, a ruler who listens to the guidance of the stones.'

Roh suddenly recalled how the topaz had pulsed in the warrior warlock's presence, as though to reassure her of his sincerity. But she shook her head. 'That's not what your mother said.'

'I don't want what my mother wants. And as you saw, I have my clan on my side. I want to help you. I have proven that much, no? I think you can be the queen we need. Were I to rejoin you, you have my word that I will stay for as long as it takes, and I will use my power and influence and rank to help you get the gems.'

Even now, the topaz pulsed true in Roh's crown. But if one gem alone told her she could trust a water warlock, what had all three birthstones and the *Tome of Kyeos* told the rulers who came before her?

'Or what?' Yrsa interjected, her sling still loaded and aimed.

'This isn't a threat,' Deodan told her. 'But the alternative is that without my aid, the warlocks will try to take the gems by force. They will either beat you to the others, or take them from you directly. The Warlock Supreme wants to unite her considerable army and march on the cyren territories. They're biding their time. Akoris will be taken easily enough, given the state of its citizens. And then the warlocks will come for you, and Saddoriel. They're waiting for the terror tempests, then they'll strike. I'm offering you protection from that. While I'm at your side, they will make no move.'

The hum of the topaz was constant. It told her there was sincerity in Deodan's words.

What does this mean? Roh's gut churned. But she knew exactly what it meant. That the kings and queens of the past had ignored the gems, the very tools supposed to guide them towards a better Saddoriel. And yet, she didn't want to believe him. Not after everything.

'I was told the terror tempests haven't happened for decades,' she claimed boldly.

'That's not strictly true. And even if it were, it's all the more reason that they're imminent. And they'll break Talon's Reach wide open, Roh,' he stressed. 'The realms have adapted to face you. They've learned from the Age of Chaos. Just as we learned from the Scouring of Lochloria. Human settlements are scattered all around these lands, full of people who would stop at nothing to end the likes of you. You are not as strong or as invulnerable as you think. You know this, you have seen it already. And what of the Akorians? You would leave them to face a battle against my mother? Or arguably worse, leave them in the hands of Adriel?'

Harlyn scoffed and Roh was inclined to agree with her.

'Adriel's supply of draketail and monk's thorn has been burned to ash. I have liberated Akoris.'

'Is that all it takes?' Deodan challenged.

Roh's stomach shifted uncomfortably and Ames' words came back to her. *Sentiments like that make for shortsighted rulers.* She didn't want to be a shortsighted ruler. According to their histories, cyrenkind had had their fair share of those in the past.

'I don't trust you as far as I can throw you,' Finn snapped. 'You were to stay in Akoris.'

'And I *meant* to follow your … instruction,' Deodan admitted. 'Until I saw …' He rummaged through the pockets of his cloak. 'This.'

Roh jumped down from her horse and took the crinkled parchment from his dirt-lined, callused hands. It was a page from her own sketchbook. A precise drawing of the quadrangle she'd seen in the Rite of Strothos. She had sketched the sandstone pavers exactly as she remembered them, and the gardens, full of life, and the babbling stream at the heart of it all …

'Where did you see this?' Deodan asked as he watched Roh scan the drawing.

'I … It was shown to me, during the rite.'

'Then I must come with you, Roh.'

'Why? What is this place?' Roh asked.

Deodan took the page from her, longing etched on his face as he studied the perfect lines and beautiful detail. 'This is the scholars' city … My home, in Lochloria. Only it no longer looks like this. It's been in ruins since the Scouring.'

'And why does that mean you should join us?' Harlyn piped up.

'Because … Perhaps Roh can offer us a future where it looks like this once more.'

The topaz sent a pulse of warmth down from the top of Roh's head. She had witnessed a lot in her mere seventeen years, both in Saddoriel and now in the realms around it. From a lair made of bones, powered by human music, to the drugged fanaticism of Akoris and the blood-thirst of the Warlock Supreme … She did not want to be another careless ruler. She would not. Then and there, Roh decided she would be a queen of change. A queen of action.

'We will put it to the group,' she heard herself say, knowing she had not done so the first time Deodan had asked to join them.

Deodan shook his head. 'No, we won't.'

Roh opened her mouth to argue. Who was he to tell her —

'I told you there would come a time when I would ask something of you.' Deodan's gaze flicked to Harlyn, who still wore her sling but indeed stood before them, whole and healthy. He turned his palm upwards, where a thin scar signified their exchange. 'You said I could name my price. This is it, Rohesia. Are you a queen of your word?'

Heat tingled at Roh's fingertips, where her talons threatened to slide free. She *hated* feeling cornered, but it was a corner of her own making. She had been rash with her pleas for help. However, Harlyn was alive because of the warrior warlock before her.

'You only have one price to name,' she said carefully, all too aware of the cunning of her own kind. As Deodan would be. 'This is what you choose?'

There was no hesitation. 'It is.'

Roh chewed her lower lip and Deodan, as though sensing Finn's incoming objections, faced the Jaktaren. 'I am no stranger to companions who detest my kind,' he said.

Nor am I, Roh mused.

'But I will do all I can to earn your trust and respect. I know things have got murky in that regard,' he added, crouching suddenly. Unsheathing his dagger, he dragged it through the earth. When he was done, he looked up, offering the dagger handle-first to Roh. At his feet was a sketch: half a pair of wings. A proposal of alliance.

Roh took a deep breath and gently pushed Deodan's dagger away. 'One thing at a time,' she muttered. She looked to Odi, who was sliding his sword back into its scabbard, and to Harlyn, who gave her a subtle nod of approval. Yrsa's attention was on Finn, whose eyes raged with fiery fury. But ultimately, this was Roh's choice, and she had given Deodan her word. She swiped her boot across the dirt and the mark of the alliance.

'So be it,' she said at last, hoisting herself back into her saddle.

'Good,' Yrsa retorted matter-of-factly.

The fury in Finn's gaze softened. 'As you like, then.'

Deodan remounted his horse and waited. 'Then lead on, Jaktaren.'

Roh could have sworn Finn rolled his eyes, but he said nothing more.

As Finn guided them inland, the winds grew cooler and they rode at a steady pace across the stretching flatlands. With Akoris long behind them and out of sight, Roh found herself relishing the idea that they could be the only ones out here in all the realms.

Mere hours later, a film of clouds covered the sun as they approached the Endon River, the scent of smoke still trapped in their noses. This section was much wider than its south-west counterpart and its current raged across the rocks and boulders in a thick, white foam.

'Let's rest here a while,' Roh told the others, noting the sheen of sweat on her horse's neck. She dismounted and led him to the water's edge to drink. As she crouched to cup the fresh water herself, something flickered within her … That same restlessness that had bothered her since the ritual, the strange sensation of foreign magic stalking beneath her skin. But the topaz gave no sign that there was something untoward afoot. Frowning slightly, Roh went to her pack where she'd left it by a boulder and fished out the drake egg, instinct telling her she needed to check on it. She gasped as her fingers brushed against its shell.

It was ice cold.

'Yrsa,' she yelled. 'Come quick!' She held the egg close, trying to share the warmth of her body with it.

Yrsa appeared at her side, panicked. 'What is it?'

Roh held out the egg. 'It's gone cold.'

'That can't be.' Yrsa took it from her, pressing her palms against its icy surface, the colour draining from her face. 'This can't be,' she said again, rotating the egg in her hands. 'We did everything we were supposed to. It shouldn't be cold – not even in the depths of the sea, let alone here.'

The two cyrens huddled over the egg, running their hands across its shell, Roh even going so far as to blow hot breath on it, trying to heat it, willing it to pulse hot as it had in the dunes of Akoris.

But the shell remained cold against her fingertips as Yrsa cupped it and the hard realisation settled deep in Roh's chest. She could sense nothing beyond the shell, no flicker of movement within.

'Deodan, Deodan! Do you have something?' Roh rasped desperately. 'We have to get it warm, we have to —' She watched Yrsa cup her hands around her mouth, as Roh herself had done moments before, trying to generate whatever heat she could.

'I don't understand, I don't understand,' the Jaktaren muttered over and over.

Dread pooled in Roh's stomach, her voice cracking as she spoke. 'It's dead, isn't it?'

Yrsa didn't respond right away – she only gently handed the egg back to Roh. 'I'm sorry,' she said softly at last.

Roh clutched the egg to her and fell to her knees. Here was yet another thing she had poisoned with her greed, her ambition. A rare, beautiful creature, dead before it could even hatch, thanks to her. A strangled cry burst from her, and suddenly, hot tears were sliding down her cheeks. She couldn't remember the last time she had cried, if she ever had, but this … this was the final straw for her. That fault line within her cracked wide open as she wept, the sensation utterly foreign and unnerving.

Closing her eyes, Roh lifted her head to the sky.

Song erupted from her. An unleashing of all that restlessness and magic that had simmered for so long beneath her surface. She didn't think about what she was singing, only that the sound was coming from her very core, every single note a reflection of her, of everything she had ever gained and everything she had ever lost, a fluid dance between love and sorrow and magic.

Tears flowed freely with her song. Birthed by a cyren, fathered by a warlock and named for a human girl ...

Maybe you are the one to bring us together ...

Ames had been speaking of fate, of destiny falling into place. Note after note escaped Roh, the melody wrapping around her. But she was not some chosen figure. There were no larger forces at work, bringing her to each crucial moment in time. It was her choices and hers alone that led her. As it had always been, as it always would be.

A crunch sounded. The vibration in Roh's hands jolted her from the rapture of her deathsong. She looked down in utter disbelief, the final note of her melody caught in her throat. A ragged gasp escaped her.

Tiny dark wings flared, breaking through shards of shell.

And a pair of molten-gold eyes stared up at her.

ACKNOWLEDGEMENTS

As a reader, I have always loved poring over the acknowledgements of a book I've enjoyed. I love knowing who helped pull the writer through those darker days until they got to the long-awaited final two words: *the end.* As an author, though, writing acknowledgements is *hard.* It's a big task to summarise the countless people who helped bring a book from an idea to the very finished product you hold in your hands. Nevertheless, here we go again …

To Claire Bradshaw and Aleesha Paz, you championed this book (and this series) from the very start. Both of you have been the most thoughtful, reliable and generous beta readers I could ever imagine. Your enthusiasm for this sequel was infectious, and during a time when I found everything difficult, it was your words that kept me going. Thank you for every comment, every question and every ounce of support.

To Gary Ditcher, your encouragement, faith in me and your love mean the world to me. Thank you for being by my side through books and life, always.

To Anne Sengstock, you've become a dear friend to me over the years and your messages have seen me through many a hard day. Thank you for your kindness and for your contagious love of stories. I hope one day we can meet in person.

To Mum, Yas and Dad – thank you for holding down the Sydney branch of the author business. Without you fulfilling orders and dashing to the printers and the post office, my stories might not reach my local readers.

Ev and Lisy, thank you, as always, for sharing my victories and defeats as though they were your own. I'm so grateful to have grown up with such creative and driven friends.

Fay Wood, thank you for your letters (both snail mail and via Facebook) and for inspiring me daily with all that you do.

Hannah Jermyn and Aleesha (again), how I miss talking books with you over several wines. Thank you for the stellar recommendations whenever I'm in need and for your ongoing support.

Thank you to my fellow author, Benjamin Stevenson – your persistence and perseverance in this industry always motivate me to do better. And apparently, I can't write a blurb without you, so thank you for that, too.

Special thanks to Margot Butler, the O'Shea family, the Mulhollands, the Zapperts and Delzoppos, Natalia Hunter, Erin Mealey, Brad Davis, Mel Clarke, Liam

Casey, Emily-May Norman, Jordan Meek (and Jordan's mum, hello again!), Danielle Noah, Phoebe Woodward, Maria Carroll and fellow author, Nattie Kate Mason.

Thanks to the Supertrampers; for drinking wine way more than we tramp and helping with that 'work-life' balance thing.

More special thank you to these incredible bookstagram friends: itsmejayse, thebooktweeter, bookbookowl, apapergarden, bookscandlescats, bookishbron, leezland, elle.cheshire, emilyandherbooks, just_perfiction, queenof_midnight, labsandliterature, missdysfunktion, readingmadly, catsandpaperbacks, zanybibliophile, books.and.hangovers, clareapediabooks, coffeebooksandmagic, devoured_pages and readthewriteact.

And finally, as always, I want to thank you, my readers, for where would I be without you?

ABOUT THE AUTHOR

Helen Scheuerer is the YA fantasy author of the bestselling trilogy, *The Oremere Chronicles,* and the *Curse of the Cyren Queen* quartet. Often likened to the popular series *Throne of Glass* and *Game of Thrones,* her work has been highly praised for its strong, flawed female characters and its action-packed plots.

Helen's love of writing and books led her to pursue a Bachelor of Creative Writing at the University of Wollongong and a Masters of Publishing at the University of Sydney. Now a full-time author, Helen lives amidst the mountains in Central Otago, New Zealand and is constantly dreaming up new stories. You can find out more via her website: www.helenscheuerer.com